Bonded Blood

THE SENSE OF BELONGING SERIES
BOOK 2

BRENDA BENNING

Bonded Blood
Copyright © 2025 by Brenda Benning

ISBN: 979-8895313046 (sc)
ISBN: 979-8895313053 (e)

All rights reserved. No part of this publication may be reproduced, distributed, or transmitted in any form or by any means, including photocopying, recording, or other electronic or mechanical methods, without the prior written permission of the publisher and/or the author, except in the case of brief quotations embodied in critical reviews and other noncommercial uses permitted by copyright law.

The views expressed in this book are solely those of the author and do not necessarily reflect the views of the publisher, and the publisher hereby disclaims any responsibility for them.

Writers' Branding
(877) 608-6550
www.writersbranding.com
media@writersbranding.com

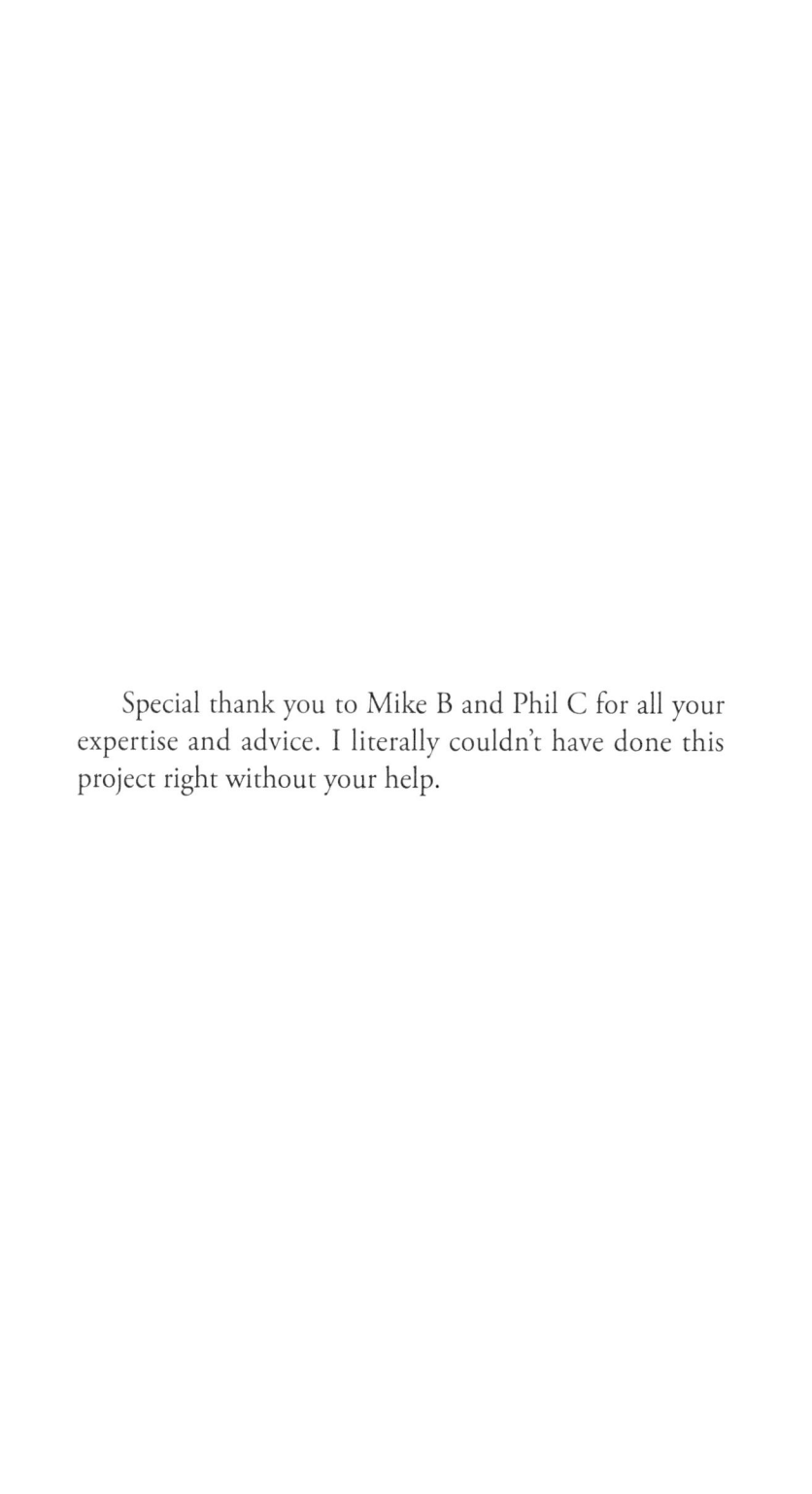

Special thank you to Mike B and Phil C for all your expertise and advice. I literally couldn't have done this project right without your help.

Disclaimer

This is a work of fiction. All characters, names, places, and descriptions are strictly a product of the author's imagination and used solely in a fictitious way. Any resemblance to a real person or situation is purely coincidental. Any trademarked name, place, or otherwise referenced are not a reflection of the holder of the trademark and are used without permission and do not reflect on said owner.

Contents

Chapter 1	1
Chapter 2	17
Chapter 3	28
Chapter 4	47
Chapter 5	62
Chapter 6	77
Chapter 7	89
Chapter 8	108
Chapter 9	122
Chapter 10	137
Chapter 11	152
Chapter 12	167
Chapter 13	183
Chapter 14	198
Chapter 15	213
Chapter 16	229
Chapter 17	244
Chapter 18	259
Chapter 19	274
Chapter 20	290
Chapter 21	304
Chapter 22	317

Chapter 23 336
Chapter 24 351
Chapter 25 366
Chapter 26 381
Chapter 27 395
Chapter 28 410
Chapter 29 427
Chapter 30 443
Chapter 31 454
Other works by this author 458

Chapter 1

Raelynn groaned as she tried to roll over. When her body resisted, she slowly opened her eyes. The space she was in was completely dark without even the slightest light anywhere. She scanned the darkness frantically with her eyes, her head not cooperating with her will to move just like the rest of her body. She closed her eyes again and tried to breathe to calm herself down. *Think, Rae, think,* she thought. She didn't dare speak, unsure if she could but more importantly, she had no idea where she was or if she was even alone. She concentrated on slowing down her heartbeat attempting to take deep breaths. She was relieved to find she wasn't completely restrained since she could take in a deep breath of air easily.

Focusing solely on her breath, Raelynn slowly opened her eyes again. She made a slow scan of the space with her eyes, trying to find any detail that would give her a clue as to where she was. But the thick darkness made that impossible. She tried to think of what she was doing before she fell asleep. Nothing came to mind, which scared her more than the knowledge that she was somewhere unfamiliar, tied up and unable to move. Frustrated, she closed her eyes again.

"Ok, next sense to try. Listen, Rae, listen," she whispered into the darkness. Squeezing her eyes shut tight, she tried to listen to any sound she could identify. At first, she heard nothing. Then she began to pick out the faintest of sounds. A bird, maybe? It was very quiet and probably far away. Or for all she knew the walls where she was were made of solid concrete and the stupid thing was right on the other side of it.

Grumbling silently, she cursed the free bird as she lay completely restricted in total darkness. Huffing, she focused on listening again. Getting frustrated with a bird wouldn't help her out right now. Raelynn closed her eyes tight and suddenly heard a click and something sliding against a concrete floor, like a heavy door. But was it here, where she was? Not wanting to turn her head, she kept her eyes closed and waited for a red hue on the other side of her eyelids to show the lights were turned on. But that didn't happen. Instead, she heard silence again.

Raelynn let out a long breath of air as slowly as she could so as not to draw attention. She suddenly realized her mouth wasn't restricted in any way, which was weird. Why would someone take her, tie her up, and not tape her mouth shut? Did they want her to scream? Were they sadistic freaks who wanted to hear her panic and cry? Well, they didn't know her well then because the last thing she would do was give into that! No, she would wait until they came to her. She never lived for anyone else, and she surely wouldn't start now.

She let her imagination run a little while she tried to decide how she would make these idiots pay for this, which aside from kidnapping her she wasn't sure what else yet. She shuddered slightly as she considered what else they could have done while she was unconscious. She moved her leg as much as she could to try to determine if she had clothes on or not. She wasn't cold, which again seemed weird she thought. She sighed in relief as she realized that she did in fact have clothes on. *Thank god*, she said in her mind.

Suddenly a light was flipped on, and Raelynn cursed herself for not keeping her eyes closed. Now they would know she was awake because she flinched at the brightness of it. Groaning, she kept her eyes closed, willing them to adjust to the light quickly.

Were these crazy people connected to her search? That couldn't be it. She had taken time off from that months ago. She hadn't even reached out to the officer again. She just did as he said and put it aside for a while. *But who else would want to kidnap me*? Raelynn questioned, racking her brain for any clue.

She suddenly heard a deep snort and resisted the shiver she felt. Before she could open her eyes to see where the sound came from, she felt a wetness on her cheek. Horrified, she screamed.

Raelynn jumped and sat up abruptly, earning her a growl. She looked around and discovered she was in her own bed with no restraints and her almost three-year-old English Mastiff glaring at her. *Ohhh,* she thought and couldn't resist the giggle that escaped her mouth. What felt like restraints must have been her dog laying on top of her as he was prone to do now and then. When that hundred and sixty pounds of love "cuddles" it could feel like a rib crushing event.

Raelynn reached over and scratched his chin, earning a little forgiveness. She twisted in her spot to see the time. It was three in the morning. "Ugh, way too early to be up, Timmy," she said with a grin, giving him another scratch behind his ear. She had gotten the dog for herself just a couple of months ago. She found out his birthday was Christmas Eve and thought it would be hilarious to name him Tiny Tim from *A Christmas Carol*.

Living alone, Raelynn wanted a little extra security in her apartment after the crazy summer she had. And since Mastiffs need little to no exercise, he was perfect. The slobber thing though, well, that was a whole other deal. Grabbing the towel she kept by her bed, she wiped her cheek. The wetness from her dream was just her dog dropping a glob of love, or something like that. Good thing she had a strong stomach.

Timmy stretched out and laid back down when Raelynn decided to get up and use the bathroom since she was awake anyway. Her small apartment was perfect for her. Even with Timmy, she had plenty of space to move around. The bedroom was probably the smallest of the spaces, but she had always wanted a king-size bed and when she finally got out on her own it was the first thing she bought. Unfortunately, it filled the tiny bedroom with barely enough room to walk around the bed. But with her ridiculously large puppy, the bed was a necessity.

She walked past the closet door, thankfully it was a large walk-in, so she didn't need a dresser or other furniture. The only thing she lacked was an ensuite bathroom, but since it was just her, it wasn't a big deal. Who wanted to clean two bathrooms anyway, she thought. After doing her business, she grabbed a cup of water and flicked off the bathroom light, heading back to her bed. Raelynn laughed as she felt around trying to get back into bed, now blinded by the sudden darkness again. Timmy had spread out at the foot of the bed, taking up about half of the bed. She would have to lay sideways if she was going to sleep at all.

She scratched his head and chuckled at him, as he burrowed further into the comforter. It didn't take long for him to start snoring loudly.

"Who needs a man when I got your snoring to keep me awake," she said with a laugh.

She arranged her blankets and pillow across the head of the bed, not even trying to move the pup. He was not aggressive at all, the rescue shelter had told her, trying to reassure her that he would be a good pet in spite of his size. The family that had him decided he was just too big for their newborn baby. Raelynn just couldn't imagine this huge ball of fluff and love would be dangerous, but she could understand the fear. He had a tendency to be unaware of his body in space, but she hoped he would start to figure it out. It reminded her of her teenage years when she had a huge growth spurt and couldn't seem to walk anymore. She still ended up being a very average five-foot-five, but that one summer was not fun.

Timmy's size was just what Raelynn wanted. He was big and intimidating and still lived up to his gentle giant nickname. She wasn't a scared person and didn't mind living alone, but she had a summer that made her question a few things, mostly her safety. She wanted to make sure she was protected. If Timmy has shown her anything it's that he can pin someone down with one paw behind his back. The last thing she wanted was to be surprised in the middle of the night by an intruder.

She had done a little research on what kind of dog to get and knew she needed an easy one with a low energy level. She quickly discovered Timmy was very lazy, which she loved. Even though she liked to be busy and out and about, she loved that he would cuddle, well more like smother her, when she sat on the couch to read or watch TV. It didn't take long for her to expect, and actually look forward to, his lazy head to look up from his spot on the couch when she walked into the apartment. She had a vision of him tackling her when she walked in the door from work, making her giggle. He was definitely capable of it, if he had the energy or desire to move.

Raelynn fell back asleep quickly, even after the weird dream. She hoped it was just triggered by her dog's weight and not something else. Her dreams didn't normally predict anything, at least not that she ever remembered. She had been thinking about restarting her search again, and maybe this was her brain's way of telling her "not yet" or something.

When her alarm went off a few hours later, she smacked the bed next to her, frustrated that it wouldn't shut off. She didn't remember she was sleeping sideways until she sat up. She glanced at the foot of the bed, still smothered in light brown fur. Timmy groaned in his sleep but didn't bother to move. Raelynn shook her head and threw the covers off.

She stood and stretched her shoulders out. "What a life, Timmy," she said as she scratched his head, earning her a slobbery lick of his massive tongue. She resisted pulling back, knowing she would be getting in the shower anyway. She didn't want him to think she didn't love his affection, even as gross as it was sometimes.

Making her way to the bathroom, she looked briefly around her room. She had just moved here right before she got Timmy. She had decided the student housing should be for students, even though the landlord said it was fine for her to stay a little longer. Raelynn had contemplated grad school to get a license in psychology instead of just a bachelor's degree, but decided she didn't want to quite yet. She had other things to tackle, and grad school wouldn't be the first thing on her list. When she went back to school, she would have to be able to devote more mental time to it and ever since meeting her new friend, she had been obsessed with something else.

Raelynn turned the shower on hot and waited a few minutes for it to actually get warm. A downside of moving out of student housing, she thought. Hot water wasn't easy to come by for some reason.

She stared at her reflection in the mirror. Her barely wavy, dark brown hair was messy and laying in knots around her shoulders. The stormy deep blue eyes stared back at her. For the millionth time, her thoughts drifted to her parents. She never knew her mom, the one she shared DNA with anyway. She had died during childbirth, which seemed weird in this day and age. But Raelynn had seen a picture or two and knew she had carried many of her mother's genes.

The white genes shined through in almost every aspect of Raelynn's appearance. The only thing she inherited from her father was his wide bridged nose. She did get some of his skin tone, she supposed. Her pale olive skin tanned easily and although she could get sunburnt, it quickly turned to tan after a day. She wasn't a hundred percent sure where all the god-forsaken freckles came from, making her look even more white than mixed.

Letting out a deep sigh, she dropped her eyes to her hands resting on the bowl. "One of these days, daddy.

I promise," she whispered to the empty white sink. She raised her eyes again and was surprised to see a single tear fall from her eye.

Raelynn shook her head and wiped it away, moving to get in the shower. There wasn't time today, she thought. She had to get ready and go to her friend Ashley's. They were meeting up together one more time before her friend took off back to Minnesota. She would miss her so much, but Raelynn knew she had things to get done. She reminded herself again not to say anything to Ashley about her plans because she had no doubt her friend would stay and try to help. But this is one thing she needed to do herself. Plus, Ashley had been through enough with the summer "adventures" and Raelynn knew she was looking forward to going home.

She had tried to convince her to stay a while longer, but Ashley said it just didn't feel like home. She would love to visit a lot though, as long as it wasn't in the summer she had joked. It was funny to listen to her complain about the weather and how "god-awful hot" it was all the time. Raelynn chuckled out loud as she remembered those conversations.

Raelynn made quick use of the shower and brushed her teeth and hair. She decided to let it air dry and put a tiny bit of gel in it to fight the crazy that could result from the still humid air of the Eastern Shore. She had lived here her whole life and never thought about it much. Meeting someone from Minnesota's much different climate opened her eyes a little bit to the weather—at least more than if it was a good beach day or not.

She heard her phone ring from the other room, forgetting she had left it out there the night before. Thinking it was likely Ashley she didn't really hurry to answer it. She threw her blankets over the bed as best she could. Timmy had moved, but instead of making it easier for her, he was now taking up the entire middle of the bed.

Giving up, Raelynn moved to the kitchen, glancing at her phone sitting on the counter. She wasn't a breakfast person and knew they were going to be eating soon anyway, so she just decided to get Timmy outside and fed before she left. She glanced at the microwave and realized she only had about thirty minutes before she was supposed to be at Ashley's.

"Timmy, come on buddy!" she called. She could hear her bed creak with his weight as he stretched. *Lazy boy*, she thought with a smile. While she waited for him to lumber in, she prepped his food dish and cleaned and refilled his water bowl. She was thinking of getting him a fountain type bowl. She knew he probably would drink more water that way. His bowl now held almost a gallon of water, and he seemed to go through it quickly.

It took almost a whole five minutes more before he lazily made his way out of the bedroom. He stretched his front legs out in front of him and then shook his body out, from his head all the way down to his tail. He walked to the sliding door, which led to the small outdoor space Raelynn had. It was why she had chosen this apartment actually. Now with Timmy it was even better.

Raelynn rushed to the door before he sat down, because that would be another chore to get him up. She quickly latched the chain to his collar and then moved outside after him to sit in the lawn chair she had left outside for this reason.

She watched as he sniffed around for a while and after finally finding the perfect place he peed and then moved quickly back to the door. She knew he wouldn't need to do the other until after he ate his food, so she let him back in to eat. She would do whatever else she could before letting him out again for that business.

If there was one thing Timmy wasn't lazy about, it was eating. He finished his bowl in record time and then moved to his water bowl to make a huge mess of dripping water from his jowls while he looked side to side in between drinks just for fun it seemed. Raelynn hadn't yet figured out his reasons for this behavior, but she kept a towel under his bowl now to soak up some of the waterfall.

She picked up her phone and poop bag container and headed back outside with Timmy. This process took a little longer, so she sat and pulled up her voicemail from earlier. She was surprised it wasn't from Ashley but her stepmom. Honesty was really her mom by all accounts since she basically had been caring for Raelynn since she was little.

"Hey Rae. It's mom. I just wanted to see what your plans are for the day. I don't have your work schedule yet. But anyway a package came for you early this morning and wanted to let you know. Love you. Call me back."

Raelynn chuckled out loud. Her mom always said who she was, as if Raelynn wouldn't know. She thought for a second, wondering if she had ordered anything recently. But she didn't think she had.

"Huh, oh well, guess I'll find out soon enough," she murmured.

A heavy weight landed on her foot, and she looked down to see Timmy had finished his business and was lying at her feet ready to nap again.

"No, no buddy, get up!" she laughed. She ushered him into the apartment and then went back out to find his mess. She kept his chain short so she wouldn't have to scour the grass too far away to find it, not that it was difficult to find. His droppings were like a horse's, and hard to miss.

She picked it up and tied the bag shut and then tossed it in a small container she kept outside for this purpose. She went back inside, closed and locked the door behind her and pulled the shades closed as well. Being on the ground level did have its issues too. She didn't need anyone to know when she was and was not home.

After she washed her hands, she gave a now sleeping Timmy a kiss and whispered, "See you later, Timmy. Be good!" He barely moved his head as she made her way out of the apartment. She couldn't help but chuckle as she walked to her car.

It was a bright sunny morning. The weather was starting to cool off, but she still didn't need a jacket all day. Sometimes in the morning, but by lunchtime it was up around seventy. It was just a few days until Halloween. The trees had begun to change colors, and the nights were getting colder now. Even though the days still averaged close to seventy, people didn't really go out to the beaches anymore. Ashley complained that now would be the perfect time to go when you weren't dying of heat exhaustion. The memory made Raelynn laugh again. She was going to miss her new friend.

Raelynn connected her phone to her car's Bluetooth system and then called her mom back. Honesty had been the only mom Raelynn had ever known. She had always treated Raelynn as her own biological daughter and made it clear to everyone that Raelynn was her daughter in every sense of the word. Raelynn's dad and Honesty had another daughter, Sahara. The two girls were very close and just under five years apart.

Honesty had another child due to a sexual assault she had endured who was now twelve. She had been adamant that God had wanted her to have this baby for some reason and she would not abort him even though she knew it would be a constant reminder of what had happened to her. She had admitted to Raelynn once that Honesty was actually afraid she would die if she had an abortion because one of her friends had many years ago. The health care system wasn't really in her favor as an African American woman who was already a single mother and didn't have great health insurance. She couldn't bear the thought of potentially leaving Raelynn and Sahara as their father had.

She had gone through extensive therapy and had developed an amazing support system around her. Now Honesty was able to reframe what happened to her as something she had overcome and survived. Not only survived but she had also flourished and grown in so many ways. And even Raelynn had to admit Jericho was a pretty decent little brother.

Raelynn always admired her mom for all she had to endure over the years. Not only the assault but the disappearance of Raelynn's father, and having to raise three kids all on her own. But she never gave up hope of her husband coming home one day. Honesty rarely complained about all she had on her shoulders and stayed very connected to her faith and church. She worked three jobs at one time just to make sure everyone was fed and often went without her own dinner for the kids.

That was one of the main reasons Raelynn moved out and stayed in student housing while she was in school. She had hoped it would lessen the burden on Honesty. Sahara had also started working and helping out. It made it possible for Honesty to finally get down to one full-time job and a part-time one that was only two days a week instead of five.

Her mom's chipper voice answered on the first ring. "Hi sweetheart," she greeted.

"Hey Mom. I'm on my way to Ashley's then I can swing by after we have lunch if that's ok," she said, watching the traffic and signs as she looked for the entrance to the development.

"That should be fine. I am already at work, just on a short break. I left it on the porch in a trash bag so hopefully no one steals it thinking it's trash and not a package." She laughed at her own sneaky trick making Raelynn smile.

"Is anyone home?" she asked, turning down a wide tree lined street. Ashley had been living in a third-floor apartment for the last few months while she did her own informal investigation into her family. Raelynn stifled a laugh at how that turned into something so much more than Ashley had bargained for, but definitely for the better. Raelynn couldn't deny that it had jumpstarted her own desire to resume the search for her father.

"I think Sahara is home but has plans around one thirty. I have no clue what Jericho is doing to be honest." It was

Saturday and Raelynn knew he was likely either gaming or sleeping, such is the life of a twelve-year-old boy.

Raelynn smiled. "Ok, I'll stop in after a little bit. I'll let you know if the house is burned down or anything."

Honesty chuckled. "Ok. Love you girl. Gotta go. Have a fun visit with Ashley and tell her 'hi' for me."

"Love you too, mom," Raelynn said and disconnected the call just as she pulled into the driveway of the three-story home.

Sharon, the owner, was outside watering her flowers. She looked up and waved as Raelynn put her car in park and stepped outside.

"Hello Raelynn, dear. How are you?" Sharon asked.

"I'm good, Ms. Sharon. How are the flowers doing? Hanging on still?" Raelynn looked around the yard and couldn't help but wonder how long they would continue to live. It wasn't too bad yet, but it would get cold enough to kill the flowers soon.

Sharon followed her gaze and shrugged. "They seem to be doing ok. What are you girls up to today?"

Raelynn shrugged. "Goodbye lunch I guess?" She hated to admit her friend was really leaving.

They had been spending a lot of time together since they met in August. Ashley's boyfriend Jacob was here as well, but he was skipping lunch so the girls could spend time together. She still couldn't believe they shared that small apartment. It was great for one person, but she thought it would be cramped for two. She thought about herself and Timmy and knew there was no way she would be able to survive. Plus, the three levels for potty breaks made her shudder.

As if on cue, Ashley appeared in the yard. "Hey Rae!" she called, drawing Sharon's and Raelynn's attention to her entrance.

She made her way over to Raelynn and they turned to Sharon. "Can we bring you anything back, Sharon?" Ashley asked.

Sharon waved her hand. "No no, I'm fine. You two have fun!" Then she disappeared into the house.

"I'm going to miss this place," Ashley mused next to her.

Raelynn grinned. "I know what you mean. It's going to be weird without you here, you know."

"Now don't start that, ok?" Ashley said with a light slap on her arm. "I'm not going to start crying."

"Well, you're in luck then 'cause I don't cry," Raelynn said with a proud smile and lift of her chin.

Ashley narrowed her eyes at her friend. "Never?"

Raelynn shook her head. "Nope!"

"I don't believe it. Not even during really sad movies? I bet you would if you watched a movie where the dog died." Ashley gave her a pointed look, knowing her weakness, even if Raelynn wouldn't admit it.

Raelynn shook her head again. "I bet not." She crossed her arms in front of her defiantly.

Ashley watched her for a few seconds and then shrugged. "Ok, but I bet one day you will and then you won't be able to stop because you have all this pent-up sadness that you have never released."

Giving her friend a shrug, Raelynn looped her arm through Ashley's, and they made their way to Raelynn's bright red four-door Civic. She had bought it right after graduation when she had finally saved enough money from her job to put a downpayment on it. She was able to keep her monthly payment low even though it was a newer car. She wanted something reliable for a long time, so the sacrifice was worth it. Now she was glad she had because when she had to take Timmy to the vet, he filled the whole back seat. She's not sure what she would have done if it was a two door.

"So where are we headed?" Ashley asked.

Raelynn shrugged. "What haven't you tried yet since you've been here?"

Ashley snorted. "You're asking me? I thought you were supposed to be my tour guide."

"True, true," Raelynn said as they buckled their seatbelts, and she started the car. "How about simple?"

"OK. What do you have in mind?" Ashley asked, with a side-eye and hint of reservation.

"The best cheesesteaks on the shore," Raelynn said with a smile.

Chapter 2

"Jericho! Where are you at?" Raelynn yelled in the entrance to the house where her brother and sister lived with their mom. The house was quiet, and no one answered when she knocked—not that she expected anyone to. She had used her key to get inside instead of waiting for someone to come to the door. Knowing her sister probably wasn't home and it was just Jericho, it was likely he wouldn't answer the door, especially if he was gaming. He probably wouldn't even hear the knock or doorbell.

A loud thump and crash sounded above her making her groan. "You aren't still sleeping, are you?" she called out with a "mom" edge to her voice. With as much as Honesty worked when they were all young, Raelynn did a lot of caregiving for her little brother. Sometimes she felt like a second mom to him.

"No! No! I'm awake! I'm awake!" a muffled voice called from above her. A few more bumps came from the second level.

Raelynn grimaced and she stared at the ceiling. Either he was messing around upstairs, had a friend over (and he would be in trouble), or he really was still sleeping. She knew she would have to investigate since her mom would expect a report, especially if he was up to no good. Hopefully he was just rolling himself out of bed, she thought, almost crossing her fingers. The last thing she wanted to find was him doing something a twelve-year-old had no business doing. Raelynn cringed just thinking about the possibilities.

With a sigh, she climbed the stairs, avoiding the squeaky one that she discovered when she was fourteen and got caught sneaking in at three in the morning. Not a pleasant experience by any means. Finding that step saved her a few more run-ins with her mom's angry and tired face through the rest of her years at home. Getting caught, and subsequently grounded, didn't stop the sneaking in and out though, she thought with a grin. She just got better at it.

It appeared as though her siblings had not yet found the step or just didn't care because while she was home, they hit it every single time. Sahara was the worst at sneaking in and out of the house at night. Raelynn would literally hear the step before her sister actually stepped on it because she heard every step up to it. Needless to say, she wasn't light on her feet. Jericho wasn't quite old enough to start sneaking out yet but he didn't avoid the step now so she figured he wouldn't later on either.

She approached her brother's door, the first one from the steps, and listened. When she didn't hear any other voices, she breathed a little sigh of relief. She didn't know what she would do if he had a girl in the room. *He's only twelve*, she reminded herself.

As she raised her hand to the knob, it swung open. Her brother let out a high-pitched squeal and fell backwards into the room.

Raelynn giggled hysterically as she watched Jericho's body fall to the floor while he clutched his chest trying to calm down.

"Rae! You scared me!" he yelled angrily.

She just shook her head and continued to laugh. "Bro, you sound like a little girl screaming like that." She bent over and rested her hands on her knees, trying to calm herself.

"Do not!" he said with a sulky expression on his face. He crossed his arms in front of his chest and glared at her still sitting on the carpeted floor. At least he had a soft fall she thought with a smirk.

She leaned on the doorframe and narrowed her eyes at him. "What were you doing?" She looked around the room. It wasn't big enough to hide anyone. Even the closet was tiny and barely fit all his Lego and comic book bins while still being able to shut the door. Jericho never closed it anyway, so it was pretty clear to see no one was in there with him. She didn't resist the relief she felt as she avoided that confrontation.

Jericho scratched the back of his head and shrugged. "I was sleeping."

"Really? Sleeping at two in the afternoon?" Raelynn asked.

He looked down and mumbled something she couldn't understand.

"What?" she asked him, stepping into the room.

He looked up and scowled at her. "I said I was up late gaming. Mom doesn't know so don't tell her!" He had a pleading look on his face, but his posture was just plain defiant.

Raelynn shrugged. "Like I care what you were doing. But mom is working really hard to keep this place running and food on the table. The least you can do is get off your stupid games and help out. Especially since both me and Sahara are out working now."

Jericho hung his head. It wasn't the first time his sister had scolded him about helping out more. "Ok. I'll try. But it's easy for you guys. You're girls. You're supposed to do the housework. Not boys." He scrunched his nose and looked up at her as if the thought made him sick.

"What did you just say?" She looked at him hard. "Who told you that crap?" She knew if her mom heard that she would have a complete meltdown about it. Heck, she was about to herself.

Jericho looked up at her and shrugged. "Everyone knows that. At Jamal's house his mom does everything, and his dad just gets to watch TV. He said that's the way it's supposed to be." His tone was matter of fact as his arms crossed his body.

Raelynn stared at her brother. Never in her life had she given him or anyone else that idea, especially since her mom was the only one in the house and she was working her tail off to bring in enough money to pay all the bills and still cook and clean. When they were old enough, she and Sahara took over some of the tasks but as she thought about it, it was mostly the cleaning because Honesty loved to cook. She said it gave her a tangible way to take care of everyone, not just paying the bills.

Jericho was a lot younger than Sahara, so she figured he probably did get to avoid a lot of the tasks simply because of his age. But never had they made it a gender issue. The idea that this friend was putting in his brain made her angry. *Equality, right?* she thought angrily. *That means men should be doing the same as women. It's not just one direction and no reciprocity. This isn't the nineteen fifties!* she thought, trying to calm her frustration. She would have to set her brother straight about this. And letting her mom know about this friend of his was part of that.

Maybe it was hearing about Ashley's father and how abusive he was when she was little, but this whole conversation upset her, and she couldn't even figure out where to start with Jericho.

"I can't even talk to you right now. I don't ever want to hear you say something like that again. Mom has been doing everything for all of us and no one has helped her. If you want to grow up to be a good man, you better start by treating mom better. You should be bending over backwards for all she does for you!" She tried to keep her temper in check. He was just a kid still. But she wouldn't allow some chauvinistic idiot to give her little brother that idea if she could help it.

"You mean men like yours and my dad?" he scoffed and turned around retreating back into his room.

Raelynn was about to turn and leave when he said those words. She spun on her heel and stared at him. "Yes, Jericho," she bit out. She took a slow breath in and closed her eyes for a second to calm herself. "Look, I get those are the only examples you have here." She moved her hands around to signal their small world. "But you should strive to be better than them. Better than Jamal's dad. Just…*better*. Do you hear me?"

She was seething mad as she went back downstairs and out to her car. She had to get away before she said something hurtful. Jericho doesn't know the circumstances of his conception, just that he has a different father than she and Sahara. But she also knew her own father before he disappeared. She knew if he could, he would have been a fantastic role model for Jericho. But she couldn't change any of that right now.

Thankfully she had already put the package from her mom in the car before she went to investigate her brother's activities. She buckled her seatbelt and quickly headed toward her own place. It wasn't far, but then again, nothing was far from anything around Salisbury.

Her thoughts were jumbled as she made her way through the streets. She had lost count of all the things her dad had missed out on since his disappearance fifteen years ago. Sahara was barely two years old when he left and didn't come back. Raelynn was a few weeks shy of eight. She remembered that morning like it was any other morning. She couldn't shake it from her memory actually.

Her dad had kissed her forehead and then gave Honesty a kiss and hug. Sahara was in the back seat of the car playing with her sippy cup. He climbed into the driver's seat and waved as he pulled out of the driveway. Honesty had to go to work too, but she always waited until Raelynn caught the bus. Her dad was responsible for dropping off Sahara at daycare on his way to the chicken factory near downtown.

Raelynn had to go to school that day and wasn't feeling good. But the rule was simple. If you threw up or had a fever you could stay home. Otherwise, you had to go to school. And even then, if you had to stay home it was spent entirely in bed and mom would bring bland food, nothing special. The only time she remembered being treated special when she was home from school was after she had her tonsils out when she was five.

She spent that fateful day at school as if nothing had happened but when she got off the bus. Honesty was already home and not Mommom. Honesty was crying and running through the house, but Raelynn wasn't sure what was going on. She never really got any answers, just that her dad was gone, and they didn't know when he would be home.

Raelynn remembered saying the special prayer she and her dad did every night and then asked God to please send her daddy home as soon as possible because Honesty was very sad. It didn't take long for Honesty to take over everything and pretty soon Raelynn and Sahara were spending most days and some nights with Honesty's mom. They did the best they could to keep things going as normal as possible. Raelynn now understood Honesty didn't have a choice. She had to push her grief aside and hold things together for the three of them.

The only time Raelynn remembered Honesty ever crying about his disappearance after that one day was when her father died, which wasn't long after. Poppop was the best substitute for a father, but even Raelynn had to admit he wasn't her dad. Although she missed him terribly, she would rather have her dad.

Over the years, Raelynn learned to accept things as they were, at least that was what Honesty had modeled to her by example. Honesty seemed to accept things the way they were and just plod along. But the older Raelynn got, the more she wanted answers. She had never accepted that her father had died or that he abandoned the family of his own free will. He was too devoted to "his girls", as he used to say.

Raelynn's thoughts were interrupted when she realized she had pulled into her spot in the apartment parking lot. She wanted to go hug her enormous ball of love and just sit and read for a while. She was off work today but had to work tomorrow, opening at five am no less. She would take it easy today and try to go to bed early. Maybe she would find a different book than the murder mystery she had started before bed last night. She didn't need a repeat of that dream.

She unlocked the door and put the package on the table by the door. She half expected her pup to come running and then laughed when she remembered who she was thinking about. *Timmy wouldn't run anywhere, even if he was being chased*, she thought with a giggle.

"Timmy, boy. Where are you?" she called, peeking into the living room and then the bedroom. He wasn't in his normal places, which made her a little worried. She closed her door and looked to see if the patio door was still closed and locked. When she saw it was, she slid off her shoes and went into the kitchen to see if he was on the cool floor. It was pretty warm outside today and she had read that these dogs don't like extreme temperatures. She had left the air conditioning unit on low for him though.

Raelynn suddenly heard a loud thump coming from her bathroom. *What the heck?* she thought. She moved slowly through the apartment and down the short hall to the bathroom. As she tried to peek around the doorway, she was pushed backwards and felt the wall behind her holding her up. A sharp gasp escaped her mouth.

She glanced down to see her massive puppy sitting and staring at her. She looked around him in to the bathroom, wondering where he was or what he was doing in there. Making sure there was no one else in there, she looked back at him again. His bored expression just made her laugh as she gave him scratches. She surprised herself at her sudden paranoia. She must still be getting used to having him around, she thought.

"Come on, let's go potty," she said with a grin.

Timmy dutifully followed her to the door and soon she had him connected to the chain outside. She settled on the lawn chair as she waited for him to do his business. Raelynn looked around the small yard. It wasn't hers, but it was fairly private, and she was alone out here most of the time. There was a larger courtyard with a playground for kids in the front and there wasn't a sidewalk out here, so most folks stayed away from this back area. A small pond was a little off in the distance and there were trees along the edges. She loved the peace of the area.

Timmy had come and lay at her feet before she realized it and she looked down at him. Her attention suddenly drifted back to the box from her mom's. She decided to take Timmy back inside as her curiosity was starting to get the better of her. She unhooked the chain from his collar, and they went back through the door. She closed it tight, locked it, and pulled her blinds across the wide span.

Her thoughts about the box started to go in a wild direction. She hoped it wasn't something sick like her dad's finger or something. *OK, too many really violent movies*, she scolded herself. She took the package from the counter and looked for her scissors. *Stop being paranoid*.

She opened the plastic bag and pulled out a medium size brown box, like what an Amazon package would come in. There wasn't any information on it, just the address label from UPS. The return address was left blank, but her name and her mom's address were printed on it. *Weird*, she thought. Why wasn't there a return address? She didn't think you could send anything without a return address in case something was undeliverable.

Slowly, she cut through the tape on the box and opened the flaps. The box itself was pretty light, like there was something tiny in it or maybe even nothing at all. If it wasn't for the slight rattle, she might have just thought it was some stupid joke and it was actually empty.

Inside she found a bunch of rolled up brown packing paper. She pulled out each piece and unrolled it individually trying to figure out what was inside. Nothing showed up so far and she had gone through about four of the papers. She had two left to unravel.

As she picked up the second to the last one, she felt some weight to it. Raelynn carefully unrolled the paper. It wasn't super heavy, but it was definitely not weightless. She couldn't figure out what it was. Once all the paper was gone, she looked at the small glass figurine in her hand. It almost filled her palm, and the bright colors were beautiful. She lifted it to get a closer look and saw how it reflected the light.

Raelynn set the small statue on the counter and stared at it. Her eyes wandered to the small shelf she had bought right after she moved in. On it she had put all of the different kinds of turtles she had collected or created during her first seven years—with her dad. Her eyes drifted back to the small turtle sitting on her counter, involuntarily filling with tears.

She had quit collecting the little trinkets after her dad disappeared. It was *their* thing. Only Honesty knew about it. The first Christmas he was gone, Honesty gave her a new one, a pretty crystal one that was probably expensive. But Raelynn told her not to buy anymore. Her heart wasn't in it without her dad. That crystal piece now stood in the middle of the rest, as if standing guard over all of them until her father would return and resume their favorite activity.

She picked up the new turtle and held it up again, wiping her eyes. She wouldn't cry. She didn't cry. Raelynn carefully moved to place the new animal next to the rest on her shelf. She set it off a little bit to the side. She wasn't sure who sent it or why, but she would have to find out.

Looking back at the box, she found one more piece of brown paper to unfold. Gingerly, she bent down. It didn't feel like anything was in it, but she unrolled it anyway to make sure. Maybe whoever sent it included a note or something. As Raelynn unrolled that last fold, a tiny card like you would find with a flower delivery fell to the ground. She held her breath as she picked it up. *Of course it had to land upside down*, she grumbled silently.

Raelynn picked up the tiny card and flipped it over in her hand. The words made her heart almost stop beating completely.

"For your collection, baby girl," she read out loud. She felt her knees grow weak and she leaned against the counter for support. Her dad always called her his baby girl. His little miracle. She never felt any anger from him about the loss of her mom or that it was her fault she had died. He always showered her with so much love to make up for the missing piece in Raelynn's life. She wondered sometimes as she grew older if her parents were really great together, but she wasn't old enough when he disappeared to even think about asking him.

Now as she stared at the words, she wondered if he was trying to send her a message. Her breath caught in her throat. "Finally," she said quietly.

Chapter 3

Raelynn had a fitful night's rest. She didn't get into a deep enough sleep to dream, which she was actually thankful for, given her dream the night before. But she was sluggish when her alarm went off at four. She had continued to work at the small coffee shop by the university campus while she looked for a more permanent type of job. She was planning to go into child psychology, so she hoped to find a job as a receptionist in a private practice somewhere. Then she could possibly get some on-the-job training, or at least a mentor out of it.

After dragging herself through her morning routine, Raelynn took Timmy out and then fed him while she made herself a quick piece of toast and cup of coffee. She knew she could wait and get a much better cup at work, but she needed the extra caffeine this morning. As she waited for him to finish eating, Raelynn's eyes were drawn to the new turtle on her shelf.

"How am I going to find the sender?" she mumbled quietly.

Timmy let out one of his deep single barks, drawing her attention back to him as he waited semi-patiently by the door. She laughed and let him out again. Raelynn glanced one more time at her shelf and shook her head.

She was too tired to think about it right now. She moved outside once she had her trusty poop bags.

Her pup must have been just as tired as she was because he was quick to go about his business and showed up back at the door almost before she got outside. She laughed when he lumbered in and moved quickly to the couch. He was sleeping before she even had the door closed and locked again.

"Lucky dog," she whined. Raelynn gave him one more scratch on his head and then headed out. Sahara would be by in a few hours to let him out for her, so he wasn't alone all day or had any accidents. She was lucky he was already house trained when she adopted him and hadn't had any issues in the house yet.

After making sure her apartment was all locked up, she made her way to her car. The sun was about thirty minutes from beginning to light the sky as she looked around the quiet and darkened parking lot. Normally Raelynn liked this early shift. The people coming for coffee right before work were the ones she liked the best. Today would be different since it was a Sunday, but there would be enough people coming in for pastries and a cup of coffee before or after church.

The people who came in around eight or nine on the weekdays were the worst. They were often running late and in a hurry and tended to be rude--like their poor planning was somehow her fault.

Today would be a slower start, but it would give her time to get some of the baked goods out and in the display before anyone came in. There were a few regulars who came in religiously at six am, no matter the day of the week. Those were her favorite people. Most were retired and had nothing to do all day, so they loved to sit and chat. Or they met up with friends in the back corner and complained about the young "whipper snappers" or gossiped about the ones not there.

Being an extrovert, Raelynn loved to talk to people. The regulars were so used to the other people coming and going, and knew who was a regular and who wasn't, that they loved to chat and gossip about people when they left the small café. It made Raelynn laugh. She didn't care for the gossip, but it was entertaining and kept her distracted. She hoped she was like them when she was old and retired. The idea of sitting at a sidewalk café table with her bestie, gossiping about the local hoodlums sounded just wonderful, Raelynn thought.

The worst time of the day was between one and three. Since they closed before five every day, whoever opened at five would get off around two and the closer would come in around nine-thirty. Raelynn had always preferred the early morning, so she rarely closed. Once in a while she would be asked to run the café for the full eleven hours, but the owner always paid her well so she would easily agree—on occasion. She made it clear she would not do it all the time and allow herself to be taken advantage of though.

As she pulled up in the parking lot of the café, Raelynn sighed. It was going to be a long day, even with the coffee. Glancing at the clock on her dash, she saw she was seven minutes early. The sun was just starting to peak over the horizon, and she leaned back against her headrest. The weather was going to be nice today so maybe people would be in a good mood. This was definitely a summer and beach place and when it got even a little chilly outside, people had a tendency to get crabby.

She finally slipped out of her car and welcomed the sixty-degree breeze hitting her face. She thought of Ashley as she pulled her jacket closed in front of her. Being from Minnesota, Ashley struggled with the hottest days of the summer, but when it hit seventy-five, she was all about the summer life. Raelynn wouldn't be surprised to see her in shorts, if Ashley was even awake at the moment that is. She hated mornings as much as Raelynn did. That conversation made her laugh when she remembered the shock on Ashley's face when Raelynn told her she preferred working mornings.

She couldn't help but wonder what Ashley would wear in the winter here. A car's beep broke her from her rambling thoughts. She looked up to see her boss smiling at her and waving. This woman never seemed to be in a bad mood, she thought.

Raelynn smiled and waved back then moved to stand by the doors. The breeze felt good at first, but now the cool wind was a little too cool. She stood off to the side to wait for her boss to unlock the door for her.

Susiana appeared next to Raelynn, as chipper as ever. "Good morning, dear. How are you today?" she asked as she put her key in the door.

"I'm good, Miss Susiana," Raelynn replied with a grin. She picked up one of the two bags her boss had set on the ground to fish out her keys.

Her boss shushed her. "Please call me Susie like everyone else." She opened the door and mumbled, "Silly girl." Susiana mumbled something about not being old, making Raelynn chuckle.

Susiana wasn't actually much older than Raelynn. She had a small child, but she had told Raelynn at one time that she had established her business before jumping into parenthood, and even that happened a little earlier than she and her husband had planned. It was part of why they had shortened hours and cut out the evening dinner hours not long ago.

Raelynn moved behind her and set the bag next to the others Susiana had already put down. She then moved to the back and hung up her light jacket where they had staff lockers. It also served as a small break room with a tiny counter that held the smallest microwave she had ever seen. There was a fridge that wasn't huge but was big enough to hold their extra ingredients for coffees and other drinks. A wire bookshelf stood next to it with four shelves. Each one had a few extra ingredients for coffee mixtures. There was an open space on the top shelf for lunches, but Raelynn typically ate at the café. Susiana made amazing bagel sandwiches that Raelynn was a sucker for.

She went back out to the dining room and grabbed an apron on the way past the small office that was opposite the break room. The stiff black fabric was heavy, but it seemed to block any and all stains that could occur while she was making lattes for the college kids, although today most of those customers wouldn't be coming in until later, unless they had papers to write or exams to study for.

Susiana allowed students to hang out for up to two hours to use the free Wi-Fi. But she did ask that they purchase something each hour they were there. She didn't even care if it was a bottle of water for a dollar fifty. Raelynn tried to monitor that, but even Susiana didn't push it too hard unless they were really busy that day. The students seemed to respect the rule, and there were rarely any issues. She figured they were happy to have a place to study outside of their room or library and would often purchase more than just a bottle of water in gratitude.

She turned on the various machines to warm them up and then got to work filling the display cases with the fresh pastries Susiana had just brought in with her. They didn't have a huge kitchen at the café, so she made most of the baked goods at her home and then brought them in each morning. Raelynn didn't even want to think about what time she was up each morning baking because these were still warm in her hands.

The first customers started trickling in about forty minutes later, just as Raelynn finished refilling all the supplies and the display cases were full.

"Good morning, honey," a kind old man named Al said as he hobbled to the counter, depending on his cane for support. "How are you today?"

Raelynn smiled. She loved Al. He was an old air force vet and loved to talk about his experiences. His wife had passed away a few years ago, before Raelynn started working there. He told her they used to walk to the café every morning, even while she was sick. It was a short walk from their tiny house just a block away. Mister Jones especially loved to provoke his friends who were army vets, bragging about how much better the air force was than the "grunts" in the army.

"Can't complain, Mister Jones. How are you?" She quickly forgot her tiredness as she jumped into action getting him his usual cup of black coffee and a strawberry Danish from the case.

He gently set his bills on the counter. Raelynn took it and gave him a smile as he walked away, carrying his breakfast. He stacked his pastry on top of his cup, insisting he can manage on his own. He called over his shoulder, "Better than horizontal, isn't it?" He chuckled at his own joke and sat in his usual spot by the window.

Shaking her head, she turned her attention to the next customer with a smile. Once Mister Jones came in it was like a signal to everyone else that the doors were open because there was a steady stream of people after that.

Raelynn finally looked at the clock at close to ten. The morning had flown by. She started to straighten up the counter, finally having a free minute, as the new girl came over to her. Chrissy had started just a couple of months ago and she had impressed Raelynn with how quickly she picked everything up. She may have been new, but it didn't feel like it with how well they worked together.

"Kinda busy for a Sunday, huh?" Chrissy said, wiping down the counter in front of them.

Raelynn nodded. "It is actually. I'm hoping the rest of the day goes by like this—pleasant and without any snotty kids." She snorted as she watched Chrissy's nose scrunch up. She glanced around the small dining room and noticed it was still about half full. The older folks had congregated in the back corner and were in perfect position to watch everyone who came in through the doors. The men sat together sharing fishing stories—literal and figurative—while the women watched people and gossiped. She noticed an older lady had cozied up to Al and she smiled as he leaned over to tell her something.

The little jingle above the door brought her attention back to the entrance and she scowled. "Ki, why are you here? I was having a good day," she joked with her sister's boyfriend.

Feigning hurt, he clutched his chest and sighed. "Oh Rae, you hurt me so much!"

She rolled her eyes at him and put her hand on her hip. "What do you want? I know you hate coffee and so does Sahara. So..." she waved her hand as if to tell him to get on with it.

"Wow, cranky today," he said and turned to Chrissy. "I'm sorry you have to deal with this on a beautiful Sunday."

Chrissy laughed and walked away. Raelynn was grateful that Chrissy wasn't one of those girls who chased the jocks around, even though she was a student at the university. Kiah was the star of the lacrosse team and the goalie. So, he was well known around Salisbury—and very popular with the girls. Thankfully he was completely taken by her sister and would never cheat on her.

"Tough crowd," he mumbled.

"Really, what are you doing here, Kiah?" she asked again.

He leaned on the counter and became a little more serious. "So, Beau wanted to do something for Ash before she headed back to Minnesota tomorrow. We were thinking about arranging a little surprise thing for her tonight. What time are you off?"

"Supposed to be two-thirty, but might be later if it stays this busy," she replied, looking at the crowd still in the dining room. Even though most were older folks, the students usually trickled in around eleven or twelve. "I'll know more in about an hour or so. What are you thinking?"

"Ok, so do you think you can keep it quiet? Beau is talking to Jacob about trying to do a little surprise thing. Maybe like seven tonight? I think Beau wants to go down to Alley Oops, but Jacob is thinking somewhere a little quieter."

"How about we just go to the bowling alley in Salisbury? That'll be a little quieter than OC," she suggested, knowing the place in Ocean City will be crazy even though it is now technically off season for tourists.

Kiah brightened and nodded. "That's a better idea. I'll let them know. See you later, Rae! Remember, don't tell Ashley!" he sang over his shoulder as he left the café.

Raelynn watched him leave and just shook her head. Remembering her friend was leaving tomorrow dampened her mood a little. She had other friends, but she and Ashley had bonded quickly over the few months she was there. She was going to miss her. Thinking of the other friends she had introduced Ashley to over the summer and fall, she pulled out her phone and texted Kiah. She could invite the other girls if this wasn't just a family thing. His quick reply had her nodding, and she sent out a message to her friends in their group chat, remembering to remove Ashley from it. She invited them all to Southbound at seven, and emphasized it was a surprise.

Suddenly she remembered that it was almost Ashley's birthday, which meant it was also Beau's. Ashley and Beau had discovered just a couple months ago that they were part of a set of triplets. Ashley's identical twin was back in Minnesota. Their story fascinated her and renewed her hope that she could find her dad and they could be reunited again. Her thoughts drifted to what that would be like.

The bell ringing again broke through her thoughts. A man walked in wearing dirty clothing and a shaggy beard. His hair looked scraggly and in need of a haircut. He looked homeless, but he didn't look sick or starving. His gaze was laser focused on Raelynn. He walked right up to the counter and stood in front of her, but he didn't order right away. She felt immediately uncomfortable, but she wasn't sure why. She didn't usually get bothered by people and their behavior. But this man stared at her and didn't even glance at the menu above her head once. She hadn't seen him before, so he wasn't a regular who didn't need to look at the menu to know what they wanted.

"Hi," she said nervously. "Can I help you?" She tried to brush aside her anxiousness as she waited for him to respond. It was then that she noticed the long scar going from his left temple to his chin. It was a thin black line, so she knew it wasn't new, but it was ominous looking. She resisted a shiver, thinking of her crime shows and the stereotypical "bad guy" look this man gave her.

He broke eye contact with her to glance above her and then his eyes immediately found hers again. "Black coffee," he said with a quiet but gravelly voice.

Raelynn nodded and then rang it up for him. He set two crumpled bills from his pocket on the counter and then reached into his front pocket and pulled out an oval rubber looking thing that he squeezed open and removed three pennies, setting those on the counter as well. She stared at the money in front of her and gazed back at his now empty hand. She had only seen those coin cases on two other occasions. Once with her father and once with Poppop. She had never seen anyone else carry one.

She looked up to meet his eyes again and a throat cleared next to her.

"Rae, are you ok?" Chrissy asked, looking between the two.

Raelynn jumped slightly and looked over at her. She picked up the bills and straightened them out on the edge of the counter. She swept up the coins and put them in her register. Chrissy had poured the coffee for the man, and he had moved to a table across from the counter but hadn't taken his eyes off Raelynn.

"Chrissy, I'm going to run to the bathroom real quick," she told her coworker. "Be right back."

Giving her a worried look, Chrissy nodded, and Raelynn hurried to the employee bathroom in the back. Once inside the small room, she locked the door and leaned against it. She did not recognize the man. But he seemed to know her. She calmed her breathing and moved to the sink to splash some cold water on her face. There was something about him, but she wasn't sure if it terrified her or not. He didn't smile but he didn't look threatening either. She didn't know what to think about it.

It didn't take long before Chrissy was knocking on the door. "Hey, Rae? Are you ok? That guy left, if that's what's wrong."

Raelynn dried her face with the paper towels and took in another deep breath of air. She opened the door to a very concerned coworker.

"Sorry, Chrissy. I just got a little freaked out. That was really weird, right?" she asked. "Tell me I'm not the only one who thought it was weird."

Chrissy nodded. "Yeah, he was creepy. Once you left, he literally got up and left the café. Do you know him?"

"No way!" Raelynn almost yelled. "Sorry," she muttered. "I don't know who he was, but he acted like he knew me." She let out a small shudder. People didn't usually get under her skin. Normally she would just stare back at someone like that.

She shrugged her shoulders and stretched her neck. She was fine, *this was nothing to worry about*, she tried to convince herself, looking in the mirror at her reflection.

She joined Chrissy at the door, and they walked back to the front together. Raelynn noticed it was nearly empty in the small restaurant when she looked around.

They separated at the counter. Chrissy went back to the bakery display and continued to refill the items that were low. Raelynn moved to the cash register and checked her supply of change and added to the already full stacks of cups and lids. It wasn't too long before the lunch crowd would start coming in. Susiana came out to double check everything, completely oblivious to the previous customer and what happened with Raelynn.

"Are we all set, girls?" she asked looking at their work over their shoulders. With a satisfied nod, she moved back to her office again. Raelynn laughed lightly. Susiana was rarely involved in the everyday workings of the café, but she did make amazing desserts and treats and did all the financial stuff. Raelynn liked her job and was paid well so she didn't mind. She also appreciated that Susiana trusted them to do their job without her worrying about it.

If she could make a living from just working there, she would in a heartbeat. Maybe she would win the lottery or something and then she could just work with Susiana and not worry about money or bills. *Wishful thinking, Rae*, she thought with a snort.

The ding of the door brought both Raelynn and Chrissy's attention to the newcomers. A group of three students walked in with bookbags over their shoulders and computers in their hands. The two girls shared a look and then returned their attention to the new customers.

Raelynn greeted the group as they reached the counter. The three of them ordered simple coffees with creamer making it easier on Raelynn than she had expected. *It must be close to midterms*, she thought. Typically, the students would come in with complicated latte or cappuccino orders. But during test times, they seemed to just want the caffeine of straight coffee.

The rest of her shift went by without much excitement. She was grateful to finally be off work and walking to her car. The sun was shining and there were few clouds in the sky. The temperature had warmed to a comfortable seventy-six and Raelynn carried the jacket she had worn in the morning instead of putting it on. She tossed it in the back seat as she slid behind the wheel.

It was almost two forty-five when she finally escaped work, but she didn't mind. She just needed to get home to let Timmy out and give him some cuddle time before the little party tonight. It should be fun for Ashley and Beau to spend their first birthday together. She had no doubt they would FaceTime Aja, Ashley's identical twin, for the party too. It was a bummer she couldn't stay to share the day, but she had a job with her uncle in Minnesota with an FBI unit there.

She thought back to those two weeks that Aja and Ashley were there together during the summer. They were so much fun, and aside from appearances, they were complete opposites. Ashley was more like Raelynn, outgoing and loved to go out and do stuff while Aja was quieter and didn't mind spending time alone. But she did come out of her shell a little bit while they were together.

The drive back to her apartment went by quickly. She hurried inside to let her pup out. Just as she was putting her key in the lock, she heard voices from inside her apartment. She leaned in, her hand frozen in front of the keyhole, listening. She heard Timmy's single deep bark and knew who was inside.

With a smile, she unlocked the door and saw her sister sitting on the couch with Timmy standing in front of her, wagging his tail so hard it looked like a blur. Sahara looked over and smiled.

"I love this dog," she said. "Why didn't we ever get a dog when we were little?"

Raelynn shrugged. "Maybe because mom could barely afford to feed us."

Sahara scowled. "Oh yeah. There's that." She turned back to the attention hound in front of her and scratched under his chin, murmuring how good of a dog he was.

"I'm gonna go change," Raelynn said over her shoulder as she made her way to her bedroom. She could wear casual clothes to work; Susiana didn't mind as long as it was clean, no holes, and nothing outrageous. She was a pretty laid-back boss and even Raelynn had to admit she had good employees who wouldn't abuse the leniency Susiana offered. She still liked to change out of the clothes she worked in once she got home.

She quickly found some shorts and a t-shirt and threw her work clothes in her basket. It was Sunday and usually her laundry night, but she knew that wouldn't happen tonight with Ashley's birthday/goodbye party. She quickly checked to make sure she had clean clothes for work the next few days, so she didn't have to rush to get something clean at the last minute.

Walking back out to the living room, she plopped down next to Sahara. "How long have you been here?" she asked her sister.

Sahara shrugged. "No idea. Maybe a couple hours. This big lug is so lazy! I tried to get him to go on a walk and he was so excited to go out that he almost ran out the door! But then by the time we got to the end of the driveway, he just laid down and wouldn't get up!" She shook her head at the pup now sound asleep at her feet.

Raelynn laughed. "Yep, sounds about right! That's why I love him. Low maintenance and loves to cuddle. Maybe too much though. He takes over my bed most nights," she said with a chuckle.

Her sister had been just as excited as Raelynn was to get Timmy. She spent a lot of time at Raelynn's, using the excuse she missed her sister being around all the time, but Raelynn knew it had more to do with the dog than her. One would have thought Raelynn had a baby, not a pet.

"I'm surprised you're not out with Kiah, planning this party thing he has going on." Raelynn turned to face her sister, resting one leg on the couch between them.

Sahara sighed. "Yeah, well I was kinda kicked out of the party planning," she said with a resigned tone.

Raelynn furrowed her brows. "What? Why?"

"Apparently the boys wanted to do this themselves," she said with almost a sneer in her voice, doing air quotes with her fingers.

Not holding in her laugh, Raelynn patted her arm. "I don't think I'd worry too much about it, 'Sha," she said gently. "This is their only chance to celebrate with Ashley.

And Beau had never known about his sisters so I'm sure he is really trying here."

Sahara sighed. "I know, but it's still annoying. I mean I'm a *girl*. I should be helping plan a party for another *girl*." She looked over at her sister and narrowed her eyes. "And you know I hate that nickname."

Raelynn nodded and smiled. "I know."

"Brat," Sahara said and smacked her arm, but Raelynn just laughed.

"Hey, at least it's not like you have to worry about Kiah going after Ashley anymore, right? He's still all yours. Let him plan the party for his sister and brother. And if it turns out terrible, we can just use that for eternity to taunt him." She shrugged and Sahara nodded slowly.

When they all first met Ashley, everyone had thought he might have a thing for her, but after it turned out they were related, that thought was quickly dismissed, much to Raelynn's relief. She knew she would kick anyone's ass for hurting her sister.

"Hey, when does Kiah start lacrosse practices?" Raelynn asked suddenly.

Sahara and Kiah were both freshmen at Salisbury University and Kiah was going to be the starting goalie as a freshman, which was unheard of. The team had multiple championship titles, so it was a big deal for him to be a starter just coming in. It was one of the reasons Sahara had become less confident lately, worried he wouldn't still be interested in her when he was basically going to be a celebrity on campus. So far nothing had changed, but she still seemed worried, especially since the season hadn't started yet.

Sahara sighed. "He's doing workouts with the team already, but I don't know when practices actually start. Why?"

Raelynn shrugged. "Just curious. So, what is the plan for tonight? Kiah came in and just told me seven. How do they plan to get Ash there and maintain the surprise?"

A snort came out of Sahara as she stared at her sister. "You really think they will be able to pull this off as a surprise? I have no doubt Jacob will be able to keep it quiet, but these idiots told everyone to be there at seven but haven't taken into account when Ashley will get there. I highly doubt it will be a surprise in the true sense of a 'surprise party', Rae."

Raelynn could see her sister resist an eye roll which made her laugh. "It'll be all fine, madam party planner. Tell you what, we have just a few days until my birthday. How about you plan a party for me?"

"Really?" Her excitement quickly vanished, and she glared at her older sister. "Right, like you would let me throw you a party. You never celebrate your birthday, Rae," her sister argued.

This wasn't a lie. Raelynn didn't like celebrating her birthday because it was a reminder of her dad not being there. He had gone missing not even a month before her eighth birthday and she never really felt like celebrating. That first birthday without him had almost gone unnoticed, but Honesty had remembered at the last minute and threw together a homemade cake and candles, but it didn't feel the same. Her birthday was when her dad would take her out to get ice cream at Island Creamery, their secret place and her favorite ice cream on the shore. She hadn't even been back since her seventh birthday.

It was also when he would give her a special new turtle for her collection. Usually, they made the turtles out of things they found on their beach walks or somewhere the two of them went. But the birthday ones were ones he made, whittled out of wood or sparkly rocks he found and cleaned. She glanced at her shelf and noticed the new turtle. It was just under a week until her twenty-third birthday and the turtle showed up yesterday. Could her dad really be trying to tell her something? Was he out there and not able to contact her directly so he sent her a message the only way he knew how?

"Rae?" Her sister's concerned voice intruded her thoughts.

"Huh? What?" she asked looking at Sahara.

"You were off somewhere in Lala Land. Are you ok?"

Raelynn nodded. "Yeah, just thinking."

Sahara sighed. "I know. I know what you think about this time of year. And it's fine. I won't plan a party for your birthday since I know you are just trying to make me feel better." Her face lit up as she added, "But when you are ready for an epic birthday party to make up for all the ones that you have skipped, I will be there with swatches of fabric and catalogs of supplies ready!" She wiggled her eyebrows, making Raelynn grin.

"That is a deal!" she said and held out her hand as if to shake on it. She knew someday she would want to celebrate her birthday again, but she wasn't sure when that would be because of the grief still associated with that day.

Timmy let out a snort from his spot still firmly planted on Sahara's feet making both of them laugh out loud.

"I think my foot is going to sleep, Rae," Sahara said with a grin. "This dog is so heavy!"

Raelynn just laughed.

"Let's get some dinner and get ready for this party, shall we?" she asked her sister.

At the word dinner, Timmy suddenly sat upright, like he hadn't just been sound asleep. Raelynn laughed again. "Oh yes, and you too, Timmy. I would hate for you to miss a meal!"

Chapter 4

Sahara and Raelynn arrived at the bowling alley a little before seven. They still weren't sure what time the boys had planned for Ashley to arrive, so they decided to meet earlier. Raelynn had invited a few of the girls she and Ashley had hung out with while she was there. Raelynn spotted the small group sitting at one of the tables just inside the doors.

"Hey girl!" one of them called as Raelynn and her sister entered.

Raelynn waved and moved to one of the open seats. "Hey! How are all y'all?

It had been a while since they had all been able to hang out with everyone now working full-time jobs and trying to get out on their own.

Sahara hung back by the doors, apparently waiting for anyone else to show up—namely Kiah, Raelynn knew without asking. She wished her sister wouldn't be so self-conscious. The guy wasn't going anywhere. Maybe she would try to corner Kiah and remind him that her sister might need a little extra TLC and reassurance.

An arm wrapping around her from behind made Raelynn jump. She turned to see Ashley's smiling face and spun to get up.

"What are you doing here already? We were supposed to yell surprise and all that!" She pulled her friend in for a hug, shooting Sahara, who was still at the door, a knowing look and grin. She had guessed it right.

Ashley laughed. "Yeah, you have a bunch of guys planning a party and aren't very slick, this is what you get." She lifted her eyes to the rest of the table and waved at everyone. "Hey guys! It's been a minute! What's new with everyone?"

Jacob, her boyfriend, came up next to her and looked around. "The other two aren't even here yet, are they?"

Ashley laughed and shook her head. "Nope!" Then she started to introduce everyone at the table to him.

The group decided to get a couple of lanes to bowl a game or two while they eat and visit. They got rental shoes and were settling back down at the tables when Beau and Kiah finally arrived, with balloons and a cake in hand.

They walked to the group with huge grins on their faces. Raelynn's eyes drifted behind them, and she let out a gasp, drawing the attention of everyone else. Ashley turned and then jumped up into her twin sister's arms. *So, the surprise wasn't the party apparently*, she thought. *Brilliant*. Getting Aja here for the triplets to celebrate their first birthday together couldn't have been easy and keeping it from Ashley had to have been hard since the twins are so close.

Sahara was standing next to Kiah now and he had his arm around her, holding her tight to his side.

"How did you pull this off?" Ashley exclaimed to Beau, giving him a light smack on his shoulder.

He just shrugged. "I thought it would be fun to celebrate a birthday before you disappeared from my life again."

She bumped into his side playfully and scoffed. "That's never going to happen. We are now connected. Even if we wanted to disappear, we couldn't. We are connected by blood, never to be separated again!"

The three of them shared a group hug and then moved to get shoes. Raelynn watched with a little bit of envy. She hoped she would be able to share a hug with her dad again someday. She loved her sister and brother and mom, but she missed her dad so much. Beau didn't know what he was missing until he found Ashley and Aja. Raelynn knows what she has been missing out on. The bond she shared with her dad was so much deeper than just blood. They were deeply connected, so tightly bonded together she didn't think she would ever find another person she could be that close to.

She was pulled from her thoughts again by another entrance. Beau and Kiah's parents had joined the party.

"If you think I was going to miss having all my kids together for this epic birthday, you were sadly mistaken!" Shay, their mom, exclaimed to the group. She pulled the triplets into her embrace and then Kiah as well, who reluctantly let go of Sahara to hug his mom. "I never thought I'd see this day," she mumbled, wiping a single tear from her cheek.

The group let out a sigh all together, like something out of a movie, making them all giggle.

"Ok, let's bowl!" Kiah said, pulling Sahara back to him. "Are you and dad bowling too?" he asked his mom.

They both shook their heads. "Nope, we are just here to watch," his dad, a professor at the university, said.

Raelynn quickly joined in the festivities, brushing aside thoughts of her dad for the night. This would be the last time she would see her friend for a while, and she wanted to enjoy every minute of it. Plus, with Aja here, she wasn't going to waste the fun.

She found herself watching Beau. He had always seemed to be around since Kiah and Sahara got together, but she never really had a chance to get to know him. He always seemed a little more reserved than Kiah and just kind of hung around, not talking much. As she looked at the triplets, she realized he was a perfect mix of Aja and Ashley. He didn't seem totally uncomfortable around the large group, but he also seemed to prefer the smaller groups. He seemed to move between everyone easily, whereas Aja was a little more reserved and followed Ashley's lead. She definitely didn't seem comfortable venturing out on her own.

Beau wasn't exactly a recluse he was just quieter than Ashley and Raelynn were. Before last summer, he would hang around a little more and it would be the four of them doing things. She suspected Sahara didn't want her to feel left out and that's why Beau hung around, but truth be told, she didn't mind being a third wheel. Kiah was entertaining and the banter between the two of them was pretty fun. She never really felt out of place and loved to see her sister happy and how well Kiah treated her.

The group had ordered pizzas, actually their parents had, and then they made a big deal about the cake. They all acted like the triplets were turning five with how big a deal they were making this. There were so many pictures taken in so many different poses and mixtures of people it was comical. Raelynn just watched and laughed at everything. The familiar pang was there, but she brushed it aside.

Sahara came over to her side and gave her a side hug, seeming to understand her thoughts. Raelynn patted her sister's arm, glad for her embrace. But she wasn't about to take anything away from this family. It was still a little unbelievable to her. She couldn't imagine finding out about a whole new group of people who turned out to be so connected. She couldn't help but wonder if her dad had another family somewhere. If he had run off, he could easily have a different wife and kids. But Raelynn dismissed the idea very quickly; she refused to believe he ran off on his own.

The "Happy Birthday" song rang through the entire building as the group sang loudly. One would think they were all drinking heavily with how crazy and loud they all were. But no one had a drop of alcohol. Laughter rang out and Shay cut the cake, giving everyone a huge piece. The cake itself was decorated in three separate sections, each of the triplets getting their own little tribute. It was cute, Raelynn thought.

As the night wore on, everyone began to take their leave. Pretty soon it was just Beau, Ashley, Jacob, Aja, Kiah, Sahara, and Raelynn. They were spread out at one of the tables reminiscing about the last few months. It amazed Raelynn how quickly they had all connected and got along. There didn't seem to be anything awkward about their little group from the very beginning.

"I guess we should get going," Jacob announced. "We have to be up and on the road by five." He glanced over at Ashley for confirmation.

"Yeah, I guess," she confirmed. "This was so much fun. I am glad you guys did this," she said to Beau. "And to pull off the ultimate surprise by getting Aja here undetected, amazing!" She pulled her twin in for another hug and laughed.

Aja smiled. "I am so excited for the drive back. An actual road trip!" She was almost giddy in her seat.

Raelynn had learned that while they had traveled a lot with their uncle growing up, they didn't get to go on vacation much. She could relate to that. Honesty had never had enough money saved to be able to do a vacation. She was literally working to put a roof over their heads and food on the table. Maybe someday she will be able to drive to visit her new friends and experience that vacation thing too.

"I should get going as well. I have a hot date with my pillow," Raelynn chimed in, suddenly feeling the lack of sleep catch up with her.

The group stood and exchanged hugs all around. They made sure they all had phone numbers and social media connections before they left.

Beau suddenly appeared by Raelynn's side. "Hey, are you gonna be ok? With your new bestie leaving and all." He smirked, a look she hadn't seen in a long time on his face.

She laughed at him. "Really? You make it sound like I am losing my sister or something." She gave him a little shove with her arm and grinned. "I am ok. How are you though? This has been a lot in the last few months. Are you doing alright?"

Beau shrugged. "I guess. It was weird at first, but now it seems like the missing pieces are all in place, the way

Bonded Blood

it always should have been. Does that sound corny and stupid?" He cringed as he squinted his eyes at her.

Raelynn laughed. "Not at all. I would still be reeling I think." She stepped back from him and crossed her arms in front of her. "You know though, you seem to be a little different."

"What do you mean different?" he asked, his tone genuinely curious.

Raelynn shrugged. "Like not so sulky and angry…" She waited a beat before she waved him off. "Then again, maybe you are just on a high from the sugar and party atmosphere. I'm sure that sulkiness will come back." She shrugged again and turned away from him, heading for the rest of the group that had gotten ahead of the two of them.

"Seriously? Have you always been this annoying?" he asked from behind her.

She could hear the teasing in his voice and his footsteps quickly catching up to her. Raelynn smiled to herself. She had never really thought about Beau as anything other than a friend to hang out with while her sister and his brother hung out. They didn't really talk much then either.

But since he had been spending more time with Ashley, Raelynn had gotten to know him a little better and really liked hanging out with him. She wasn't sure if his broodiness was from all this family stuff and now a weight had been lifted from his shoulders, but she liked this new Beau. She could tease him, and he wouldn't get frustrated and huff at her.

She reached the rest of the group and gave Ashley a tight hug. "I am going to miss you, woman!" she said with a smile.

Ashley giggled. "I know. I will miss you and this place. I have a feeling I shouldn't be leaving now though. The weather is finally getting nice!"

Raelynn laughed. Ashley and Jacob were both wearing shorts and t-shirts while everyone else was in jeans and light jackets. She just shook her head. "I don't understand your temperature gauge, that's for sure!" Raelynn gave Jacob and Aja quick hugs and then turned to leave, nearly bumping into Beau who had moved to stand right behind her without her noticing.

Beau grabbed her shoulders to steady her, so she didn't stumble backwards. "Hey, are you in that big of a hurry to get out of here?" he asked, that smirk back on his face.

She scowled at him. "Maybe." Raelynn glared at him, trying to hide her embarrassment.

The girls exchanged a few more promises to stay in contact and to visit when they could and then Raelynn headed to her car. Sahara was going back to campus with Kiah, so Raelynn headed off by herself. Her thoughts were tumbling around in her head, drifting from the family Beau and Kiah now had to her own family.

She startled in her seat when there was a knock on her window. She turned to see Beau standing outside her door. She started her car and then put the window down. "Hey, everything ok?" she asked.

Beau nodded and leaned against her window, his forearms resting on the frame. "Yeah. I was just going to see if you wanted to grab dinner or something sometime." He shrugged slightly and avoided her eyes. He may have been a little like a cranky old man before, but he never lacked confidence. He looked a little nervous as he asked her out, but he still held himself with that confident air. Not in the cocky way Kiah acted, though.

Raelynn studied him and then slowly nodded. "Sure. But I have to tell you if you are using me to get to Ashley, it won't work." She grinned with a wink.

His laugh rang out in the darkness, his eyes rolling at the same time. "Ok, noted. I'll text you if that's ok. I have to work for the next few days so maybe this weekend?"

"Sounds like a plan," she said. "I am off Saturday for… well, I'm off. So, Friday or Saturday would be good." She didn't want to tell him she was off for her birthday. It would sound a little like she was asking for a gift or something. That wasn't it. She just decided to do something for herself this year. She had asked to be scheduled for the second shift on Sunday, but she wasn't positive what the hours would be for Sunday anyway since it was Halloween. Susiana had a little boy who would likely be trick or treating later so she may not have to work at all. She'd be lying if she said she'd be upset for the extra day off, though.

Either way, she wasn't really sure what she would be doing, if anything. She would probably be spending it with Timmy, maybe cuddling and watching old movies. She knew she could work if needed and didn't mind the schedule being up in the air. She would likely have to make up for the weekend off, but she didn't care. She was going to take the time off and enjoy it.

Beau nodded. "Ok. See you later, Rae." He smiled, tapped the roof of her car, and stepped away.

She waved and pulled slowly out of the parking lot, heading to her place. She and Sahara had left about five hours ago, and it would be perfect timing to get Timmy out and then take a nice long hot bath. She hoped she could sleep since she hadn't the night before. Her body seemed to be getting the message already because she was starting to feel a little sleepy.

She was grateful for Susiana's weird hours. Mondays she opened earlier than normal but closed by noon. She liked to hit the early work crowd and then business seemed to die off by lunch. She didn't have a huge lunch menu anyway, so Mondays were typically Raelynn's day off. She tried to convince her boss to do the same on Sundays, but they tended to have quite a few people come in on Sundays after church, so she kept it to Mondays only.

Susiana had another person who wanted only Mondays because it worked with her other job's schedule, and Raelynn didn't mind having that day off. She was looking forward to sleeping in. She tried to take off another random day of the week but usually wasn't picky. Susiana just picked a different one to give her off based on everyone else's schedules. It worked for Raelynn, since she didn't have any other obligations to worry about.

Raelynn found her thoughts drifting to Beau. She had once thought about him in a dating option kind of way but had written it off a while ago because of his moodiness. He just always seemed angry or annoyed. She wondered if it was about her and decided it wasn't what she wanted to get involved with regardless of what was going on with him. She didn't like getting involved in any drama and he seemed to be completely immersed in it.

She had to admit he seemed so different tonight though. He was smiling more than she ever remembered before. She wondered if the family stuff was what was wrong before and now he was ok. She couldn't help but wonder

Bonded Blood

if the unknown wore on him, like she knows it has on her with her own family. Maybe he would share that with her on their date, she thought. It would make sense though.

Realization hit her as she parked in her lot. *I have a date with Beau? Like for real?* She suddenly felt like the high school girl who just got asked out by the school's hottest, most popular guy. She knew if she looked at her cheeks they would likely be bright red. She was being ridiculous, but she couldn't help the grin on her face. She honestly couldn't remember the last time she went on a date.

Raelynn nearly skipped into the building, fully aware that she was being silly. As she put her key in the lock she heard Timmy bark. She smiled. He knew it was her at the door and she couldn't wait to get in and cuddle him. She wondered if one day he would meet her at the door and jump on her like Dino from the Flintstones when Fred came home from work. She actually hoped not after she remembered how big he was.

She opened the door and then relocked it after she got inside. Dropping her keys on the table, she moved into the kitchen for a glass of water. Timmy was sitting in front of the fridge, and she swore he was glaring at her.

"What?" she asked him. "Was I out too late?" She bent down and scratched behind his ears, his weakness. She giggled when he flopped over on his side and stretched, begging for more pets. She gave him belly rubs and then Raelynn laid down next to him, draping her arm over his thick body.

They laid like that for a while. She felt herself starting to fall asleep, so she jumped up. "Come on, buddy. Let's go potty and then get to bed."

Timmy moved to sit, lazily, and then almost reluctantly followed her to the door. She chuckled at his slow pace. When she finally got him outside, she didn't even bother to sit outside and wait. He walked to his favorite pee spot and then came right back in. He didn't even wait for her to close the door before he was in her bedroom stretching out on the bed.

"You know, I think I might get tired of you taking up the whole bed one day, but for now, I love it," she said with a grin. She rubbed his head with her forehead and then headed to the bathroom to change and get to bed herself.

* * * * *

Raelynn awoke to a wet nose in her face. She opened her eyes and was face to face with Timmy. "What time is it?" she asked him, as if he would answer. She rolled over to grab her phone just as it alerted her to a text. The light was streaming in through the slats of the cheap blinds on her bedroom window, so it couldn't be too early, she thought. Since she didn't work she wasn't in any hurry to get anything done anyway.

She opened her texts and saw her mom had texted her. She must be on her break at work because it was after nine o'clock, she noticed.

Good morning, honey. Just wanted to check in. I'll be at work until late tonight so I was wondering if you could come over later on and make dinner for your brother and sister. Or pick up pizzas or something. Sahara is working until six too or I'd ask her.

She could guess what that really meant. Typically, Kiah and Sahara would go out after she finished working. Sahara didn't have a car yet and Kiah liked to pick her up. She worked close to the house and could walk, but he had the luxuries of not having to work and a car. Kiah claimed he didn't like her walking even the four blocks to the doctor's office where she worked as a receptionist.

Sahara had been working there for a couple of years and they had been great working around her high school schedule, and she really liked the doctor and other staff. They had already agreed to keep her on while she was in college. She planned to go into the medical field but wasn't sure she had it in her to go to medical school. Maybe a physician's assistant or a medical assistant. She wasn't sure yet. And since they were such different degrees, she was just doing a heavy load of sciences this year to see if she was even cut out for the field at all.

"No problem," Raelynn said slowly as she typed it to her mom. After she pressed the send button, she turned back to see an expectant face staring at her. "What?"

Timmy tipped his head to the side making her laugh. "I know, stupid question. It's breakfast time, isn't it?"

She flipped the covers off and Timmy immediately jumped off the bed and walked alongside her as if he was guiding her out of the room. "Guess we are going right outside then," she mumbled as he made his way to the door to be let out, not giving her a chance to get to the bathroom first.

Raelynn held her arms while she waited for Timmy to finish. It was a chilly morning, and she just had her pajama shorts and shirt on. Thankfully he didn't take long, he must have been waiting for a while, she thought. She got his breakfast ready and then bolted to the bathroom. The cold air and then having to wait for Timmy didn't do her any favors.

By the time she came back out, dressed and ready for whatever the day would bring, Timmy was lying by the door waiting to take care of his second round of business.

When he saw her walking toward him, he lifted his head, but didn't make a move to stand. Raelynn stood next to him and crossed her arms.

"Are we doing this or not, big guy?" she asked with a smile. When he didn't move, she lifted her hand to open the sliding door, and he finally moved. She hooked him up to his chain and then followed him out. It was much more comfortable now that she had a sweatshirt on. She looked at her phone while Timmy did his thing.

She had a text from Ashley that they had left around five-thirty. She didn't say goodbye, only that she would see her soon. She promised to come back and visit after Christmas—and emphasized probably not in the summer again, making Raelynn laugh. She would love this morning's temperature and was probably driving through the mountains at this point, loving the cool air. Raelynn on the other hand preferred the heat of summer. She figured that probably came from spending her whole life on the Eastern Shore.

Timmy appeared at her feet and looked up at her expectantly, and a little impatiently. "You are definitely the laziest dog I have ever met," she said with a grin and shake of her head. She followed him and then headed for the kitchen to make herself something to eat.

She had started to get some basic cooking lessons from Susiana at work. She liked to bake but didn't always have the time. She had learned to make simple things like egg and bagel sandwiches and omelets. She hated how long it took to make pancakes, and she resorted to store bought waffles for the same reason. When she was growing up, she relied on easy dinners like pasta and sandwiches. Peanut butter and noodles were cheaper than meat and potatoes. Even seafood wasn't inexpensive, in spite of living in a geographical area where it was abundant and fresh.

Looking in her fridge, Raelynn opted to throw together an omelet. She made a mental note to go shopping for groceries. She hated that task and avoided it until she absolutely had to go—which sadly looked to be now. Groaning, she grabbed a pen and notepad. Since she had the day off, it would be a good day to get that annoying job done. Typically, she just walked through the store to see what spoke to her, but she was out of almost everything so she would need at least a partial list. If she shopped without one, she would definitely go over her food budget.

Raelynn checked on Timmy's supply of dog food and treats and then decided she might as well get this undesirable task done with. She could make something better when she got back and had more choices. Maybe that would be motivation to stick to her list and get in and out quickly. She could pick up something for dinner at her mom's house too, making that request even easier for herself. Satisfied with her plan, Raelynn gave Timmy one last scratch and then headed out.

Chapter 5

After packing away the groceries back at her place and having a quick, but small lunch, Raelynn headed to her mom's. As she pulled up to the house, she let out a sigh. She had lived in this house as long as she could remember. Honesty had formally adopted her the year after her dad went missing so the county wouldn't step in and take her away. Raelynn had always been grateful for the protectiveness Honesty felt over her. Maybe that's why she always saw Honesty as her mom and nothing less. Her DNA didn't matter, Raelynn was always treated the same as Sahara by Honesty.

Her dad and Honesty had married shortly before Sahara was born but they had never done the official adoption process because it was an extra expense. Raelynn didn't really think much about it when she was younger, but when Honesty spent the extra money to legalize their relationship, she realized how much it meant to have that piece of paper. She appreciated it now more than ever as she looked at the small rundown home in front of her.

Honesty took good care of it and made sure any repairs were taken care of as quickly as she could afford. One of the neighbors had offered a long time ago to cut her grass for her every week. He always said it was easy because the lawns were pretty small, and it saved him turning so much at the property lines. Raelynn thought he might actually have a crush on her mom, but Honesty had made it clear a long time ago that she wasn't interested. Either way, it helped Honesty out with the upkeep of the property.

The day had warmed up to close to seventy-five, but Raelynn kept her jacket on as she made her way to the front door. She noticed a small box on the porch next to the door. It wasn't a huge space, with just enough room for two lawn chairs. She would have stepped on it if she hadn't been looking down. She picked it up and then unlocked the door.

The house was quiet as she had expected since Jericho was still at school and Sahara was working. She set the box down and then moved to the kitchen to drop off the bag of groceries she had brought. It wasn't much, just a frozen lasagna, bagged lettuce, and a loaf of French bread to heat up. She wasn't sure who would be eating but if there were leftovers, she would leave them for Jericho to have the next night if Honesty was working late again. *It's about time for him to learn to use the microwave to feed himself,* she thought.

Raelynn started to unpack the bread and got the lasagna ready to bake. She preheated the oven and then looked around for what else she would need for serving. It didn't take long before she had everything ready to go. Since the lasagna was frozen it would take the longest to be ready.

She glanced at the clock and saw that it was almost four. Her brother should have been home by now. "Where is he?" she asked the empty house.

As if on cue, Jericho opened the front door. "Hey Rae!" he called from the entrance. He walked into the kitchen with the box in his hand. "Why's this by the door? It has your name on it."

Raelynn turned around and looked at him. "What? Really?" She moved to his outstretched hand and once she took it, he turned and ran up the stairs. "Dinner in an hour, Jericho," she called after him, just before his door closed.

She eyed the package in her hand. She hadn't even looked at the name when she picked it up earlier. Now she was curious. The address label was like the last one—no sender information. But Jericho was right. It was again addressed to her with Honesty's address. Part of her was glad this person didn't have her new address, but the other part was curious as to why they were sending anonymous packages. And how did they know Honesty's address? How did they know Raelynn would get the package at this address? She hadn't lived here in a few years. But most importantly on her mind was what was in this one?

"Only one way to find out," she muttered as she moved to get a pair of scissors. She gave the box a light shake before she set it down and started to cut the tape. It felt slightly heavier than the one on Saturday with a similar rattle. But this time it sounded like multiple things were being bumped together instead of just one thing knocking against the sides.

"Hm," Raelynn said. "Weird." She set the scissors aside and pulled the flaps open. Like the last box, this one was full of brown paper. But there were two distinct bundles in it, with some crumpled pieces surrounding them.

She pulled the first bundle out of the box and started to unravel the paper. This bundle was slightly bigger than the other one. Raelynn continued to unwrap the object until a dull red turtle was staring back at her. Her breath caught in her throat as she turned it around in her hand. "What the hell," she muttered. This one was made of some sort of plastic, and it looked like a preschooler had made it out of some sort of upside-down bowl. It was so different from the beautiful one she received on Saturday, which was clearly store bought.

She turned it over in her hand and there was a number scratched on the bottom. "Forty-four? What?" She shook her head and set it down. It was slightly bigger than her hand but still not heavy at all.

Raelynn turned her attention to the other bundle. This one was smaller and very light. As she unwrapped it, she felt sharp edges, so she slowed down even more with her unraveling. She dropped the paper and held something she had to assume was another turtle. This one was made out of seashells. She furrowed her brow looking at it. The biggest shell was the turtle's shell and then there were smaller ones that were its head and legs. *In a weird way it's kind of cute*, she thought.

"The hell is that?" Jericho yelled from the entryway.

Raelynn turned to him and scowled. "Language, Jer." She wasn't about to tell her brother about the strange deliveries or her turtles. He was way too young to understand anyway.

"Pfft, whatever. What is that?" he asked again, waving his hand and headed for the fridge.

"Hey, we are having dinner in…" she ignored his question again and checked the time, letting out a groan, "dang it, thirty minutes!" She put the strange new turtles back into the box and closed the flaps of the top. Then Raelynn turned back to the oven. Thankfully she had preheated it before, but she hadn't put the food in yet. She slid the lasagna pan into the heat and then turned to make the salad. The bread could go in just at the end of the cooking time.

Raelynn mixed up the salad and took out plates and cups for herself, Jericho, and Honesty. There was enough food for Sahara and Kiah if they chose to come back in time. Remembering that, she sent a quick text to her sister letting her know there was dinner available. She looked around and sighed seeing that Jericho had disappeared again. She was going to have to get him to start helping out somehow.

By the time she had things close to ready, it was almost five-thirty. She knew her mom was working until six. But she would be home right after, and Raelynn knew she would appreciate dinner being ready. Once everything was done, she turned her attention back to her "gifts."

She removed the two statues again and set them next to each other. Raelynn sat on the chair and put her chin in her hand, biting her lip. What was she looking at and what was going on?

The timer on the oven startled her out of her thoughts and she looked up surprised at the time. How long had she been staring at these things? She got up and checked the lasagna and added the bread to the shelf and reset the timer. With a sigh, she picked up the two turtles and carefully put them back inside the box again. She crumpled up the paper and put it in the recycle bin.

Raelynn leaned against the counter and stared at the box. She was annoyed. She didn't like not knowing something and this package thing was irritating her so much. The worst part was she didn't know what she could do about it.

Her thoughts drifted to the officer she had been in contact with a few months ago when she started her search for her father. He had actually warned her that she should back off for a bit since it seemed to be stirring something up. But he never told her what that something was, he just told her to hold off and put it aside for a while. She was caught up in the stuff with Ashley at that time, so she was fine with it. And then she just never started it up again.

Maybe this was her sign to contact Officer Milton again. She had met with one of his undercover guys during the summer too and he was helping her put feelers out about her dad. They hadn't found anything substantial but then she had to back off. Maybe he would help her out again. She made a mental note to give Officer Milton a call after work the next day.

The oven timer went off breaking into her thoughts. She noticed that Jericho hadn't reappeared after he grabbed what she thought was a soda from the fridge. Her face lit up with a mischievous grin. Now would be a good time to do a little life teaching for him.

She turned off the timer and went to the entrance of the kitchen to call for him.

"Hey, Jericho!" she called. "If you wanna eat, you better get your butt down here and do something to help out!" She heard a groan from upstairs and laughed quietly at her brother.

She moved back to the kitchen and grabbed the oven mitts to take the dinner out of the oven. She set the tray of bread on one side of the stove and lasagna on the other. Then she pulled the salad out of the fridge—she didn't even realize she put it in there—and set it next to the other things. Then she pulled out the salad tongs, serving spoon, and a spatula. She cut the lasagna into squares and waited for her brother to drag his lazy behind down the stairs.

She suspected that he thought if he waited long enough she would have it all done.

Raelynn leaned against the counter and folded her arms across her chest, crossing her ankles one over the other as well.

Jericho finally made his way down the steps as slowly as possible. His shoulders were slumped, his arms hanging past his waist as he dragged himself toward her. Raelynn chuckled at him but waited to say anything until he was in the kitchen.

He looked around and shrugged. "You don't even need me, Rae. Why did you call me down?"

Raelynn straightened and looked around. "Well, I have the food ready, but the table needs to be set and the milk needs to get put on the table. And the butter. You can do some of this Jericho. Be helpful instead of expecting to be waited on like some royalty or something."

Her brother shrugged and gave her a smirk. "It's the perk of being the baby in the family."

Her mouth dropped open staring at her brother. She couldn't believe he had just said that, and she was at a loss for words.

Jericho pointed at her and laughed. "See? You got nothin' to come back with, so you know it's true." Then he moved to the counter where she had laid out the food and looked around. "Hey where are the plates and stuff?"

Raelynn shrugged, finally getting a hold of herself. "I don't know, *baby* boy. Maybe you need me to cut up your food and feed it to you too? Since you can't even reach the plates. Wait, I don't think we have any sippy cups anymore. How will you drink your milk? Should I go get a bottle for the *baby*?" She gave him a pat on the cheek and grinned.

By the time she finished with her teasing, Jericho was visibly irritated. "Ok, ok, I get it. Stop with the baby stuff! God. I was joking. Learn to take a joke, Rae," he grumbled at her.

She stood in the same spot waiting for him to ask again about the dishes. She knew he still wouldn't take the hint and set the table, but she would wait and see how long it took. Raelynn realized she and Sahara had a lot of work to do to get him in shape. She had stacked the plates on the counter behind her, but even if she hadn't taken them out of the cabinets, he hadn't hit his growth spurt yet so he still couldn't reach the shelf they sat on.

Jericho stood in his spot in the middle of the kitchen and turned in a complete circle. His shoulders dropped and he turned to glare at his sister. "Rae!" he whined, making her laugh.

She moved to the side and grinned back. She waved her hand over the plates and cups neatly stacked on the counter like a game show model.

"These, my dear brother, are plates and cups. They are just waiting for you to set the table for everyone." Raelynn moved further to the side and positioned herself at the corner of the cabinets and crossed her arms, staring at Jericho.

Being the defiant and annoying little brother, he smirked and moved to grab a single plate and cup.

Raelynn jumped faster than he expected, knowing he would do something like that, and he dropped the plate before it was more than an inch above the stack. Jericho huffed and took a step back and crossed his own arms.

She almost laughed as he tried to look intimidating, but she was almost five inches taller than he was and had about thirty pounds on him. He didn't stand a chance in the standoff.

The front door opening drew both their attention away and they heard a commotion from the other room. Raelynn turned her attention back to her brother, who did the same. She didn't move though. She knew from the noise it was likely Kiah and Sahara, and she needed her sister's backup to get Jericho to help out.

Sahara seemed to notice the standoff between her siblings as soon as she entered the kitchen. She gave Kiah a jab with her elbow that Raelynn didn't miss. Sahara smirked at her brother, now glaring at her. Raelynn gave her sister a quick nod of her head to show the plates hoping her sister would catch on.

"You know the sooner you set the table, Jericho, the sooner we can all eat," Sahara said with a glint in her eye. Raelynn's grin grew glad her sister knew what was happening. They were always close growing up and now she was glad they could share understanding without words.

Jericho's scowl grew. "You can't make me. Besides, I am a kid. You can't deprive me of food. It's the law." He obviously felt like he hit his jackpot because his scowl turned into a triumphant smile. He crossed his arms over his preteen chest, as if he was some big tough guy now.

Raelynn and Sahara burst out laughing at the same time. "No, Jer. I am not your mommy. Only your mommy is required to feed you. I am your sibling. So, if you want to wait to eat until mom gets home, fine. If you want to eat now, then I suggest you set the table like a good little boy." She ruffled his hair, making him swing his arm at her.

Bonded Blood

"You're a jerk, Rae," he said with annoyance. "I'm just a kid. I can't be expected to take care of you adults."

Sahara came and stood next to her sister. "You know, Jericho, when Rae was your age, she was helping mom cook and clean because mom was working three jobs just to feed us and make sure we could stay in this house. And she was even making sure you were fed when mom couldn't. I don't think you can sit here and argue about your age. Rae was doing as much as mom when she was even younger than you."

Raelynn nodded in agreement. "When I was twelve, you would have only been like three. Back then you couldn't do anything for yourself. But I am starting to wonder if you even can now. Maybe you shouldn't be left alone all day when mom has to work." She turned to her sister and tapped her lips with her finger. "Maybe we should look into a nanny or babysitter for him, Sahara. I don't think the little guy should be left alone for so long."

Raelynn gave her brother a little pout and Kiah laughed from the entryway, drawing their attention to him. The two sisters raised their eyebrows at him.

"What? You guys are funny. I'm hungry so if the little dude isn't going to eat, that's fine, but can us big people?" Kiah asked, lifting his hands in surrender. His voice was almost as whiny as Jericho's.

Sahara and Raelynn looked at each other with wide eyes. Sahara turned to her boyfriend and popped her hip. "Maybe you should help him set the table, Ki."

Kiah waved his hand. "Sure. I don't have a problem setting the table. Beau and I trade off all the time." He looked down at Jericho who thought he had won the debate and grinned. "Figure it out little man. Women are the bosses. The sooner you figure that out the better your existence will be."

Sahara and Raelynn shared a shocked expression and then watched as Jericho grudgingly followed Kiah to the stack of plates and cups and proceeded to set the table.

Honesty walked in just as Jericho set the last fork by the plates. She gasped as she watched. When he had finished, she walked to him and gave him a hug, thanking him for helping out. Jericho's smirk said all Raelynn knew he wanted to say. She would deal with that later, she thought, rolling her eyes.

She brought the tray of lasagna to the table while Sahara brought the salad and bread. The five of them then sat while Honesty said a short prayer. Raelynn listened to her mom once again pray for the safety of everyone they loved, knowing it would hurt Jericho to specify her father and not his, but she knew Honesty's intent. They had talked about it numerous times before and Raelynn understood. They shared a tiny nod, and Raelynn saw the sad smile on her mom's face. *She still missed him as much as me*, she thought.

Her thoughts drifted to the box that was now set aside on the counter. She made a mental note to talk to Honesty about the turtles and see what she thinks. Honesty knew she was doing some digging into her dad's disappearance and had been worried about Raelynn's safety, especially since they didn't know what had happened to her dad. They both had a hard time believing he was mixed up in something that would get him killed. But so much time had passed that they couldn't be sure of anything, especially since he hadn't come back yet.

Bonded Blood

The chatter during dinner was light and Raelynn tuned most of it out, lost in her thoughts. Sahara and Kiah getting up from the table jarred her focus back to the family around her.

"Come on Jericho. Learn how to clean up after yourself now too," Sahara said with a grin.

Jericho grumbled as he stood from his chair, earning him a chuckle and pat on the head from his mom.

"It's good for you to know how to take care of yourself son. You never know, you might be a single guy forever and then who would cook for you?" Honesty asked.

Jericho straightened his back and grinned. He leaned over his mom's shoulder and gave her a hug. "Oh momma. I will always have you to take care of me. It would be your greatest honor I am sure to take care of your *youngest child* forever."

Raelynn laughed, knowing full well where that would get him. She leaned back and crossed her arms, giving him a small nod and tipped her head toward Honesty, as if to say, "listen up, buddy."

Honesty pulled out of his arms and gave him a stern look. "Now listen up good, child. I will not be your maid and cook after you turn eighteen. You need to learn how to take care of yourself. In this day and age, no woman wants to have a useless man around. You got to stand up straight and be a good man, a man any woman would be proud to have by her side."

Jericho scoffed. "Yeah, right. Like the losers who aren't here?"

Raelynn's heart skipped a beat. Again, knowing the truth about his beginnings and the suffering Honesty had gone through, she held her breath. She was about to step in when Honesty spoke up.

"Yes, Jericho. And have you noticed that they are not around? I wouldn't put up with a useless man either. Learn from their mistakes, son. Be a better man." She stood and disappeared through the door.

Raelynn locked eyes with Sahara who had watched her mom walk out the door as well. They knew it wasn't their place to say anything about Jericho's conception, but Raelynn knew she would have to talk to her mom. He needs to know sooner rather than later. He was starting to have the same mentality that women are to be used and not appreciated. His friend's parents weren't helping the situation either. The girls also knew their mom still harbored strong feelings about her missing husband and their father. But they couldn't say any of that to Jericho either.

Kiah stepped up and tugged on Jericho's shirt. "Come on. Let's load the dishwasher."

Jericho didn't fight him this time and just followed behind him. Maybe he realized he had struck a nerve with his mom, Raelynn hoped anyway.

Raelynn was thankful for Kiah being there and showing her brother that it was ok to do the housework and help out. She might have to enlist his help with Jericho after all.

Sahara gave Raelynn a nod and motioned for her to go talk to their mom and make sure she was ok. "I got this," she mouthed to her sister and who then turned to the boys who were working on clearing the table.

Moving quickly from the kitchen, Raelynn headed to her mom's room. It was a small bedroom on the main level. It had been converted from the dining room when Jericho was born. Raelynn actually wondered why her mom hadn't moved back upstairs to her old bedroom, but then she remembered she had taken the bigger room that belonged to her parents. She guessed it was probably still too hard to be in that room for her mom.

As she approached the door, she was struck again by the amount of sacrifice her mom had willingly given for her family. There was just a sheet hanging over the former dining room entrance, they couldn't afford to put a proper door in when she moved to that room. It made Raelynn even more annoyed that her brother was so selfish.

She gently knocked on the wall next to the makeshift door and pushed the thin material slightly to the side to walk through. Honesty was sitting on the double bed looking out the small window.

"I know I should tell him, but I just don't know how," her mom said softly when she saw Raelynn standing in the doorway.

Raelynn moved to sit next to her mom and pulled her hand into her own. "He does need to know, mom. But in your own time. I wish we could find dad. He would set him straight about what's right and how to behave like a man, not this Jamal's dad he's hanging around with." She didn't hide the disgust in her voice at the mention of Jericho's friend.

Honesty let out a small chuckle. "Yeah, that family is somethin', in this day and age." She shook her head and let out a sigh. "I know you are still hoping for a happy reunion, Rae. But I think you need to start facing the fact that your dad is gone." Her voice was low and barely audible.

Raelynn stared at her mom for a second and then shook her head. "I don't know, mom. I need to talk to you about something, but not with everyone here."

That drew her mom's attention, and she studied Raelynn's face. Then she slowly nodded. "Ok, Rae. When Jericho goes to bed tonight we can talk."

"I don't think I can wait that long. I have to get back and let Timmy out," she said, thinking.

Honesty laughed, "That dog." She smiled and shook her head. "How about this? You go get the beast and he can run with Jericho in the backyard since it's fenced and then we can talk."

Raelynn laughed. "Well, I can go get him but he will not run!"

Honesty laughed with her and nodded. "Ok, he can sit or lay in the yard with Jericho."

"Ok," Raelynn said, still chuckling. "I'll be back." She stood and moved to the door. "Mom? If you need help talking to Jericho, I will be there."

"I know you will sweetheart. Thank you." Honesty gave her a smile and then stood to follow Raelynn out of the room.

Chapter 6

Raelynn didn't have to convince Timmy to go for a car ride. It seemed like that was the only thing he moved faster than a snail for. She grabbed her poop bag container and his leash, and then headed back to her mom's. Timmy laid down on the back seat and propped his head on the door so he could look out the window.

She just shook her head and smiled. Her big buddy was so adorable. Adopting him was arguably the best decision she had ever made.

Jericho met her outside when she got to her mom's. He opened the door for Timmy and Raelynn tossed him the leash over the seat. He clicked it on the pup's collar and then Timmy dutifully stepped out of the car and followed Jericho to the backyard.

Raelynn glanced in the yard as she walked by and saw that her brother had set a bowl of water on the ground and had a pocket full of treats. She snorted. Just what her lazy dog needed. Then again, it would be good for Jericho to try to do something other than play video games. If he could get motivated to just hang out with a dog it was a win. She doubted he would be successful in teaching Timmy any tricks, but she applauded the attempt.

She wandered to the back following her dog and brother and then entered the house through the kitchen door. Honesty was sitting at the table looking at one of the statues from the box. She held the one made of shells up in both hands while her elbows rested on the table. Honesty had her eyes squinted as she studied the small figure.

Raelynn stepped in to the kitchen and sat across from her mom. "Hey."

Honesty looked up and furrowed her brow. "Is this what you wanted to talk about?" Her eyes drifted back to the turtle in her hands.

"Yep," she said simply. Then Raelynn pulled her bag up into her lap and removed the one that came on Saturday and set it on the table next to the new box. Then she took the second one out and moved the box with her bag to the floor.

Silence took over the room as Honesty picked each one up and turned it around in her hands and then set it down to pick up the next. She examined each one as if it were made from fragile glass. Raelynn just sat watching, not sure what to say. She was sure the same thoughts were going through Honesty's mind as went through hers.

After what felt like an hour, Honesty put the three figures next to each other and lifted her eyes to meet Raelynn's.

"What do you think, Rae?" her mom asked.

Raelynn shrugged. "I'm really not sure what to think. I'd love to believe it is Dad, but I am also aware of how crazy that would be. I mean if it were him, why would he send me some weird statues and not just come home?"

Honesty nodded slowly. "I don't even want to entertain this as being your father, Rae. It seems too risky to get our hopes up." She bit her lip and stared at the turtles. With a sigh, she added, "But he was the only one who knew about your turtles. Sahara doesn't even know and you two are as close as sisters could be, more like best friends even." She reached across the table and took Raelynn's hands into her own.

Raelynn stared at her mom's hands in hers and sighed. "So, what do we do?" she asked, her eyes burning. She refused to let any tears fall, but she could feel the pressure behind her eyes.

"I don't know," Honesty said with her own sigh. "What about that officer you talked to during the summer? Do you think he would be able to help?"

"I'm not sure. I mean there really isn't anything here. Just three little turtle statues." Raelynn swung her hand over the small collection. "I thought about calling him tomorrow, but I'm not sure when I can even meet up with him. I work the rest of the week. If I remember right, his schedule was similar to mine. I hate to bother him during his time off."

Raelynn dropped her mom's hands and picked up the turtle made of seashells. She turned it over in her hand, studying the shells. Something caught her eye as she turned it over again. A faint marking on the underside of the main shell drew her attention.

"Mom, what's this?" she asked, giving Honesty the statue.

Honesty turned it over and ran her finger through the inside of the shell. "It looks like a number." She wrinkled her nose. "That's weird." She turned it back and forth and twisted it. "I can't tell. It looks like a one and an eight, but there's a faint line too. Here, what do you see?"

Raelynn took the shell and turned it over. She squinted, trying to see the inside clearly. Frustrated, she took out her phone and turned on the flashlight. "I think you are right. It could be eighteen or eighty-one. I don't know if this is a line or not, but if it is, it would make the number eighteen." She turned it around in different directions to get a better look. The faint line looked similar to what might be printed under a number for clarification, like the six and nine in an Uno game.

She flipped it over and set it on the table beside the glass one, which she picked up next and flipped over. She had noticed when she first got it that the price tag was blacked out on the bottom of it. Thinking about the other statues, Raelynn decided to take a closer look at it. Nothing was etched into the glass, but she now noticed that not all of the tag was blacked out. There were only two numbers that she noticed were still visible: a three and an eight.

"Look at this one. There's thirty-eight on it. At least I think it is. Those are the only numbers not blacked out anyway." Raelynn handed it to her mom.

Honesty took it and looked at the bottom. "You're right. Is there anything on the other one?" She pointed to the third one as Raelynn picked it up to check.

"It looks like a four and a four. Forty-four?" She handed it to her mom who confirmed it.

"Yes, that does look like forty-four." Honesty put the statue down and set them in a line. "What do you think that all means?"

Raelynn crossed her arms on the table and then put her chin down on them, staring at the little group. "What are you trying to tell me, dad?" she mumbled to them.

Honesty slid from her chair and moved to stand behind Raelynn. She put her hand on her daughter's shoulder and gently rubbed circles. Raelynn reached up and held on to Honesty's hand tightly in her own.

The door suddenly swung open, and Jericho ran into the kitchen screaming, jolting both of them out of their own thoughts.

"Rae! Rae! It's Timmy!" he screamed and then ran back out.

Raelynn looked at her mom and then took off after him. Honesty was right behind her. But what they found in the backyard made them stop in their tracks.

"What the…" she started.

Jericho laughed like a crazy hyena and was jumping up and down. "Watch Rae, watch!"

Timmy was sitting like a pro, waiting patiently for his next command. He didn't move and he didn't lay down. He barely even turned his head when Raelynn came running out of the house.

"Timmy, shake!" Jericho said and put his hand out. Timmy looked at him and then at Raelynn and then lifted his paw into Jericho's, earning him a treat from Jericho's other hand.

"Did you see it, Rae? Did you see it?" He continued to jump around and laugh, while Timmy just watched.

"How did you get him to do that, Jer? I mean he's not even laying down like he normally does. You're a dog whisperer, Jericho!" Raelynn was impressed and so pleased that Timmy was so smart.

Timmy eventually got tired of the antics and lay down on the grass. He flopped onto his side and took a deep breath, making them all laugh.

"Seriously, Jer. I think you should take him to obedience classes and then you can train him and maybe get a job training other dogs." Raelynn gave her little brother a light shove, making him laugh.

Jericho shrugged. "Maybe."

Raelynn turned back to Honesty. "I should probably get this big guy back home. He'll be good and tired after working so hard and being such a good boy." She scratched his chin earning a roll to his back for additional belly rubs.

Honesty laughed. "I guess so! I'll grab your box of treasures while you get him in the car."

"Hey, Timmy! Wanna go for a ride?" Raelynn asked.

Timmy jumped up and sat at attention and waited for Raelynn to clip the leash to his collar. Laughing, she snapped it on, and he stood up and moved toward the gate with her. Raelynn just shook her head and followed him, barely holding the leash.

After her dog jumped in and settled in the backseat, she closed the door and moved to meet Honesty in the front yard with the box of turtles. Raelynn took the box in one hand and then gave her a hug.

"Call or text me when you get home, Rae. I want to make sure you get home ok. I'd be lying if I said I wasn't a little worried about your safety right now." Honesty's voice was low, so Jericho didn't hear her.

Raelynn nodded. "I know, but the address on the packages is still yours, so at least they don't know where I live. Well, hopefully anyway."

"Just be careful, ok?" her mom pleaded. Her eyes held so much concern that Raelynn almost felt guilty about bringing her into this mystery.

"I will. I promise." She gave her mom another hug and then turned to her brother who was feeding Timmy treats through the window. "Ok, Jericho. When's the next lesson?"

He shot her a grin and shrugged. He gave Timmy one more head scratch and then ran for the house.

Raelynn gave her mom a wave and then headed home.

* * * * *

Raelynn sat on her bed with the turtles laid out in front of her. Timmy was sound asleep on the floor, snoring away. Suddenly she had an idea. She took out a notebook and wrote down the turtles and the numbers. She also thought it might make sense to put them in the order she received them, in case there was some significance to that. *Nothing was off the table at this point*, she thought.

She let out a sigh and grabbed the box. She knew the new turtles would be going on her shelf, so she decided to move everything to the kitchen. Raelynn put the statues in the box and carried it to the table. She pulled them out again and then pulled the last of the paper out of the box. Something fell to the floor as she shook it out to fold it for recycling.

Squatting down, she picked up the small card. It was similar to the last one, but the message was different. The first one sounded like it was from her dad. This one made her think it was definitely not her dad. But the style of card was the same and the writing was similar. The ink even looked the same. She wasn't an expert by any means, but "similar" gave her hope.

Raelynn stared at the card again. "Two for two," she read. She furrowed her brow. "Two? What did that mean? Two for what 'two'?" For what seemed like the millionth time, she wondered what these messages could mean. She couldn't help but hope it was really her dad trying to get a message to her. Two turtles, that part she got, but what were the two turtles for?

"Why not just come to us, dad? Why all this?" She asked out loud. "Ugh. What am I supposed to do with this?"

Just then her phone rang from the bedroom. She ran to grab it before it stopped ringing. A small part of her hoped it was her dad answering her question, as crazy as that sounded.

The caller ID showed Ashley was calling and she couldn't resist a sigh. "Hey, girlfriend," she said cheerfully as she answered the call.

"Hey yourself! How are things Rae? I texted a couple times, but you didn't text back. Is everything ok?" As good as it was to hear her friend's voice, she couldn't help the disappointment that hit her heart at the same time.

Raelynn scolded herself for even considering it might be her dad. She stifled a sigh and put on her happy face. "Everything's good. How about you? How was the long trek back to Iceland?" A genuine smile came across her face.

Ashley snorted. "You know, Iceland is actually a really beautiful place, Rae. And I couldn't exactly drive there." The sarcasm in her friend's voice was a welcome distraction from her current thoughts.

Raelynn let out a small laugh. "So, what's up? It's only been a day, Ash. Miss me already?"

"We just stopped for dinner, and I noticed you haven't texted me back. I just wanted to make sure you weren't missing me so much that I had to come back and get you and bring you back to Minnesota with me." Raelynn could hear Jacob laughing in the background.

"No, she's just tired of me and Aja already and misses you," he yelled from the background.

Raelynn chuckled. "So how far are you? It takes almost two full days, doesn't it?"

"Yeah. We are somewhere around Chicago, I guess. Since Aja took time off to come for the party, she needs to get back, so we haven't done too much stopping," Ashey explained.

"Hey, put me on speaker," Raelynn said. Once the phone switched over, she heard Aja say hi. "So, what are you guys doing now, besides eating?"

Jacob spoke up first. "Since I am the designated driver while Ashley sleeps and Aja just watches everything as if she's never seen it before, we will be stopping for the night soon and then drive the rest of the way to the Twin Cities. Should be there early in the afternoon tomorrow."

Raelynn laughed. "Boy you guys are great company it sounds like!"

"No, not really," Ashley said sheepishly. "I actually switched places with Aja and am all spread out in the back, well as much as possible with all the stuff, and am sleeping most of the time."

"Wow, sad you guys. Jacob, you can call me anytime if you need some company," she volunteered sympathetically, making the other three laugh.

"Hey! We promised to be better tomorrow," Aja chimed in.

Raelynn smiled again. "Well, the offer still stands."

"I might have to take you up on it, Rae," he said. "These two aren't very good with conversation and I caught myself drifting off now and then because I was so bored." He dragged out his words dramatically, making her laugh.

She heard Jacob make a sound like Ashley may have just jabbed him and she laughed again.

"Hey Rae, have you talked to Beau? I tried calling him too, but he hasn't responded to me either," Ashley said.

Raelynn suddenly remembered the night before when he had asked her out. Did Ashley know?

She cleared her throat. "Um no, actually. I saw Kiah tonight for dinner, but that's pretty much it. Is something wrong?"

"No, I don't think so, but I just wanted to make sure. We are going to get back on the road. I'll talk to you soon, ok?" Ashley said, as she turned the speaker off. And then she whispered, "Let me know how the date goes." She giggled and then hung up the phone, not giving Raelynn a chance to respond.

Raelynn looked at her phone in disbelief and then shook her head. "Well, I guess she knows," she mumbled and with a shake of her head.

Tossing her phone aside, Raelynn looked at her statues again and the tiny cards lying next to them. She studied the numbers she had written down, tapping her fingernail on her chin as she tried to make sense of the numbers. A thought occurred to her as she looked at the numbers.

"Four-four, April fourth. That's Sahara's birthday." She turned to the other numbers.

The one and eight confused her, so she set it aside. She didn't know anyone with a January or August birthday. "March eighth…" she mumbled as she stared at the three and eight. Honesty's birthday was in March, but it was the third, not the eighth. *Maybe it was an anniversary*, she thought. But Honesty's and his anniversary was in September. "Ugh," she said frustrated.

She couldn't connect the numbers to any more dates, so she gave up. Leaning back in her chair, she closed her eyes and tipped her head up. She had to work in the morning, so she decided to sleep on it for now. She put the turtles on the shelf next to the others but kept them slightly apart for now. She wasn't sure if any more would come based on the last note, so she wanted to keep them a little separate from the rest.

Raelynn made her way back to her bedroom and quickly changed. She plugged in her phone and saw it was almost ten and she had to be up early. It wasn't super late, but it was late enough after the emotional toll the last few days had taken on her.

She lay in bed thinking about Ashley. When she was there, they had so much fun together. She was already starting to miss that, even though it had only been a day since she had seen her last. They had just connected so quickly and easily. She felt very early on that she could talk to Ashley about almost anything, some things she didn't even talk to her mom or Sahara about. One of those things was about her dad and how much she hoped to bring him home one day. Sure, Honesty knew that too, but she didn't know how serious Raelynn was, or the lengths she had already gone to causing some potentially dangerous people to notice her.

Stepping back from her search was more about Officer Milton suggesting she lay low for a little while for things to calm down than anything else. Only Ashley knew that truth though. She made a mental note to give him a call the next day on her break. She wasn't sure how much good it would do, but she could at least check in and see if it would be a good time to start looking into things again.

She drifted off to sleep thinking about her dad when she was little, before Sahara was born and it was just the three of them. She never felt jealous of Sahara's arrival though, and she was actually thrilled to have a baby sister. She remembered when they told her Honesty wasn't her "real" mom and how her biological mom had died when Raelynn was born. Unfortunately, they had told her when Honesty was pregnant with Sahara so she had worried something would happen to Honesty too.

Raelynn rolled to her side and felt her big dog at her feet. She couldn't stretch out, but the security he brought her made it worth sharing her bed. She drifted off to sleep listening to the snoring of Timmy, with a smile on her face.

Chapter 7

The chime above the door rang out as Raelynn was crouched down pulling out some supplies from under the counter.

"I'll be with you in a second," she called out to the customer as she finished grabbing the things she needed.

A grunt responded to her making her scowl to herself. She hated Tuesday customers. Well, customers after nine anyway. She glanced over to look at her coworker. Chrissy had a strange look on her face and Raelynn shot her a questioning look.

Chrissy gave her head a slight nod and then she cleared her throat and walked to the bakery displays to see if anything needed to be refilled.

Weird, she thought. She set the cups on the counter, and then stood to meet the green eyes of the creepy man from the other day. She shivered slightly as she gave Chrissy a pleading look. She seemed to understand because she came over and stood next to Raelynn busying herself with something.

"Good morning. Can I help you?" Raelynn asked slowly.

The man stared at her like he did on Sunday. She held her ground and lifted her chin slightly, not to be intimidated or whatever he was trying to do. Finally, he looked up for a split second and then back at her. A tiny smirk played at the corner of his mouth and Raelynn resisted a shiver.

"Black coffee," he said simply. His voice was rough and gravely like he had been smoking three packs of cigarettes a day for a century.

Raelynn forced a smile and gave him a nod, turning away from the counter to fetch his cup and fill it. She almost wished the spout would speed up so she could get out of this man's piercing gaze.

She set his cup on the counter and slid it toward him. His eyes did not shift but he raised his hand to set down two bills and some coins, picked up his cup and finally turned and walked away. His eyes never left hers until he moved to find a place to sit. The encounter was eerily similar to the last one they had and left Raelynn feeling unsettled.

Raelynn let out a breath she didn't know she was holding. What was it about him that had her stomach all knotted up? Chrissy came up behind her and put a hand on her shoulder. She moved around her and then leaned her back against the counter so she could face Raelynn.

"Do you know him, Rae?" she asked quietly, not looking in his direction.

Raelynn shook her head. "Never seen him before in my life." She felt a shiver run down her spine as she tried not to look at him, still feeling his eyes on her.

Chrissy gave her a sympathetic look. "He seems to know you. Maybe we should let Susiana know."

"No, there's nothing really to tell. He hasn't even said anything aside from his order. He just stares, which in and of itself isn't a big deal." Raelynn tried to convince herself it was nothing, but it was hard to set it aside.

"Ok, but I am going to watch him from now on. He didn't come in yesterday and you weren't here. Maybe it's a coincidence, but I don't trust him." Chrissy chanced a glance over her shoulder at the man who had chosen a seat directly across from the counter again. When Raelynn followed her gaze, she found his eyes still on the two of them. She quickly looked away and started to clean up around the counter.

She suddenly remembered she was going to call Officer Milton today. Now she really felt like she should make that call. Something wasn't sitting right with her, and she wanted to be sure she was safe. This man hadn't done or said anything threatening, but his constant gaze was creepy and didn't sit right in her heart.

Raelynn racked her brain trying to figure out if she knew the man from somewhere. Working at the coffee shop she sees a lot of people come in and out. But no one has ever made her feel this uncomfortable. She would have remembered that.

Maybe it was someone from school, but again, his look was unmistakable. His almost jet-black hair was in long thick twists, well past his shoulders and unkept like he needed a retwist a long time ago. She didn't notice any smell, so maybe he had showered, and just didn't care about his hair. His clothes weren't dirty, at least not as bad as the last time he was in, but they were wrinkled and looked way too big for him. As if an attempt to cover the scar, his face was almost fully covered with a thick beard. *At least he has a change of clothes*, she thought, not that it meant a lot. But despite the way he looked, he might not actually be homeless.

Chrissy whispered to Raelynn, "I'm going to run to the bathroom. Are you ok here alone?"

Raelynn glanced at the stranger and nodded to her coworker. "Go ahead. I'm good." Two customers came through the door and approached her. She was relieved to see someone else come in. The rest of the café was empty except for the strange man across from her, still staring.

Ignoring him, she turned to the new customers. They looked like students, and she was actually glad for a complicated drink order for a change. It would give her something to focus on instead of the piercing emerald gaze behind them.

Almost immediately after the two students grabbed their drinks, the man approached the counter again. Raelynn didn't break eye contact with him while he stood for a moment, not doing or saying anything. He finally set something down in front of her, gave her his half smirk again, and then quickly left the café.

Raelynn stared as he left, feeling the air rush out of her lungs. She didn't even look down, just watched until he was out of sight. He didn't get into a car, he just walked until he disappeared down the busy street.

"Oh, good Creepy Guy is gone. Hey, what's this?" Chrissy asked as she came up next to Raelynn.

Looking over, she saw something in Chrissy's hand. She remembered that he had dropped something on the counter, but she hadn't taken her eyes off him to look before Chrissy came back.

"I don't know. What is it?" she asked. Chrissy had a small envelope in her hand, turning it over.

Handing it to Raelynn, Chrissy's brow furrowed. "It has your name on it, Rae. Is it from Creepy Guy? He knows your name?" She leaned over the counter trying to see if he was actually gone.

Raelynn felt a cool sweat break out across her neck just as one of the students came to the counter and asked a question.

"Um, excuse me, Chrissy? Could I get some extra napkins?" she asked, hesitating.

The two baristas made eye contact with their eyes wide. Then they looked down and laughed. "Our name tags," Raelynn said, the relief she felt was instant. Of course that's how he knew her name.

Chrissy handed her the napkins and then moved back to the bakery cases to restock everything. Raelynn looked down at the abandoned envelope that Chrissy had set back down and gingerly picked it up. Her relief about how he knew her name was quickly gone as she stared at the wrinkled and tattered paper. It looked like it had been crumpled up as small as possible and shoved in a pocket before making its way to her.

She lifted her eyes to look around the nearly empty café and sighed. It was getting close to the lunch rush. Maybe she should wait to open this until she gets home, she thought. Then if it was something upsetting, she would be in her own space and not at work trying to fake that everything is fine. Then again if it was a threat, she should tell someone which would make being at work ideal.

The decision was made for her when a group of people walked in, making the little bell jingle multiple times, as if someone was holding it and just swinging it back and forth. Raelynn put the envelope in her apron pocket and straightened. *Well, guess I'm waiting*, she told herself. She couldn't look lazy at work, especially with Susiana also being there.

The lunch rush made Raelynn completely forget about the envelope until it was time to clock out. She was grateful for the distraction, but as she removed her apron and felt the crinkled paper, she realized she now had to face whatever it was. She had decided to hold off on calling the officer for now. She wanted to see what Creepy Guy had left her first. She shook her head at the nickname Chrissy had given him but had to admit it fit. The turtles might not be enough to call the officer in, but the envelope might be something that she really needed help with. *What*, she wasn't sure yet, but who would innocently give a complete stranger a letter?

Raelynn dropped her apron in the basket to be washed and grabbed her jacket. She had been so busy at work that she didn't even know if it had stayed cool outside or warmed up during the day. She gave her boss and coworker a wave and headed out into the bright sunshine. The day had been busy aside from two very brief periods. That only lasted for about a half hour in total though. She always preferred it to be busy. It made the time go by so much faster than when it was slow.

She quickly reached her little red car and unlocked it. She slid inside and put her key in the ignition. She didn't have one of those fancy ones with a keyless start like Ashley had. But she was ok with that. Raelynn had paid for her car on her own which she was so proud of. Honesty wouldn't have been able to help her anyway and she didn't want that extra burden on her mom.

That's why Sahara didn't have her own car yet—and why she stayed close to home for college. Sahara didn't work enough hours to save much money, and she was ok with that. Raelynn just hoped she wasn't putting too much pressure on herself to be with Kiah instead of working just to feel secure in that relationship. She really didn't think her sister needed to be that worried about Kiah, but you couldn't exactly tell someone to stop feeling a certain way.

Raelynn felt the envelope in her pocket the entire ride home. She now understood the whole "burning a hole in your pocket" saying because she was so aware of the paper she literally felt as if her leg was on fire.

She parked quickly and headed into her apartment to find it empty. Her sister must have had something to do today, she thought. Raelynn dropped her keys on the table and whistled for Timmy. He wasn't in his usual places again and she furrowed her brow. She walked toward the bathroom and peeked in since that's where he came from on Sunday.

The sight she saw made her laugh. Her massive dog had tucked himself in the tub and was snoring, making the sound echo throughout the room.

"Oh, Timmy, you goof," she said, still chuckling.

Timmy raised his lazy head to look at her. He let out a little snort and then put his head back down on the edge of the tub.

Raelynn couldn't help the giggles that came out. "You weirdo," she said leaning over the tub to give him head scratches. "You are definitely not an attentive guard dog, are you?"

She straightened herself and stretched her back. She took one last look at her lazy pup and shook her head, heading back to her kitchen. A loud thud let her know her dutiful pet was following her, likely to go outside. She walked to the door and waited for him to appear and then she let him out. She hadn't taken the paper out of her pocket yet and was starting to actually get impatient as she waited for Timmy to do his business.

As quickly as she could, she got Timmy settled back inside and then sat on her couch, tucking her feet under her legs. She pulled out the envelope and stared at it. Turning it over and over in her hands, she couldn't believe it was still tightly sealed.

Nothing was on the front except her name and plenty of dirt. The writing was as creepy as the man. It looked like a ransom note out of a kidnapping movie or something. The only thing that would have made it worse was if the letters of her name were cut out of a magazine or something. She shook her head to get rid of her ridiculous thoughts.

Raelynn stuck her finger under the flap and carefully slid it along the edge, trying not to get a paper cut. The paper flipped open slightly as the glue gave way and just as she was about to take the contents out, her phone chimed from the table. She ignored it for a moment and looked inside the envelope.

She pulled out a piece of paper that looked like a lined loose-leaf page one would use in high school or something. It was dirty and crumpled, similar to the condition of the envelope. She carefully pulled out the folded paper and set the envelope aside. She wasn't sure what she would find inside, but it felt like there was something wrapped inside the paper.

Bonded Blood

As she unfolded it a small piece of cardstock fell out. She stared where it fell and let out a groan. A familiar looking card. "Ugh," she thought. Picking it up, she suddenly felt a cold chill. Was the creepy guy from work sending her the turtles? She flipped the card over in her hand and noticed this card was a little different. It was the same small size, but it had a symbol printed on it; a circle with four hands connected. She wrinkled her nose as she stared at it. It looked slightly familiar, but she couldn't place it.

There wasn't any other writing though. She flipped it back and forth but there was nothing else on it. *That is bizarre,* she thought. She stared at the drawing again. It was hand drawn and actually done well, she thought, because she could make out the four hands clearly. She couldn't make out what was drawn in the center of the hands though. It was some sort of symbol or something. Whoever made it was talented, maybe even an artist. It was a simple sketch, and looked freehand, but there were no erase marks showing it took multiple attempts to make it look right.

She dropped the card on the couch next to her and picked up the paper that was wrapped around the small card and laid it flat. She couldn't tell if the markings on it were from writing or if it was just dirty. She flipped it over and found the same thing on the other side. "This is so frustrating," she complained to her ceiling, dropping back against the cushions.

Raelynn suddenly remembered her phone had chimed earlier. She moved to grab it and see what else the universe wanted to throw at her on this lovely Tuesday.

There's another package, hon, her mother's text said.

Raelynn sighed. *Yay*, she thought sarcastically and scowled at her phone. Knowing she had to work the next day, she thought about stopping over for dinner again tonight to see what the new mysterious package held. She decided to call her mom and see if she had plans. Maybe bringing dinner over would work. Then Jericho could play with Timmy again too.

She pulled up her mom's contact and pressed the call button. It rang four times and then went to voicemail. Thinking maybe Honesty was still at work and just got a quick break to text Raelynn, she decided to ask the question through text instead of leaving a voicemail. Her text was quick and simple, then she set her phone aside and tried to think of something simple to make for dinner. *Maybe picking up pizzas would be a good idea tonight*, she thought. Nodding to her sleeping giant at her feet, she got up from the couch and moved to the kitchen. She knew she had mailer coupons from a few of the pizza places around town, her favorite being Salisbury Pizza.

Locating the one she was looking for, she slapped it in her hand with a grin. Her phone dinged again from its spot on the couch. Raelynn nearly tripped over a sleeping Timmy who had spread his large body across the entry to the living room. She playfully scolded him for just flopping wherever he felt like it as she stepped over him.

Honesty's response about dinner confirmed that she was still working. Raelynn sent a quick text to her sister and then decided to change and head to their house. Maybe her sister would be around. She had a fleeting thought that maybe Beau would come with Kiah, but then quickly dismissed it. He hadn't come to dinner before, and she hadn't invited him so it didn't make sense that he would just show up.

Raelynn couldn't help but wonder if she should invite him. But then what would that suggest to Honesty. And actually worse, she knew her sister wouldn't let any teasing opportunity go by easily.

He had only just asked her to go out. And the date hadn't even happened yet, she groaned to herself. "Getting a little ahead of ourselves aren't we?" she muttered under her breath.

She quickly changed and took a hoodie from her closet. She grabbed the card from Creepy Guy, chuckling again at the new nickname, and shoved it in the back pocket of her jeans. Raelynn pulled Timmy's leash off the table and clicked his poop bag container to the loop.

"Hey Timmy, wanna go for a ride?" she asked in her playful voice just for him.

The enormous dog jumped to his feet from a dead sleep and then sat up straight, waiting for her to click his leash. She just shook her head and laughed. "Now if only we could get you to move like that when the front door opens, that would be amazing." She scratched behind his ears and clicked her tongue.

The drive to her mom's went by quickly as her thoughts started to move to the new package her mom had texted her about. Her thoughts had skipped right over the package when she started to think about dinner but now it came back to her as she maneuvered the streets in her hometown.

She had let Jericho know she would be coming over, too. He should be home by the time she got there since it was already after four. He would have been home around three forty-five from school if he went straight home because he walked from the middle school.

As she pulled in, her little brother jumped out of the front door. Raelynn rarely saw him move that fast and Timmy seemed to be the only motivation for that. She shrugged slightly, deciding she was ok with it. Timmy got some much-needed attention—and probably a little discipline—while she was able to stay longer with her family. She loved her dog, but she didn't like having to always leave early to make sure he gets outside and doesn't have an accident in the apartment. This seemed like a win-win for everyone.

Jericho was turning out to be a great asset, she decided as she watched him take Timmy out of the back seat with the big dog dutifully following him to the back yard. Raelynn couldn't hide the smile on her face as she watched her brother carefully make sure the gate was latched tightly before he took off Timmy's leash and then disappeared out of sight.

Instead of following them, Raelynn walked to the front door. She noticed the package right away sitting on the small table just inside the door where everyone left their keys. She picked up the brown box and moved into the kitchen to grab a knife or scissors to open it. As she was pulling the scissors out, she glanced out the window to the backyard. She stopped for a second to watch as her brother was trying to get Timmy to roll over on command. She watched with humor as Jericho rolled over, showing Timmy what to do while the pup yawned and watched him with a bored look.

She laughed when Timmy eventually lay down in the grass and continued to watch his trainer. Raelynn moved away from the window when she saw that Jericho thought taking a break was a good idea too and rested his head on

Timmy's side. The dog had flopped over and the two of them looked content and comfortable. She took out her phone and snapped a quick picture of them.

Moving to the table, she set down the scissors next to the box. She sat down in front of it and sighed. Usually getting a package was exciting and fun, forgetting what she had ordered until it came. But these packages have been growing increasingly more difficult to open, emotionally anyway. She didn't know what they were trying to tell her and the new information about the creepy guy possibly being involved had her a little more on edge.

She carefully ran the sharp edge of one of the blades along the tape and then pulled the top free of the adhesive. She took a deep breath as she opened the flaps. This box was about the same size as the others, but the package was heavier. It made her wonder if this would be something different. The others were small and light. She thought that all of them together might not be as heavy as this one was.

Gingerly, she lifted the paper from the inside of the box. Nestled inside the box, with newspaper wrapped tightly around it to keep it from moving, sat a round silver piece of metal, like sheet metal. She carefully lifted the object out of the box and set it on the table. Raelynn stared at it for a minute before she squatted on the floor to look at it directly.

There was a round "shell" of metal with four tiny metal pieces for legs and a larger piece in the front for the head. There was no doubt what the thing was, but what it was made of was interesting. It looked like scrap metal, with the sharp edges folded over to make them smooth. The shell looked like it had taken a beating before it was used for this purpose. The circle looked rough, like it was cut into its shape with a dull tool. It could have been the same tool that smooths the edges of the other parts, namely the head and legs.

Raelynn picked it up and held it higher. "This is so bizarre," she mumbled, plopping back down into her chair.

She thought about her collection before her dad had gone missing. The ones on her shelf were not expensive pieces, aside from the one Honesty had purchased and the sea glass one that came on Saturday. The ones they had made together when she was little were not at all costly. She had one made of paper that her dad had helped her roll and glue together. The metal one in her hand was oddly similar to that one, she thought.

She had one that they made from shells they had found on the beach one day, too. She thought about the one she had gotten yesterday that was also made of shells. It was definitely nicer than the one they had made together, but they were similar. Raelynn felt her face flush as she thought about the others she had gotten. Were they all recreations of turtles she already had? Because if they were, then it could only be her father who was trying to contact her, right? Otherwise, she had a very invested stalker, which she dismissed immediately because she didn't want to even consider that.

Her thoughts went to the others, wondering what they all had in common. *Numbers*, she remembered, snapping her fingers.

Carefully, she turned the new turtle over and inspected the inside of the shell. She furrowed her brow when she didn't see anything. All the others had numbers in that location. Why didn't this one have numbers? Frustrated, she set it back on its feet and put her chin on her folded arms. Why wouldn't this one have numbers?

Raelynn leaned against the back of the chair. Maybe there were only the three numbers that mattered, she thought. Then there must be something important about them. None had her birthday, but one had Sahara's. She thought about Honesty's birthday and their anniversary. But she couldn't shake the hurt that her birthday wasn't one of the important numbers. Sahara was just a baby so maybe it was fresh in his mind, she tried to justify. But she was slightly upset, and she couldn't deny it. Her father meant everything to her, why didn't he feel the same?

She knew she was being selfish and acting like a spoiled child, but the hurt was hard to deny and just let go. Raelynn tipped the turtle toward her and scowled at it. She stared at the head, and then realized there were markings on it, almost like a face was carved in it. She tipped it toward her to get a closer look and saw that there were eyes scratched and a third circle for a nose. Above the eyes were tiny eyebrows carved into it.

"That's weird," she thought with a shake of her head. "Eyebrows? Really?"

Turning the turtle slightly to get a better look at the two little humps over the eyes, she realized when she turned the structure to the side, it looked kind of like a three. She turned it a little more and saw some squiggly lines that looked like it could be another number above it. But it could also be weird curly hair too, since the carver had given this thing eyebrows. She let out a soft laugh as she thought about how ridiculous it was. The rest of the turtle was basic and rough. But the details on its head were just crazy. She couldn't help but look at the legs to see if there were toes carved into each one, but no such luck.

Raelynn turned it so the head was facing away from her, and she studied the lines. She could definitely argue that the eyebrows looked like a three. The lines next to it she realized could actually make a four. "Thirty-four?" she asked out loud. When she turned it away from her, she realized it could also be an "h" and an "E", which confused her even more. None of the other ones had letters, just numbers.

A howl from outside took her attention away from the statue and she moved to the kitchen window. Timmy was chasing Jericho while Jericho laughed. Raelynn couldn't help the smile that played on her lips. Timmy never ran and Jericho was clearly enjoying his babysitting job. She glanced to the side, catching the microwave clock with her eye, and realized she should have already ordered the pizzas. She quickly grabbed her phone and saw she missed a text from Sahara, too. They were coming for pizza and bringing Beau, if it was ok with her.

Raelynn sighed. *Good thing I haven't ordered yet*, she thought. She quickly typed back that it was all good and she was ordering right then. She searched for her coupon and then went online to place her order. She had about thirty minutes before it would get there, and she needed to get things ready for everyone. Thinking about what they had around to drink, she sent her sister a text asking her to pick up some drinks. They didn't have much milk, not that they drank a lot of it, but she didn't want to leave her mom without any for Jericho's cereal in the morning.

She quickly put her newest statue in its box and then decided to run it out to her car, so it was out of the way.

She could tell Honesty about it later; she didn't need Sahara or anyone else asking questions. She wasn't ready to talk about it to anyone else yet. Raelynn wasn't absolutely sure she should tell her mom about the new one either yet.

After getting Sahara's confirmation text, Raelynn moved around the kitchen gathering paper plates, napkins, and cups. The only dishes they would have to wash would be the cups and that was easy. She took one more look outside and laughed when she saw the two boys lying together on the grass again. Timmy apparently had energy, but only for a short time it seemed. She wondered how many treats her brother had given him so far.

Raelynn decided to try to get Timmy fed before the pizza came so she called out to Jericho from the kitchen door. She had the box now closed in her hand.

"Hey, Jer? Will you take this to my car and grab Timmy's food and bowl? He can eat now before our pizzas get here." She watched her brother nod and get up from her dog's side. She set the box down on the step for him.

Timmy raised his head and huffed his annoyance, giving Raelynn a look that made her chuckle. "Oh, settle down, boy. He'll be right back." Then she ducked back inside. It was almost five thirty and her mom would be home soon. Sahara and Kiah were on their way according to her last text, after they grabbed drinks from the store. She wasn't sure if Beau would be riding with them or on his own. She was actually looking forward to seeing him again. She was a little confused by her feelings but decided to just go with the flow and not force anything. She had enough going on with this turtle business and Creepy Guy.

There was no denying Beau was attractive. His dark hair and eyes held an intense depth to them. His face was usually serious and held so much tension. The other night was the first time in a really long time that she didn't see the standing scowl on his face. His skin tone was much darker than hers, but not as brown as the rest of her family's. Thinking about the differences in skin tone made her think about her own family again.

She always felt a little out of place in her own family. Even when her dad was around, she was the one who stood out the most, and not like she was more attractive or anything. She just looked so different from the rest of the family. Honesty never treated her differently, but Raelynn's light skin full of freckles and bright blue eyes made people do a double take when they were out together. It wasn't any of their business, but people did ask stupid questions, like if she was adopted or a foster kid.

Wanting to feel like she belonged has weighed on her soul for a long time. She wondered if her father had been there while she was growing up, maybe she wouldn't have felt so alone. Plenty of her friends had mixed parents. But even they carried more black characteristics than she did. It was like only her mom's white genes were passed down to her. Maybe it was a way of honoring her mom or something, but she always wished she had just a little darker skin. In the summer she spent a lot more time outside and since she tanned to a much darker tone, she felt a little more "normal" that time of year.

High school was rough though. People said stupid things like "You don't act black enough to be black," or "you are white, why are you trying to act black?" Raelynn never really knew what to say. She carried her dad's wide bridged nose and her hair, while brown and not black, did hold curls, if she took the time. But that was about it. Everything else screamed "white girl."

Honesty used to tell her to embrace her differences and be proud of them. They were what made her the unique person she is. She isn't like everyone else and will always stand out. Until she got out of high school, she never really felt those things. But in college she met so many more people who shared similar stories as hers, specifically also had mixed parents and looked more white than black. It helped a little bit, but the words she heard growing up didn't just disappear. Maybe someday she would feel like she belonged right where she was. At least her family never treated her differently, and for that she was very grateful.

Chapter 8

The family sat around the dinner table chatting while they ate. The three pizza boxes were nearly empty, and everyone was almost finished. Raelynn sat back in her chair and looked around the table at her family. Sahara and Kiah had scooted their chairs close together and were holding hands, laughing at something Honesty had said. Jericho was still stuffing his face with pizza and Timmy was stretched out on the floor under the table, sound asleep.

Raelynn's eyes shifted to Beau who was sitting next to Kiah. She was startled to find he was watching her. She shot him a small smile and then looked around the table again. She decided to start cleaning up, so she stood and began to gather the paper plates and cups. They had left the pizza boxes on the counter so she could just fill the empty ones with the dirty dinner plates, making cleaning up a breeze.

Beau got up and started to help her stack plates. She leaned her hip against the counter and watched him as he brought a stack to where she was standing.

"What?" he asked with a grin. He looked around and then wiped his face with his free hand as if he had something on it. "Do I have sauce on my face or something?"

Bonded Blood

Raelynn smiled back and shook her head. "Nothing. Thanks for helping." She waved her hand toward the table. "It's not like these guys will help," she added, a little louder so they could hear her.

The chatter at the table ended abruptly and all eyes turned toward Raelynn. Smirking, she gave an exaggerated flip of her long brown hair and turned away from the table. "Come on Beau. This is going to take forever." She dragged out the last word and started to make her way across the short distance to the trash bin.

Beau let out a chuckle as he followed her with a stack of plates to go into the second empty pizza box.

"Wait a minute, Miss Goody Two Shoes," Sahara called from the table. She pushed her chair away from the table and moved to stand in Raelynn's way as she tried to pull out the trash bag.

Raelynn jumped back, surprised at how fast her sister was. Regaining her composure, she gasped dramatically and pretended to almost drop her stack of dirty dishes and empty pizza boxes.

"Geez, Sahara! Be careful," she playfully admonished her sister. "I could have dropped all this and then I would have had even more to clean up while you all just sit around and chit chat."

Sahara groaned. "Oh, shut up, you poor deprived Cinderella wanna be!" She grabbed the stack from Raelynn, drawing another exaggerated gasp from her sister.

"Oh, do be careful, Sahara!" Raelynn said with a really bad southern drawl. "I wouldn't want to be blamed for ruining your perfect manicure." She put her fingertips to her lips as if she were really concerned about something happening to Sahara.

"Mom, tell her to shut up," Sahara whined to Honesty, who just sat back and watched her daughters with amusement.

Leaning back in her chair, Honesty chuckled. "Oh no, I think it is only fair that you clean up. After all Rae bought and served the dinner." Her gaze drifted to Kiah who was still sitting at the table.

When he made eye contact with Honesty, he jumped up and started to help clear the table. Jericho lifted his hands up in surrender when she turned to him.

"Hey, I'm still eating," he said as he grabbed his fifth slice of pizza.

"Yeah, and you'll eat all night long if it means you don't have to help, *baby* brother," Raelynn said as she lightly slapped the back of his head, emphasizing the word again just to irritate him.

Jericho smiled, his teeth full of cheese and sauce. "Ya gotta do what ya gotta do," he said with a lift of his hands.

As they finished cleaning up, Timmy seemed to be aware of movement and lifted his head lazily from the floor.

"I suppose I should get going," Raelynn said looking at her dog. "You wanna go, Timmy?"

Timmy sat up straighter and watched her expectantly. But he still didn't make the extra effort to fully sit just in case she decided they weren't leaving yet. *He would definitely hate to put in any extra effort for nothing*, she thought with a grin.

"No, not yet. Let me try to teach him a new trick, Rae," Jericho pleaded. "He almost has 'lay down' mastered."

Raelynn snorted. "Jer, he has it mastered already. Look at him. He's been laying down all through dinner."

Jericho glared at her. "Not that, stupid." He continued to mumble under his breath. He picked up his half-eaten pizza and bag of treats from the counter, gaining the attention of Timmy, who had scooted himself out from under the table fully and stood at attention watching his little trainer with interest. Jericho didn't even have to say anything. As soon as Jericho headed toward the back door, Timmy stood and followed him outside.

"And he escapes cleaning up again." Sahara mumbled under her breath. She shook her head and threw away his plate.

Raelynn sat back down at the table and the rest of the group followed. Everything was cleaned up and the trash bag was taken outside already. Raelynn had no idea who did it or when it was done. The atmosphere was relaxing, and everyone was in good spirits.

"So, what's on the agenda tonight, girls?" Honesty asked, looking between her girls.

Sahara shrugged and looked at Kiah. "I don't know. Did you want to go see that new movie, Ki?"

"It's Tuesday, Sahara," Raelynn said with a shake of her head. "You should really get a job."

"I do have a job, Rae," Sahara grumbled with a slight pout. "I just don't have to get up at four am, like some crazy person."

Raelynn laughed. "Or work full time to pay for everything like an adult." Her teasing was met with a stern look from Honesty.

"You know that I would love to have you back here too, Rae. You chose to move out." Honesty gave her daughter a knowing look.

Raelynn sighed. She was just teasing her sister, and her goal was not to upset her mom. "I know, but she's also an adult now. I chose to live on campus to help out by saving you money. You should be able to work less now that you have two adult kids, Mom. Take some time off for yourself." She swung her hand at her sister and added, "And she could help out too now."

"But I do help out, don't I mom? Tell her I help out," Sahara complained, sounding like a toddler and making everyone at the table laugh.

"Pfft. Whatever. Seems to me I am the one getting dinner ready and I'm don't even live here anymore." Raelynn reached around the table and bumped her sister's arm. "Way to get me in trouble again with your whining, *baby* sister," she said, dragging out "baby" like she did with Jericho.

Honesty stood up and stretched. "Well, you guys can continue your sibling bickering. I do have an early morning, so I'll see y'all later. Thanks for getting dinner again, Rae. Love you all, goodnight." She disappeared quickly into the bathroom and Raelynn heard the shower start.

Leaning back in her chair, she looked at her sister again. "Seriously though, Sahara, you should think about it. Giving mom a break from providing for everyone would help out a lot. She has been working two and three jobs for as long as I can remember. She's still doing a full time and a part time job. It's not like she's getting any younger."

Sahara sighed. "I know, but I want to focus on school too so I can get a decent job as soon as I'm done and can either help out more financially or move out on my own. That would be helpful, too."

Raelynn didn't miss the quick look Sahara gave Kiah as she talked. She wondered what that was about, but assumed it had to do with her insecurities about him and their relationship again. She made a mental note to talk to Kiah later. Maybe she can give him a heads up about her sister's insecurities. She rarely can get him alone though when Sahara isn't around. Then again, maybe she should just stay out of it.

"I could go for a movie. How early do you have to work Rae?" Beau was watching her from his spot next to Kiah.

"Are you asking me out again, Beau?" she asked with a smirk. She put her hand on her chest as if in shock. "'Cuz I think I already agreed to go out this weekend. Can't wait until then huh?"

Sahara and Kiah gasped. Sahara's wide eyes made Raelynn laugh. "When were you going to tell me he asked you out, Rae?"

Beau shot Raelynn a look and she couldn't help but notice a tiny bit of redness staining his neck. She hoped she didn't just embarrass him too much. She actually thought Kiah would know about their impending date, but maybe he didn't share everything with his brother like she normally did with her sister.

"Sorry, I thought you guys knew," she apologized, staring at Beau. She hoped he knew she was almost exclusively talking to him. She had a lot to learn about Beau it seemed.

Kiah and Sahara thankfully became absorbed in a back and forth about who knew and who didn't and who kept it a secret. Raelynn gave Beau a slight nod of her head, asking him to follow her out the front door. It would be better to talk away from the other two.

Once outside, Beau chuckled. When Raelynn looked over, her eyebrow raised, he shook his head.

"They're like a couple of preschoolers. Give them a tiny distraction and they are completely oblivious to who took the toy first," he explained with a laugh.

Raelynn nodded and quickly agreed. "Oh yeah. Sahara can't stay focused on anything longer than four minutes." She hesitated and then added, "I thought maybe we should talk." She wrung her hands together, not sure what to say.

A hand covered hers, drawing her attention to Beau's concerned eyes. "Hey, is everything ok?"

Raelynn let out a sigh. "Sorry. I just wanted to say sorry for letting the cat out of the bag. It didn't even occur to me that they wouldn't know about you asking me out." She let her hands drop to her sides and leaned her back against the railing.

Beau lifted her chin with his finger and reluctantly she met his gaze. "Um, Ki knows already, Rae. I told him I was going to ask you out before we even went to the party." He shrugged and gave her a smile.

She narrowed her eyes. "So, then are you embarrassed to be going out with me? 'Cuz I can cancel, or you can cancel if you need to save face." She intended it to be a joke, but suddenly realized she hoped that wasn't the case. Raelynn was almost afraid to look him in the eye again.

"No way, Rae. I am looking forward to it. But I was serious about going to a movie with the *children* tonight, if you are game." He had tipped his head down so he could see her face, a smirk playing on his lips as he referenced the younger two inside. "What do you say?" he almost whispered.

Raelynn looked up and met his dark brown eyes with her own blue ones. Slowly she nodded. "I guess so, since they probably need a babysitter anyway," she said with a small laugh.

Beau's face lit up and he stood straighter. Raelynn stood up too and they turned to walk back into the house. Kiah and Sahara were gone from the kitchen and Raelynn looked around to make sure everything was cleaned up. They were most likely in the backyard with Jericho and Timmy. She glanced back at Beau behind her and tipped her head toward the back door.

"I'm sure they're outside now. I should probably take Timmy home and then I can meet you if you want. Not to be a bummer, but I don't really want to go to anything too late," she commented. "Ugh, I sound so old," she added with a groan.

Beau laughed. "No worries. I also have a full-time job and need to be up and gone by seven thirty. Early is good for me." He paused as they headed out the door. "Or… we could just stay in and watch a movie." His voice was quiet and a little hesitant.

Raelynn realized he wasn't exactly shy, but he was definitely not the outgoing person she was. It made her smile for some reason. A lot of the guys she had dated in the past were outgoing and very confident. Not that there was anything wrong with being confident, but sometimes there was a fine line between cocky and confident. *I guess someone could be shy and confident at the same time*, she mused.

Pretending to think about it, she tapped her finger on her lips. "Hmm. Maybe that is your plan, get me alone in private and take advantage of me," she teased, wiggling her eyebrows.

He just shook his head with a knowing grin on his face. "I am not even going to get sucked into your mind games, Rae. I don't think I would be much of a match for your quick wit. But…I would like to spend some time with you. And in private would allow us time to talk instead of sitting in silence in public." He shrugged and then walked by her into the small yard.

Raelynn just watched him walk by. She surveyed the yard. Timmy was stretched out in the grass again with Jericho right next to him. Sahara and Kiah were sitting on the old swing set that probably should have been taken down years ago. It probably wasn't even safe for the young adults to be on. Beau had made his way over to the sleeping dog, who barely lifted his head as Beau scratched between his ears.

Looking around, Raelynn suddenly realized she missed being here with everyone. She was a people person and would much rather be in the middle of chaos than all alone. But then again she liked having her own space and privacy that she didn't get here. The house was small with too many people in it. She couldn't help but wonder how Jericho would do being the only one in the house. Sahara had decided to live at home for college, but Raelynn suspected she might decide to move on campus for spring semester, especially with lacrosse picking up and Kiah's time being divided even more.

Raelynn took a breath of air in and smiled as she smelled the freshly cut grass of one of the neighbor's yards. That probably meant her mom's neighbor would do theirs the next day. The neighborhood was like that. They tended to all work together to keep the block looking nice and well maintained. She sometimes wondered if

Bonded Blood

they had a schedule or if they just had some sort of silent communication.

When she was younger and Honesty was working almost all day every day, the women around them would act as second and third mothers. Honesty couldn't afford daycare and Raelynn was almost ten, so she was technically old enough to babysit her sister, but the people on their street rallied around the family and made sure she and her sister were always fed and taken care of. Raelynn was sure it had to do with the sudden disappearance of her father. She also had her mommom who would come take care of them as well.

"I should probably get this lug home, Jericho. Are you finished with your training today?" she asked her younger brother.

Jericho shrugged. "I think he decided he's done." He stood up and then called out to Timmy to see if he would move.

Raelynn laughed when he barely lifted his head. "I guess that's a no. Ok, come on Timmy. Wanna go for a ride?"

The entire group laughed as the dog jumped to his feet and wagged his tail waiting for Raelynn to take him to the car. She clipped his leash and then walked him to the front. Jericho followed and opened the door for Timmy, closing it once he was inside and his leash was removed. Raelynn reached in and put her key in the ignition and started it, then closed her door as well.

She needed to find out what Beau had in mind before she left. She thought maybe she should get his number too. Hopefully it wouldn't be so weird to ask for it since they already had plans.

Jericho stayed by the car, talking to Timmy through the now open window.

"I'll be right back, Jericho. I need to talk to Sahara quick." He nodded to her as she made her way back to the back yard again.

Sahara and Kiah had moved off the swings and were standing by the back door. Beau was leaning over the small rail talking with them when Raelynn came back around the corner. She moved to stand next to him.

"So, what's the plan, kids?" she asked the little group with a grin on her face.

Beau stepped away from the rail and swung his hand at the younger two. "These guys want to go see that new horror movie. I'll admit I'm a baby and have no interest in horror movies at all. So, I am out. What do you want to do, Rae?"

He looked almost embarrassed to say he didn't like horror movies, and any other time Raelynn may have teased him about being a chicken, but she hated that genre of movies more than any other. Action was her favorite. When she found out Ashley was the same way they tackled a few movies and Netflix series together in the short time she was there.

"Rae hates horror movies too," Sahara bluntly volunteered, and Raelynn suddenly had a suspicion they chose that because she knew Raelynn and Beau both disliked them. Whether it was to be alone or to force her and Beau together, she wasn't sure though.

Raelynn narrowed her eyes at her sister who gave her a bright smile. But she didn't have it in her to be upset. Truth be told, she'd rather hang out at her apartment and watch anything than spend a ton of cash at a movie theater.

She had gotten popcorn during her grocery expedition, so she was set.

"Not a fan," she said with a scowl. "My place it is then. You wanna follow me or meet me there?" she asked Beau.

Beau shrugged. "If you're ok entertaining me, I can follow you."

"I need to say goodbye to my mom. I'll be right back." Raelynn pushed past her sister on the steps and disappeared into the house.

She could hear the low chatter of the others still outside but ignored them to find her mom, who was likely on her way to bed. Raelynn knew her mom would be working almost fifteen hours the next day and going to bed before the sun went down was normal. When they were growing up, Honesty was in bed most days before them and was gone for work hours before they woke up. Raelynn only remembered seeing her mom for about an hour or two while they ate dinner before she either had to go back to work or to bed.

Honesty's room light was still on, but it was a soft glow, letting Raelynn know it was her bedside lamp. She lightly knocked on the doorframe and waited for her mom to tell her to come in.

"Hey mom. I'm going to head out. Do you need anything before I go?" she asked quietly.

Honesty was lying on her bed with a book in her hand, something she always said she wished she had more time for. It made Raelynn happy to see she was finally getting that wish.

"I'm good. You know maybe you should pick Jericho up tomorrow after school and let him hang out with Timmy at your place?" she suggested. "Then you don't have to spend so much time here."

Raelynn shrugged. "I don't mind, but he might like to hang out there anyway. I'll ask him. What time do you work tomorrow? Do you want me to just keep him for dinner and then bring him home?"

She knew she would be finished with work long before Jericho got home so it would work out well to just pick him up. And Timmy would love the snuggle buddy too; she doubted he would do any more training.

Honesty sighed. "That would be helpful. I have to work until almost eight between the two jobs tomorrow." The regret in her eyes was clear.

"Don't worry about it, mom. I got him. You should really think about cutting back to just one job. You deserve to have a little fun, you know," she said with a smile.

Honesty laughed. Raelynn knew she wouldn't date, still believing like Raelynn did that her dad would show up one day. But she could go out with friends or something.

The thought of her father brought the turtles back into her thoughts. She hadn't told Honesty about the newest one but decided she wouldn't unless her mom asked. She wasn't sure what to make of the deliveries and didn't really know if she should do anything anyway.

"Thank you, Rae. I'll let you know tomorrow when I will be home. But he is old enough to be alone too, so if you have things to do, you can drop him off." Honesty nodded to her daughter and Raelynn gave her a hug.

"'Night mom," Raelynn said.

"Goodnight, baby," Honesty said with a soft smile.

Bonded Blood

Raelynn dropped the curtain between the rooms and headed back outside, silently grateful her mom didn't ask about the latest package. She opened the door to the yard and saw that no one was around. She pushed the door shut tightly and locked it. Then she made her way out the front door. She found Beau and Jericho leaning in the car window giving Timmy some much needed attention. *Poor dog*, she thought sarcastically with a roll of her eyes. *He was so deprived of love.*

Chapter 9

Raelynn picked up the empty bowl with a few unpopped kernels of popcorn rolling around in the bottom. "Should I make some more or are you heading out?" she asked Beau, who was sprawled out on her couch with his socked feet crossed on the coffee table in front of it.

"Hm, are you kicking me out, Rae?" Beau asked with a smirk on his face.

They had just finished watching the latest *Mission Impossible* movie. It was almost ten and she knew she really *should* be kicking him out and getting to bed, but it had been so much fun that she hated to make him leave.

"Well, I do have to be up in six hours for work…" she said slowly. "But this has been so fun, I hate for it to end if I'm honest." She was almost embarrassed to say her thoughts out loud.

She sat back down next to him on the couch and fiddled with her hands. Timmy had gone to bed a long time ago leaving the two of them alone. Raelynn had no doubt he was spread out on her bed which would make it difficult to get it tonight.

"How about this?" Beau started slowly, watching her carefully. "I have an early morning too. And I have had a great time as well. I am off around five tomorrow, so maybe we can grab dinner or something."

Raelynn smiled. "That could work. Oh wait, I have to take my little brother tomorrow after school for my mom." She bit the side of her lip, knowing having Jericho around would be less than romantic.

To her surprise, Beau shrugged. "So? He's alright to have around and he loves your dog. We can do something easy and just hang out. No pressure, just more of this. Having a good time together." He sat up straighter to sit next to her and moved his hand in a circular motion as if to summarize their night with a simple hand gesture.

"Hmm," she dragged out, teasing him a little. "I guess that could work." She nudged his shoulder with her own and smiled. "No pressure though, right? Just having a good time?" Her eyes were teasing, and he seemed to pick up on it.

"No pressure," he said with some weird hand gesture that she knew was nothing even close to the "scout's honor" thing, assuming that's even what he was going for. Jericho did boy scouts for a short time in grade school as a way to keep him occupied after school, so she vaguely remembered it. "I promise."

Raelynn laughed. "Ok, a boy scout you clearly were not. But I agree to your terms then. I will be back here long before you are off work, so just shoot me a quick text when you're on your way and I'll figure out dinner."

They stood together and Raelynn picked up the bowl again and Beau grabbed their empty soda cans. After setting everything on the counter, Beau moved toward the door.

"I really did have fun, Rae. I am looking forward to tomorrow." He gave her a wide smile and headed to the door.

Smiling back, she followed him and opened the door. "I did too. Who knew the broody brother could be so much fun," she said with a wiggle of her eyebrows.

Beau snorted. "Yeah, it's been a rough year if I'm honest. Maybe something I can share another time. See you tomorrow." He gave her a mock salute and with a laugh, headed out the door and down the hall.

Raelynn watched as he rounded the corner and disappeared from her sight. Locking the door behind her, she leaned her back against it. It suddenly occurred to her that she probably shouldn't have said what she did. She hoped he wasn't hurt by it. Sometimes stuff just comes out without thinking first. *He seemed ok though*, she thought, biting her lip.

Pushing off the door, she went into the kitchen to clean up the few things they used. She didn't like leaving things lying around. Not rinsing the cans could easily lead to ants and other bugs. Maybe not in October, but you never knew what would find its way inside. Being on the ground floor she felt like she was more likely to get bugs than those on the upper floors.

As Raelynn moved through the apartment turning off lights and the TV, she noticed her collection on the shelves. She had brought in the new box from her mom's today, but it was still sitting on the kitchen table. Turning around, Raelynn went back into the kitchen to take the newest statue out. "If you could even call these statues," she mumbled to the empty room.

Setting the newest addition on the table, she sat down and eyed it like it was some secret or suspicious thing. She couldn't think of any reason for the deliveries and the numbers weren't adding up either. They weren't all birthdays because hers and Honesty's were more than two numbers. There wasn't any way to make October 30 into two numbers that she could come up with. And why only have Sahara's? Her parents' anniversary wasn't even one of the numbers.

Maybe it was the dates they were made, she briefly thought, but she decided that didn't make much sense either, since they were all over the calendar. Then again, maybe it was some sculptor who was marking them somehow like any artist would. That thinking led her to wonder why someone would make a bunch of turtles out of random items.

A thought suddenly came to her. What if these weren't connected to her father at all? Was it just a coincidence that she and her dad had collected them? What if someone was setting her up to think it was her dad to lure her into some dark and twisted plot from one of her dark mafia novels?

Suddenly Raelynn laughed out loud. Her brain was going in all kinds of random directions, and she knew it was her exhaustion spinning out of control.

"Yep, time to go to bed," she said with a sigh. "My mind is spiraling into weirdness."

Shaking her head, she got up and turned off the light, leaving the little guy sitting on the table. Four would be coming very early tomorrow and now she slightly regretted having Beau over. But only slightly, she thought, as she made her way into the bathroom. She glanced at Timmy who was indeed spread out across her entire bed.

Raelynn paused, wondering if she should tease her dog with treats to get him to move over, but then thought better of it, deciding to just sleep on her couch. She was too tired to worry too much about it by that point. She finished up in the bathroom and slipped on her pajama pants and t-shirt. Then she grabbed her pillow, which Timmy had thankfully stayed away from, and a fleece tie blanket she had made with her mom and sister years ago.

Once she was settled on the couch, she looked over and found that her shelf of turtles was in her direct line of sight. She let out a sigh as she looked at the ones from when she and her father had been collecting them. She had forgotten why they had even started the collection, but she knew she was very young when they got the first one. She didn't remember the details since she was around two years old. The story she remembered being told was that she had picked it out at a gift shop by the beach, surprising her dad.

Back then she had been obsessed with the movie *Finding Nemo*. But unlike everyone else, she wasn't fascinated with Dory or Nemo. She loved Squirt, the baby sea turtle. When she saw the tiny statue in the gift shop she had to have it. Her dad was surprised she didn't find a stuffed one instead, but she'd insisted this was what she wanted.

Suddenly not tired anymore, Raelynn flung the blanket off of her body and sat up frustrated. She rubbed her face and thought about taking something to help her sleep. The turtles seemed to be taunting her, and she let out an annoyed breath. Standing, she moved to grab the crystal one Honesty had given her so many years ago. She had always loved it, even though she requested her mom not purchase any more. It reminded her of her dad and made her miss him even more.

She sat back down with it and held it up into the small stream of moonlight coming in from the tiny opening between the shades. Even with the limited amount of light, it still sparkled with the entire rainbow of colors. The intricate cuts and angles made it a beautiful piece. Raelynn knew Honesty must have saved for a long time to be able to buy it. And while she appreciated it, she also felt incredibly guilty about the amount it took from her mom's income.

Honesty always told her it was not as much as Raelynn thought and it was worth every penny it cost to see her little girl happy again.

As she stared at it, Raelynn thought back to her childhood. She had grown up without her biological mom but never felt like something was missing. Her friend Ashley had lost her mom at a young age and said she always felt like there was a part of her missing. Honesty was amazing in that she never let Raelynn feel less than Sahara and always treated both her daughters equally. She once told her that Raelynn was half of her dad and he was Honesty's everything, so how could she not love his daughter as much. They may not have shared blood, but Honesty always said their bond was stronger than DNA.

The love that she saw in her parents' relationship always solidified the fact that he did not, would not, have left on his own. She never believed that he had run off or lost hope he would come back to her. He wouldn't have left the three of them alone to struggle like they had if he wasn't forced to. She just wished she knew what it was that kept him away. Maybe she could help now that she was an adult.

At some point, Raelynn had laid down and drifted off to sleep. Her dreams were all over the place, replaying memories of her and her dad. She awoke with a start, feeling the weight of the crystal piece on her chest. Looking over, she picked up her phone from the table, surprised her alarm hadn't gone off. It wasn't light out yet, but she still felt a moment of panic that she had overslept.

Raelynn was relieved to find that she was only two minutes ahead of her alarm. Taking in a breath to calm her racing nerves, she stretched and dropped her legs off the couch. It wasn't the worst place to sleep, but she definitely preferred her bed.

"Timmy, boy," she called once she was upright. "Let's go potty."

She listened as he obviously stretched and then flopped off the bed with little less than a thump. She cringed, thankful she didn't have anyone below her. He slowly made his way out of the bedroom and when he saw Raelynn, he stretched his front paws out in front of him in a massive stretch.

"Yeah, I'm sure you're sore, you spoiled beast," she said sarcastically. "You could have shared you know."

She moved to the door to let him out. Once he was clipped to his chain, she sat in the chair and breathed in the fresh air. It was a crisp morning, cooler than it had been. She figured it was probably at least sixty, but it smelled fresh and clean.

Timmy made quick use of his business, and they were back inside pretty fast. She poured food into his bowl and moved into the kitchen to make her coffee. Raelynn chuckled at her leisurely pace given she was only up a couple minutes before her alarm. She was also relieved that she felt awake and not sluggish given her late night.

Thinking about Beau and their relaxed evening brought an unexpected smile to Raelynn's lips. She wasn't really looking for romance, but she couldn't deny how much she enjoyed the time with him. She and Beau had actually known each other for a long time. They went to high school together but were never really friends. It wasn't until Sahara and Kiah started dating that they actually hung out. Raelynn wouldn't say he was the guy she admired from a distance either, like some romance novel trope where she always had a secret crush or something. If she was completely honest, she had barely thought about Beau more than what his name was back then.

Raelynn shifted her thoughts from Beau as Timmy began to make noise licking the bottom of his food bowl. He had finished it all and always acted like he was starving. She thought he would probably eat all day if she kept filling his bowl. She shook her head at him and smiled, giving him head rubs and chin scratches.

She refilled his bowl with fresh water and then let him out again. As Raelynn watched him sniff around for his perfect spot, she wondered what would make someone relinquish such a sweet and well-mannered dog. She felt so lucky to have gotten him when she did, and they had settled into their routine quickly. She didn't know what she would do without him anymore and he had only been with her a couple months.

Timmy lazily made his way back to the door, bringing Raelynn's attention back to her pup. She moved into the grassy yard to clean up after him and quickly bagged it up. She tied the bag closed and dropped it in the container and then headed inside.

"Come on buddy. I gotta get to work." She kneeled down and scratched his ears with a hand on each side of his head. Timmy lifted his chin and closed his eyes.

If he was a cat, she had no doubt he would be purring like crazy.

Raelynn closed and locked the sliding door and pulled the curtains closed again. The sun was still hiding beneath the dark sky and the temperature felt pretty mild even without its heat. It wasn't so cold that she was uncomfortable in her long sleeves, which was a good omen for the rest of the day.

Timmy lumbered into the hallway, and Raelynn just shook her head. The crazy dog seemed to really like the bathroom lately.

She made her way back into her room and finished getting ready for work, after thoroughly washing her hands. It was a typical Wednesday. Since only Monday's hours varied, Raelynn's schedule was pretty much the same every day. Raelynn didn't mind working every day, and she had an agreement with her boss about overtime. The last thing Raelynn wanted was to stress her boss's finances by requiring her to pay overtime.

This week would be weird, she thought, with her taking Saturday off and then Sunday being up in the air. At least she would still get paid her normal paycheck regardless, per Susiana's insistence, for her birthday. She didn't give her employees any kind of bonuses for their birthdays, but she did kind of give them a gift in the form of the day off and pay for almost a full shift. For a small business it was a big deal for her, and Raelynn never forgot to thank her for it—even if she didn't really need the whole day off.

Raelynn locked up her apartment and then made her way to her car, officially beginning her day. She paused outside her car and looked up into the clear sky. The sun was just at the very beginning of rising, but it was still dark

Bonded Blood

out. She always loved the sunrises here in her hometown. This was the time she knew to come outside and start watching the sun rise. It was the start of her favorite time of the day.

When she started driving and was allowed to take the car, she and Sahara would drive down to the ocean and watch the sunrises and sunsets. They would get up early in the morning to take Honesty to work and then drive to Ocean City before the sun came up. Jericho was still little and would fall back asleep in his car seat and never even know they went anywhere. Raelynn's only camera was her phone, but the skies were so vivid that any camera would work. They would repeat the process for the sunsets when they could.

As Jericho got older, it was harder to drag him out of bed and Sahara decided she agreed with his desire to sleep. So, Raelynn would sometimes go alone. Once she started college and moved out of the house, she would pick early classes so she would have to get herself up and drive to watch the sun literally rise from the water and then be wide awake for class.

Even though she wasn't an early riser naturally, when she had something to get up for, she didn't have any issues with getting out of bed. Sahara on the other hand hated getting up early the older she got. Jericho is very similar as well. But Raelynn liked the solitude of watching the sun rise or set by herself. For some reason she felt her dad's presence the most when she was by the sea.

As she opened her car door, she glanced back at her apartment building. The lot she parked in was small and a lot of people parked on the street if they even had a car. Many people walked around here since a lot of students lived in the building as well. It wasn't an exclusive residence for students, but the rent was more reasonable than some other places.

"Hey Rae!" a voice called from her left.

She turned and saw one of her best friends from high school, her silhouette lit up by the parking lot light in front of her. She didn't know that Serenity had moved into her building. Where had she been that she didn't know this?

"Hey Reni! What are you doing here?" She closed her car door and moved to greet her friend. She hadn't seen her in a while and was happy she called out to her.

They shared a hug and Serenity smiled. "I just moved in last weekend actually. I didn't know you lived here. How long has it been? Man, we used to be inseparable and now we hardly talk."

Raelynn shook her head. "I know! I've been here a couple months I guess, I don't remember. A lot is going on in my head. How are you? Where are you off to?"

Serenity and Raelynn had gone to school together from third or fourth grade on through high school. She had lived just a few blocks from Honesty's house, and they had always rode the same bus. Since they lived close together, they would often walk to each other's houses, meeting halfway to appease their parents. Since Honesty was usually working, Serenity's mom would sometimes look after Raelynn and her siblings for her as well. Serenity had two older brothers, so her mom was able to work nights and Serenity's dad worked during the day, when he was around. If there was any crossover in schedules, one of her older brothers would watch them all. So, there was always someone there to keep an eye on all the kids.

Raelynn was glad to see her friend again and felt a little guilty for neglecting their friendship. "I am off to work. What about you?" She leaned against Serenity's car and crossed her arms across her chest.

Serenity shrugged. "Just heading to grab a quick breakfast with my mom and then try to find a new job. I hate the one I have and am looking for something else," she rolled her eyes and groaned.

"Where are you working now?" she asked her, with a lifted eyebrow. It wasn't really hard to find jobs around here, but during the fall and winter it can be a little more challenging.

During the spring and summer, the jobs were abundant and paid well due to the abundance of tourism. Once seasonal businesses started to close in the fall, the job market slowed down. This was why she was thankful for Susiana and her job. She had kept it for a long time and didn't plan to quit until she had to—or the perfect "adult" job came up.

Serenity scrunched her nose. "I'm working at one of the smaller pharmacies downtown by the hospital. I just don't get enough hours and then they close early now and then because it's slow, and I lose money. I need something more stable and consistent."

Raelynn nodded. "I guess that makes sense. So where are you going to look?"

"I love the pharmacy *job* I just need more consistent and reliable hours. They basically trained me. So, I didn't have to go to school for all that. I only have my AA from Chesapeake, which is fine, but I don't want to have to take any more classes. I am hoping to find something at one of the bigger pharmacies that doesn't require me to get more education." She sighed and leaned against her car next to Raelynn.

"Hm, wish I could help but that's an area I know nothing about," Raelynn told her. "I'm still at the coffee shop over on College, probably will be forever. Let's get together soon. I have to run now though, or I am going to be late."

Serenity nodded. "Yeah, I better get going too. I'll text you my address, well apartment number," she said with a small laugh. "I still have the same phone number. But you know that. I got your text this weekend, but I couldn't get there. Hope all is good with Ashley. Did she leave then?"

Raelynn quickly filled her in on Ashley and then they hugged again and went in opposite directions.

Raelynn gave her friend a quick wave as she opened her car door again. She missed her friend more than she realized as she watched Serenity drive away. By now the sun was a little more than a sliver against the darkness of the early morning sky and the colors were starting to show up in the muted streaks of the clouds. She sighed and slid into her car and started it up.

Driving to work was such an everyday thing that she rarely thought much about it anymore. She arrived with only three minutes to spare. She liked being more like ten minutes early, so she didn't feel rushed. She also liked to be there when Susiana drove in because punctuality was important to her boss.

Raelynn was glad that Susiana was running a few minutes late as well because she was just getting out of her vehicle when Raelynn parked. She hurried out and waved to her boss as she jogged to catch up to her at the door.

"Sorry, I'm late this morning. I ran into an old friend," she explained quickly so Susiana wouldn't think she had overslept or something.

Her boss waved her hand. "Oh no worries. I had a rough night with Anton anyway. I think he is coming down with something."

She noticed Susiana's tired eyes and felt bad for her. Raelynn picked up one of the bags her boss had set down to unlock the door. She knew it had to have been a long night because the bags of pastries were fewer than normal.

"Thank you, Raelynn. I am not sure how long my energy will keep up. I didn't even have much time to bake because he was so fussy and wanted to be held almost all night. I hope we have enough to get through the morning rush." Susiana tried to hide a yawn behind her free hand as she pushed the door open with her hip.

"Well, I am here and will do whatever you need me to. Except bake. I'm not much of a specialty baker. Basics I can do, but that's it," Raelynn said with a smile.

Susiana laughed. "No baking today. I'll just make sure to get my husband to cover Anton tonight since he is off the next two days." She sighed. "I hope he is better by Sunday."

"That would be a bummer if he was sick for Halloween. Let me know what I can do to help. I'm here and I think Chrissy comes in later, right?" she asked over her shoulder. Raelynn set the bag down on the counter and moved to the back hallway, with Susiana right behind her, to grab her apron.

"I think so. I'll be right up, you go ahead, Raelynn. And thank you," she said with a small smile. Susiana disappeared into her office and quietly closed the door.

Raelynn wasn't sure if she should go ahead and move the contents from the bags into the display case or if Susiana would be right out like she said.

The bell above the shop's front door brought her attention to the front and she decided to leave them for now. The door shouldn't have been left open, she thought. Raelynn took a quick glance behind her to see if Susiana was still in the office.

"Can I help you?" she asked, her head down as she tied her apron around her waist. When no one answered, she looked up. "We aren't actually open—"

She froze in her spot as her eyes locked with the dark green ones of someone that she didn't want to be alone with.

Chapter 10

The man gave Raelynn that creepy smirk and dropped an envelope on the counter in front of her. He looked up and raised his eyebrows at her. When she didn't move to take it, he leaned closer and pushed the paper toward her with a dirty finger.

Raelynn looked up and studied his face. He looked creepier up close and she resisted a shudder. His eyes were so dark they barely looked green anymore. Those eyes were deep and penetrating, and clearly hiding something. They made her feel a little scared as he continued to stare at her. His thick locks fell in front of his face, the long and unkept strands shined in the lights of the café, almost as if they had been oiled recently. His clothes were mismatched and too big for his frame. He definitely looked like he didn't have access to regular showers. But she noticed again that he didn't smell bad, like she would expect looking at him.

He grinned at her, revealing surprisingly white teeth. Raelynn furrowed her brow looking at him. Who was this person? It didn't make sense to her, was he actually homeless? She didn't know what to think about her observations. Not only did he not smell bad, but his teeth were bright and clean. She would have expected him to have dirty, broken, or even missing teeth. But that's not what greeted her.

Confused, she raised her eyes to meet his again, but she quickly shifted her gaze away from his scruffy face to his dirty finger as he tapped it on the paper.

Raelynn slowly reached out and put her hand on the envelope, sliding it closer to her. He gave her a slight nod and then quickly left. She was still stunned staring after the man. He had disappeared so fast she didn't even see where he went after he left the café.

Susiana walked into the front area and picked up the bag Raelynn had left on the counter.

"Who was that?" she asked absently, looking inside the bag.

Raelynn jumped, not aware that her boss had reentered the space. "Oh, I don't know but he didn't want anything." She grabbed the envelope and stuffed it in her apron and picked up a washrag to wipe the already clean countertop. It wasn't even wet, she quickly realized and let out a chuckle at herself. Thankfully her boss was just as distracted. *Or maybe she was just too tired to care*, Raelynn thought.

Susiana looked up and nodded. "Ok. I'm going to get these set out and then get some paperwork done in back. Let me know if you need any help before Chrissy comes in." And then she quickly disappeared again.

Letting out a sigh, Raelynn reached back into her pocket and felt the paper. Her mind drifted to the strange man who kept appearing at her workplace, leaving her now a second note. She would have to wait for her break to see what was inside this one. She moved to the sink and got the cloth wet and grabbed a bottle of spray cleaner. The counter didn't need to be cleaned, but she wanted to keep busy.

She hadn't relocked the door since it was only a few minutes before they would open anyway. She was all set up, thanks to Chrissy refilling everything the night before. Now it was just a matter of waiting for people to trickle in.

A quick glance at the time showed the morning rush would be starting any minute. Once that started, she would be busy for the rest of her shift, aside from a few short lulls and her break. She liked the time to go fast. It wasn't that she didn't like her job. Raelynn just hated being bored and standing around. She needed something to keep her mind occupied.

She finished the counter and tossed the rag into the sink just as the bell rang above the door. She looked over to see a group of three students walking in. She smiled at them and noticed they all wore weary expressions. *Definitely must be midterm season*, she thought silently. She remembered those days all too well.

"Good morning. How can I help you?" she asked with her most sympathetic tone.

One of the guys leaned against the counter and groaned. "Anything that is super charged with dangerously high levels of caffeine."

A girl next to him punched him lightly in the arm and laughed. "You still have to be able to sit long enough to pass the exam, TJ."

"I don't even know why I took this class to begin with," the third one complained.

The girl stepped up and ordered all three of them black coffees with the promise of something else later on. Raelynn suspected that was to pacify the two guys with her though.

She gave the three a nod and after running the card through, started to get their drinks.

The rest of the morning moved along steadily. The stream of customers was constant and never reached an unmanageable level. The regulars occupied their table in the back corner as usual and continued their gossip from the day before. Susiana made an appearance once to refill the pastries and was relieved to see that they still had plenty. Usually that would upset her but after her night, and limited ability to bake more than she did, Realynn figured her relief was justified.

By the time Chrissy came in, Raelynn had completely forgotten about Creepy Guy's visit and was cleaning up the tables. There was one couple sitting at one of the tables by the window, but the rest of the place was empty. She wiped down the tables and then made her way back to the counter to restock supplies when her coworker walked through the door.

"Mornin' chica!" Chrissy called from the door.

Raelynn smiled. "Hey, girl. I'm so glad to see you! I gotta make a bathroom run in the worst way." She waved her hand toward the back, letting her colleague know to move quickly.

Chrissy shot her a mock salute and laughed as she disappeared into the hallway.

When she finally reappeared at the counter, Raelynn bolted for the bathroom. She could have asked Susiana to cover for her for a minute, but she knew her boss was trying to get other things done.

Raelynn made her way back out front as she retied the apron strings around her waist. Smoothing the front,

Bonded Blood

she felt the envelope in her pocket. The memory of the early morning visitor flooded back to her mind, and she nearly ran into Chrissy as she rounded the corner to the front. Her coworker grabbed her shoulders to keep them from colliding.

"Hey, everything ok?" Chrissy asked with concern. Her hands were still on Raelynn's shoulders.

"I'm fine, just distracted. It's been a busy morning, I was glad for the break," she answered, still a little frazzled by almost running into Chrissy.

Looking at her carefully, Chrissy finally nodded and dropped her hands. "I was just going to ask Susiana a question since it was empty out front. I'll be right back." Then she disappeared behind Raelynn.

Sighing and holding her chest trying to calm her rapidly beating heart from being startled, Raelynn moved back out front. She looked around and saw that it was in fact empty in the dining room area. It hadn't been this quiet since they opened more than three hours ago. It was typical to have a midweek lull on Wednesdays but today was steadily busy all morning.

Chrissy came walking back out of the hallway and gave Raelynn a nod before moving to the bakery cases. Even with the steady stream of customers in the morning, the bakery case wasn't empty. She suspected that was what Chrissy went to ask Susiana about. Raelynn hadn't had the chance to clue her in on what their boss told her earlier.

Raelynn loved working with Chrissy. They worked all but two of her shifts together. They had a routine that worked well for both of them—Raelynn stayed in front of the cash register and handled the coffee drink orders while Chrissy managed the baked goods. If Raelynn got overloaded with orders, Chrissy would step over and help out without being asked and vice versa. They worked well together. Susiana rarely came out of her office when they worked together, showing her confidence in the two of them handling everything.

The bell above the door jingled just as Chrissy came back to the front. Raelynn shot her a quick glance as their eyes met. She smiled, knowing they were thinking the same thing.

Two women came through the door. They looked like they had never been there before, staring at the menu and didn't even notice Raelynn waiting patiently for them to reach the counter.

Smiling widely, she waited for them to make their way to her. "Can I help you with any questions?" she asked as one of them finally made eye contact with her.

The woman sighed. "I'm sorry. I've never been here before but was told I *had* to try it." She shot a look over her shoulder at the other woman with her, who smiled widely at Raelynn. "I'm new here," she added, as if to justify why she hadn't been there before.

Chrissy appeared next to Raelynn and leaned over the counter. "If you haven't been here before, then you absolutely have to try Susiana's cinnamon rolls. They are the absolute best on the Shore—and I promise you won't regret the calories." She whispered the last words with a wink.

"Agreed!" The other woman chimed in.

Raelynn and Chrissy helped with their orders and then watched as they found a table by one of the big windows. After they had left, Chrissy leaned over.

Bonded Blood

"I wonder what it would be like to live somewhere else and then come here. I've lived here my whole life. Have you?" she asked Raelynn.

Raelynn nodded. "Yep, I'm a lifer too. Haven't actually been off the shore much in my life. Not a lot of money to travel. Even going over the bridge was a big deal for me growing up." She was referring to the Bay Bridge that connected the Eastern Shore to the mainland of Maryland near Annapolis. Raelynn had only been over the bridge once in her life and it was when she was really young. She vaguely remembered the experience if she was honest.

After the ladies left, the café was quiet, a more typical Wednesday actually. Raelynn took an earlier lunch break since it was quiet. She grabbed a bagel sandwich from the display and made herself a Frappuccino. Once in the break room, she sat down and felt the paper in her apron pocket crinkle. She had forgotten about it again.

Taking a breath, she pulled it carefully out of her pocket and set it on the table next to her lunch. She had an urge to wash her hands again after looking at the filthy paper. Deciding to just jump in and read it, she pushed her food aside and picked up the envelope.

Raelynn turned it over in her hands a couple of times, debating what to do. Her name was scratched on the outside in pencil and was faded, as if it was written a long time ago and had been in a pocket or something for a long time. The envelope from the day before was pretty much the same, only instead of pencil scratching it was written in pen. She wasn't sure if the penmanship matched, but she knew she would have to check.

Screw it, she thought and ripped open the top. She gently pulled a folded piece of paper out of the dirty envelope.

The paper inside was surprisingly white—and clean. She furrowed her brows, thinking it was strange. Yesterday's paper was much dirtier. This page looked almost brand new. How is the outside so dirty while the inside is almost perfectly white?

She was expecting another card to fall out of the folded page. As she held the paper, she closed her eyes, unsure of what was waiting for her inside the note. She slowly opened her eyes then spread the paper flat and pressed her hands across it. When nothing fell out of the folds, she just smoothed out the wrinkles as best she could. Raelynn furrowed her brows as she squinted at the single sentence on the paper, and then read it out loud.

"The time is nearing."

"What the hell?" she mumbled as Susiana walked in.

"What's wrong?" her boss asked. She reached into the fridge and grabbed a bottle of water. Susiana leaned against the closed door and looked at Raelynn, waiting for an answer.

Shrugging, Raelynn folded the paper again and said, "No, everything's fine. How are you holding up?" She didn't want to get her boss involved in whatever was happening in her life. Changing subjects was the best option.

Susiana rolled her eyes. "I'm still here but I'm dragging. Not gonna lie. I'm so glad I have you two up front today. I might catch a nap if I'm completely honest." She gave Raelynn a sheepish smile.

"We got it, if you need to go ahead," Raelynn said with a sympathetic smile.

She knew she and Chrissy could absolutely run the café if needed. She was also confident if Susiana needed to leave, they could handle it as well. Susiana would never leave though. This place was her baby and even as much as she trusted Raelynn and Chrissy, she wouldn't leave someone else to lock up unless it was an emergency.

Susiana smiled. "I know you two can handle it. You are my best two employees, but don't tell anyone," she whispered, as Chrissy appeared in the doorway.

She leaned against the door frame and crossed her arms. "What aren't we telling anyone?" she asked with a grin.

Susiana waved her hand and moved out of the room back to her office. "Oh, you know, work stuff." She laughed as she walked by Chrissy and closed her office door.

"Should I be concerned?" Chrissy asked, looking back at Raelynn.

Raelynn laughed. "Nope. She was just saying she trusts us to handle the front in case she needs to take a little nap."

"Oh. Yeah, no problem. It's so you-know-what out there. Not gonna say it out loud, but since I can hear the bell from back here, I'm gonna hang out here for a minute." Chrissy shoved off the wall and moved into the space to grab a drink from the fridge. Susiana stocked it with water bottles and a few cans of soda for her workers.

Raelynn opened the note again and stared at it. Chrissy had moved to stand behind her and read the words out loud.

"Rae, what's going on? Are you being followed or stalked or something?" Chrissy moved and sat down next to her.

"I don't know. This whole thing is weird, but I don't think anyone is following me or threatening me. I just keep getting…things." Raelynn sighed and motioned to the paper in front of her. She really didn't want to get into this with her coworker, but she thought maybe she needed to bounce it off someone.

Just then they heard the jingle of the bell and Chrissy gave her a look that said the conversation wasn't over yet and then hurried to the front. Raelynn got up and washed her hands and started on her lunch. She didn't have much time and didn't want to leave Chrissy alone for long, plus she didn't want to be starving later because she didn't eat when she had the chance.

Raelynn stared at the paper again. None of the notes so far had made any sense. This one sounded a little more ominous than the others, which actually did make her a little nervous. She tried to think of what was in the last notes. The first literally sounded like her dad was talking to her. The others were like some sort of riddle. Maybe together they meant something, she thought. She made a mental note to pull them all out that night and see if she could see a pattern or something. She was always up for a good puzzle.

When she was learning how to read, one of her and her dad's favorite things to do was watch Wheel of Fortune on TV every night. She never won over her dad, but she learned a lot about putting letters and sounds together. When they went to restaurants, which was rare, she would work on the word games on the kids' menus/placemats and see how many she could get without asking for help.

After her father disappeared, they didn't go out to dinner at all. But at one point Honesty worked at a local diner and she brought home a stack of old ones for Raelynn because they had changed their menu. Raelynn spent an entire afternoon working on the different games, since there were multiple versions and not every menu was the same. She even tried to teach Sahara how to play the words games, but she was just too young.

She had discovered she really liked to try to figure things out, from puzzles to crime shows. Maybe her dad knew this about her before she even did and this whole thing was some kind of puzzle for her to figure out. None of it made sense at the moment though, so that theory was a little questionable.

Chrissy plopping down next to her pulled Raelynn from her thoughts, and she jumped slightly.

"Everything ok?" she asked, shooting a scowl at her coworker.

Chrissy nodded. "Yeah, just hate it when it's slow. The time drags. So, tell me about this note thing. That outta liven things up a little." She grinned and nodded toward the paper in front of Raelynn.

Raelynn stood and put her trash in the bin and stretched. "Let's go back out front in case anyone comes in and I'll fill you in on the little I know."

They made their way back out front and found a small group of students walking in the door just as they got to the counter. They were busy for the next two hours with a steady stream of students and a few other single people who came in for takeout orders.

Before Raelynn knew it, the clock rang out two dings. The cute little clock on the wall, with a chef's hat and spoons for the hands, made a dinging sound like a timer going off every hour. She realized she and Chrissy never got the chance to talk about the notes. The steady stream of customers had slowed, and she looked over at Chrissy who was studying the almost empty bakery case. She leaned against it and raised her eyebrows at Raelynn.

"I'm not sure we are gonna make it with what's left, Rae. It's pretty slim pickings now." Chrissy gestured toward the glass.

Raelynn shrugged. "Not much we can do about it. At least we made it this far into the day. If we had one cookie left at the end of the day, I am sure Susiana would be happy we didn't run out completely." She grinned and Chrissy nodded.

"Yeah, you're right." She let out a sigh and then added, "You never told me about the notes though. Are you working tomorrow?"

Raelynn nodded. "Yep. I'm off Saturday so I am working the rest of the week."

"Then I will expect an explanation tomorrow about all this. You might want to get the authorities involved though, especially if this has been going on for a while. People are crazy. Don't take a chance with your life, Rae. Besides, I kinda like you," she said with a shrug and a wink, making Raelynn laugh.

"Don't worry. I have people in my corner. You're not gonna get rid of me." Raelynn moved to the back and started to undo her apron as Susiana came walking up front.

Raelynn stopped in case there was something her boss needed before she left. Susiana looked around and then moved to the bakery case. She leaned over it and nodded.

"Thank goodness. I promise girls, I will have more tomorrow. I already gave my husband the warning." She looked around the mostly empty café and smiled. "You two are so great, you know that? I don't know what I would do without either of you." She pulled Raelynn in for a side hug and gestured for Chrissy to come as well.

Raelynn chuckled as she thought Susiana acted more like a grandmother than a late-thirties mom of a toddler.

"So, are you ok if I take off, Susiana? Or do you want me to hang around for a little longer?" Raelynn asked.

Susiana shook her head. "Nope, we should be good. Have a good night, Raelynn." Then she spun on her heel and disappeared back into her office, leaving Raelynn and Chrissy staring after her.

"She must have gotten that nap," Chrissy said with a laugh.

Raelynn laughed as well and nodded. "I'm glad she trusts us like that."

"Can't argue with that!" Chrissy agreed. "See you tomorrow, Rae."

While Chrissy turned to the front, Raelynn went the opposite way to put her apron away and grab her stuff to head out. She removed the note from her apron pocket and shoved it in her back pants pocket and glanced at the clock again. She had plenty of time to go let Timmy out before going to her mom's house to pick up Jericho.

She waved to Chrissy and Susiana who was now up front with Chrissy as she walked out to her car. She was pleasantly surprised by the warmer temperature outside. The sun was still shining brightly with only a few clouds blocking it.

As she got in her car, she started to think about the night ahead. She had been busy enough at work that she forgot about her date, if you could call it that, with Beau. They really hadn't defined anything, but she wasn't about to overthink it. He was fun to hang out with and she was good with that for now.

Dinner was a different thing though. What would she make for the three of them? She was tired of pizza, if that was possible. She wanted something different. She liked to cook but wasn't so great at it that she could impress anyone with her skills. Maybe something simple like spaghetti would work. The thought occurred to her that she didn't even know what Beau liked. If she was cooking for Sahara and Jericho, it would be easy. But what did Beau like? Did he have any allergies she should know about? An allergic reaction would definitely be a bummer.

Raelynn suddenly realized there was a lot she didn't know about Beau. Maybe she should text him to make sure before she decides on what to make. She started her car and then sent a quick text. If he was busy, he could just answer whenever, and then she could decide. As she thought about Beau more, she realized she also doesn't know what he does or where he works.

They had a lot of opportunities to get to know each other and she had to admit she was looking forward to it. He had definitely changed in the last few months, and she suspected it had to do with discovering family he didn't know existed, maybe he felt something was missing like Ashley did. She wondered if missing her dad was affecting her mood like it had seemed to affect Beau.

All she could hope for was answers to the lingering questions about her father. Hopefully he was still alive somewhere, but she hoped for *any* information about him at this point. Maybe he had died so many years ago. Would that change her too? She hoped not. She tried continually to keep her hopes in check. He didn't seem like the kind of guy to just up and abandon his family, but there were always stories about that. Maybe he just got caught up in something or was in the wrong place at the wrong time.

But no one knew what happened to him. Not even the officer who was trying to help her last summer. She couldn't get any information about him. It was frustrating and weird, she thought. How can someone disappear in this day and age without a trace. A sudden reality struck her as she drove, lost in her thoughts.

If someone didn't want to be found, they would do everything they could to disappear without a trace. She felt a shiver as she wondered if her dad *wanted* to disappear and not be found. Did he plan this in such detail that no one would ever find out what really happened?

Chapter 11

As usual, Timmy needed no extra encouragement to jump in the backseat of Raelynn's car. As she closed the door, she thought maybe she should get one of those car seat covers they make for dog fur. It was close to three thirty and Jericho should be home from school by the time she got to the house. She had confirmed with her mom that she was taking Jericho and Honesty would pick him up around seven thirty, since she was going to be able to leave a little earlier than she thought.

Beau had also texted to check about plans, which she was grateful to find out he didn't have any allergies or anything he didn't like. Even though the blue crab was the state's declared crustacean, not everyone liked it. And just because they had the freshest seafood around, plenty of people didn't enjoy that either.

Even through text, he seemed unsure if she still wanted to get together, which she had to think was just because he was being considerate. He seemed like he still planned to come over though. Either way, it made her smile. She wasn't going to overthink it though. They were just two friends getting together for dinner. Informal and fun, she thought.

Raelynn had decided to make a simple meal knowing her brother would be the one to make a fuss about anything.

Bonded Blood

She took out some meat to thaw while she ran to pick up Jericho. She would have plenty of time to get everything ready before Beau got there. It wouldn't take long anyway. She wished she had her mom's cooking skills, but she was pretty limited to pasta dishes. Or chicken tacos. The chicken was about as top notch around here as the seafood.

Honesty's fried chicken was the best on the Shore, according to Raelynn anyway. It got her thinking that maybe she should help her mom out a little more with dinner so she could learn. When Honesty was working so much when they were kids, Raelynn's kid-friendly menu of grilled cheese, PB&J sandwiches, macaroni and cheese, didn't really sound as appetizing as an adult—especially for entertaining other adults. She needed to grow her resume to include more adult dishes. Maybe she and her mom could do some bonding over cooking classes, she thought with a grin.

She wondered for about the millionth time how life might have been different with her father still around as she grew up. Maybe she would have helped Honesty make dinner every night and she would know how to make so many dishes by now. Honesty definitely wouldn't have had to work so many jobs. They might have been able to do other things, maybe take a family weekend at the beach or something.

Feeling sadness start to creep in, Raelynn shook her head to clear it. No use in wishing for something different. All they could do now was move forward. All the wishes in the world wouldn't change how things had happened. She needed to focus on the present and the evening ahead.

As she got closer to her mom's house, she realized she forgot about dessert. Even with the limited supply that Susiana had brought, Raelynn could have grabbed something for the two of them early in the day. Then again, maybe that would have been too stressful for her boss with how worried she was about running out of baked goods.

Shrugging to herself, she decided if they wanted something later, they could go to one of the ice cream places around. She didn't even know what kind of desserts Beau would like anyway. When Ashley was still there, Raelynn had become her self-declared tour guide, taking her to all the important places in Salisbury and Ocean City. Important *food* places at least. Raelynn wasn't a real adventurous food connoisseur, but she did know the best restaurants around to get the good stuff—especially ice cream.

Her thoughts drifted quickly to the choices she had offered her friend and then she brushed aside the one major place she intentionally left off her tour. She wouldn't bring up that place unless Beau did. She had been able to resist going for almost fifteen years and she wasn't going to cave now. Raelynn silently hoped Beau didn't challenge her resolve, she wasn't ready to tell him why it wasn't an option.

She arrived at her mom's sooner than she realized. They didn't live far apart, but it seemed to go by especially fast this time. She sighed as she parked in the small, single lane driveway. She left the car running as she exited the vehicle and glanced back at her lazy boy in the back seat. He lifted his head when the car stopped but didn't move so she just figured it was easier not to disrupt him and just run in for Jericho.

Slamming the door shut, she jogged to the front door. Her brother opened it just as she reached the top step and before she could open it herself. He grinned at her and pushed a small box into her belly. Then he took off, not even waiting for her to take the package from him before he had climbed into the backseat with Timmy.

Raelynn smiled and shook her head at her brother. They never had an opportunity to have a dog growing up and Jericho seemed to be making up for that loss. She dropped her eyes to look at the package that she almost dropped when the handoff happened from Jericho. She frowned and bit her lip as she studied it.

Once again there is no return address and just her name and her mom's address printed on it. It didn't get past her that she had literally received a package with a new turtle in it every day the last four days. Even on the weekend when there wasn't delivery on Sunday, she got two on Monday. It's Wednesday now and she had collected five, counting this one, assuming it's another statue or turtle or whatever they were.

Letting out a sigh, Raelynn made her way back to the car. She had watched Jericho lock the door to the house behind him, so she knew it was ok to leave. As she opened her door, she snuck a peek at her brother and dog in the back. The chuckle that slipped out drew a scowl from Jericho. The two boys in the back were cuddled up, Jericho definitely not wearing a seatbelt as he laid across the big lap dog, who appeared as content as if he were made for this, an oversized body pillow.

She settled into her seat and lightly tossed the box on the front passenger seat next to her. She maybe should be a little more careful, but she was struggling with the whole thing and didn't really give it much thought—aside from frustration. Maybe if she knew for sure they were from her dad she wouldn't be so irritated. But she was becoming increasingly worried it had to do with Creepy Guy from work and not her dad at all.

Raelynn glanced back at her brother in her rearview mirror as she started the car. "Hey, bro. Buckle." She raised her eyebrows at him, and he gave her a huff similar to what her dog gives her when she forces him to move.

After a few grumbles between Jericho and Timmy, they were finally on their way back to her place. Glancing at the clock she saw it was almost four, which was about what she had planned. As she drove, she decided to give her brother a choice for dinner, something she rarely did.

"Hey Jer, tacos or spaghetti tonight?" she asked, looking in the mirror.

Jericho scrunched his nose. "Spaghetti?" He looked at Timmy and cocked his eyebrow at the pup. "What do you think, buddy?" He acted like he was having a silent conversation with his dog and then finally he nodded as if they had come to some sort of agreement.

"Tacos it is. I don't like beef, you know that Rae," Jericho said with a knowing look on his face.

Raelynn nodded. "I kinda figured." She let out a sigh. She did know he preferred chicken and was going to just make him deal with it but then thought maybe she was in the mood for chicken too. *Tacos it is*, she thought in agreement.

"We are gonna need to stop at the store though. Will you stay in the car with Timmy? I won't take long but I don't want to leave him alone." She hated leaving him in the car ever and would always make sure she did her running before she got home or when she didn't need to have him with her. Even though it wasn't hot outside anymore, she didn't like to take any chances of anything weird happening.

Jericho shrugged and scratched Timmy's head. "We'll be fine, won't we buddy?"

Raelynn bit the corner of her lip. She would have to make this a quick trip in and out. She made a mental list of what she would need. She had tortillas and hard shells, as well as a couple different kinds of rice. She would just need some cheese, lettuce, peppers, and maybe some black olives and that should be good. She had sour cream and taco sauce at home if Beau wanted the extras. Thankfully, she knew the store had taco supplies in the first aisle after the produce. *Easy in and out*, she thought.

She drove to the store and parked close to the entrance. Looking back once more to make sure everything was fine with the boys in the back, she exited the car and quickly walked inside. The cold air from the building was overwhelming as she walked through the automatic door. It wasn't even summer anymore, but the store management seemed to be confused with how cold it needed to be inside. She wished she had grabbed her sweatshirt.

Taking a small basket off the stack, Raelynn quickly moved toward the produce. She made record time through the vegetables and fruits and then headed for the "Hispanic Foods" section. Looking through her basket's contents again, she nodded and moved quickly to the self-checkouts. The line was only two people long, and the regular checkout had a line of three. Either way she would be waiting.

As she waited, she stood on her tippy toes to look out the windows. She saw her car there and even though she couldn't see inside, knowing it was there and she could see it, gave her some comfort. Raelynn moved her attention back to the line in front of her.

It didn't take as long as she thought before she was in front of the register. Raelynn looked up once more to see her car in the same spot. Turning her attention back to the task at hand, she scanned her things and slid her debit card into the reader. Before long, she was on her way back outside.

Pulling her car door open, she felt a sudden chill run over her skin, like she was being watched. She glanced around her, but didn't notice anyone in the parking lot or anywhere near her either. *Weird*, she thought. Maybe it was just the cooler than expected breeze she decided and slid into her seat. A quick look in her backseat made her forget all about that weird feeling.

Jericho and Timmy were again cuddled together, and both were sound asleep. She couldn't remember the last time her brother took a nap. She chuckled and shook her head. Raelynn just left them be and started the short journey to her apartment. It was less than five miles, even though everyone knew an accident could happen at any time. She smiled hearing her mom's words in her mind from any time she left while living at home.

As she parked her car, both Timmy and Jericho woke up. Her brother stretched and let out a groan.

"I needed that," he said with a grin. He scratched Timmy under his chin and the dog obliged him by lifting his head.

Raelynn turned to look at him. "Tough day at school, little bro?" She sounded a little cheeky because she knew he was a smart kid. School wasn't hard for him, and they both knew it.

Bonded Blood

"Eh, just boring," he snorted back. He latched the leash on Timmy and then opened his door, leading the big pup out.

She laughed as she walked after them, carrying her box and bag of groceries. Since her apartment was on the first floor, she wished she had a door directly to her place with a secure lock. Without that security she had to walk to the front of the building. Jericho and Timmy were already waiting for her to unlock the large glass door at the entrance when she got there.

"You know, you could help me out here, Jer," she grumbled as she tried to juggle the things in her hands and get her key out.

Jericho shrugged. "You got it. Besides I got Timmy."

They both looked at the dog who was patiently waiting for her, completely ignoring everything else around them.

Raelynn rolled her eyes. "Yeah, he's such a handful." She finally got her key in the door and held it open for them with her foot.

The two ran ahead of her, making her laugh. Timmy wasn't a runner but whatever Jericho was giving him, the dog gladly took. Her brother laughed as they made their way down the hall to her door. Once in front of it, the boys stopped again and waited for her to catch up.

"I'm coming," she said with a sigh. Raelynn set the box down this time and unlocked the door.

Jericho swung it open, with Timmy lumbering in after him. Once inside, the dog went to his water bowl and emptied it. Her brother jumped in and filled it again right away and then went to fill his bowl with food.

"He can wait to eat, Jericho. He usually eats when I do." Raelynn set her bag and box down in the kitchen and then turned to lean against the counter.

"He's hungry now, Rae. Can't you see?" He swung his hands in the direction of Timmy scarfing down his bowl of food as if he hadn't eaten in a week.

Raelynn scoffed. "Jericho, this massive beast will eat constantly if you let him. They warned me at the shelter to only feed him twice a day or he would get even bigger, and that much harder to handle. He's already over a hundred and sixty pounds!"

Her brother shrugged again. "Not my problem." And then he smirked as he ran around the corner into the living space.

Groaning, she picked up Timmy's now empty bowl and put it in the sink. As she turned back to follow her brother, her eyes landed on the small brown package. She bit her cheek thoughtfully. Should she wait to open it until later? She knew curiosity would get to her if it was in plain sight, but Timmy's howl took her attention to the other room before she could think twice.

Running into the room, she saw her dog and brother in a wrestling match on the floor, with Jericho laughing uncontrollably. She leaned against the doorway and watched them roll around and couldn't help but admire the gentleness of her pup. He had to outweigh Jericho by at least sixty pounds and yet he never put all his weight on the boy. They said these were gentle giants, and seeing it for herself now, he definitely lived up to that description.

Raelynn's phone chimed from the kitchen, so she moved back that way. She looked at the clock as she opened her texting app and saw that she needed to get going on dinner.

Bonded Blood

Her message was from Beau, letting her know he was off work a little early. He was going to make a stop on the way over, but if it was ok, he would be there a little earlier than planned. Looking at the clock again, she nodded absently.

Raelynn typed out a quick "ok" and then moved to prep the chicken. Thankful that she decided to make tacos now, she started to get things ready. It wouldn't take long, so Beau coming early would work out ok. The chicken was almost completely thawed, which would make it easier to cook and shred. She heard the TV turn on at some point but didn't think much of it. Jericho knew his way around her place, and she knew he wouldn't do anything he wasn't supposed to. She had caught him in a few things that made him realize she would probably find out and then he'd be in trouble with his mom.

While the chicken cooked, she started to remove the other ingredients. She cut up the one green pepper she had and a couple sweet peppers. The tomatoes were grape sized ones, so she just cut them in half. The cheese, black olives, and lettuce were easy. Raelynn took out a pan and filled it with water for the rice. She decided to just make white rice for now. She could add seasonings to that if the boys wanted it spicy.

She had both kinds of taco shells, and since she wasn't sure what Beau preferred, she took both out and set them aside. Turning on the burner for the rice, she looked over at the chicken that was browning perfectly next to her. She stirred it up, shredding it as she went, and reached for her taco seasonings.

"Hey, Jericho?" she called to him as she added the seasonings to the chicken. When he didn't answer, she turned the heat down and leaned around the wall. "Jer?"

She found him staring at the television, lying on Timmy's side with his arm above his head. "Jericho!" she said louder. This time he looked up, a bored look on his face.

"What?" he grumbled out, turning back to the TV.

"Will you please come set the table? Beau is coming and I am trying to get the rest of dinner ready." She turned back to the stove and waited. After the last conversation they had about helping out, she wondered if he had taken any of it to heart.

After about three or four minutes with no movement heard from the other room, she set her spoon down and turned the heat down even more on the stove. The last thing she wanted was to burn anything.

Raelynn leaned against the door frame and stared at her defiant little brother, trying to decide how to teach him a lesson. She also didn't want Beau to think she wasn't a good sister by being really petty. She let out a sigh of frustration.

"Jericho. What did I tell you about helping out?" She tried to keep her tone in check since she knew he had never had to do anything before.

Her brother looked up and shrugged. "That's at home. I'm here now and a *guest* so I shouldn't have to help." His smug look made Raelynn want to scream at him. Lucky for him, a knock sounded at the door.

She scowled at him and moved to the door. "Maybe I won't feed you, you ungrateful brat," she called over her shoulder.

Raelynn opened the door and found Beau standing with one hand propped against the doorframe.

"Hey," he said. "I hope you weren't talking about me." he raised his eyebrows at her and grinned.

Fighting off the blush from being caught taunting her brother, Raelynn waved her hand. "Don't make me mad and you won't have to worry about it. But that was intended for my annoying and ungrateful *baby* brother." She said the end of her sentence loudly so her brother could hear her.

His grunt from inside the apartment signified he heard her loud and clear. Now that there was company, he appeared next to her at the door.

"Hey Beau," he said with a cheeky grin. "I was just going to set the table. Wanna help me?"

Jericho nearly skipped back into the kitchen, drawing a scowl from Raelynn. "Unbelievable," she muttered.

Beau raised his eyebrows at her, humor written all over his face. Raelynn narrowed her eyes. "Don't you dare help him," she said quietly. "Unlike him, you *are* a guest here tonight."

He laughed and gave her a mock salute as they moved inside, and she closed the door. They stepped into the kitchen and Raelynn couldn't help but notice the neatly stacked dishes on the small table, with silverware in the cups. Shaking her head, she moved to add the rice to the now boiling water and then get the rest of the food ready while she waited for that to cook.

Beau followed her and leaned against the counter not far from where she was cooking. "Can I help with anything?" he asked, looking around.

Raelynn looked back. "I think my annoying brother got it all out now. It just took you coming in to get him moving," she said with a smirk. "I just have to wait for this and then we should be good to start."

Nodding, Beau pulled out a chair and sat down. Raelynn turned back to the rice and then moved it from the burner, turning it off.

"I should probably get Timmy out before we start. Wanna come out with me or hang out with the preteen monster?" she asked with a smile and a swing of her thumb at the living room wall.

Beau let out a chuckle. "I'll come with you. Can I use your bathroom quick though?"

Raelynn nodded. "Sure, down the hall to the right." Then she headed to gather her massive ball of fur to go potty.

"Timmy, boy, let's go outside," she called from the door, as she grabbed his discarded leash on the floor by the front door. No doubt another of her brother's thoughtful gestures. "I gotta do something to teach this kid some respect and responsibility," she mumbled to herself.

"Huh?" Jericho asked, looking up from some show on TV.

"Nothing," she said dismissively back to him. "Come on boy." Timmy had slowly made his way to her and once she clipped his chain to his collar, she followed him outside. It was cooling off and she wrapped her arms around her middle, holding her sweatshirt closer. It was probably closer to fifty-five than sixty now, she thought. While she liked the fall, she preferred the summer months. She hated being cold and would rather be hot than the alternative.

She chuckled as she thought of the conversations she and Ashley had. Ashley would laugh at her and tell her things like you can always put more layers on in the cold, but you can only take so much off in the heat. While Raelynn couldn't ever come up with a good argument, she still preferred the heat over being cold.

Timmy seemed to be taking his sweet time, so she sat down on her chair and waited for him to finish. She felt another sudden chill similar to before, like she was being watched. She looked around and didn't see anyone. The small yard was empty aside from her and Timmy. This side of the building was mostly hidden from most people's view anyway. She suddenly felt a little exposed and vulnerable. While it was quiet and private, it was also secluded and easy for someone to sneak up on her.

Raelynn shook her head hard trying to dispel the spiraling thoughts. She looked at Timmy, who was finally doing his business, and she took in a deep breath of air. He didn't seem phased or like someone was around who shouldn't be so maybe it was just in her head. Or he really wasn't a good guard dog, she thought.

"Come on boy," she called, wanting to get back inside quickly.

As if there was no hurry in the world, her dog took his sweet time getting back to her. Frustrated, she slid the door open and quickly closed it along with the curtains.

"Everything ok?" Beau asked, startling Raelynn.

She grabbed her chest in surprise and managed to hold in the shriek from her throat. Beau rushed over to her side and put both his hands on her shoulders. His eyes were full of concern.

"Rae? What happened?" He looked around her, as if he could see through the now closed curtains.

Raelynn closed her eyes and took in some air to calm her rapidly beating heart. When she opened them again, she tried to give him a reassuring smile.

"Yeah, just got spooked by some animal or something." She moved away and into the kitchen. "I gotta get dinner ready. Come on, boys." Her voice returned to normal as she tried to brush aside the strange feelings. She reminded herself she was fine, and it was probably an animal in the trees. No one was out there watching her.

Chapter 12

Dinner went by quietly. Jericho was preoccupied with something on his phone and Raelynn was lost in her thoughts. She felt Beau gently touch her hand, drawing her eyes to meet his.

"Is something wrong, Rae? You seem kind of out of it," he asked, his voice low and full of worry.

Raelynn shook her head. "No, everything is fine. Sorry, I'm just a little distracted." She gave him a small smile and looked over at her brother, who had finished eating and was focused on his phone, playing some game. "Jericho, why don't you clean up your spot and go see what Timmy is up to?"

Jericho looked up from his game and scowled at her. "When I'm done." And then he turned back to his phone.

Raelynn was about to say something when Beau jumped in. "Hey, come on, bro. I'll help you. Then we can find a movie or something." He pushed his chair out and stood, prompting a grumbling Jericho to reluctantly put down his device and stand as well.

Beau gave Raelynn a wink and the two boys started to clean up the table. Raelynn grinned and gave him a slight nod of thanks and then moved around the kitchen putting away the leftovers. She could use them for her dinner the next night. She looked at the clock on the microwave and noticed it was close to six already. That meant she only had a little over an hour before her mom got there for Jericho.

She wasn't sure why, but she was looking forward to him leaving. Typically, she got along great with Jericho, and it wasn't like he was particularly difficult tonight. Her mind was just all over the place and she wanted space to think. Raelynn put her now partially filled containers in the fridge and closed the door. She leaned her back against it and crossed her arms over her chest.

Raelynn was startled to see Beau standing in front of her, his pose similar to her own, making her smile. "Hey," she said shyly.

Beau smiled back, his brown eyes slightly squinted as he observed her. "You gonna tell me what's up or are we waiting until your brother leaves?"

She sighed. "I don't really know if I'm completely honest. Can we wait until he leaves?"

"Yep, that's why I asked. But something's clearly not right so please let me help if I can," he said, his voice full of sincerity.

It had been a long time since Raelynn had felt this comfortable talking to anyone about something so personal. She didn't know why, but she wanted to tell him what was going on. She was going to tell Chrissy at work earlier, but customers had interrupted them before she could. She knew she had to talk to someone and make time to call the officer as well. This was more complicated than just a couple of turtle statues being delivered to her, and Raelynn couldn't help but worry about what all this meant. More than the turtles though, she worried if the deliveries were connected to Creepy Guy and the recent feelings that someone was watching her.

Her eyes drifted to the box behind Beau, drawing his eyes to follow hers. He stepped away from the counter and lifted it in his hands.

"Does it have something to do with this?" He lifted the box and looked at the address label. His eyebrows furrowed and he looked up at her expectantly. "There's no return address."

His tone almost made her laugh. It was a question she asked herself as well. How did someone deliver it or even ship it without a return address?

All Raelynn could do was nod and shrug. "I thought the same thing. It's weird, right? I mean I didn't think they would take anything without a return address, and then to take it and mail it, it's just odd."

Beau stared at the box, quiet as he thought. He finally raised his eyes to meet hers and lifted his brow. "This is definitely not normal, Rae. Have you opened it yet?"

It was obvious the box was unopened, so she didn't answer his question, just watched as he turned it over and over in all different directions. Beau bit his bottom lip in concentration. Raelynn smiled unconsciously as she observed him.

Eventually he looked up and met her eyes, which were full of humor. "What?" he asked, lifting his hand with the package in it. "Am I the only one who is curious about what's inside?"

Raelynn let out a sigh without thinking, drawing his brows closer together. "Rae?"

She let out her breath and shrugged, dropping her eyes to the floor. "It's not that I'm not curious, it's just that…" her voice trailed off, as she tried to find the right words.

"It's not the first one, is it?" Beau asked suddenly, making her eyes lift to his face again.

"Can we talk about this later, Beau? I don't want my brother to know." Raelynn's voice was just short of pleading. She didn't want her brother to catch wind of any of this. He was too young and wouldn't understand. She also didn't want to stir up anything with him about her dad, drawing more questions about his own father that her mom wasn't ready to tell him yet. So many unexpected layers to this mystery, she thought.

Honesty had never told him about his own conception, actually she didn't tell anyone what had happened to her that horrible night. The only reason Raelynn knew was because when she found out that Honesty was pregnant, Raelynn had accused her of cheating on her father and that she had given up on him. Raelynn was almost twelve and her dad had been gone for close to four years. But she hadn't given up hope that he would come back.

Honesty had come in from an appointment and ended up staying home that day, spending most of it in bed. She missed another day after that, and she never missed work. They couldn't afford for her to miss work. Raelynn had thought she was sick and couldn't work, but when Honesty told her she was pregnant, Raelynn became angry and nearly turned the house upside down with her rage.

She had just had the whole lesson at school about reproduction and puberty. Honesty had also never shied away from her questions. So, Raelynn knew what had happened, well, that Honesty and some man had sex and now she was pregnant. She was crushed. She was still holding out hope for her father's return and thought that

Bonded Blood

Honesty was as well. She'd be lying if she said she wasn't hurt and felt betrayed by everything at the time.

But what she didn't know was that Honesty had been assaulted, and the man was never caught. Honesty said she didn't know who it was, that it was a random attack as she was leaving work one night, but Raelynn always suspected there was more to the story than she let on. She had never asked her mom though. She thought her mom would tell her if she wanted. But to this day, Honesty still hadn't said who it was, so Raelynn let it go.

As she grew up, Raelynn met several people, friends, who had been sexually assaulted or abused within their own family. She knew the scars those people carried. She had found out in eighth grade that her best friend had been sexually abused for years by her uncle. When Raelynn found out, she confessed to Honesty who then gave her some help with how to help her friend. Eventually Serenity and her mom pressed charges, and he ended up in prison. Raelynn had held her friend's hand during the entire trial, and they formed a bond like no other that Raelynn had ever had before.

Throughout high school, Serenity had difficulty dating or even being around the boys in their school. But Raelynn stood next to her, and she walked the halls with her, went to the bathroom with her and everything else that Serenity needed until she healed, as much as one could from that kind of trauma and violation. Serenity was eventually able to find a really great guy. The three of them hung out a lot until Serenity was comfortable alone with him. He ended up moving away their senior year, but Raelynn was pretty sure they stayed in contact.

It wasn't long after that that Sahara and Kiah met. Serenity hung out with them all for a while but then she started working to help her mom out at home. Her dad got laid off from his job and started drinking a lot, making it even more difficult for him to find work. Serenity and Raelynn started to drift apart after that.

They tried to hang out at least a few times over the last summer. Serenity was part of the group at the beach when they had met Ashley. It was one of the few times she had been off work for an entire day. Throughout college though, it was hard to find time to do much of anything besides work and study for Raelynn.

"Rae?" Beau's voice snapped her out of her random trail of thoughts.

"Sorry," she mumbled. She cleared her throat. "I just don't want to talk about it with Jericho here. Let's go find something to watch on TV or something while we wait for my mom to get here." She grabbed a hold of his hand without thinking and pulled him into the living room.

Timmy was again sprawled out on the floor with Jericho laying on the dog's side, his hands behind his head. The TV was already on with some anime show playing on the screen.

Raelynn let out a groan drawing his attention to her. Jericho had a mile wide grin on his face, knowing she didn't care for this type of thing. Not that there was anything inappropriate about what he was watching, she just didn't have any interest in it.

"Jericho, don't you have any homework?" she asked, hoping she could get control of the remote somehow.

Her brother just laughed and turned back to his show. "I don't get homework, Rae."

"I know, but I had to try," she grumbled, sitting down on the small couch behind him. Beau sat next to her with a grin on his face, watching them.

"Why do we have to watch this stuff Jer? It's just a big kid cartoon. I mean you might as well watch Mickey Mouse on Disney channel or something," she said, taunting him.

Jericho sprung up from the floor, making Timmy jump as well, looking for danger or maybe just annoyed that his cuddle buddy moved. It was actually a toss-up with this dog. "Blasphemy! This is not a cartoon, Rae. This is way better than anything else! I mean watch this. These are the good guys and they are—"

"I don't care!" she interrupted him. "Are they real people? No. Are they drawn characters? Yes! See? Cartoons." She sat back crossing her arms in front of her with a satisfied smirk on her face.

Jericho just stared at her. His looked over at Beau and pleaded, "Come on, bro. Talk some sense into her, will you? She's so messed up."

Beau put his hands up in the air. "Oh no, I'm not getting in the middle of this. Nice try kid, but not gonna happen." He grinned and waved his finger between the two of them, trying not to laugh.

Admitting defeat, Jericho huffed out his frustration and muttered something about Beau being chicken and then settled back down on Timmy, who had settled as well and was snoring softly.

Raelynn laughed. It wasn't long before there was a soft knock on the door and then it opened, revealing Honesty's smiling face.

"Hey kids," she called as she moved further into the apartment. The living room was directly across from the door, so she saw everyone gathered there before she got very far. Plus, it wasn't a large apartment anyway.

The only one who moved was Timmy, who stood up, swiftly pushing a grumbling Jericho off his side.

"Timmy! Traitor," he said as he stood and stretched.

The big dog didn't give him a second look but trotted over to Honesty to get head scratches. Raelynn laughed as Jericho continued to complain. "Hey, now you know how I feel when you come around," she said, throwing a pillow at him.

Jumping out of the way, Jericho sneered at her. "You have terrible aim sister."

"Maybe I wasn't aiming at you. You are kind of fragile. I would hate to hurt your little ego from getting hit by a girl." She shrugged, earning a glare from her brother.

"Ok, let's go before you start something that I have to finish," Honesty interjected, with a knowing look at both of them. "Hi Beau," she added with a wave.

"Hi Misses Jacobs. How are you doing?" he asked politely.

Honesty waved him off. "Enough with the 'misses' business. Ugh. Makes me sound old," she mumbled.

Beau laughed. "You sound like my mom."

Timmy drew everyone's attention back to him with a groan and stretch. Raelynn jumped up and decided to take him outside.

Bonded Blood

"I'll see you guys tomorrow, ok, Mom? I'm going to let the beast outside," she said as she moved toward the door, with Timmy quickly catching on and following.

Honesty nodded and turned to see Jericho walking out the door behind her. "I guess he's ready. Thanks for getting him today, Rae. I worry about some of the kids in the neighborhood and I don't want him getting caught up in anything. See you tomorrow!" She waved and then disappeared behind the door.

"Mind if I come with you?" Beau asked, standing from the couch.

Raelynn nodded, suddenly remembering how she felt the last time she let her pup outside. Maybe Beau remembered and was being protective, she thought, as a warm feeling filled her heart.

They moved to the door while she explained Timmy's process to Beau. She clipped the chain and then moved to the chair. She couldn't help but glance around to make sure no one was around, even though she hadn't seen anyone before either.

She felt Beau's presence behind her as she looked out at the darkened wetlands in front of her.

"Rae," he whispered. "Is everything ok? You seem hesitant, or scared, or something."

Raelynn let out a soft sigh as she lifted her head to stare at the stars. She would never get tired of the number of stars that could be seen here. She thought it was like that everywhere, but when Ashley came from Minnesota and shared her own awe at the multitude of them, she realized it was a feature of her hometown that she had taken for granted.

"I'm ok. Just a lot on my mind," she finally said.

Timmy appeared at her feet and Raelynn was suddenly grateful for a dog who only liked being outside long enough to do his business without running around chasing everything that moved. She unclipped his chain and they moved back inside. She quickly locked and rechecked the door twice before she moved away from it. She could feel Beau's eyes on her the whole time.

"Should I make some popcorn, or do you want something else?" she asked as she moved past Beau and into the kitchen. She opened the cabinets and looked around. "I don't have too much for snacks, but I have popcorn and a bag of pretzels."

Beau stood in the doorway of the kitchen. "How about ice cream?" he asked.

Raelynn bit her lower lip. "I don't keep ice cream around because I would literally weigh eight hundred pounds if I did."

"I didn't say here. Let's go to Island Creamery. Everyone knows they have the best ice cream around. My treat." Beau took a step further into the space.

Raelynn froze. Her fear ironically just happened. Yes, everyone did know they had the best ice cream, but she also couldn't go there. Could she tell Beau "no"? There are so many other choices, she thought. Maybe she could talk him into a different one. But then would he want to know why she didn't want to go there, and more importantly could she lie to him? Seriously why is the one place she doesn't want to go the one he picks?

"Rae?" Beau had moved closer to her and took her hand in his watching her closely. "We don't have to go. I was just thinking it might be fun. Not that I mind hanging out with you here. But Timmy should be ok for a little while alone, right?"

Raelynn shook her head. "No, sorry. My mind is just all over the place."

He watched her carefully for a second. "Do you want me to leave. I mean if you would rather be alone, it's ok," he asked, hesitation in his voice as he watched her.

"No! No, I don't really want--" she paused as she looked up at him. "I don't really want to be alone right now." She whispered the last part. She wasn't a weak person and had always been proud of the fact that nothing rattled her. But right now, she was a little.

Beau studied her for a minute and then nodded slowly. "Ok. Tell me what you want to do."

Raelynn stared at him and then nodded. "Ok, let's go get ice cream." She didn't know if she would tell him about her aversion to IC just yet, but she knew the first step was the hardest.

As they moved back through the kitchen, she saw the still unopened box. With a sigh, she picked it up.

"Maybe we should handle this first," she said more to herself than Beau.

"You definitely don't seem surprised, or excited like one might be for a package. Which tells me there's more to the story than this one," Beau said thoughtfully. "Wanna talk about it?"

"I think I need to, if you are willing to go with me on this. It's complicated and I kinda think I'm losing my mind a little bit." Raelynn suddenly remembered the envelope that Creepy Guy had given her at work.

"Hold on," she said, holding up her finger and then ran to her room. When she had gotten home earlier, she had changed out of her work clothes and put the envelope on her dresser.

She glanced around and noticed that her window shade was open, and she moved to quickly close it without looking outside. Again, realizing just how paranoid she was acting. She grabbed the dirty envelope and walked back to the kitchen, only to find that Beau wasn't there anymore. With a sigh, she grabbed the box and headed into the living room.

"What are these?" Beau's voice rang out from the other side of the room, startling Raelynn.

She didn't need to look at what he was talking about, she knew what was in that corner of the room.

"Come and sit down. I'll try to explain this without it being an epic novel type thing," she said, trying to keep her voice even as she realized this was the first time she would be telling someone else about her turtle collection and its connection to her dad.

Beau glanced back at the shelf and then reached out to take the crystal one that Honesty had given her so long ago. "Is it ok if I look at this one? It's actually really beautiful, especially in the light. I bet it's amazing in the sunlight."

When she nodded, he picked it up carefully and then settled next to her. She watched him silently as he turned it around in different directions, trying to capture the light from the single lamp in the room.

"That one is from my mom. She gave it to me the first Christmas after…" her voice trailed off as she struggled to find the words.

"Your dad left?" Beau finished for her, drawing her eyes suddenly to his.

"What?" she asked, moving slightly away from him. *He didn't leave*, she wanted to scream at him. But first she wanted to know how he knew about her dad.

Beau reached out to grab her hand before she pulled it away. "I'm sorry. Sahara had told Ki and he told me at some point. I didn't mean anything by it. Rae, I'm sorry."

Raelynn relaxed a little but was now on edge. She had forgotten about Beau's brother and her sister for a second. Of course she would tell Kiah, that made sense. But now she suddenly wondered if that was how Sahara was talking about their dad. She had never really included her sister in any of her theories. She had always felt like Sahara was too young to understand.

"Um, it's ok. But I need to make it clear. My dad did not take off as you suggest. I don't know if that's what Sahara said, but he didn't just leave. At least we don't believe he did of his own free will. Something happened to him, and I am going to figure it out." Her voice was strong and full of conviction, and she was surprised to see a look of amusement and maybe even pride on Beau's face. *What was that about,* she wondered.

Raelynn let Beau take both of her hands in his warm ones, gently moving the box to the side, and he smiled. "There is the spitfire girl I was trying to take out," he chuckled. "I admire your strength, Rae. I can't imagine losing my dad and not believing that he left on his own. We all know what kind of man my biological father was. There was never any doubt who he was though. My mom never tried to hide what kind of person he was. But you had the privilege of knowing yours before this happened. Your tenacity and resolve are amazing."

Trying not to let his words get to her, she wasn't the blushing kind of girl after all, she just nodded and looked away. "He was an amazing dad actually. Honesty has always been in my life though. And she is just as amazing. My biological mom died giving birth to me and Honesty came into our lives before I turned two. She never treated me as anything other than her daughter. Aside from our drastically different physical looks, no one would ever know we weren't blood."

Beau nodded. "My mom came up with the analogy that me and my stepdad don't share blood, but we have bonded blood instead. So, we are still deeply connected. He's the same as your mom. I have always been treated like Ki, who is his blood. I remember once when I was younger, my mom was mad at me for how I had treated my dad. I don't even remember what I did or said, but she played me a song, an old country song called 'He Didn't Have to Be' about a guy who chose to be a dad to a kid that wasn't his. It made me realize that he really didn't have to choose us, but he did. I was so angry at my biological father that I was blinded to every other dad."

Raelynn listened quietly as Beau talked, surprised at how much he was openly sharing with her. They were friends, but they never really talked much one on one before. Maybe it was to make her feel more comfortable to tell her story, but she suddenly realized that she and Beau shared something that others maybe never experience; kindred spirits Honesty would probably say.

Bonded Blood

He had stopped talking and she realized he was now looking at her intently. Flustered, she smiled and nodded, not knowing what to say exactly.

Suddenly the weight of the box felt like pounds instead of ounces. She looked down at it leaning against her leg. Raelynn dropped his hands and picked up the box. Lifting it slightly, drawing his attention to it, she gave a weak smile.

"This is a whole other thing," she began. She couldn't help but steal a quick look at the tiny crystal turtle sitting on Beau's thigh. Until recently, she had always resisted taking a good look at it because it just seemed to strike a nerve and cause her heart to ache when she looked at it. But now, settled on his leg, she couldn't help but take it in. She knew it sparkled in the light. And with the colors, she knew it would be gorgeous in the sunlight. She had never thought to put it somewhere that would allow it to literally light up a room though.

Raelynn dropped his other hand and pulled the tape off the box, since she forgot her scissors to cut it. She was surprised at how easily it peeled away from the flaps and she had it opened in no time. She peered into the box tentatively, not sure what she would find this time. Her eyes moved to Beau's and then back to the contents of the box.

Taking a deep breath, she reached in and pulled out a small structure made out of plastic tubes. She set the box aside and then held up the little thing to get a better look at it. Staring, she suddenly felt like she was maybe trying to make something out of nothing. This did not even look like a turtle. *What the heck*! she thought with frustration.

"Uh, what is it?" Beau asked slowly.

A laugh escaped her lips, sounding more like a snort. "Ok. I don't know honestly."

Beau took the structure from her and squinted his eyes. He turned it this way and that and finally gave up. "I have no clue, Rae." He set it on the couch next to her.

Raelynn sighed and threw herself backwards into the cushions of the couch.

"Wait, there's a note." Beau's voice rang out and Raelynn sat up again, watching as he pulled a folded paper from the inside of the box. Carefully he opened it and read out loud, "A safe place to hide in."

Chapter 13

"Ok, so that's not the weirdest part," Raelynn said slowly. She stood from her spot and went back into her room. She had stashed the notes in one of the boxes from her deliveries. She grabbed it and walked back into the room. Beau was staring at the two letters, one in each hand, as she made her way back over to him. Dropping the box on the table, she moved around the small piece of furniture and sat next to him again.

His eyes tracked her movements, and his brow furrowed at her words. "What do you mean?" he asked when she came back. His eyes drifted to the box in front of them and then back to hers.

"So," Raelynn started, wringing her hands together nervously. She couldn't help but wonder if he would think she was crazy. But at the same time, she needed to process this with someone. She took a deep breath and closed her eyes. After a moment, she opened them again, a new resolve went through her. She had to talk this out. "Ok, so every time I get a box, I get a note." She lifted the notes from the inside of the box and then pushed the box aside.

Beau raised his eyebrows as she held the papers out to him. He gingerly took them and glanced at each one. "These are…creepy, Rae," he said slowly. "Who do you think is sending them? And what does it have to do with your turtles?" His eyes drifted up to her shelf and then back at her.

"Ok, so hear me out, please," she said, looking away from him. How was she going to tell him she thought her dad was trying to contact her when even she had a hard time believing he would be this difficult about it? If he wanted to contact her, why didn't he just tell her where he was in one of these notes? And then there was the strange man at work she didn't even want to think about. The biggest question on her mind now was whether this was her dad or the creepy man's doing.

Beau laid the papers back on the table and turned to face her. He put his ankle under his knee and turned his body in her direction, giving her his complete attention.

When she didn't talk, he let out a soft chuckle. "Rae, after the last six months, I assure you nothing will surprise me. I promise. Just lay it on me. Let me help if I can. Even if it is just to support you, ok?" He spoke quietly, and she knew he was still processing his own family situation after the bombshell was dropped on him not long ago.

"So, a couple days ago I started getting these packages. I think I have five now. Anyway, each one was a different kind of turtle and then a note," she began, tapping the top of the stack of notes.

"Why turtles, though?" Beau asked.

Raelynn cleared her throat nervously and shrugged. "My dad and I used to collect them when I was little. We loved to go to the beach and collect random things that he would then turn into turtles." She waved her hand to the shelf for emphasis. "When Honesty was pregnant with Sahara, she hated being outside. She was so hot and overheated easily. So, just my dad and I would go. I guess when I was about two, we saw baby turtles heading out to sea and I was so excited. It started something way back then I think. I don't remember it, but Honesty talks about it and my dad always brought it up before…well, before." She took a breath of air in and calmed herself.

After a few minutes, she continued, "Maybe that's why Squirt was my favorite character." She had never made that connection. It was like a light bulb went off in her head as she remembered how excited she was when she saw the movie for the first time. She remembered her dad laughing while she watched and clapped her hands at the baby turtle on the screen. Raelynn felt the sadness creep back in as she thought about her dad twirling her around in the small living room to mimic the current in the movie.

Beau squeezed her hand, and she looked up grateful for the encouragement. "Anyway, ever since then, whenever my dad saw a turtle, he would get it or make one for me. He used to whittle things out of wood with his pocketknife and he carved a turtle for me once." She stood and picked up the small wooden one from her shelf and handed it to Beau. She smiled as he examined it.

"He used to tell me when he got good, he was going to learned how to do chainsaw carvings and he was going to make a huge turtle for our yard. I think he was just being funny, but he did love to carve things." She shrugged and took the small carving back from Beau's outstretched hand.

Waving her hand to the rest, she said, "The rest we just collected here and there. Some we made ourselves because the actual ones were too expensive to buy." She picked up the bigger one made of shells that she had done with her dad to show Beau. These are the ones that came with the notes.

One by one, Raelynn took down the last four she had received to add to the one from today on the table. After the collection was complete, she sat down next to Beau again.

"So, you think your dad is sending these to you?" Beau asked.

Raelynn looked at him and nodded. "You don't think I am crazy to think that's a possibility?"

Beau laughed softly. "Again, after the last six months? No. I don't think you're crazy, Rae. But I do wonder why the secrecy? I mean, if he's sending all this, why not just send whatever it is he's trying to tell you?" He looked back at the turtles now gathered around the table. "I don't understand that part." Beau tapped his chin with his fingernail.

"I don't know either," Raelynn mused. "I don't have any idea what he is trying to say, if it is even him. But-" she stopped short as she thought about the creepy guy at work. Her thoughts drifted again to the possibility this wasn't her dad at all, and someone was trying to lure her into some weird and demented trap. But then again, *why*? It's not like she was famous or rich or had some strange skill, like a specialist in bomb making or something. She chuckled at herself. *Too many spy and action movies*, she thought.

She felt Beau's touch on her arm and her eyes met his. "But what, Rae? What else has happened?"

Raelynn's chuckle was out loud this time. "Nothing. At least I don't think anything." She took a deep breath and tried to smile to brush it off as nothing. "There's this creepy guy at work who keeps showing up during my shift. At least I think it is only my shift. Chrissy said he didn't show up on Monday when I was off. Anyway, yesterday he gave me this envelope," she reached through the stack and took out the notes Beau was looking at when she first came back from her room, and then today he gave me this one. He gives it to me and then he just leaves. It's weird. But he doesn't say anything and he's not like stalking me or anything. He leaves and then just disappears.

Beau's expression was a mixture of curiosity and worry. "We?" he asked.

Nodding, she explained, "Yeah. Me and my coworker Chrissy. She's been there every time he has shown up."

"Hm. Weird. I mean if he was stalking you, he wouldn't just leave. It's almost like he's a messenger or something," Beau said thoughtfully.

They were quiet for a few minutes, lost in their own thoughts. Raelynn wondered what the man was really up to. She remembered he was dirty, but didn't smell bad like she would have expected by his appearance.

"Weird," she whispered, again thinking about what he looked like, drawing Beau's focus to her.

"What else is weird, Rae?" he asked gently.

Raelynn looked at his face, from the letter in her hand. "The creepy guy at work. He's really dirty, like he's homeless or something. But when he got close to me, he didn't smell bad, like he hadn't showered in a long time. It was just weird. I can't think of a different word."

She looked closer at the note from the envelope he left. The paper was smudged, but it was also not like a dirty piece of paper from a trash can. It almost looked like someone took their fingers in dirt and smeared the paper to make it look dirty. The prospect of this being an intentional illusion wasn't something she had considered before.

The sudden realization made her gasp. She looked up at Beau and opened her mouth as if to say something, but nothing came out. *What was going on*? she thought, panicking a little bit in her mind.

Beau grabbed both her hands in his and squeezed. "Rae, look at me. It's ok, we're going to figure this out. I'll be right by your side, ok? Raelynn, please look at me." His voice was strong with resolve but filled with worry at the same time.

Slowly, Raelynn nodded her head. "Ok," she whispered. "But I don't even know where to start, what to do." She looked back at her hands and noticed they were shaking, even in Beau's tight grip.

Beau let out a breath. "Maybe we should see if Uncle Sam wants to come back out for a visit?" he said with a small smile, half joking.

His words brought a slight smile to Raelynn's lips as she thought about her friend. She always thought it was funny that they had an uncle named Sam. Thinking of her friend coming back already made her almost want to call right away. Then she realized Ashley had only just left a few days ago. Had it even been a week yet?

"As much as I would love to see Ash again, I don't think this is something the FBI is going to be interested in. I mean that whole thing this summer was a bit more involved than this." Raelynn grinned wider and she felt her body calm down, grateful for the distraction. The worry about someone being deceptive and possibly trying to hurt her didn't go away, but at least Beau had managed to bring her anxiety down a little bit so she could think.

Raelynn dropped his hands and turned to the table of papers again. "Ok, so all I have right now are five letters and five kind of demented looking turtles—being generous calling some of them turtles I think," she said with a soft snort. She picked up the latest one and studied it.

The "body" was made up of a single piece of plastic tubing, like PVC for plumbing. There was a tiny piece of something hanging from it, fabric of some sort. As she turned it over, she noticed the bottom had four notches out of it, almost as if the person was trying to create feet.

Raelynn laughed as she shook her head. "I think I am trying too hard to make them into turtles." She handed the structure to Beau and pointed out the "feet" she had discovered.

"I think you might be right, Rae," Beau said, still studying it. "If we look at the rest," he put the little thing down and picked up another, "they all seem to have been made out of materials that you wouldn't think would make good statues and some improvising had to be made." He picked up another one and pointed at it. "Look. This is like some sort of plastic bowl, but they added stuff to make it look like a turtle. This one had to have been hard. Look at the tiny pieces of metal they used to make the feet. Whoever made these did a good job of making some of the details actually look like a turtle though."

Raelynn studied the turtles one by one and noticed that Beau was right. At first glance, these turtles looked like some artist who did contemporary art with whatever trash they could find. But each turtle was made from a different product completely. Almost like each one held information specific to only that one.

She shared her thoughts with Beau who nodded, as if he was thinking the same thing. "I never really paid attention in art class, but that makes sense."

Raelynn thought about her art classes and came up blank as well, other than what she just realized. Was there some sort of message in the types of materials or the art itself? The only person she knew who had ever had an interest in art and actually was quite the artist herself until she had to give it up to work for her family, was Serenity.

"I think I know someone who could help!" she suddenly exclaimed, jumping from her spot to find her phone. Was it a coincidence that they just met in the parking lot earlier that same day? She didn't think so. The universe was helping her, she was convinced of it. She felt warmth inside her chest as she thought maybe it was her dad helping her out to solve his mystery. For the first time in many years, she felt like she was close, really close. And her conviction that he was alive after all this time finally settled in her heart.

She knew it was emotionally dangerous for her to let herself get caught up in the idea that this was her dad after all this time, but Raelynn had no other ideas who it could be. No one else knew about her turtles. And even if the rest of the notes didn't sound like him, the first one definitely did. She was going to hold onto that until she had reason to doubt it. She just had to right now.

"Rae, we need to be careful." He paused and then added, softly, "Do you know why your dad has been missing for so long?" Beau's voice jolted her back to reality.

She looked back at him, still sitting on the couch. "No. I don't know why. We were never told anything actually. He just didn't come home from work that day." She slowly moved back and sat next to him. "What if…" her voice trailed off as she pondered worse case scenarios of why her father hasn't been around the last fifteen years.

"I just think we need to get the right people involved to make sure this isn't a trap or a trick to get to you. I don't know why someone would do anything to hurt you, but we don't know what we don't know right now." Beau's voice of reason made sense, but it didn't help Raelynn's resolve.

She was convinced her father was still the same man she knew him to be. He didn't get caught up in drugs or something dark and sinister like that. He didn't abandon his family for a different one. He didn't just disappear to start a new life somewhere else. He loved his family, he loved her. He wouldn't leave on his own.

Her resolve again solidified even more in her heart. "My dad is not like that, Beau. He's a good man."

"I know, Rae. I know," he said, patting her hand comfortingly. "That's not what I mean. I'm worried this isn't your dad and someone is posing as him with the turtles to lure you somewhere unsafe, for some weird reason that we don't know yet."

Realization dawned on her, making her suck in a breath. "Oh. But, why?"

Beau shrugged his shoulders. "Who else knew about the turtles with you and your dad?"

"No one," she replied. "Only mom. I never even told Sahara."

"Ok, well that's not helpful then, is it," he said with a rueful grin. "Maybe the clues are in the notes?" His statement sounded more like a question as she tried to wrack her brain for who might know about her and her dad's collection and who might want to hurt her.

Raelynn felt like she was in some crime show, trying to figure out all the pieces to the puzzle. None of it made sense right now. If only she could fast forward to the end where everything finally makes sense, and it all turns out perfectly.

"Hey, Rae?" Beau's voice broke into her thoughts. "Do you know why some of these letters are bolded?"

"What?" she asked, leaning over to see what he was talking about.

Beau pointed to one of the notes and then she noticed that some of the letters in the words were in fact darker than the others. She picked up one of the other notes and noticed the same thing.

"That is bizarre. Why would only a couple letters be made to stand out. Do you think they mean something?" She looked over the other notes as she studied the letters that were bold. Nothing stood out as significant to her and while they were bolder than the other letters, it wasn't like they were written with a black marker to make sure they stood out. "Maybe it's nothing, just a coincidence," she decided, shrugging.

"Maybe. Maybe not. Let's just keep it in mind for now. If it spells something, it could give us an idea of who or where this person wants you to go," Beau suggested.

Raelynn nodded. "Maybe. I'm going to text Reni and see if she can offer us any help with the art stuff. She was going to be an art student before her mom needed her to work to help support the family. I doubt she ever let it go completely though. She was an amazing artist." She picked up her phone again from the table and pulled up her friend's number, firing off a quick text.

Maybe she can give some insight into what kind of art this was and maybe lead to a department at the university or an art studio nearby. It was kind of a long shot, but at that moment she was looking for any place to start.

After she sent the text, she set her phone down again and leaned back against the couch. Beau looked over at her and then settled back as well. They were both lost in their own thoughts as her phone alerted her to a text. She looked over and met Beau's eyes.

"That was fast," she thought out loud.

They both leaned forward as Raelynn opened the text. "She's gotta work tomorrow but she said she could come by after, around eight." She looked at Beau with a grin on her face. "Are you tired of me yet? Wanna spend another evening here?"

Beau laughed. "Not tired of you at all, Rae. I'd love to come back. I do have to work as well, but I can be here any time after six. How about I bring dinner this time?"

Raelynn nodded. "I have to work too, but I'll be done by two-thirty, as usual. I can cook too though. I will have more time than you will after work."

Waving his hand, he shook his head. "Nope, I got it and it's my turn anyway. I don't cook much, but I can call in takeout and pick it up on the way over. Where does Reni live?"

"I guess she just moved into my building this past weekend. I ran into her in the parking lot this morning. I haven't seen her much since summer, but we used to be super close," Raelynn explained with an almost apologetic tone. She felt bad that they had drifted apart, but their friendship was also one that she knew would stand the test of time.

Beau nodded and looked down at the table full of 'treasures'. "Ok, we have a plan. I'd put these away somewhere, so your beast of a dog doesn't decide to use them as chew toys or something." He laughed, letting her know he was kidding.

Timmy looked up from his spot in front of the table and let out a huff as if he understood what Beau said, making both of them laugh.

"I don't think it'll be a problem. It would require some motivation for him to reach up and grab something. But I will put them away anyway. I don't want anything to get messed up." She glanced shyly up at Beau and added, "Thanks for helping me, and not thinking I'm crazy."

"Hey, I have seen crazy, and it doesn't look like you, Rae. I hope we can solve this and find your dad safe and sound. And I really hope you aren't being misled. I know you want him to be the good guy still, and I sincerely hope he is." He said the last part with compassion in his eyes as he held hers.

Raelynn nodded. "Me too, Beau. Me too." She knew what he was saying and she knew she should be careful, but her heart was telling her this was her dad.

They sat lost in their thoughts for a few minutes before Raelynn looked over.

"Hey, is it too late for a movie? We never did get ice cream either." She was silently grateful she dodged the bullet of having to tell Beau why she didn't want to go to his favorite ice cream place. Maybe one day, but she wasn't sure she was ready yet. Maybe with Beau, though, she could try making a new memory. She didn't miss that his favorite place for the sweet treat was the same as her dad's either. What did they say about little girls ending up with men who are similar to their fathers? She shook the thought from her head. It was way too early to be thinking about Beau like that.

Beau stretched next to her. "I should probably get going actually. And you have to be up early too, don't you?"

Reluctantly, Raelynn nodded. "Yeah. Four a.m. is stupid early."

"That is a little crazy early. Why don't you find a job with later hours? Do you like the early mornings?" Beau asked.

Raelynn snorted. "No, I'm actually not much of a morning person. But I like the job and being done by two thirty in the afternoon is nice. It's like having the whole day to still be able to do stuff. Plus, I like my boss." She finished with a shrug. She knew she would be looking for that "adult" job soon, but she was making enough to make ends meet and have a little extra, so she wasn't in a huge hurry.

Because she had been doing the research into her dad's disappearance last summer, she had decided to put the job search on hold. But then she suddenly had to back off because she was getting the attention of some "people who were dangerous," but that's all she knew.

The reminder of Officer Milton brought her eyes back to Beau. "Oh my god, Beau. I just remembered something. Last summer when I was doing some digging, I had actually started to get information. Not a ton, but it was a start. And then the cop who was helping me told me I had to back off because I was getting some unwanted attention. He only said they were dangerous people, no other details. What if…" Her voice trailed off as she thought about the possibility of someone actually being after her.

Nothing about what she had discovered meant anything to her, it wasn't even very informative if she was honest. She was only able to figure out a rough timeline, and even most of that was a guess. She tried to think of who she had talked to but could only remember the officer and their conversations.

"Do you remember talking to anyone or finding out anything that would make you think someone from then was after you now?" Beau asked carefully.

Raelynn shook her head. "I don't remember anything weird. That's the thing. Nothing I found out made me think I'd uncovered some magical missing piece. It barely even registered as something in my mind. I don't feel like I even learned anything if I'm honest. His warning was really odd and came out of nowhere."

Beau nodded. "And have you talked to him since then?"

"No. But I was going to call him tomorrow. He used to work the same shift I did so it was always hard to get a hold of him. I'll leave him a message tomorrow on my break and see if he calls me back."

"Good idea. Maybe he can give you more information about who the people were. You might want to be careful who you tell stuff to though, since we really don't know who is doing all this. I mean, just in case it isn't your dad." Beau's reasoning made sense and Raelynn just nodded her agreement.

She narrowed her eyes at him suddenly and tapped her cheek. "How do I know I can trust you, Beau? I mean you aren't the same person you were a few months ago. You are being a lot friendlier with me lately." She gave him a look that made him laugh.

Bonded Blood

"Funny, Rae," he said with a grin. "But I guess if you suspect me, we'll have to figure out some sort of rigorous test to prove my loyalty."

Raelynn laughed. "Ok, I think of something. But for now, I am not telling you anything else. At least not until tomorrow. But you will have to feed me and prove there's no poison in my food for starters."

Beau nodded seriously. "Ok, deal. But you better tell me if you have allergies first. Otherwise, that's not a fair assessment of my loyalty."

They laughed as Beau stood and held out his hand for her. She smiled and took his hand.

"I'll see you tomorrow, Rae," Beau whispered.

Raelynn nodded. "Tomorrow, then, sir. And don't be late. I'm sure I'll be famished by six o'clock," she added, dramatically putting the back of her hand to her forehead.

Beau laughed and pulled her in for a hug. "Have a goodnight, Rae," he whispered.

Chapter 14

Raelynn went to bed thinking about everything she and Beau had talked about. She felt a warmth inside when he hugged her that she hadn't felt since her dad had held her in his strong arms. She missed so much about him, and she tried to keep her emotions in check. But it was getting too difficult. She felt like she was finally closer than she had ever been. The nagging in the back of her mind tried to keep her grounded and remind her that it might not be him. But the little girl inside missed her dad too much to believe it was a trick.

When she finally fell asleep, with her pup lying across her feet, she dreamt of that little girl and her daddy. It was like her mind was on repeat as she watched him push her on a swing and run on the beach. Things she had forgotten were played out in her dreams like the time they built a sandcastle big enough for four or five kids to play with until a group of teenagers playing football tripped and smashed it.

She laughed in her sleep as her dad chased them away, thinking his little girl would be upset. But Raelynn had already smoothed out the sand and started to dig a new hole that one of the new kids insisted on getting buried in. Her dad had sat down in the sand next to her and just pulled her in for a hug. Raelynn wasn't ever an angry or short-tempered child. She had always been able to go with the flow and adjust where she needed to. That attitude has helped her weather the storm of her childhood without her dad and her mom not being around much due to working.

Even though the loss of her dad crushed her, she never gave up, even at eight years old. She knew in her heart he would come back. It was only as she got older that she began to consider that he might not come back, or he may not come back alive. He had been her whole world.

When she woke up, Raelynn's eyes were sore and scratchy. As she got up and looked in the mirror, she noticed they were bloodshot. She must have been crying in her sleep, she thought. Pulling out a washcloth, she soaked it in cold water and then pressed it to her eyes. She didn't need to go into work looking like she was hung over or something, she thought with a snort.

She got in the shower to wash away the rest of her sleepiness and thought about her dream. Maybe it would even be considered a series of short dreams. All the memories she held close to her heart were replayed for her as if a movie reel was spinning for only her to watch. She couldn't help the stray tear that fell down her cheek as she remembered those happy times.

She quickly washed her thick and knotted hair and then rinsed off, getting out of the shower to keep moving. She didn't want to get sad and teary before work. She had just managed to clear her eyes. Raelynn quickly dried off and peeked at Timmy who was still stretched out on her bed. She chuckled and got herself ready for the day. Once she was ready for work, she could get him moving too. He was usually pretty motivated in the morning so she knew it wouldn't take him long to take care of his own business.

Not one for a lot of makeup, Raelynn decided to put just a little mascara on her eyes today, maybe draw away from the redness a little more. Her blue eyes popped a little bit more and she gave her reflection a satisfied nod. She had given up trying to cover all her freckles with makeup years ago. Moving to the kitchen, she got her coffee ready and put Timmy's food in his bowl.

As if on cue, the lazy dog made his way into the kitchen and stretched his front paws in front of him. Raelynn stifled a laugh as his paws nearly reached end to end of her small kitchen. He sniffed his food and then turned toward the door.

"Creature of habit, eh, Timmy?" she said out loud as she followed him to the sliding door. She quickly clipped his collar and then grabbed her Crocs from inside the door to follow him out. She was about to sit down, watching Timmy make his way to his spot, when Raelynn stopped short and stared at her chair.

A cold chill ran down her back as she stared at a small brown box sitting on her chair. It was a good thing she wasn't holding Timmy's leash because it would have fallen from her hand. She looked around and saw nothing out of the ordinary and no one around, as per usual. Her eyes focused back on the box, almost like it was taunting her.

Holding her breath, she slowly moved and picked up the box. This one was heavier than the others Raelynn noticed. She gave it a hesitant shake and could feel something moving inside. This one didn't have an address label on it, only her name in black Sharpie marker. She narrowed her eyes, trying to see if the writing gave anything away. She tried to think if it was the same as any of the notes. She doubted she would remember her dad's handwriting, but she knew someone who most likely would.

Tucking the box under her arm, she thought maybe she was a little crazy because it could be a bomb or something. *Again with the action movies*, she scolded herself. She looked up to see Timmy standing at the door expectantly.

Raelynn hesitated. She opened the door for Timmy but glanced at the box in her hands again. "Whatever," she mumbled. "If someone wanted to give me a bomb, they would have had it go off by now. Stupid," she chastised herself and moved inside, taking one last look around to see if anyone was there. As expected, she didn't see anyone or anything unusual.

Feeling a little unnerved, she moved inside and closed the door tightly behind her. Timmy would still need to make one more trip outside, so she didn't immediately lock it. Raelynn sat down at the table where she and Beau had laid everything out the night before. She set the box on the table and stared at it. She didn't realize how long she sat there until Timmy whined at the door.

Startled, she looked up and then at his bowl, which was now empty. Shaking her head, Raelynn stood and grabbed her roll of poop bags. "Ok, buddy, let's go."

She took her phone off the table as well, *just in case*, she told herself and then moved to the door again. Raelynn was grateful for the consistency of Timmy's morning routine. She knew exactly how much time she needed to get him settled for the morning before she had to leave for work. It helped her gauge her time.

Once they were back inside, Raelynn looked at her phone. She noticed she had a missed call and when she opened it up, the number was unknown. Who would be calling her in the middle of the night. A million thoughts ran through her head, but she brushed them all aside. There was nothing she could do about it anyway and since they didn't leave a message, she pushed it from her mind. At least that's what she told herself.

Raelynn had about four minutes until she had to leave. She looked at the box once more and then decided to wait to open it. She would have time before Beau came over and even more time before Serenity came.

She gave Timmy a few more scratches, as he stretched himself across her couch, and then headed for the door. She double checked that the sliding door was locked and made sure all her curtains were closed tightly. Satisfied that her apartment was as secure as it could be, she left, locking the front door behind her.

Raelynn never considered herself a paranoid person. She remembered when she first met Ashley. She didn't know Ashley's uncle was an FBI agent at first, one of the best in the country actually. But she would laugh at all the things Ashley did that her uncle taught her for safety. If Raelynn hadn't known about her friend's uncle, she would have called Ashley paranoid.

But now, as she walked across the parking lot, the lights above still bright against the dark sky, she couldn't help but look around every which way to make sure no one surprised her as she made her way to her car. Raelynn tried not to look like she was crazy as she looked around, but she felt the uneasiness settle in her body.

Before today, the packages were delivered to her mom's. That made sense because that's the address her dad would have known. It made her feel safer somehow. She could tell herself that they didn't know where she lived. But now, whoever was delivering the packages knew where she lived. And not just her address but which apartment was hers and how to get in. She remembered the chill she felt the night before, twice, as if someone was watching her. Everything left her feeling unsettled.

She drove slower than normal to work because she was so distracted. Her thoughts were running in a million different directions, and she couldn't make sense of a single one of them.

Raelynn arrived at work before she really even realized it. She parked and sat in her car for a few minutes, getting her bearings again. She looked around the lot and saw that Susiana wasn't there yet and she was alone. The sun was starting to lighten the sky with pinks lining the horizon above the trees. She wasn't sure how she made it work as early as she did, especially since she didn't remember any part of the drive aside from pulling out of the parking lot at her apartment.

She didn't have to wait long for her boss to show up. She felt her breath release, unknowingly holding it. Raelynn wasn't sure if she was scared or just felt uneasy. She looked toward her boss and noticed Susiana had a large stack of containers with her baked goods in them, making Raelynn smile. She must have held her husband to kid duty like she promised the day before. Or her son was feeling better. Either way she was grateful for the distraction.

Jumping out of her car, she hurried over to help Susiana with her load. Her boss gave her a smile of thanks and then reached for her keys.

"Did you get any sleep last night, Miss Susiana? Or did you stay up all night baking?" Raelynn asked with her own grin.

Susiana sighed. "A little of both maybe?" she said with a laugh. "And seriously you need to stop being so formal."

Raelynn just grinned back and caught the door with her free hand as her boss unlocked it. Once inside, she remembered to turn the lock on the door, unlike yesterday. She didn't need any repeat surprises like her run in with Creepy Guy before they even opened again. She chuckled to herself about the new name for the man she couldn't identify. He probably wouldn't appreciate the name, however.

She got to work right away, determined to focus on something other than the possible appearance of said visitor again and the box sitting at home. Actually, both boxes now that she remembered the one with everything in it from the last five days. Shaking her head, she put her things away and grabbed an apron from the rack. She refocused her attention on work and put on a determined face. She moved out of the break area and to the front to help Susiana load up the bakery cases.

They worked side by side until the cases were full and everything else was stocked and ready for the morning customers. She leaned against the glass case and crossed her arms over her chest.

"We are set, I think," she said as she watched her boss unlock the door and flip on the "open" sign.

Susiana nodded. "Yep. As efficient as ever, Raelynn. Thank you for your help. I'll put the rest in the coolers in back. Let me know if you need help up here."

Raelynn nodded and watched Susiana carry the few boxes that were left to the back and disappeared from her sight. With a sigh, she turned toward the front door and watched the parking lot continue to grow brighter. Soon the sky looked bright and clear. She suddenly realized she didn't even notice the temperature as she made her way to work earlier.

She shook her head. She needed to get focused. She would worry about the rest later. She wouldn't let anything distract her from her job, especially when Susiana depended on her to handle everything up front until Chrissy showed up. She busied herself with double checking the supplies for drinks and pastries. Typically, the night crew, if you could call them that, refilled a lot before they left for the day. They were responsible for taking trash out and cleaning the equipment. Raelynn rarely worked the closing shift, but on occasion she would be asked to cover for someone.

Chrissy always preferred that shift and Raelynn liked being off before three, so it worked out. If something happened the night before, Chrissy always left a note letting her know what she wasn't able to get to. They had a few college kids who picked up shifts here and there, and Chrissy always made sure they did the tasks that she and Raelynn agreed didn't matter too much if they were missed. But trash was always taken care of to prevent any unwanted visitors from surprising them in the morning.

When the bell above the door finally rang for the first time, Raelynn was relieved. She was looking forward to being busy so she could keep her mind occupied on things she could actually control. She was running out of things to keep her busy.

It was a little later than normal for the first customer to come in, but she didn't mind. What made it even better was that it was an actual customer. She didn't realize until that first person came in that she was subconsciously worried that Creepy Guy would come in again.

Thankful that it wasn't him, Raelynn moved to greet the customer and take their order. An older gentleman greeted her back and smiled, tipping his hat.

"Good morning sweetheart," he said. "Is my nemesis here yet? I need to get the right seat today."

Raelynn laughed. "Nope, you beat him in today, Mister Adler. Your usual?"

"Of course. Can you be a dear and bring it to me? I want to get my seat before he gets here." He was already turning around, after laying his cash on the counter.

"Yep, no problem. I'll have it to you in a moment," she said with a grin. She loved these older folks. They were sweet and always had cute pet names. Then again, most people around here rarely use first names. It was more likely a "dear", "sweetheart', or "honey" than an actual name.

Mister Adler smiled and waved at her as he walked away. "As always, keep the change!" he called over his shoulder with a wide grin. One thing she always found funny was not only were these older folks always competing about silly things, like which seat was the best, they also liked to argue about who was the best tipper. She didn't make a lot off any of them, but it was cute. And they made it clear they appreciated her either way.

Shaking her head, Raelynn turned to make his coffee and put the creamer he likes with a couple packets of sugar on a tray. As she was about to move away from the counter, Al came wandering in. As he looked around, he let out a few curse words, making Raelynn and Mister Adler chuckle.

"Late again, old man!" Mister Adler taunted.

"What did you do get up at the crack of dawn to get here first? Don't you have anything better to do with your time?" the man grumbled. Raelynn grinned at the men. They were always giving each other grief and it just made her day to see and hear them banter back and forth.

Mister Adler laughed loudly. "Like you do either. Come on, get your coffee. I have a game to beat you at."

Raelynn set the tray down on the table and moved back to the counter to take the new man's order. She knew what it was, as these two were regulars most days. Every time they came in, they teased each other. They reminded her of the old movie "Grumpy Old Men." She thought they were actually old friends from way back in high school. They had both lost their wives years ago to illness and had reconnected over "the Facebook" as they called it.

The newcomer waved at Raelynn and motioned with his hand to bring it to the table. She nodded and collected the things he needed for his coffee. Al had insisted a long time ago that she call him just Al. He hated formalities, and she could tell from his attitude that the more informal the better for him. She delivered another tray to their table and then went back to her counter just in time for a new group to come in.

The morning flew by with a few different groups of students coming in and spending a couple of hours in the café. They had multiple refills and ordered plenty of pastries, so Raelynn knew Susiana wouldn't mind that they stayed as long as they did. She also knew when it was finals or midterms, Susiana was more lenient with students hanging around for long periods of time.

By the time Chrissy came in, Raelynn realized that she had been steadily busy all morning. She was glad when her coworker showed up though because right before she appeared, a large group had come in and Raelynn was swamped with orders. Thankfully Chrissy knew to just jump right in and help out.

As the group moved on, Raelynn took a second to thank her. Chrissy waved her off and grinned. They went about the rest of the morning restocking as Raelynn finally had a lull in customers.

"Wow, you must have had a busy morning, Rae," Chrissy commented. "Everything is almost empty. You never let it get this low."

Raelynn grimaced. "Yeah, it was a little nuts. Sorry. But I am so glad you are here now. I could use a bathroom break." She grinned as she slipped off her apron and headed for the restroom quickly.

When she came back out to the front, Susiana was with Chrissy, and they were taking stock of the bakery cases. Raelynn threw her apron back over her head and walked up to stand in between them. Susiana nodded to her.

"Things are busy today," Susiana commented. "I'll grab another container for this and then we should be good." She disappeared again. Chrissy and Raelynn laughed as they watched her go.

Leaning against the counter, Chrissy studied Raelynn. "So, how are things? I mean besides here." She swung her hand around them.

Bonded Blood

Raelynn shrugged. "Good I guess." She wasn't sure what her coworker was getting at, so she waited for her to ask more questions.

Chrissy leaned in and whisper-yelled, "Has Creepy Guy come in today?"

"Chrissy! Shh!" Raelynn whispered back. She looked around and was relieved no one was looking their way. Straightening, she shook her head. "Actually, no. I haven't seen him at all today. Huh, that's weird."

She was surprised that she hadn't even thought about it until Chrissy brought it up. Raelynn startled when the bell above the door suddenly chimed, as if Chrissy had summoned him somehow. Her shoulders relaxed when she saw it was a couple around her age.

Shooting her colleague a glare, she turned to take their order. Chrissy grinned back at her and shrugged, as if it wasn't a big deal.

After getting their drinks, they moved to Chrissy for their pastries. Once they moved away from the counters, Raelynn moved back to stand next to Chrissy.

"I am actually surprised that he didn't show up today. I mean the day is early, but still." Her thoughts drifted to the unopened box waiting for her at home. Was it possible that he was the one who delivered it to her house? It would explain why he hadn't shown up at her workplace. As much as she didn't want to think about this stranger knowing where she lived, she couldn't help but wonder who he was and why he was giving her these things. Was he behind the other packages too?

Chrissy was studying her thoughtfully. "You know you never told me about the note he gave you yesterday."

Raelynn raised her eyes to meet Chrissy's. "What?"

"Yesterday. Creepy Guy came in early and gave you something. You were going to tell me about it, but then it got busy and we both kinda forgot." She watched Raelynn, still leaning against the counter.

Realization finally dawned on her. She had completely forgotten about it until Chrissy just reminded her. "I actually forgot about that. It's a long story that will probably have to wait for another time," she said, motioning to the door where another group had just come in.

"Ugh, ok. But don't forget this time!" Chrissy said with a pointed look.

Raelynn nodded and then turned to the new group. The next time she got a break, she turned to Chrissy. "Hey, I need to make a quick phone call. Can you handle this for a second or two?"

"Yep, no problem," she said absently, focused on the almost empty case in front of her again. Her face was twisted in a scowl, probably trying to figure out how they went through so many baked goods in a short time.

Raelynn quickly made her way to the break room to make the call she had forgotten about all day. She quickly pulled up the contact and was not shocked when she got his voicemail, she left a detailed message for him to call her at his earliest convenience. She sighed as she put her phone away and thought about everything again. She hadn't been able to think much since she started work, which she was grateful for.

Her phone alerted her to a new text message. She turned her phone over to look at the screen. Furrowing her brow, she hesitated before she opened it. Relief poured through her as she saw it was a note from Beau asking about plans for later. Thankfully nothing had changed on her end, and he thought he might be able to get out a little earlier again. She made a mental note to ask him more about himself. She still didn't know what he did for work. She wondered what else she didn't know. They had been spending a lot of time talking about her issues and she felt a little guilty only talking about herself.

She sent a quick text to Serenity to make sure she could still come over too and was relieved when she got a message back right away. Satisfied that she had done all she could so far, she tucked her phone back in her pocket and went back out front to help Chrissy.

Raelynn was glad to see it was still quiet up front. She watched Chrissy finish filling the bakery items and then she moved to refill her cups and lids. It had been a busy day and Raelynn was actually looking forward to leaving work. It wasn't that she didn't like being there. She was just looking forward to making some progress on this mystery. Hopefully.

The rest of her shift, Raelynn and Chrissy stayed busy with a steady stream of customers. Aside from passing words, they didn't even get to chitchat much. Raelynn didn't mind though. She welcomed the busyness of the café during the last part of her shift.

Before long, it was time for her to clock out and she made a quick exit. She gave Chrissy a wave and then hurried out to her car. The cooler than expected air caught her off guard and her breath caught in her chest. She took another deep breath and then slid into her car. After she buckled, she held her cold steering wheel tightly in her hands.

She had plenty of time before Beau would be there. It suddenly struck her that they had been together the last three nights. Trying not to overthink anything, she chalked it up to him just wanting to help her out. Her thoughts drifted to the box sitting on her table at home. Then she remembered that it only had her name on it, and that reminded her about the writing.

Raelynn pulled out her phone and texted her mom, asking if she was home. When she got an immediate response, she smiled. A plan formed in her mind. If she made good use of her time, she would be able to get home, grab the package, and then bring it to her mom to see if the handwriting was familiar to her; if it was her dad's.

With her plan ready, she pulled out of the parking spot and headed home.

Chapter 15

Honesty stared at the writing on the box and sighed. "Sorry, Rae. I don't think that is your dad's handwriting. I mean it is actually hard to tell for sure. It has been so long…"

She suddenly stood and disappeared into her room, the curtain swaying after her. Raelynn leaned back in the chair. She had picked up the package and Timmy after work and headed straight for her mom's house. She didn't intend to upset her mom, but she had to know about the writing. She couldn't think of anyone else who might recognize it.

Honesty reappeared in the doorway with an envelope in her hand. She was visibly shaking as she stared at the paper in her hand.

"Mom? What is that?" Raelynn asked as she stood and met her mom in the doorway. Honesty handed Raelynn the worn paper and without taking her eyes off of it, Raelynn hesitantly took it. "Are you ok?"

Honesty slowly nodded. "Yes. I forgot your dad sent me a letter once when he was gone on a trip. It was a long time ago, obviously," she added grimly. "But his handwriting would be on it. This was before we texted everyone. You can compare it if you want."

Raelynn nodded and moved back to the table. She held the paper up to the box and squinted her eyes. Dropping it down, she let out a frustrated groan.

"I can't though, I wish I knew someone who could tell," she mused dejectedly. "It was a long shot anyway."

"Maybe not," Honesty said. "Maybe it's not as far-fetched as you think."

Raelynn looked up. "What do you mean?"

Honesty sat down across from her. "Did you call the officer from the summer yet? I would think he would have contacts who would be able to make that kind of determination, right?"

"I guess. I left him a message today but haven't heard back yet." Raelynn thought about it for a second and realized her mom was right. She could ask him if he knew someone, or maybe he could even make a judgement about it from his experience.

"Keep the letter, Rae," Her mom said, patting her hand. "Just make sure I get it back. It is one of the few things I have left that I can still feel his presence in."

Raelynn nodded. "Ok, I'll take extra special care of it. Thanks, mom. I should get going." She stood and gave her mom a tight hug. "Love you, mom. I'll let you know what else I find out."

Honesty smiled and gave her a nod. "Thanks, sweetie. Good luck."

Moving toward the back door, Raelynn smiled at her mom. "Hopefully this gets figured out sooner rather than later. I'm already starting to get tired of the riddles and questions." *And I just want my dad back*, she added in her head sadly.

She opened the door and spotted her brother "training" Timmy again. She chuckled as she watched the two work. She was so glad that Jericho had taken so well to her dog. It would have been much more difficult to bring him around if they didn't get along, although she suspected Timmy would sleep anywhere without a problem.

After a few minutes, she noticed her mom behind her. "They are cute together aren't they," she said quietly.

Raelynn nodded. "I was just thinking that myself. I should probably get him and get home before Beau comes over."

Honesty smiled a knowing smile. "So, Beau has been over a lot lately." She left the suggestive tone hanging in the air and Raelynn tried her best not to groan.

"Yes, mom. But he is just being nice. There is nothing there. And don't go getting any crazy ideas about your two daughters and two brothers." She pointed her finger at her mom, trying to be stern.

"Uh huh. Ok, Rae," Honesty said with a laugh. Then she turned to the yard and called, "Hey Jericho, time to help me with dinner." Jericho groaned but slowly made his way to them. Honesty gave her a smile and wink, knowing they had all been trying to get him to help out more.

At the same time, Raelynn called to Timmy, who looked up and then jogged toward her. Raelynn met him at the bottom of the steps and clipped his leash on. They made their way through the gate to the front and her car.

"See you later, baby brother," she called over her shoulder, earning herself a nasty glare. She laughed and then got Timmy loaded into the backseat.

She looked at her phone quickly to see that it was almost four. "How did the time go so quickly?" she mumbled out loud.

Raelynn started her car and then made her way back to her apartment. She couldn't help but glance at the seat next to her where the letter and box sat. Her thoughts wandered to what was written in the letter and then wondered if it would be an invasion of her parents' privacy if she read it. *She wouldn't have given it to me if it wasn't ok to read, right?* she rationalized.

She shook her head hard. *Not gonna get caught up in that,* she thought with a smile. She would respect their privacy and not read it, she decided. Her thoughts drifted to what she would want if it was her letter, and she knew she wouldn't want someone else to read about a private moment between her and her spouse.

Before long, she was pulling into the driveway of her parking lot. Raelynn turned off the ignition, but stayed in her car for a second, just looking around. She suddenly wondered if someone was lurking around watching her. The memory of the package outside her sliding door flooded back and she let out a small shudder.

Timmy had sat up on his seat, looking intently out the window. She couldn't help but wonder if he sensed it too or if he was just waiting patiently for Raelynn to come and get him. She let out a chuckle and shook her head. She was just being paranoid, she decided. She grabbed the letter and moved quickly out of the car. Timmy waited nicely while she hooked up his leash and then jumped out. She hurried toward the door. It was then that she remembered Creepy Guy didn't show up at work at all during her shift. Was it because he had followed her?

Raelynn sucked in her breath at the thought that he might know where she lived. It actually bothered her more than realizing someone followed her home. *And it's probably the same person*, she thought grimly. What kind of danger was she in that she was being followed?

Maybe she should go stay at her mom's house for a little while. But then that would put her mom and brother in potential danger, wouldn't it? If only she and Beau were closer, she could ask him to stay. Raelynn felt her face heat up at the thought.

As she fished out her keys, she noticed Timmy sitting next to her, facing away from the door. It almost felt like a protective stance. She scratched his head, but he didn't move. She wondered if she had misjudged his protective instincts. He never faced away from the door. He always waited patiently for her to unlock it, looking up at her the entire time. But this was different.

She quickly unlocked her door and Timmy ran, as much as he ran anyway, inside and plopped down on the kitchen floor, looking at his bowl. His belly was flat on the floor and his head rested on his front paws. His eyes were the only thing moving as he watched her move, the look on his face was the definition of sad puppy eyes.

"Oh my, Timmy. You are so dramatic," she said with a laugh. She wondered if he would even protect her if someone broke in. She noticed he didn't do anything when she felt that chill outside yesterday. She was probably overthinking his behavior earlier. He was probably just hungry. Raelynn scooped food into his bowl and refilled his water. Then she leaned against the counter and watched him eat as if he was starving, resisting a laugh.

Her phone buzzed in her pocket, and she pulled it out to see who was texting her. She grinned when she saw it was from Beau, letting her know he was on his way and would be grabbing Mexican shortly. She had a favorite

Mexican place but wasn't sure if she told him what it was. When he called earlier and suggested it, she quickly agreed and gave him her favorites.

Timmy finished his food quickly and moved to his water. He splashed it everywhere and had plenty more dripping from his massive jowls as he moved away from his now empty bowls. Raelynn pushed off the counter and laughed again. She grabbed the towel just for these events and wiped the floor as he moved to the door, leaving a trail of water drops.

Raelynn sighed as she followed him to the door, glancing at the still unopened box sitting on her coffee table. She gently pushed the curtains aside and looked outside quickly to make sure no one was nearby. She honestly didn't know what she would do if someone was actually standing outside her door. She wasn't a horror movie fan for a lot of reasons, but the fear that it would put in her already wild imagination would make it impossible for her to live alone again.

Timmy waited patiently for her to hook up his chain and went about his business quickly. Raelynn didn't sit like she normally did. Being outside didn't feel as serene as it did just yesterday and she wanted to be back inside as soon as possible. She was glad she was on the ground floor even with everything going on because if she was far away from her apartment every time she had to take Timmy outside, she would be even more worried.

Once back inside, she locked the door, and pulled the curtain closed again. Running her hands down the front of her jeans, she closed her eyes and tried to calm her racing heart. Beau would be arriving soon, and she needed to get herself together again. Her eyes instantly settled on the package when she opened them again.

Bonded Blood

She decided to go ahead and open it before Beau got there so she could process the new information. Timmy disappeared into her room, and she figured he would be napping shortly again. Raelynn didn't care because she knew she was in for a late night. She thought about taking the next day off but then remembered she had already taken Saturday off and didn't want to leave Susiana shorthanded by calling out with late notice. Knowing she had a couple of days off soon helped her relax. Even if she lost some sleep, she would be able to catch up on Saturday morning.

Raelynn grabbed a soda from her fridge and then settled in front of the brown package. Her scissors were still in her hand as she studied it, wishing she had x-ray vision. With a groan, she spread out the blades and slid one along the tape. She noticed the clear tape had smudges on it, making her wonder if someone could get fingerprints from tape. That would solve a lot of questions for her fairly quickly, she thought.

Thinking of this, she was more careful about opening this box. Maybe Officer Milton would call her back and she could get this to him. She decided not to disrupt it too much because she figured it would have to be taken off some specific way for it to be useful. Instead, she just cut it in the center and made sure it didn't pull off anywhere.

Finally having it free from its bindings, Raelynn opened the flaps and peeked inside. Seeing the newest addition to her collection, she crossed her brows and stared at it. It filled the entire space of the box and was flat on the top. Reluctantly, she reached in and pulled it out.

This one was significantly heavier than the last, not that it meant anything specific. But the weight was surprising.

The rest were small and pretty lightweight. She set it down in front of her and then moved to sit on the floor in front of it. Even she had to admit this one looked even less like a turtle than the rest.

It had a long "body" made of metal, not like the other metal one which was more like thin sheet metal. This one was heavy metal and barely had much of a curve to its "shell". There was a smaller piece that looked like it had been welded on top for a head and four tiny pieces that were also welded to the bottom as feet. The whole thing had a layer of dirt covering it. She looked down at her hands that now had dark smudges from just lifting it out of the box.

Raelynn flipped it over to see if this one also had numbers on the bottom. There were scratches but she couldn't make out numbers. Grabbing her phone to use the flashlight, she shined the light into the slight concave of the shell and could barely make out a four and a three.

She suddenly remembered she didn't check the PVC turtle to see if it had numbers on it. She quickly went into her room to get the box she had put the rest in the night before to check it. As she walked by, she let out a small laugh at Timmy who was stretched out on her bed. "Bed hog," she mumbled as she walked back to the living room with her box.

Setting the box on the table, she slowly took each one out and set it on the table in a row. Raelynn picked up the plastic piping one and turned it over carefully. Sure enough, there were two numbers scratched into the underbelly of the little turtle. "Seventy-four," she said quietly. *No July birthdays either*, she thought to herself. "Ugh," she groaned out and leaned back on the couch. The little structure in her hand seemed to be taunting her as she tried to figure out what the heck they all meant.

Her thoughts were interrupted by a knock at the door. She looked up and noticed the time, assuming it was Beau. She had locked her door when she came home this time, not sure what was going on with the early morning delivery. She decided it would be better to be safe than sorry. Raelynn jumped up from the couch and moved to the door, taking a quick look through the peephole before unlocking it for him.

Beau moved inside, his hands full with two brown bags and another bag over his shoulder. Raelynn took one bag from him and moved into the kitchen to get utensils and plates. Beau followed her in and set his bag next to hers and then dropped the bag off his shoulder.

"Hey, can I put this in the living room for now?" he asked, his eyebrows raised.

Raelynn nodded. "Of course. Timmy's crashed on my bed, as usual, so he should leave it alone. He's such a good guard dog, isn't he?" she added with a snort. It didn't escape her that he didn't seem bothered that someone else was in the apartment.

Beau let out a soft chuckle as he moved into the other room. While she waited for him to come back, Raelynn took out the plates and forks. She grabbed a couple of sodas from her fridge. She was guessing what he liked, but she didn't have many options anyway. She did keep a few bottles of water in her fridge just in case her options weren't acceptable.

As Beau came back into the kitchen, a shadow from the hall pulled her attention to the doorway behind him.

A large paw came into view as Timmy stretched his full length before he managed to get all the way into the room.

"Seriously, Timmy?" she admonished. "Now you make an appearance? Not the knock on the door or the extra voice in the house? Annoying."

Beau laughed and turned to scratch the pup under his chin, who gladly tipped his head up for the extra love. "Oh, he just smelled food, I bet," Beau said with a laugh. "Are you hungry, buddy?"

He reached into his pocket and pulled out a large raw hide bone. He glanced at Raelynn for permission. She just laughed and nodded. "Like he's not spoiled enough."

"I figured that would allow us to eat instead of him maybe wanting some too," Beau explained.

Raelynn shrugged. "He actually doesn't beg much, which I am so grateful for. I wouldn't be able to resist if he did and he would be about thirty pounds heavier than he already is."

"You're a good boy, aren't you, buddy," Beau cooed at the huge dog, who ate up his love. Beau laughed and then handed the dog his treat.

Timmy gladly took it and trotted into the living room. Raelynn moved so she could see where he went, not really thrilled with the idea that he ate it on the couch. But he went to the large pillow bed she had gotten for him when he first came home and settled in with his treasure.

Raelynn breathed a sigh of relief. "He's only used that thing once, but it's like he knows that's where he should take the bone."

"He's a smart dog, isn't he?" Beau said, standing next to Raelynn. "How come he was surrendered?"

"I don't really know. The shelter just said that the family had a baby and were scared of him being too big around it. I mean I guess I could see that, but he's so gentle." She shrugged. "Oh well, my gain. 'Cuz I love the big lug."

Timmy lifted his head and tipped it to the side watching Raelynn. Suddenly he gave her a yip, as if he knew what she said and agreed and then went back to his bone.

Raelynn and Beau's eyes met, and they laughed, clearly thinking the same thing.

They dished out their food in silence and then moved to the other room, settling in.

Beau spoke up first. "So, I must have done ok on the order, huh?"

"Well, I kinda gave you the things I like. But you did good. These are my favorites," she said with a grin.

Nodding, Beau smiled back. "Mexican can be tricky. Sometimes it is super spicy even when you ask for it mild. Some folks don't like spice, except old bay out here. Something I learned is not a thing everywhere it seems."

Raelynn put down her fork. "What?"

Beau laughed. "Apparently Ashley had no idea what 'old bay' was. I had to explain it to her and until she tried it—and didn't care for it at all—she had no idea what I was talking about."

"Are you serious? I mean who hasn't heard of Old Bay before? Like what does she put on her seafood or literally *anything*?" Raelynn asked, shocked by the new information.

"No clue. It was so weird and funny at the same time, if I'm totally honest," he said with another laugh.

Raelynn just shook her head. "Weird Minnesota people," she muttered. She looked over the table of all her recent deliveries and sighed.

The sound didn't get past Beau, and he set his fork down. Seeming to know what she was thinking, he put his hand on her arm gently. "We're gonna figure this out, Rae."

"I know, but it's so frustrating," Raelynn whined.

"Always is, isn't it? Trying to solve puzzles can be annoying, but it'll be worth it in the end, right?" he asked quietly.

Raelynn nodded. "I do like a good puzzle," she said with renewed optimism.

"That's the spirit," Beau said with a chuckle and exaggerated swing of his arm, as if to signal a gung-ho thing.

Snorting, she just nodded. "You're weird, bro. But yeah, we got this. Thanks for helping me, even if we haven't figured anything out yet."

Beau lifted his shoulder. "Hey, it's a good distraction from the normal every day b.s. so I'm all in."

"Yeah, until it gets really weird or dangerous, right?" she asked.

"Nope. I'll stay by your side as long as you will let me. I love a good puzzle too. Brain teasers are my jam, Rae." His voice was full of humor, and he wiggled his eyebrows, making her chuckle.

Raelynn shot him a grin. "I guess we will make a good team then."

They finished their dinner and Raelynn cleared the table, leaving only the turtles and their corresponding notes. She sat back down on the couch and Beau joined her after he grabbed another drink. He held it up as if asking if she was ok that he had taken it. Raelynn smiled and was glad he felt comfortable enough in her space to help himself.

"So, where did we leave off?" he asked, as he settled down next to her.

Raelynn bit her lip, trying to figure out how to say that a new statue came, but more importantly *how* it was delivered.

Before she could say anything though, Beau's voice rang out in surprise. "Wait a second. There's a new one—or did you find it somewhere and I just didn't see it yesterday?"

His eyes met hers and she cringed. *Guess he took the* how *out of the equation*, she thought.

"Um, so, this morning when I took Timmy out," she paused, trying to find the right words to not cause concern, but failing. She took a breath and closed her eyes, deciding to just get it out. "When I took Timmy out, the package was on my chair outside, with only my name on it." She tilted her head back, waiting for Beau to freak out.

It wasn't like they were dating or anything, but he was becoming a close friend, and she would be concerned for his safety if it was him in this position. And if he wasn't a guy who looked like he worked out every day. Even the strongest willed feminist didn't stand a chance against most men if they weren't trained or physically strong. Raelynn wasn't foolish enough to believe she wasn't an easy target.

When Beau didn't respond, she opened one eye and peered over at him. She was startled to see him just staring at her. His emotions were hard to read. She opened her other eye and turned her body to face him.

"Look, I know what you are going to say. But there's nothing I can really do. I don't have cameras and have no real idea who would have put it there," she rushed out, trying to explain why she isn't sounding very concerned or scared. In truth, she was a little scared, but what could she do about it?

Beau just shook his head. "It's ok, Rae. You don't need to justify anything. I'm just worried for your safety," he paused, seeming to struggle finding his words as well. "But I don't know if it is appropriate or would even be helpful—" he stopped talking and dropped his head.

Raelynn grinned. "You know I'm not easily offended right? Just say what you are thinking. I'm trying to figure out what to do myself. I can't go to my mom's because I don't want to drag anyone else into this if I can help it. Plus, I don't know if I even need to be concerned." She paused. Then she added, more to herself than to him, "If I was truly in danger, it seems like something would have happened by now."

Beau looked at her skeptically. "Maybe, but Rae, you never know. There's no way to know who sent the packages and the only person we know about being connected at all is some creepy guy who keeps showing up at your work."

"I know, I know. But what choice do I have? I mean it. I can't go somewhere else until we figure out who is sending them, and I can't exactly hire a bodyguard." She swung her hand toward Timmy, who was aggressively gnawing on his bone in the corner. "Now if Timmy were a little more of a *guard dog*, I might not have to worry." Even raising her voice and emphasizing the words "guard dog" didn't make her pup raise his eyes at her.

Raelynn threw up her hands in defeat. "See? Useless."

Bonded Blood

Beau laughed. "Ok, ok. But what if, I mean, maybe, if it would help," he stopped again and took in a deep breath. "I could stay here for a few days. If you want, I mean, if it would help you feel safer, I mean…"

She wanted to laugh at Beau's struggle to get that out, but she was touched that he was concerned about her enough to suggest it. She did think about it herself earlier after all.

Touching his arm lightly, she decided to tease him a little to relieve his discomfort. "Oh, that's so sweet of you Beau, but I only have one bed, and it is already taken up by the man in my life." Raelynn tried to stay serious, but the look of horror that crossed his face as he tried to say he didn't mean *that* was too funny and her giggle snuck out.

"I'm giving you grief, Beau. Seriously. It is sweet of you though." She patted his arm and smiled. "Besides what would the neighbors say?" she teased, lightly touching her chest in feigned shock.

Beau reached behind her and pulled out a pillow, smacking her square in the face. "Funny girl, huh?"

Raelynn shrugged and laughed. She tried reaching for the other pillow, but he beat her to it and tossed them both to the floor, brushing his hands together, satisfied.

"I am serious, though," he said with sincerity in his voice. "I would take the *couch,* and I wouldn't try any funny business. Scout's honor."

Raelynn snorted again. "Yeah, we already established that you were no boy scout. But I'll think about it. Thank you."

Beau nodded and picked up the new note. "Have you read this yet?" he asked, after looking it himself.

"No, forgot about it actually. What does it say?" she asked, leaning over to read what was in his hand.

She read it out loud as Beau held it, "'Almost there'. What the heck?"

Beau nodded, his face laced with seriousness and concern. "Yeah. Sounds like something some creepy stalker guy would say, doesn't it? Want to consider my offer now?"

Chapter 16

They spent the next two hours going over the notes and studying the turtle statues with no really good ideas of what it all meant. Raelynn's frustration was almost at the max and she was ready to quit and give up on trying to figure this out completely.

"Hey," Beau said gently. "I know this frustrating, but there has to be something here. Who else might have some ideas to help?"

"Ugh, I don't even know," Raelynn grumbled. She dropped her head back against the couch and closed her eyes. She didn't normally get migraines or even headaches for that matter, but she definitely felt one coming on. She closed her eyes and pressed her fingers on her forehead, trying to relieve the dull ache.

Beau was leaning forward, his elbows resting on his knees as he looked at the collection in front of him. "When is Serenity coming?" he asked finally, letting out a sigh.

She felt him lean back against the couch and she resisted a smile. Opening her eyes, Raelynn looked over at his exhausted face, his eyes now closed.

Watching him for a few minutes, she wondered if she should have left him out of all this. It wasn't fair that he had to worry about something that didn't have anything to do with him. He shouldn't have to stress about her stuff.

"Hey, Beau," Raelynn started. When he opened his eyes and looked at her, she gave him a small smile and dropped her eyes to her hands, fidgeting. She wasn't sure how to put her thoughts into words.

He shifted next to her, and she looked up, noticing he had moved a little closer and turned to face her. "What's wrong?" he asked.

Raelynn sighed. "I just don't feel right burdening you with all this. I feel like I dragged you into my mess and gave you extra stuff to worry about. I'm sorry."

Beau took her hand in his and gave it a squeeze. "Rae, we are friends, right? This is what friends do. They are there for each other. And none of this is a big deal to me. I'm glad to help out. It didn't seem like you could talk to anyone else about it, so I am happy to lend a hand. You are not burdening me with anything, ok?" The earnest look in his eyes made her feel a little better, but she still felt guilty.

When she didn't answer him, he gave her hand a harder squeeze. "Ok, Rae?"

"Ok, ok," she said, giving up. She was actually grateful he was there and standing by her, but she still felt bad getting him involved. For a split second, she hoped it wasn't putting him in danger as well.

"Ok," he repeated. "So, when is your friend coming?"

Raelynn glanced at the clock on her phone. "Actually, any minute. We should have made a list of what we wanted to ask her." She grabbed the notebook she was using to write down the numbers and flipped to a clean page.

Beau shrugged. "What is she coming over for? I mean, how do you think she can help?" he asked.

"I thought she could help us figure out what kind of art this is and then maybe we can get the name of someone local who we could interview and see if there is any connection to them or if they know of other artists in the area we could talk to." She knew it was a long shot, but she was looking for anything right now. "I was thinking maybe it could give us a lead on who might be making these I guess."

Beau just nodded. "Ok. It's a good idea actually. Downtown has some pretty cool galleries so it could lead somewhere." He turned his attention back to the collection on the table. He gently picked one up and studied it. "You know if you really think about it, a few of these are really well done—if they are supposed to be turtles. Look at the details with the feet. And that one with the crazy face carving."

Raelynn followed his finger and nodded. "I guess. So does that mean maybe it is an actual artist and not my dad just trying to put things together to send me some kind of weird message?" She hoped that wasn't it, but she also recognized that they had to look at other possibilities as well to figure this out.

"No, I'm not saying that. I guess I am just trying to see a different angle," he explained, still looking at the turtles.

They were quiet for a few minutes and then Raelynn sighed.

"How about we put this aside until Reni gets here?" she asked, her raised eyebrows in question. She needed to shift gears and think about something else for a while. "I realized today that I don't even know that much about you, Beau. What are your hopes and dreams? What do you want to be when you grow up?" Her tone was playful, as she tried to put this mystery aside and talk about something else. She wasn't lying, she had realize how little she knew about him.

Beau laughed. "Well, I don't want to be a fireman anymore," he said with a grin.

They both leaned back against the couch cushions and Raelynn smiled and nodded. "Why does every little boy want to be a fireman? So what is it these days? Doctor, lawyer or teacher?"

"None of the above," he said with a smile. "When I was little, we had a house fire. Not a big one, but it was traumatic. It was a small kitchen fire that somehow stayed within the kitchen but the damage from the water and everything was enough that we lived in a hotel for almost three months." He took a breath and looked up at the ceiling. "The firemen saved my guinea pig, and I thought he was the biggest hero in the world. I vowed I would grow up and save people's pets too." He put his hand across his chest as if saluting someone he had great respect for.

Raelynn smiled. She thought of the little boy standing by the street crying for his pet. "I bet you were a cute kid," she said. "I can just see the little tears streaking down your chubby cheeks." Her voice trailed off as she watched him.

Beau scoffed. "Really? That's what you get from the traumatic almost loss of my pet?" He shook his head at her. He dropped his eyes and tried to act hurt, but he had trouble hiding his smile at her teasing. "You're kinda mean, Rae."

Raelynn waved her hand and winked. "Thankfully you didn't lose your pet though. So, I'm not *that* mean. I was just picturing a sweet little Beau, that's all," she justified, jutting her chin out.

"Right," he said. "Anyway," he dragged out. "How long til Serenity comes over again?"

Laughing at Beau, Raelynn shrugged. "Not sure. Are you done being alone with me? You need backup?"

"Haha," he said. then he tapped his lips with his finger and nodded. "Actually, yeah. I am a little afraid to be alone with you. You are a little meaner than I thought. Who knows what else you might be mean about." As if to emphasize his point, he slid to the far side of the couch away from her.

Raelynn couldn't hold in her laughter. "You're crazy!"

As if on cue, a knock sounded at her door, drawing both sets of eyes to it. "Wow, saved by the door," Raelynn said with a smirk. She got up and moved to the door, glancing back at Beau and narrowing her eyes. "But I'll be back." She made a motion with her two fingers, pointed at her eyes and then at him, adding, "I'm watching you."

He laughed loudly from his spot on the couch and Raelynn smiled. She was enjoying spending time with Beau more than she thought she would.

A second knock sounded at the door just as she reached it to look through her peep hole. Seeing it was Serenity, Raelynn quickly opened the door and greeted her friend with a hug.

"I am so glad you moved so close, Reni! We will be able to see each other all the time again," she gushed, holding tightly to the other.

"Me too. You have no idea how much I have needed a friend, Rae," Serenity said quietly, causing Raelynn to pull back and study her friend.

She furrowed her brows and asked, "What do you mean? Is everything ok, Ren?"

Serenity let out a long sigh and then caught sight of Beau behind Raelynn. She straightened her shoulders and cleared her throat. "We can talk about it later. I didn't know you would have company. Is everything ok *here*?"

Raelynn turned and looked back at Beau. He stood and met them to introduce himself to Serenity. He held out his hand and when she reached out as well, he gave it a gentle grasp and shake.

"Hey, I'm Beau, a friend of Rae's," he said. "I hope it's ok that I'm here. We were going over some things and Raelynn thought you could help. But I can come back another time if you would be more comfortable."

Raelynn smiled at him. He was so understanding, even though he didn't know Serenity's history. She turned back to her friend and squeezed her shoulder. "Ren, it's ok. Beau is a good guy, and I will make sure you are safe, ok?" she whispered in her friend's ear, not wanting Beau to get the wrong idea or misunderstand.

"Oh, no, it's ok, Rae, I was just surprised." Serenity smiled at Raelynn and gave her a side hug back. "I am so much better than I used to be around new *people*." She stressed the last word, but Raelynn understood what she meant.

Nodding, Raelynn let go of her friend and waved toward the living room. She was annoyed that she only had a couch in her living room for the first time since she moved in. She rarely had anyone over besides her sister.

Beau seemed to read her mind and ducked into the kitchen to grab a chair. He sat it down after Raelynn and

Bonded Blood

Serenity had each taken a spot on the couch, settling next to Raelynn a good distance from Serenity. Raelynn was grateful that he had seemed to pick up on her friend's nervousness and had given her plenty of space. She shot him a smile, hoping he knew she appreciated his actions.

Beau gave her a slight nod back and settled in his chair, waiting for Raelynn to dig into their dilemma. Their teasing banter now long gone and she felt the seriousness of her situation weighing on her.

Serenity leaned forward and picked up one of the turtles on the table and scrunched her nose. "Uh, Rae, what are these?" She didn't look disgusted, but curiosity was clearly written on her face as she studied the small piece. Her eyes suddenly widened, and she looked at Raelynn.

"Rae? These aren't part of your collection. What are they? Where did you get them?" Serenity's voice took on a slight edge as she turned and stared at her friend, the turtle still in the palm of her hand.

Raelynn stared at her friend. She wondered why Serenity had a strange look on her face as she looked between the statue and Raelynn. She suddenly remembered she had told Serenity about her turtles one night when they were in middle school because she was missing her dad, and her friend had wanted to help comfort her. It was around one of her birthdays she thought as she tried to think back.

"I forgot I told you about my turtles, Reni," Raelynn said, shaking her head. This might make it easier for her to explain the new ones, since she already knew Raelynn's story about her dad and his disappearance.

"What do you mean? Nobody else knows about them?" Serenity glanced at Beau who gave her the slightest of nods.

Raelynn shook her head. "I only told you, and I even forgot about that. The only other person besides my mom who knows is Beau, and that's because of everything happening now." She looked up and gave Beau a small smile.

Serenity just looked between them, her forehead crinkling in the process. "So…what is going on, Rae?" She looked again at the turtle in her hand and then back at them.

Gently taking the small statue from Serenity's hand, Raelynn held it up and scrutinized it. "I guess the only place to start is why we asked you to come over. I need your help, at least I am hoping you can help us figure this out." She set the turtle down next to the others and waved her hand above them. "I started to get these in the mail, and I am confused about all of it. We are trying to find a place to start, and I was wondering if you have any idea about what kind of art this might be?"

"Wait, what? I don't understand," Serenity stared at her friend.

Raelynn turned to face Serenity. "So, it's kind of a long story. But I have been getting these statues since Saturday." She swung her arm over the collection and then looked at her friend again. "There seems to be a theme, besides the fact that they all look like turtles anyway. We are trying to figure out a way to find out who is sending them but haven't had any luck. I thought maybe it was a certain kind of art that could lead us in a direction. I'm not sure if it is anything, but I need to start somewhere, you know?"

The room was silent for a long time, no one knowing what to say. Beau cleared his throat suddenly and then moved out of the room. Raelynn watched him go but was unsure where he was heading. Maybe the bathroom, she guessed.

Bonded Blood

Turning back to Serenity, Raelynn sighed. "Reni, I am worried that my dad is trying to send me a message somehow and I need to figure this out as soon as I can. It's ok if you don't know anything in particular about this type of art, if it's even a thing, I guess. It was a long shot to begin with." She didn't want her friend to feel guilty about not being able to help.

Serenity was never able to actually study art like she had wanted to, but she was always reading about different artists and her reports in high school were always about famous ones. Raelynn just hoped she would be able to remember something from back then.

She felt a sudden sadness overcome her as she stared at the turtles on her table. She couldn't think of what their next step might be. The officer hadn't called her back yet, so she was still sitting with no leads.

Scooting closer to her, Serenity gently set her hand on her friend's arm. "Rae, that was a long time ago. But if I can look closer at them, I might be able to do a little research." She paused and picked up the one made of PVC piping.

Raelynn watched as she studied the creature. Out of the corner of her eye, she saw Beau returning. Timmy seemed to sense a shift in the room and decided he needed a potty break. Raelynn wasn't even sure where he came from. Beau gave her a nod and moved to let the big dog outside. She sent him a grateful look and turned back to Serenity. Raelynn was suddenly aware of how much nonverbal communication she and Beau already seemed to share.

"That is a huge dog, Rae," Serenity gasped quietly as she pressed her back into the couch cushions slightly.

Raelynn noticed her friend's unease and moved a little closer. "He is but he is literally a teddy bear. I promise he won't hurt you," she said soothingly. She had never known Timmy to show any aggression or even bark at anyone. She had forgotten about how big he was to strangers since she knew him so well. "I'm sorry, I should've asked you about dogs before."

Serenity didn't take her eyes off Timmy as he lumbered toward the door, seemingly unaware that she was even there. Beau followed him out and then closed the door after he had him hooked to his chain. "It's ok, I guess."

Raelynn watched her friend closely. She trusted Timmy, but she could see why Serenity was apprehensive. She resisted the irritation she had that another new person was in the home and Timmy seemed completely unaffected. Thinking back to her last delivery, she again worried that maybe he wasn't the best guard dog. Sure, he was big and intimidating, but he didn't seem the slightest bit interested in strangers or potential danger.

Trying to change the subject, she turned back to the statues on the table again. "Do you have any thoughts at all, Ren?" she asked, desperate to find something to start with.

Serenity set down the turtle from her hands and sighed. "I don't know. I mean it just looks like the artist used a bunch of junk to make them. But each one is used with different stuff. It's weird." Her eyes didn't leave the group on the table as she talked.

Raelynn noticed a far off look in her friend's eyes as she stared at the collection. Just as she was about to reach out to her, Serenity jumped up. She looked like something spooked her, her face flushed and her eyes wide.

"Uh, Rae, I gotta go, I'm sorry. I'll text you later," she said as she hurriedly gathered her purse and rushed to the door. She didn't even put her shoes on but grabbed them and disappeared through the door before Raelynn could say anything to stop her.

She was still staring at the door when Beau and Timmy came back in from outside.

"Everything ok, Rae?" Beau asked. "Where did Serenity go?" He sat back down next to Raelynn as Timmy made his way to his water bowl.

Raelynn snapped out of her shock and looked up at his concerned face. "I have no idea what just happened to be honest," she said, turning back to the door. Serenity obviously got triggered by something to rush out like that, but *what*?

Reaching out his hand to touch hers, Beau waited for her eyes to meet his before he said quietly, "Tell me what I missed." He raised his eyebrows and gave her hand a squeeze.

"I really don't know. She was looking at the turtles and then we were talking about the kind of art she thought it might be and then she literally bolted." Raelynn groaned and leaned back. "I wish I knew what went through her head. Not only because she's my friend, and she was clearly upset by something. But also because it might have triggered something that could possibly help us. Is that selfish, Beau?"

"I don't think so. There is a lot going on right now and I think you are desperate to find out any answers," he reassured her. "But you should probably check on her as a friend first."

"I know. I will text her in a little while. I just need to get my own thoughts together first." She sighed and then continued, "Can we talk about something else? Tell me more about you, Beau. I know you went to UM Eastern Shore for college, but I have no idea what you even studied." She needed to focus on something else for a little while. Anything but these statues.

Raelynn looked over at him and Beau nodded, leaning back against the couch. He still hadn't let go of her hand and her eyes drifted to the connection. She wasn't sure how she felt about it yet but was slightly surprised it didn't feel awkward.

"Well, in all fairness, I don't know what you studied either," he said with a grin.

Raelynn chuckled. "Fair enough. I'll go first. I studied psychology. I guess I went through a lot as a little kid with my dad going missing and everything. I turned out ok, I think, but I could have used some extra help when I was growing up. I want to help other kids with some of their difficult stuff," she shrugged as if dismissing her past difficulties.

"That's actually really cool, Rae." Beau's voice was quiet, and she could feel him watching her.

Finally, she looked up and gave him a small smile. "It's a start anyway."

Beau nodded. "It's kinda weird how we pick careers around something we experience in childhood isn't it?"

"I guess so," she agreed. "So, what happened to you when you were little that drew you to UMES?"

"I studied animal science. I started out there and then moved into poultry science," Beau said, matter of factly.

Raelynn wrinkled her nose. "Um…why?"

"Hey, I didn't criticize your major, Rae," he said with mock hurt. "Why are you going after mine? There's that meanness coming out again."

Trying to control her laugh from escaping, Raelynn put her hands up defensively. "I'm sorry. But why would you go into the science of chickens? It seems just so weird, that's all. Are you an aspiring farmer, Beau?" She crossed her arms and raised her eyebrows at him with a smile.

Beau shook his head and grinned back. "Ok, it does sound weird, but it was actually because my best friend growing up had grandparents who were chicken farmers. One summer we went to help them on the farm and the whole thing just fascinated me." He shrugged and then laughed. "But I guess studying a chicken's digestive system is actually kinda weird."

"Seriously, that's what you studied?" Raelynn asked incredulously. "Like, for real? Its digestive system?" She shook her head and wrinkled her nose again. "Yuck."

Beau laughed. "It is actually pretty interesting. But I won't bore you with details."

"Oh please, bore me. I have to know what is so interesting about studying a chicken's stomach and poop." Raelynn feigned interest and leaned forward in her seat, settling her arms over her knees and resting her chin on one hand.

Beau, acting as if he didn't catch her sarcasm, leaned forward as well and started to talk about all the things that go into a chicken and how it is processed and then expelled from its body. He knew she was totally grossed out, but he acted as if he didn't notice, just to tease her back.

"So, I can tell by looking at poop from different chickens what kind of feed they ate and even what some of those chemicals are and where they came from. Pretty cool, right?" he asked, looking at Raelynn's disgusted expression.

Slowly she shook her head. "No. Not cool at all, Beau. That is utterly disgusting. Don't ever talk about chicken poop with me again. The last thing I need to visualize when I eat my favorite fried chicken is that picture in my head!"

"Oh, come on, it's not that bad. Wanna hear about their circulatory system?" Beau asked, enjoying her discomfort entirely too much in Raelynn's opinion.

"Nope, nah uh, I'm good. I'm going to go grab a snack. Want something?" she asked as she pushed off the couch.

Beau shook his head. "I'm good actually. Maybe a Pepsi or Dr Pepper if you got it." He watched her walk to the kitchen and then chuckled again.

"Hey, do we need to do anything with the beast, Rae?" Beau called to her from the other room as she opened her fridge.

Raelynn glanced around. She sure was the neglectful owner tonight, she thought. She wasn't sure where he had spent most of the night. "Do you know where he is?" she called back.

Beau was quiet for a second and then said, "Nope actually. But he did his business outside a while ago. Is he in bed already?"

Raelynn laughed to herself. Most likely he has already taken over her bed, she thought. "I'll check in a minute." She started a bag of microwave popcorn and then made her way out of the kitchen. "Will you listen for the popcorn for me? I'm going to use the bathroom and make sure

Timmy didn't sneak out while we weren't looking," she snickered as she moved toward her bathroom.

Knowing he had to be in one of two places that he preferred, she guessed correctly. He was sprawled out on her bed, thankfully once again nowhere near her pillow. She loved her dog, but the idea of him slobbering all over her pillow disgusted her—though now she had something worse in her head thanks to Beau.

Chapter 17

The alarm rang out way too early, she decided. She and Beau had stayed up much later than she had planned just talking. It was a relaxing and fun night after Serenity abruptly left. They spent the whole time talking without a movie or TV on and munched on popcorn and drank soda. She had planned to go to bed well before midnight, but the time had flown by, and she found she really enjoyed being with Beau. She wasn't going to jump to the relationship thing, but she was more than willing to see where it could go. She was just glad he hadn't pushed to spend the night after the evening's earlier events. She didn't want things to be awkward.

As she rolled over and hit her phone's screen to turn off the annoying sound, she groaned. Hopefully she'd make it through the day. There was no doubt she would be tired. She finally got up with the thought that she was off the next day, possibly up to 3 days in a row depending on her boss's Halloween plans. If she did end up working it would at least be a shorter day.

Her loyal companion was sleeping, and snoring, at the foot of her bed. He took up half the bed still, but she managed to get him shifted enough the night before to have some space for herself.

Bonded Blood

Raelynn made her way to the bathroom and as she sat on the toilet, she tried to wake herself up. *A cold shower should do the trick*, she thought grimly. Groaning again, she finished her business and started the shower, leaving the temperature lukewarm. It would be interesting to see if she could even handle it.

She hurried through her morning routine, taking advantage of her pup still being asleep so she could get ready first. Raelynn mused that this is what it must feel like to have a child. Typically, Timmy demanded her morning attention for eating and taking care of his own business. These kinds of mornings were rare. But she was also aware that she only had a limited amount of time before he would be awake and demanding her attention.

Of course, her line of thinking brought thoughts of her dad again. As she stared at herself in the mirror, her mind wandered. The memories of her dad were fading, and she hated that more than anything. It was more like watching an old choppy black and white film instead of the brightly colored memories of a small child.

Her phone's ringing broke her from her thoughts, and she exited the bathroom, shutting off the light as she passed by. Timmy was still stretched out on her bed, but he lifted his heavy head and gave her a massive yawn. Raelynn chuckled at him as she grabbed her phone.

The caller ID showed an unknown number, but without thinking she pressed the green button.

"Hello?" she answered, as she looked around to make sure she had what she needed for work.

A throat cleared on the other end before a male voice spoke. "Miss Raelynn?"

Raelynn hesitated for a second and then hesitantly confirmed, "Yes, this is." A quick glance at the time showed it wasn't even five in the morning. *Who calls at this time of day?* she thought. If she wasn't already up and getting ready for work, she wouldn't have even answered.

She stood still and waited for the voice to say more. She was about to hang up when he cleared his throat again and finally spoke.

"Miss Raelynn. This is Officer Milton. I honestly didn't expect you to answer at this hour but wanted to at least leave a message for you." Raelynn smiled in relief at the now familiar voice.

"Officer Milton, I'm glad you called actually. I'm just getting ready for work but have a few minutes. What's up?" Raelynn motioned to her dog to come with her to the kitchen.

The reluctant animal followed her after an epic stretch and plop down from the bed. Once again, Raelynn was reminded of the benefit of living on the main floor.

She made her way into the kitchen to fill his bowl while Timmy walked to the sliding door. The phone was still quiet on the other line as she waited for the officer to speak again.

A deep sigh crackled across the line. "Well, I am, uh, sorry to bother you, but I got your message and, uh, I just, uh, wanted to let you know that I, uh, won't be able to help you out." He paused and Raelynn froze as she watched her dog outside.

"What do you mean, you can't help? Did something happen?" She could feel her heart rate spike suddenly as she worried that something had happened.

Bonded Blood

The line was quiet again as she waited. She wasn't sure what to even say in response to what he just said.

"Uh, no nothing *happened* but I just won't be able to help you look into this," he paused and then continued, "I'm sorry Miss Raelynn. I just can't help."

Raelynn felt her eyesight grow foggy. What was going on? She was planning, or at least hoping, that he would be able to help her figure out who was sending these *gifts* to her and maybe start up their investigation again. Something was up with the officer and Raelynn was stunned at this news.

Timmy's wet nose on her hand drew her attention back to the present and she moved back inside with him.

"Um, ok, Officer Milton. I guess I am just stunned right now. I have had some things hap—"

"No, no, Miss Raelynn," he interrupted her. "Don't say anything else. If you agree, I can send you the info of a person who can help you. I just can't anymore. I'm sorry. Good luck." Then the line suddenly went dead.

Raelynn stared at her phone's black screen. Should she be worried about something bigger again and that's why he can't help? Her frustration was at its peak just as Timmy let out an annoyed bark to get her attention.

She jumped and then shook her head at her pup. Nothing got in the way of his food apparently. She dropped her phone on the counter and put Timmy's food bowl on the floor with his now full water bowl. He made quick work of emptying both and then headed back to the door. Raelynn operated on routine and just followed him.

By the time she had made her way to work a few minutes later, she had not even realized what she had done until she snapped out of her stupor by a car horn behind her. Raelynn shook her head and glanced in her rearview mirror, scowling at the impatient car behind her. She made her way into the intersection, now clearly seeing the bright green light.

It didn't take much longer for her to arrive in the café parking lot. She parked and sat in her car, since her boss wasn't there yet. Looking at her phone, she saw that she was actually about ten minutes early. She was surprised since it felt like she had woken up later than normal and had gone through her morning in a bit of a fog after the phone call.

Watching the light from the slowly rising sun start to color the sky ever so slightly, Raelynn leaned against her headrest. What was she going to do now that the officer cryptically told her he couldn't help her?

A sudden text came through, making her look at the device still in her hand.

Contact Sharon. You know who I mean.

Raelynn bit her cheek. Sharon? Does he mean the one who Ashley stayed with? She didn't know anyone else named Sharon, so she would have to take a chance with that. Later though. It was too early to bother anyone at this hour, she thought with a sigh.

A car coming into the lot made her look up again. Susiana waved as she turned and parked her car a couple spots from Raelynn's. With another deep sigh, she made her way out of her car to help her boss with her bags.

"Good morning, boss," she said with a forced smile.

Susiana was already pulling things out of her back seat as Raelynn arrived at her vehicle. "Good morning, Raelynn. Beautiful day, isn't it?" She set two large bags full of containers on the ground and grabbed a third and fourth from inside the car before she closed it.

"Wow, Susiana, you have more than normal. Busy night?" Raelynn asked as she picked up the two heavy bags from the ground while her boss locked up her car.

Susiana nodded. "Maybe. I thought maybe we would just do a shorter day Sunday with Halloween and all that, so I spent some extra time baking Halloween cookies. I'm hopeful that we can get some special orders of them and that will make up for the shorter hours on Sunday."

"That's a great idea actually. That gives you all day today and Saturday to get the baking done." Raelynn nodded and waited for Susiana to unlock the door. There was a small kitchen inside the café, but it wasn't big enough for the kinds of items Susiana liked to make, so she only used it for some last-minute things or special orders.

"Yep, that's the goal!" she agreed with a smile.

They moved into the dark café and her boss quickly switched on the lights, flooding the small space with bright light. Raelynn got busy right away setting up for the morning. It was Friday, and it could go either way as far as how busy it would be. Sometimes it was really quiet and other times it was busier than Sundays after church.

She restocked the front supplies while Susiana loaded the bakery cases with all her goodies. Raelynn suddenly realized she didn't get a chance to eat that morning, and the pastries looked amazing. She might have to buy one before lunch with how her stomach was protesting its emptiness already.

After she had everything ready, she looked over at Susiana, who was busy setting up a display for the cookie orders. She was once again grateful for the job she had and how easily they worked together. When Susiana was satisfied with her displays, she turned to Raelynn, hands on her hips and a smile on her face.

"I think we are ready," she said with satisfaction. "What do you think?"

Raelynn nodded. "It looks great. We should have done this earlier in the week though."

"I know, but we'll see how this goes. Next year maybe we'll do it sooner," her boss said with a shrug.

It briefly crossed Raelynn's mind that she might not be there next year, if she decided to actually buckle down and look for that adult job. Instead of bringing that possibility up, she just nodded and smiled. If only she could come into some magical money, she could work here forever, she thought with a sigh.

The first customer came in as soon as the door was unlocked, and Raelynn didn't stop moving until roughly fifteen minutes before Chrissy walked in. The sigh of relief that escaped her lips wasn't missed by her coworker.

"Rough morning, Rae?" she asked as she rounded the corner with her apron in one hand. Her face was lit up in a smirk as she surveyed the messiness around her coworker.

Typically, the mess annoyed Raelynn, but she had been so busy, she didn't even have time to notice—until Chrissy pointed it out.

She grimaced and then groaned. "It has been crazy. I think everyone is off today and needed to buy a coffee instead of making one at home," she said with a sigh as she dropped onto a nearby stool. Raelynn looked around and took in all the things that needed restocking. "Ugh, I better get to it, huh?"

Chrissy just chuckled from her corner and slipped the apron over her head. "I'll start here. It looks like Susiana's baking has been a hit. Everything is almost gone and it's not even ten." She clucked her tongue and stood with a notepad and pen to take note of everything she needed to grab from the back.

Giving Raelynn one quick look to let her know she was going to restock, Chrissy disappeared. Susiana came out a few minutes later to survey their supplies as well. She let out a sigh, but didn't say anything.

"Everything ok, Susiana?" Raelynn asked her boss, both of her hands full of straws and stir sticks.

Her boss waved her hand. "Oh yes. I just can't believe how busy we have been. How have the cookie orders been?" Her attention was drawn to the small display she had put together when they first came in. She had put out about twenty order forms and a small box for them to be put in when filled out. Both she and Raelynn were surprised to see there were only two forms left.

"Wow, looks like this was a hit," her boss said, pleased with the numbers. "I guess this confirms that we will have shorter hours on Sunday. My little man will be thrilled." Susiana took the slips of paper and nearly skipped back to her office.

Chrissy appeared next to her and had a confused look on her face. "What's that about?" she asked, pointing her thumb over her shoulder at their boss.

Raelynn filled her in on what Susiana had told her that morning, which seemed like ages ago.

"Hm, ok. So, who is working Sunday? You or me? And what kind of shorter hours is she talking?" Chrissy asked, leaning against the counter facing her coworker.

"I'm not sure, but I figured since I am off tomorrow and Monday, I can pick it up," Raelynn said with a shrug.

"Ok," Chrissy said thoughtfully. "But if you are gone those two days, who am I stuck with tomorrow?" She gave her coworker a worried look.

Raelynn shook her head. "I'm not sure actually. I have been so focused on other things that I didn't even look at the schedule. I'm sure you'll be fine though." She patted her friend's shoulder and gave her a sympathetic smile.

She knew the two of them worked most of their shifts together and complimented each other well. Chrissy had only started a few months ago, but it didn't feel like it to Raelynn. After a short week of training, Chrissy had jumped right in. There were a few students who worked limited hours, something Raelynn did over the summer. Susiana allowed a few of her good workers the opportunity to work on an on-call basis instead of a regular schedule. These students were good workers, but since they didn't work all the time, it didn't always create a good camaraderie between them, and they definitely didn't have the kind of rapport she and Chrissy had.

Chrissy groaned and pointed her finger at Raelynn. "I hope you know you will hear about this on Tuesday. It better be someone who isn't incompetent!" She huffed and then turned back to her bakery cases.

Raelynn laughed as she turned to the counter as a new customer walked through the door. The break was short-lived as the steady stream of customers, mostly students, started up again a few minutes later.

Bonded Blood

By the time Raelynn was ready to leave for the day, she was exhausted. It had been a crazy day, and the steady stream of customers reminded her of the summer traffic and tourism. Those Fridays in the summer were almost always the worst day of the week. It sometimes even required Susiana to be out of the back office helping them keep up on supplies and orders. Relieved that it was over, and looking forward to a day off, Raelynn dropped her apron in the hamper and grabbed her things.

"See you next week, Chrissy," she called as she walked by Chrissy who was helping a customer with an order. Her words earned her a wave and a scowl, making Raelynn smile as she headed outside. The cooler than expected air made her catch her breath. She had been so distracted in the morning that she had forgotten her jacket. Her light long sleeves weren't blocking the cold air at all.

Hurrying to her car, Raelynn crossed her arms around her body to try to keep some warmth contained. It didn't work very well, and she was glad to be in her car just a few minutes later. She started the engine and turned the heat on and then the fan on high. Hopefully the vehicle heated up quickly. She held her hands in front of the warm air coming from the vent, rubbing them together.

Her thoughts drifted to Ashley again, as they always did when weather issues popped into Raelynn's head. Curiosity got to her, and she looked at the temperature on her car's dash. She was surprised to see it was fifty-four degrees. No wonder she was cold, she thought.

"Even Ashley would be cold at this temperature," she mumbled to herself. Satisfied that she wasn't being a baby about being cold, she buckled her seatbelt and thought about the rest of her day. It was almost exactly two-thirty.

She needed to get home to let Timmy out. Her sister had a class so she knew Sahara wouldn't be able to help out with Timmy. He would be fine, she knew, but she still felt bad when he didn't have someone to entertain him for a little while when she worked.

"Oh, who am I kidding?" Raelynn laughed out loud. "He will sleep all day anyway." Even though she knew she was probably right, she still hurried home.

As she drove, Raelynn thought about her friend. Serenity had texted her late last night, apologizing for her sudden departure. She had something come up but wanted to talk to Raelynn tonight. Beau had mentioned getting together and going on an actual date tonight, but she wasn't sure if that was still happening with everything going on. She decided to meet with Serenity earlier in the day and then she could still do something with Beau later.

A sudden thought came to Raelynn. Creepy Guy hadn't come into the café during her shift. She should have been relieved, but she felt oddly disappointed. *A new delivery might give a clue that would make everything make sense*, she thought. *Then again, why would one more make a difference?* she argued with herself.

She rounded the last corner before her parking lot came into view. She sighed as she looked at the three-story building. A buzz took her attention briefly away from the building to look at her phone. It was sitting in the cup holder, and she couldn't see who or what the alert was for, but she looked anyway. She always did her best to ignore her phone while driving and since she was so close to her place, she just looked back up at the road.

Raelynn parked in the lot and quickly moved to her apartment. If Timmy was awake, he would be waiting impatiently for her to let him outside. She grabbed her phone and locked her car. As she made her way to the big glass doors, she fished her keys out of her pocket. Just as she was about to put her key in the lock a hand grabbed her arm.

A scream escaped her lips as she spun around to find Creepy Guy staring at her, both his hands in the air as if he wouldn't hurt her. There was something in his eyes she couldn't place. Maybe it was regret, but for what she wasn't sure. Scaring her maybe. But there was something else. Something oddly familiar about his eyes.

Raelynn narrowed her eyes and studied his. He fidgeted, dropping his eyes, and then shoved a box into her hands. He gave her the slightest of nods and then moved to the side and started to walk away.

"Wait!" she called summoning as much strength as she could. She needed to know who this person was. "Please!" Maybe if she talked to him, he would help her figure this out. She had always been a little afraid of who he might be, but now with everything leading to literally nothing, she was becoming desperate.

He turned slightly and shook his head and then hurried away from her. She glanced down at the box and then when she looked up again, he was out of sight, and she had no idea which direction he went.

She wanted to yell and scream and throw a tantrum, but she knew it wouldn't do any good. She stared at the package in her hands. She was just thinking about how she didn't get anything today. *Karma*, she thought gloomily.

She looked around again and when she saw no one was around, she sighed and continued inside to her apartment. She wondered why he came to her directly and didn't leave it outside, assuming it was him last time she found one on her chair. Shaking her head, she unlocked her door and noticed it was eerily quiet.

Of course, Timmy would still be asleep while she was worried about keeping him waiting all day. She closed the door behind her, set the new box on the kitchen counter, and went in search of her dog.

She was slightly alarmed that he didn't come when she called him but knowing her pup, he was sound asleep and couldn't be bothered. She looked through her entire apartment and couldn't find Timmy anywhere. It's not like he's a small animal that could easily hide.

Raelynn stood in the middle of her living room with her hands on her hips, trying to figure out what to do. Did someone take him? And if so, she was actually curious to find out *how,* when she should have been more concerned with who had been inside her apartment.

Something caught her eye as she looked around. Her front door had something stuck to it. She pulled the note off the wood and read it out loud.

"Hey Rae. I stole your dog (smiley face). I sent you a text, but you didn't answer so I thought I better leave you a note too. Love you, S"

Raelynn breathed a sigh of relief. Her sister must have gotten out of class early. At least she knew he was safe and not dog-napped or something. She grabbed her phone from her pocket and sure enough there was a text from her sister. She confirmed what Raelynn suspected, and that Jericho wanted to see him.

"I guess I don't have to worry about him for now," she said out loud. She opened a new thread and texted Serenity

Bonded Blood

to see when she was free. Next, she texted her sister and mom in the same conversation and asked about their plans to figure out how to get her dog back.

Her sister responded immediately. "Ransom to get your dog back is dinner. Six o'clock sharp."

Laughing, Raelynn was about to respond when her mom beat her to it. "Be nice Sahara. Rae, I'll have dinner made, no need to bring anything. Love you."

Looking at her clock, Raelynn saw she had some time. If Serenity could meet soon, then she would be able to make it to dinner easily. She waited a few minutes and when no response came from her friend, she decided to get changed and then see what Beau had in mind for the evening.

When there was still no response from Serenity, Raelynn decided to see what was on TV. As she moved though her apartment, thinking how weirdly quiet it was, she saw the box on the counter.

Raelynn let out a groan and reluctantly grabbed the box and scissors. "Might as well see what he gave me today," she said grimly, and then settled on the couch.

She stared at the box for a long time, debating whether she wanted to open it or not. Then she chastised herself because she was actually disappointed earlier that she hadn't gotten one.

"Ugh!" she groaned. She snatched the box up and slid the blade across the tape to release the restraint. "What surprised awaits me today?" she mumbled.

Raelynn opened the four flaps and peered inside the box. Her brow furrowed at what she saw. Gingerly she picked up the newest addition to her collection. It was the strangest one yet, and the smallest.

There was a tiny container that looked to be the body, with a piece of burlap or some sort of fabric covering it. Sticking out from under the fabric were four tiny white rocks and a slightly larger one, obviously the four legs and head. The plastic container was painted white, but when she put it down, there was a rattle from inside it.

Raelynn flipped the turtle over and then back, confirming there was something inside of it. Before she could think about what to do next, her eyes landed on the writing at the bottom of the box. Her breath caught in her throat as she read the words, "Out of time."

Chapter 18

After Serenity texted back saying she couldn't meet that day after all, Raelynn decided to go to her mom's. She needed to process what was happening and what the new and disturbingly ominous message meant. As she sat in her car again, she stared ahead at nothing. What was she going to do? She wasn't sure if Officer Milton couldn't or wouldn't help her anymore. Either way she was stuck.

Suddenly she remembered what he said about Sharon. She knew a little bit about what Sharon used to do before she retired because of the summer excitement with Ashley. She also had met her many times when she came by to see Ashley. But she wasn't sure how Sharon could help her. She remembered how she had helped them with some information last summer. When Officer Milton was helping her gather information, he had asked her to help him with an undercover assignment he was doing. He was posing as a professor at the college and needed a student to help back up his story. Sharon had been helping him for safety and information. Raelynn never really knew how that situation resolved now that she thought about it.

She decided to just stop over at Sharon's since she didn't live far from her mom's. She wasn't sure what the message from Officer Milton meant and for some reason she didn't want to call anyone in case someone was listening in. It didn't make a lot of sense since they would likely already be aware of where Raelynn was or who she talked to anyway. *Too many crime shows,* she thought with a chuckle.

A few minutes later, she made the right turn into Sharon's development. Raelynn loved this neighborhood. It had large older homes with big yards. There weren't many fences, which gave the whole area a welcome feeling. If she could ever afford to live here, she would in a heartbeat. As she drove up to Sharon's home, she looked at it with admiration. She bet about four of her mom's houses would fit in this one.

She stopped in the spot where Ashley had always parked. Sharon came out of the house as soon as she turned off the ignition. She shouldn't be surprised. This woman had an amazing knack for knowing things. Raelynn was also aware that Sharon had an extensive surveillance system around her entire property, so she probably saw Raelynn coming when she turned into the development two miles back. She grinned as she realized that.

"Raelynn dear! What a surprise," Sharon exclaimed as she greeted her guest.

Raelynn grinned as she closed her car door. She knew she didn't really surprise the older woman. "Hi Miss Sharon. How are you doing?" She glanced around the yard and smiled. "I see your flowers are still surviving."

Sharon nodded and smiled back. "They seem to be doing ok. Come in, dear. Then you can tell me why you are here."

Resisting the urge to say Sharon probably already knew, Raelynn followed her into the large home.

Bonded Blood

They settled at the table off to the side of the kitchen. The space was huge. It included a large kitchen with two islands and an informal living space with a large TV. A small table for four was set up off to the side that backed up to large floor to ceiling sliding panes of glass. There were bookshelves everywhere she looked. Some had cookbooks, others had novels. Her mom's entire main floor might fill just this space of Sharon's house. Maybe four of her mom's houses was being too conservative as she thought about the other two levels of this home.

Sharon set two glasses of lemonade on the table and then sat across from Raelynn. She reached out and grasped one of Raelynn's hands. The look on her face was one of compassion and Raelynn knew at that moment that Sharon already knew why, or part of why she was here now. Did Officer Milton call her already?

With her free hand, Raelynn was absently stirring her lemonade with the spoon Sharon had put in it, trying to figure out what to say, or more accurately how to say what she wanted to say. Now that she was here, Raelynn knew she needed Sharon's help. She knew Sharon was a huge part of what happened over the summer. But she still wasn't sure why the officer told her to contact Sharon instead of helping her himself. She didn't actually know what to ask for help with. Her dad's disappearance? The crazy turtle deliveries? Maybe even the notes, she mused silently.

A second hand covered her own, drawing Raelynn's attention to Sharon's eyes. "Just start from the beginning, dear, ok?"

"It's almost as if you have an idea already about why I am here. How?" Raelynn had to know.

Sharon chuckled. "I know things." She shrugged and then nodded. "Brad called me. He was concerned about you and wanted me to help you out if I could."

"Brad?" Raelynn asked, confused.

"Officer Brad Milton," Sharon clarified. "So, tell me what I can do to help, Rae."

Raelynn thought for another second and then sighed. "I don't know what you already know. What did he tell you to help me with?" She had to assume Sharon was just talking about her dad's disappearance. But she had to make sure. She had only told Beau, Serenity, and her mom about the turtles. There's no way Sharon could possibly know *that* is there?

Sharon leaned back in her chair. "Well, I know about your dad and that you are looking for him. But I am guessing there is more to that than what Brad even knows."

"I guess you *do* know things," Raelynn said with a small laugh.

The older woman just smiled and gave Raelynn a slight nod. "So, start from the beginning. What brought you to Brad in the first place?"

Raelynn leaned back and watched a stray droplet of water fall from her glass onto the table. She sat up straighter and began to tell Sharon the story from so many years ago about how her father left for work and never returned. She held back the emotion that was trying to come out as she grieved again the loss of her dad. She was back in that eight-year-old's mind, missing her dad and not understanding why he didn't return. She felt the anguish her mom felt at the loss and possible betrayal by the man she loved more than anything. Only now as an adult, telling the story to someone with so much compassion in her eyes, it all hit her differently.

When she finally sat back in her chair again, after retelling the story from her youth, Raelynn felt Sharon's hand on hers and tried to smile. But she knew it fell short. She finally understood the deep hurt and emptiness her mom felt whenever Raelynn brought up her dad.

She also realized the depth that grief held on to someone. Her father had been gone for so many years now. She thought it would be easy to talk about him after so much time, but she quickly learned that was not the case at all. The grief she was never really allowed to give closure to would always be there, waiting for the next situation to resurface. She wondered for the first time if she had ever been given the opportunity to grieve, really grieve, the loss of her dad.

Raelynn picked up a lot of slack at home while her mom was trying to make ends meet working so many hours. She was only eight, but she had to grow up pretty quickly to help take care of Sahara and then later Jericho. She quickly brushed those intruding thoughts away because that would mean that her mom was somehow neglectful. And Raelynn knew that was not the case. She was doing the best she could.

Sharon handed her a tissue and Raelynn wiped her face, not even realizing she had tears streaming down her cheeks. She closed her eyes tightly and took a deep breath, shame filtering into her thoughts. *Crying won't solve this*, she thought. She needed to get herself together if she was going to be able to tell Sharon about the most recent events, the things Raelynn believed were bringing the two of them together now.

"There's more, isn't there, Raelynn?" Sharon asked gently.

Raelynn's surprised eyes looked at her and she gave her a genuine smile this time. "Yep, you definitely know things," she said with a shake of her head. "I think it would be easier to show you though. Can I come back later tonight or tomorrow? I need to meet my family for dinner."

"Of course. I am going to dinner myself and then I will be back here with nothing but a good book waiting for me." She patted Raelynn's hand and then added, "I will do a little bit of looking into this and see if I can come up with anything to get us started."

Both women stood and moved toward the door. Once outside, Raelynn was again surprised by the chilliness in the air.

She noticed the sky starting to darken already, the shorter days being one of the annoying things about fall. As she opened her car door, Sharon's voice stopped her.

"Raelynn, dear," she called. "Please don't talk to Brad anymore about this, ok?"

She gave no other explanation of why and before Raelynn could ask a question, Sharon had already disappeared into her home. She slid into her seat and put the key in the ignition, but she didn't start it right away. Raelynn stared at the large brick house in front of her and wondered why Sharon would tell her not to contact Officer Milton. *Weird*, she thought, as she finally started her car and made her way to her mom's.

The drive went by quickly as Raelynn's thoughts spun, wondering if the person she had trusted with all this last summer was involved somehow. Or maybe he just got reprimanded for doing something off the books. Either

Bonded Blood

way, she had to push it aside. She trusted Sharon and had seen first-hand what she was capable of. She would just have to trust her with this as well.

The few miles from Sharon's to her mom's showed the stark contrast in the socioeconomics of the area. Her mom only lived about four or five miles from Sharon's. The houses were much closer together and significantly smaller the closer she got to her old neighborhood. She knew a lot of these people worked at the local factories, most somehow related to chicken farming. There was the actual chicken factory where they processed the chickens to the mill where the company produced the feed for their farmers. There were competing companies as well, which made the job market for factory work pretty broad.

Raelynn hated the smells by the factories, as did most people who grew up here. But she never wanted to move away like many of her classmates always talked about. Many didn't end up leaving, but that was always the talk in high school. Finding a job outside of their hometown and away from the smelly plants was the goal. Her dad used to say that was the smell of money.

Raelynn's dad worked at one of the plants when he disappeared. There was never anything in the news about his case, which led everyone in the neighborhood to believe he left on his own and there was no foul play. Even at her young age then, Raelynn knew there was more to it than that. Honesty worked at a different plant in the front office before she had to take on more jobs to make ends meet for her and her kids.

When she pulled up along the street in front of her mom's house, Raelynn sighed. The dark color with bright contrasts of the white shutters and yellow door showed

Honesty's strength and defiance. She was determined not to sink into depression after her husband disappeared. Raelynn remembered when they had the house painted the deep red. Her mom said it was always her favorite color, and she wanted the world to know she was ok. She said the white shutters were for her girls' innocence and the yellow door was the sunshine they brought her every day.

Raelynn always thought it was corny, but it reminded her every time she came home that her mom was the strongest person she knew. Maybe that was her goal after all. She looked around the street and saw that Kiah's car was parked on the small driveway. As she exited her vehicle, she heard her brother's obnoxious hyena laugh coming from the back of the house. He must have Timmy back there with him, she thought.

Instead of heading that way, she went to the front door. Her mind was a little jumbled and she just wanted to see her mom, the only other person on the planet who shared her feelings and would understand. They went through their grief and loss period together and had a bond that was unbreakable. Something she never had with anyone else.

As soon as Raelynn opened the door, she felt at home. Her mom was making her favorite fried chicken, and the smells were like a lifeline for her. The meal she was making was Raelynn's favorite comfort food. Raelynn didn't know how to make it just right yet, something she made a note to talk to her mom about teaching her soon.

Raelynn moved into the kitchen and sat at the small table, noticing once again the difference in this table compared to the one that she left just a few minutes ago. She wasn't jealous, she loved the closeness of her family and being that close to someone for meals made the relationships better too, she thought. They had to work together as a team more times than not growing up, which resulted in some fights and arguments, but it was soon discovered that if the problem wasn't worked out, things wouldn't get done.

She watched her mom in silence, wondering for the millionth time what it would be like to have her dad here right now. She remembered the two of them dancing in the kitchen and her mom getting mad because she was trying to get dinner done and he wouldn't let her. The memory made her smile.

"Oh, Rae. I didn't hear you come in," her mom said, turning toward her daughter, wiping her hands on her apron. Her mom looked a little closer and her brow lifted in concern. "Is everything ok, sweetie?"

Raelynn nodded. "Yep. Just glad you picked this for dinner tonight. It's my favorite, but you already knew that."

Honesty just nodded and smiled. "I think Sahara, Ki, and Jericho are tiring out your pup for you." She tossed her thumb over her shoulder at the window.

Raelynn stood and moved closer to see what her mom was talking about. Sure enough, the three of them were outside running around. Timmy was sitting in one spot watching them. If she didn't know better, she would say he looked bored. Jericho was trying to get him to play fetch, which was comical to watch. Jericho would throw the ball, and Timmy would watch it and then sit there until Jericho went to pick it up and try again.

"I think the only one getting tired is Jericho," she laughed and pointed out the window, drawing Honesty's attention to the group outside.

Shaking her head and chuckling, Honesty turned back to the stovetop. "Well, dinner should be ready soon. What have you been up to, Raelynn?" she asked, turning the burners down and stirring something in her pot before she turned back to her daughter.

Raelynn shrugged. "Not much really." She knew what her mom was asking, but she didn't have anything new to tell—except the additional turtles and cryptic notes. Oh, and Creepy Guy. She let out a small shudder as she remembered what happened after work just a few hours ago. Her mom didn't need to know all that. She would just worry. And with Sharon on board now, maybe she would be able to find out what everything means.

A sigh escaped her lips and Honesty didn't miss it.

"Sit down, Rae," her mom instructed.

Raelynn obeyed and sat across from her mom at the small table. She folded her hands tightly together and waited for a lecture. When Honesty didn't say anything, Raelynn looked up.

"What's wrong," she asked her mom. The concern and worry on her mom's face hadn't been there for a long time. It scared her more than she cared to admit as she watched her mom carefully. *Something isn't right*, she thought.

Honesty cleared her throat and dropped her eyes. "I wanted to talk to you about something Rae. I need you to keep an open mind and listen, ok?"

When Honesty looked up again, Raelynn met her mom's eyes and raised her eyebrows. "What's going on, mom? You're kinda scaring me."

Her mom waved her hand in the air, dismissing her concern, but it didn't do anything for Raelynn's nerves. "Just tell me, mom," she insisted.

"Ok, but promise me you will keep an open mind." She gave Raelynn that mom look she was so familiar with growing up. This wasn't negotiable and Raelynn would have to accept it for what it was, whatever *it* was.

Raelynn let out a frustrated sigh and gave her mom a slight nod.

"Out loud, Rae," Honesty insisted.

"Ugh, fine! I will accept it for what it is," she mumbled. Maybe it was childish, but she crossed her fingers under the table as well as her ankles. There was no way she would let go of anything to do with her dad if that was what Honesty wanted her to do. She was not giving up on him.

Honesty gave her a smirk and then stood from her chair and moved to the fridge. She turned when she reached the door and looked at Raelynn one more time.

"So, your sister and I decided that this year you didn't get to choose whether you had a birthday party or not. We are just having one." She proceeded to open the fridge and pulled out a chocolate cake with strawberries on top, also covered in chocolate. She brought the cake to the table and set it in front of Raelynn's shocked face.

"What?" was all she could get out of her mouth.

"Now I know tomorrow is your birthday, but I also know you wanted to do something on your own for that day. So, we decided to celebrate tonight. Sahara handled everything and in about an hour, your friends will be here to help you celebrate with a long overdue birthday party." Honesty stood up after she set the cake down and put her hands on her hips. A satisfied look crossed her face, and she smirked at her daughter, who was still tongue-tied.

"So, you planned all this. And then took my dog to get me to come over for a party?" Raelynn finally asked when she found her voice again.

Her mom shook her head. "Nope, that was your sister. She figured you wouldn't come if you didn't have a reason or if you knew what she was planning. She wanted to have a surprise party, but we both knew that would likely have ended badly for all of us," Honesty laughed.

Raelynn just shook her head and smiled. She tried to be mad, but she was actually glad her sister had done it, especially without her knowledge because her mom was right. She wouldn't have wanted it. Now that she was here and her mom made her favorite dinner, which she understood now, she wasn't going to go anywhere.

A door slamming brought both of their attention to the back door, where Sahara was standing, looking sheepishly at her big sister.

"Are you mad, Rae?" she asked quietly.

Raelynn shook her head and went to hug her sister. "No 'Sha. Thanks for this. I didn't know how much I needed it until now." She held her sister tightly against her and felt the tension leave her sister's body. *She must have been really worried*, she thought.

"But I do have to know who you invited, little sister," she said with a smile.

Sahara stepped back and twisted her hands together. "Um, I kinda went through your phone to get numbers," she said quietly.

Bonded Blood

Raelynn laughed. "Well, good thing I don't have my secret contacts in there!" She pulled her sister in for another hug. Then she thought of something. "Hey, did Ki manage to get Ashley here too like they did for Beau's birthday?"

"No, but she is going to FaceTime later. So, you're really not mad?" Sahara's face still held worry, but Raelynn just shook her head.

"Thank you. I never wanted a party because it always felt incomplete. But now I see that I was missing everything right in front of me. I love you, sis." She gave her sister one more hug and then moved to the stove to help Honesty with finishing dinner.

Soon after, they sat down for dinner. A knock at the door sounded almost immediately after they all sat. Honesty looked up and gave Raelynn a nod to answer it. She had the easiest access since everyone was crowded around the small table.

She hurried to the door and opened it to see Beau standing there. "Hey, I heard it was someone's birthday," he said with a smile.

"Not technically, but we'll count it," she grinned back. His confused look made her laugh. "It's tomorrow actually."

Beau nodded and they made their way into the kitchen. The dinner was relaxed and loud, just the way it was supposed to be, she thought. Her dog lay on the floor in the living room, having given up trying to get closer to anyone in the cramped space. Almost as soon as dinner was finished, there was another knock on the door. Raelynn moved to open it and was greeted by her friends' happy and excited faces.

"You would think we are in grade school again," she said with a laugh.

"Hey! We never got to have a birthday party for you, Rae! This is like the first time for most of us," her friend Fushia said, pushing a brightly colored package into her hands.

Four more guests showed up and then they moved to the backyard. Raelynn hadn't seen the backyard since she came, except when she watched Jericho play fetch with himself. As she walked outside, she noticed her sister had strung twinkling lights on the low-lying branches of the trees, creating a softly lit perimeter where below was a circle of chairs around a portable firepit. They had also set up a folding table where Sahara and Kiah were setting out supplies for smores and the cake from earlier.

Beau came up behind her and she looked up. "I still can't believe they did all this," she said quietly.

"It is kind of cool, isn't it? Kiah has been talking about it nonstop for like a week, and then swearing me to secrecy," he said, rolling his eyes. He looked back at her and asked, "Why don't you like to celebrate your birthday?"

Raelynn turned toward him and shrugged. "I always felt like I was missing something. But I see now that I have been neglecting what is right in front of me for what, or maybe who, isn't here. It's not fair to everyone else actually, especially my mom. I guess I have been selfish." Raelynn suddenly felt bad.

Her sister had been bugging her for years to have a birthday party. Not even a week ago she told her sister she could plan a party for her someday. She didn't realize her sister took it to heart at that time and started planning.

"Come on, Rae! Let's cut the cake!" her sister yelled from across the yard. Sahara was standing next to the card table with a knife in her hand, waving it toward her sister. Kiah grabbed a hold of her wrist and took the knife from her hand, earning an annoyed "Hey!" from Sahara.

Raelynn turned toward the group and then grabbed Beau's hand instinctively and led him to the table where her sister and his brother were waiting.

Chapter 19

Raelynn sat between Beau and Serenity staring at the flames in the fire pit. It was dark outside, and the chill was muted only by the heat from the fire. Sahara and Kiah had left a little while ago to go to a movie or something on campus. Three other friends, Jazzy, Valaria, and Fushia had left as well.

"So, I was thinking we could talk, Rae," Serenity's soft voice broke the silence surrounding them.

Raelynn looked over at her friend and nodded. "Sure, Reni. Is everything ok with you?"

Serenity sighed. "I think so. I'm sorry about before. I, well, I don't really know how to explain it. Give me a little time and I will try. But I wanted to talk to you about the other stuff. The art question you had about the turtles." Half of her face was lost in the shadows and only the light from the flames lit up the side Raelynn was sitting on.

Suddenly Raelynn remembered she was supposed to meet with Sharon again. "Oh my god," she exclaimed. "I gotta make a call quick."

She got up and moved away from the other two. Raelynn quickly dialed Sharon's number and held her breath. She hoped Sharon wasn't upset with her. She just completely forgot with everything else going on.

Bonded Blood

"Hello?" the voice on the other end of the line said.

"Hi Miss Sharon. I am so sorry, I got caught up with my family and forgot about meeting again. Can we do it tomorrow?" Raelynn rushed her words out, hoping it was ok. She knew all too well that the older generation didn't like being disrespected when it came to not following through with commitments.

Sharon chuckled on the other end. "Oh no worries, dear. Enjoy your birthday celebration. Call or text me in the morning and we can meet right away. Gary is going somewhere with his work friends, so we have the house to ourselves." She paused for a second and then added, "and feel free to bring your friends. They may be able to add to our information. See you tomorrow, dear."

The line went dead after Sharon spoke those words, leaving Raelynn staring at her phone. So many questions popped into her head as she tried to process what the older woman had said. How did she know they were celebrating her birthday and on top of that, how did she know Beau and Serenity were helping her with the other stuff?

Raelynn shook her head. There was time to figure that out later. Right now, since Sharon wasn't upset, she wanted to talk to Serenity some more. She turned back to the fire and as she was about to move in their direction, her mom's voice stopped her.

"Hey, Rae," she called softly. "Can you come here for a second?" She had a funny grin on her face and Raelynn wondered if they had something else up their sleeves.

She glanced at her friends still by the fire. Satisfied that they were comfortable with each other for a few more minutes, she followed her mom inside and through the kitchen. She stopped in her tracks at the entrance to the living room. In front of her sprawled out on the floor was her little brother and dog cuddled up in blankets. She tried not to laugh and wake them up.

"Why don't you leave Timmy here tonight?" her mom suggested. "Sahara grabbed more food than I think we need for a week and Jericho will love the company. I have to work in the morning but should be back by lunch time."

Raelynn nodded. "Ok, I can do that, but only if you are sure. I can write down what he needs with times and all that for Jericho. Giving him a little responsibility might be good."

She took one more look at the two on the floor and then shook her head. Who would have thought they would have bonded so quickly. Jericho may not help out around the house much, or at least it's a work in progress, but having him take care of Timmy would help with a little bit of responsibility. And who better to work with for the first time than this lazy and easy-going dog?

"I'm going to go to bed. Stay as long as you want, Rae. Just make sure the fire is out before you go. It's mostly contained in that thing, but I don't want to take any chances." Honesty said and then headed for the bathroom.

Raelynn stopped in the kitchen and found a paper and pen and wrote down Timmy's schedule for her brother. After reading it over a few times to make sure it was clear, she stuck it on the fridge with a magnet. She heard the bathroom door open, and she called out to her mom to let her know where her list was located. After getting an acknowledgement and goodnight from her mom, she headed back outside.

As she walked down the steps to the yard, she saw Serenity and Beau leaning close together talking quietly about something. She felt an unexpected pang of jealousy seeing them so close but brushed it aside. They were just friends after all, and Beau hadn't said he wanted anything more than that. Then again, neither had she. The feeling surprised her.

She decided to sit in the now vacant chair where Serenity had been sitting when she left. As she sat down, both looked over at her. Serenity stood up quickly.

"Sorry, Rae. You can have your chair back," she said hurriedly.

Raelynn waved her hand. "No, it's ok. You can sit. What were you guys talking about, or is it private?" she asked, looking between them.

"Not private, but maybe we should go back to your place to talk about it," Beau volunteered. "Is that ok?" He looked between both girls, waiting for an answer.

"It's fine with me. Reni?" Raelynn asked, her eyebrow raised. "I mean you are going that way anyways, right?"

Serenity shrugged. "Sure. What about your dog?" She looked around nervously.

"He's staying with my brother," Raelynn said with a laugh. "We just need to put the fire out and then we can go."

It was already starting to fade anyway, so instead of adding anything to it, they could put it out. Raelynn grabbed the bucket of water that was sitting nearby and slowly poured it over the top, trying to make sure none of the ash was blown around. Then Beau took the small bowl of sand and did the same thing. They waited a few minutes and then Raelynn mixed it up to make sure the coals were all smothered.

Satisfied, she nodded. "Ok, Let's go."

"I am going to stop at my place before I come down to yours, ok, Rae? I have to grab some stuff." Serenity said as they climbed into their vehicles.

Raelynn nodded and waved and then waited for Beau to get into his car. It seemed funny to her that they were driving three cars to her apartment, but they all needed to get home somehow, she thought. She made sure Beau was behind her, not that he needed directions, but she wanted to make sure he was ready and not stuck or anything.

The drive back to her apartment was weird. Her thoughts were jumbled with Sharon's knowledge about her party, her friends helping her, and the closeness Beau and Serenity seemed to share. Maybe that was what spooked her friend before? She decided she couldn't worry about everything and had to pick and choose. Raelynn decided the art was the most important thing to focus on at that moment. The rest would fall into whatever place it was supposed to.

She parked further away from the front door than normal so she could walk in with Beau. The last run in made her a little nervous to be back here if she was completely honest with herself. At least if Creepy Guy showed up again, she wouldn't be alone in the dark. She thought again about the familiarity of his eyes, frustrated that she couldn't place where she would have seen them before.

A knock on her window made her jump. She stifled the scream, which she was thankful for when she saw Beau standing outside her door.

Bonded Blood

"Sorry, Rae!" he said quickly. "I didn't mean to frighten you. I thought you knew I was there."

Raelynn tried to calm her heartbeat and got out of her car. "No worries, just lost in my thoughts is all. Come on." She led the way to the front, this time resisting the urge to grab his hand.

She looked around as they walked, looking for anything in the shadows. Beau must have noticed, because he sped up and walked right next to her.

"Rae?" he asked slowly. "Is everything ok? Did something happen that you didn't tell me?" Even though it was dark, and she couldn't see him very well, she knew his forehead was probably wrinkled with concern.

Raelynn just nodded and continued to move to the front door. Beau just stayed alongside her, and she appreciated his presence. It amazed her how quickly they had gotten to know things about each other, making her feel like they could be more than friends. But now with Serenity, she was worried about hurting her feelings if she pursued Beau.

Once they were safely inside her apartment, she sighed and looked around. It was weird not having Timmy with her. There wasn't anything out of the ordinary, it was just strange.

"So, are you going to tell me what happened that had you all freaked out outside?" Beau asked.

And there was the wrinkle in his forehead, she thought and almost laughed at her prediction.

Raelynn shook her head. "It was nothing really." She tried to sound convincing but then the box that Creepy Guy had given her earlier lay on the floor next to the table, where the latest treasure was sitting.

Beau followed her eyes. Raelynn saw them widen when they landed on the newest addition.

"When did you get this one?" he asked as he moved into the living room. When she didn't answer, he turned to look at her. "Rae?"

Letting out a sigh, she took her shoes off and moved around him to sit on the couch. "Creepy Guy gave it to me today after work." Her voice was quiet while she waited for him to digest that information.

"'Creepy Guy' as in the guy that's been stalking you at work?" Beau asked, sitting next to her. "Do you think it's the same person who left the box on your chair the other morning too?"

She looked up to meet his worried eyes. "I guess so," she said with resignation. If he knew where she lived, then she may be in more danger than she thought. She leaned back against the cushions and closed her eyes. These past few days have felt like months.

"Ok, that's it, I'm staying here, Rae. I would never forgive myself if something happened to you. And without your dog here tonight, I just think it will be best." Beau stood and started pacing as he talked.

Raelynn watched him with humor. "Do I even have a say in this? And besides, my dog is hardly a deterrent. He's the laziest being on earth and doesn't care if a stranger comes in. That's not enough of a reason for you to have to stay here, Beau." She was only half trying to convince herself of this as well as him.

She was a little scared, she hated to admit. But it seemed a little far-fetched that this guy was stalking her only to make contact once and then disappear. Well until the next day anyway. It suddenly occurred to her that she only ever saw him once a day. Aside from looking creepy, he never actually did or said anything threatening. If he wanted to hurt her, he'd had many opportunities already, didn't he?

With a resigned sigh, she closed her eyes and tried to focus. Would it make her feel better to have someone here with her? Absolutely. But should she really do that to Beau? Especially if he and Serenity were interested in each other? That wouldn't look good. Knowing her friend's trust issues with men, she would have to tread carefully.

"Honestly, Beau, I will be fine," she opened her eyes again and turned to look at him. Raelynn was surprised to see him studying her. She lifted her chin. "Seriously, don't look so worried. I'm fine. The security here is great."

Beau shook his head. "Rae, you live on the ground floor. Do you know how easy it is to break into a sliding glass door?" he asked. Then he added, "And I bet if your dog sensed danger, he would surprise you with his reaction. Plus, his size alone would make most people back away."

A knock interrupted their conversation. Knowing it was Serenity, Raelynn just called out for her to come in. Beau looked at her in shock.

"You didn't lock the door?" he asked incredulously. "Seriously, Rae!" He dropped his hands dramatically on his knees.

She couldn't help the giggle that escaped at his over-the-top concern, earning her a glare. She shrugged it off as Serenity came into the room.

Raelynn noticed her friend carrying two bags that were stuffed full of items plus she had a stack of books and papers in her hands. She jumped up to help her carry everything and stacked what she had on the table.

"Wow, what have you been up to the last twenty-four hours, Reni!" Raelynn asked as she looked at the overflowing table. Thankfully Beau had moved the newest creature before they set everything down. She stood with her arms crossed, not sure what she was looking at or where to start.

Serenity laughed. "I know. After I calmed down yesterday, I did some digging. I already told Beau some of this tonight while you were inside, but I thought it might be even better to just show you."

She sat down on the couch next to Beau while Raelynn sat across from them on the floor. Raelynn pulled her knees to her chest and wrapped her arms around them. "I can't wait to see what you found," she said, avoiding the couple in front of her.

"Ok, so after I left, I started to think about some things," Serenity began. "There's something I need to tell you, but let's do this first." She motioned at the overflowing tabletop and then met Raelynn's eyes that were now focused on hers.

Serenity cleared her throat and looked down again. "So, when I was a junior, I was really into art. Rae, you know this obviously." She turned to Beau as if to tell him she was saying this for his benefit. She looked back at Raelynn and continued. "My teacher started to ask me questions about my art and wanted to know if I was interested in pursuing it. I knew it wouldn't pay what I needed to make since things were still rocky at home. My dad was gone a lot more, I guess he got a job as a truck driver my mom said. He would be gone for sometimes a week at a time, but when he came back, my parents would argue about his check not being enough or whatever."

Raelynn watched her friend close her eyes tight and shifted her eyes over to Beau, watching to see if he would comfort her at all. It might give her a clue as to their budding interest in each other she thought. When he didn't move toward Serenity, Raelynn made a slight move of her head, and when he nodded and moved over, she knew he understood. Her friend needed her.

Moving to the couch, Raelynn found herself between her best friend and Beau, unsure what she felt at the moment. She grabbed her friend's hand and gave it a squeeze.

Serenity opened her eyes and gave Raelynn a small smile. "I never told you about my parents and their fights, Rae. When Griff moved, I was lost. I would come to hang out with you to get away and feel like things were normal again. My dad would be gone more than he was home. So, I lost myself in my art." She shrugged and straightened her back, seemingly steeling herself to the pain of the past.

"So, I told my teacher, sure why not? He started taking me to different galleries around town. He thought it was because I wanted to pursue art as a career, but it was really just to get away from my house. I think we went to all of the galleries in town and then even some in Berlin and Ocean City." Serenity paused and made eye contact with Raelynn again.

Waiting patiently for her to continue, Raelynn gave her friend's hand another squeeze. She was starting to get the idea that she had neglected her friendship with Serenity over the last few years. She was becoming aware of what she had missed being consumed with her own loss growing up. These were things that Serenity kept from her best friend, and Raelynn couldn't help but blame herself for not being a better friend.

"Reni, I'm sorry I wasn't there for you. You could have told me anything. We used to share everything, and I feel like I failed you," Raelynn said sincerely.

Serenity patted her hand and shook her head. "No, I kept this from you intentionally. You had a lot going on too, trying to help your mom make ends meet and take care of your brother and sister. Don't feel guilty, ok?"

"I will still feel guilty, Reni, but please tell me Mr. Davis didn't do anything…inappropriate," she said with her eyes full of worry and fear for someone else preying on her best friend.

"No, nothing like that, Rae," she said shaking her head. "He was more like a counselor to me. He listened and helped me to focus on something else and even encouraged me to apply to art school. I actually did, and surprisingly got in, but I knew there was no way I could go. I had to stay and help my mom keep a roof over our heads. My brothers helped too, but my dad actually left us with a heap of debt that was nearly insurmountable." Serenity's eyes became thoughtful for a brief moment as she added, "And then one day it all just went away. The debt, the stress, all of it disappeared. And my mom was happy again. I don't know what happened, but it was weird. By then I was already starting my first year at community college and just decided art was my past."

The trio sat in silence, each lost in their own thoughts. Raelynn tried to think back to that time and why she didn't know all that was happening with her friend. She would have done anything for Serenity. Her mom was like a second mother to Raelynn and her siblings. She was sure her own mother would have helped as well, even with as little as they had. The guilt of failing her best friend was starting to send her thoughts reeling.

Beau was the first to break the silence. "So, is this connected to our art? Did you recognize the same style or something?"

Serenity giggled. "Oops, sorry. Yes, that's where I was going! So, I actually pulled all my old art boxes out last night. I don't think I slept at all, and it was a good thing I didn't work an opening shift today. Since I just moved in, I have a ton of boxes that need to be sorted through, so I just started looking for my art ones. I found the old programs and brochures from different galleries and studios." She motioned to the pile in front of her and then laughed. "I couldn't decide what to bring so I kind of brought it all."

Raelynn's eyes widened. "Holy cow! This is a lot, Reni. Where do we even start?" She picked up a paper that advertised a revolutionary war exhibit.

"Well, I found some of what I was looking for. Most of this I brought just in case." She picked up one of the bags by her side and pulled out a small brochure. She turned it to face Raelynn.

"Last night I got a little freaked out because I remembered this one display we saw. It was a new artist and a new kind of art. These little guys reminded me of it, and I got kind of excited—but scared at the same time. I guess my teacher knew the artist, so he was excited to take me to the exhibit back then. The guy was a little weird and made me uncomfortable. Well, you know my history, and so you can guess." Serenity waved her hand around trying to dispel the discomfort she was remembering.

Squinting, Raelynn took the paper from Serenity and read out loud, "'Amateur artist displays first of its kind in Salisbury this weekend'. Ok, weird," she said with a wrinkle of her nose. She turned it over and saw a photo of what looked like a pile of trash. Her eyes met Serenity's. "What am I looking at, Ren?"

Serenity giggled. "It was a new type of art that uses trash as the sculpting material." She paused and looked from Raelynn to Beau. When neither of them seemed to understand, she sighed and moved to grab one of the turtles off the shelf.

Raelynn followed her movement with intrigue, still not fully understanding. Beau seemed to be doing the same thing.

When she sat back down, Serenity held up the turtle made from what looked like pieces of sheet metal bent in different ways. "Don't you see it?" Like a kindergarten teacher asking her class a question, Serenity waited.

With still no connection, she huffed. "Ok, come on, guys! This little guy is made from scraps of metal." She took the paper from Raelynn's hand and held it up next to the turtle. "This is a sculpture made of random things, and I guarantee there are pieces of metal in that pile."

"But metal isn't exactly trash, Reni," Raelynn said, studying the two things. "I mean I guess it could be, but—"

"Look!" Serenity interrupted. "That one is made of plastic pieces. That one is made of a different kind of metal. Do you really not see what I see?"

Raelynn looked from her friend to the collection of new turtles. *Maybe this is the connection we need to at least get started*, she thought. "Ok, I can see there is something there. Can we clear this off and put the turtles in front of us so we can see them together? Do you have anything else from the artist, Reni?"

Bonded Blood

The three of them started to clear the table off, setting most of the papers underneath it. Once it was clean, Raelynn grabbed the new turtles from the shelf. Like an assembly line, the three set the statues in a line one by one. When the last one was set down, Raelynn stared at them.

The longer she looked at them, the more she started to believe Serenity was on to something. But there was still something not right. "Reni, these all seem to be made from only one thing. Like this one is only the thinner metal while this one is the heavier one." She picked up the seashell one. "And this is only shells. Is that the same thing?"

Serenity bit her lip. "I'm not sure. I mean maybe each one has a theme or something," she suggested.

Beau, who was quiet the entire time, finally spoke up. "Maybe they are all a collection just made of different things."

Raelynn leaned back on her knees. "What do you mean? Like these are all things found in a certain spot and the artist just used one material for each? Does that mean they might all be connected too?" She looked down at each one and shook her head. "I guess, but it still doesn't make a lot of sense to me." She picked up one of the first ones she got, the one with the weird bowl. "I mean I can see how this one is just a junk statue, but the rest…" her voice trailed off as she tried to make sense of it.

"Well, I was thinking I could reach out to the head of the gallery and ask about the style. Maybe he knows who the amateur artist was then and that could help us with a place to start. At least we could ask questions that could lead us to something more meaningful." Serenity looked between them.

With a sigh and a nod, Raelynn agreed. She wasn't sure where to start either, if she was honest with herself. This was as good a place as any.

She clapped her hands together and stood up. "Ok, so where do we start?" Raelynn asked.

"Well, I have to work early tomorrow but should be off by three. I can call the gallery owner and ask some questions on my break and maybe go talk to him after work," Serenity volunteered.

Raelynn nodded. "I don't work at all tomorrow, but I need to meet with Sharon at some point. Maybe you can see what you can find out and then we can talk later tomorrow." She was distracted but felt like they at least finally had a direction to start looking instead of just sitting and spinning with nothing but a few statues.

"I don't work either, so I can help out too," Beau said, looking at Raelynn intently.

Serenity suddenly yawned making them all look at her and laugh. "I guess it is getting kinda late," she said sheepishly. "I'll text you tomorrow, Rae."

Raelynn nodded and stood to meet her friend. "I will let you know where I am at then too. I'm sorry about missing all this when we were younger, Reni," she whispered as she gave her a hug.

"It's all good, Rae. Don't worry about it. I kept it from you, you didn't do anything wrong." She looked around Raelynn and waved to Beau, who gave a small wave back. "See you tomorrow."

Raelynn closed and locked the door behind Serenity and then sat on the floor across from Beau again.

"What's wrong?" he asked.

Bonded Blood

"What do you mean?" she asked back confused.

Beau sighed and then leaned forward, resting his elbows on his knees. "You are sitting all the way over there and look a little lost."

"I guess it's just that even though we have a lead, we don't really have anything either. I don't know if I would even call it a lead. It's just a starting point," she said, deflecting her distance from him to the mystery surrounding her.

"Ok, but we have to start somewhere. Maybe this artist is still around and will lead us somewhere meaningful. And you said you are meeting with Sharon tomorrow, right?" When she nodded her confirmation, he continued, "Is this the same Sharon who helped my mom and uncle last summer?"

Again nodding, Raelynn looked up at him, waiting for him to respond.

Beau face lit up with a slightly mischievous grin. "Well then I'd say things are about to get really interesting." He thought for a minute and then added, "And I am not going anywhere tonight either."

Chapter 20

By the time Raelynn went to bed, it was well past two in the morning. True to his word, Beau slept on the couch and was a perfect gentleman. When she thought about it, she realized that it might be because of his and Serenity's interest in each other. She decided she just needed to be ok with it because she had enough going on anyway.

She stretched and was surprised at the room she had in her bed. Then she remembered Timmy wasn't there. Raelynn picked up her phone and was shocked to see it was only seven. She didn't have any messages so she thought she might try to go back to sleep. But the realization of what today might bring made her give up on that thought and take a shower instead.

The events of the last week flooded her mind as she stood under the warm stream of water. Raelynn would be lying if she said she wasn't a little bit nervous and excited for today. Realistically she knew there wasn't much that would happen today, but the idea of finally getting some answers made her feel a little giddy.

Raelynn had to admit that she agreed with Beau's comment the night before. She was able to witness Sharon and his uncle working side by side last summer and it was amazing what they had done and in a short amount of time too. It was like watching one of her crime shows on TV.

She made quick work of her morning routine thinking she should be a good host and make breakfast for her guest. Pulling her long brown, almost straight hair up in a messy bun on her head, she shrugged on a hoodie and her favorite comfortable jeans and headed out to the kitchen.

The moment she opened the door, she froze. The smell of bacon permeated the entire apartment. Raelynn slowly approached the kitchen and saw Beau standing over the stovetop flipping the bacon like a pro. She leaned against the doorframe and watched for a minute before he caught her.

"Hey!" he said. "Happy birthday, Rae." He came over and handed her a piece of crispy bacon. "Unfortunately, this is all I know how to cook," he said with a smile. "But I figured we could work together to make pancakes or something."

Raelynn laughed. "Thank you, and I actually am not much better. But I do have a solution." She moved around him, snatching the bacon from his hand with a grin.

She reached into her freezer and pulled out a box of frozen waffles and held them up. Shaking it she said, "I am not a good cook either. But this will work. Oh! I can make eggs. I must warn you though. Nothing fancy. Scrambled is as fancy I get, and actually your only option."

Beau laughed with her. "Perfect. I'm good with that."

He took the bacon pan off the stove and put the meat on a plate. Then he moved to the toaster and started the waffles. Raelynn got busy making the eggs. They were quiet as they tended to their chores.

When everything was ready, they moved their plates to the table in the living room and Raelynn went back to grab a couple of glasses of juice.

"Sorry, I'm not much of a cook. I guess that speaks to my experience with house guests, huh?" she said with a sheepish grin.

Beau shook his head. "No, I should have taken over anyway. It's your birthday after all and you allowed me to stay here. Of course, that was for your own protection and everything." He paused for a split second and then added, "So, maybe you *are* right. You should cook for me. Forget what I said before." He waved his hand and chuckled.

"Well technically you didn't protect me from anything, so I really don't owe you anything. So, since you used my blankets and now I have extra laundry to do, you *should* have cooked breakfast. Or at least have gotten something better delivered since it is my birthday and all." Raelynn tried to sound serious, but she couldn't do it.

She let out a laugh and Beau just looked at her with raised eyebrows, still attempting to be serious. "Actually, the best protection is one you don't need. See, me just being here, with my intimidating ninja physique scared off any potential threats. So, since you didn't see anyone try anything is testament to my protector prowess." He put his hand on his chest and looked off as if he were some sort of superhero.

Raelynn picked up the pillow he had slept on the night before and threw it, hitting him square in the face. He gave her a shocked expression as she dissolved into a fit of giggles.

"I can't believe you just did that! You are incredibly ungrateful, Raelynn. I'm actually—ooff!" His voice was muffled again by a second pillow.

Raelynn's laughter increased as she rolled on the couch. She didn't see Beau get up and grab two pillows of his own and move to stand over her. When she opened her eyes, they widened, and she put her hands in front of her face. She felt the first pillow and her laughter was muffled but didn't subside. When the second pillow came, she sat up again, thinking his attempt was done. But when she opened her eyes, a third hit her right in the face.

"Hey!" she shouted. "Cheap shot."

"Oh right. You started it, you know," Beaus said with a laugh.

Raelynn shrugged. "You deserved it. And now my breakfast is cold." She crossed her arms over her chest and pouted at him.

Beau raised her eyebrow and grinned wickedly. "Want me to try again?"

Just then Raelynn's phone alerted her to a text message. "Saved by the bell, meanie," she said to him. "I will get even though," she whispered, making him laugh.

She picked up her phone to see a text from Sharon asking if she would be able to come over soon. She had something to discuss with Raelynn right away.

Lifting her eyes to meet Beau's, all playfulness disappeared. "Sharon wants to see me as soon as possible," she said with a worried expression.

"Ok, let's finish up and we can go," he said seriously. "Tell her you can be there in about thirty minutes if that's ok."

Raelynn nodded and sent the message. She sat frozen for a minute as she thought about what could be so important that she needed to go so early. It wasn't even eight yet.

Beau moved to sit next to her on the couch and took her hand in his. "Hey, this is good, Rae. You are finally going to get some answers. It's going to be ok. Come on, eat something and then we can go."

Raelynn nodded absently as she stared at her phone. *Was this good news or worse than what she already knew?* she thought. Shaking her head she pushed the thoughts aside. Beau was right. She needed to eat and then get going.

Thinking of Beau, she typed out another text to Sharon asking if it was ok that he came along with her. Since she wasn't sure what kind of news Sharon had, she wanted to have support there, someone who knew everything to this point.

She glanced up and gave Beau a smile. "Ok, let's eat and then go. I'm nervous though," she admitted. "What if it's bad?"

"I don't know, Rae, but whatever it is, it's better than nothing—which is what we have right now. Right?" he asked gently.

Raelynn sighed. "I guess so."

They finished eating in silence and then cleaned up. Raelynn had a new, unused toothbrush she had kept in case Sahara stayed over so after Beau was able to shower and freshen up as well, they headed out the door. They decided to only take Raelynn's car this time because he said he wasn't leaving until he felt like she was safe.

The drive to Sharon's was quiet, both lost in their own thoughts. Raelynn was fidgety and wished she wasn't driving. She turned the radio on to try to settle her nerves but couldn't find anything to listen to. Beau seemed to notice and took hold of her hand and turned on some oldies station that neither of them knew.

"What are we listening to?" she asked him, looking over.

Beau was smirking at her and just shrugged. "I figure this way we can agree on what *not* to listen to. Besides, you couldn't find anything anyway."

"Fair enough," she grumbled, listening to the annoyingly high-pitched guitar. She cringed and looked at him again. "Can you find something else? I never understood the appeal of this sound."

Beau laughed. "I know. My dad is a huge eighties electric guitar fan." He gave an exaggerated shudder as he turned the station. "What do you like? Country like everyone else around here?"

"I don't really care honestly. I listen to just about anything." She gave him a pointed look and added, "Except *this*."

As she pulled into Sharon's driveway, Raelynn smiled seeing her outside already watering her flowers and picking at the dead ends.

"Still trying to hold on, huh, Sharon?" she joked, getting out of the car.

Sharon waved and laughed as she walked over to the couple. "Well, what else would I do with all my time? Come on inside. Good morning, Beau. Gary just left so we can go inside and chat."

He gave her a smile and nodded his head as they followed her into the house. Sharon went to the stovetop while she waved the other two toward the table. Beau and Raelynn sat next to each other on one side. Sharon carried a pot of coffee and three mugs on a tray and set it in between them all.

"Ok," she said as she sat down. Raelynn noticed she had grabbed a folder at some point in her trip from the stovetop to the table. Sharon slid the file toward Raelynn and tapped the top. "I am not sure what you know about your father's disappearance, but I'm going to guess this is new."

Raelynn suddenly felt like crying. Sharon hadn't said her dad ran off, but just that he'd disappeared like Raelynn had been saying all these years. Maybe Sharon didn't believe he left on his own either. She didn't say *when* he left, so Raelynn kept her hopes up that maybe she was right.

"I want to warn you though, Raelynn. The stuff in this file is very disturbing and may be hard to see. But it is important for you to know as much as possible if we are going to figure everything else out, ok?" Sharon reached out and put her hand on top of Raelynn's to offer her encouragement. "Are you ready?" she asked, her voice soft and gentle, her eyes watching Raelynn's carefully.

Raelynn nodded and moved her hand to open it. Inside she found multiple pieces of paper that were obviously photocopied. The first few pages were some names and locations, but nothing that meant anything to Raelynn. She put them aside, after scanning for her dad's name and not finding it.

The next pages were horrific pictures of different people who had clearly been tortured before they died. Raelynn tried to avoid looking at most of them and focused on the backgrounds, noticing that the places were different in all of them, but one stood out. She looked up and saw Sharon watching her closely.

"You recognize this one, Rae?" she asked, her gaze held understanding even though she asked the question, almost as if she expected Raelynn to know.

Raelynn nodded. "That's dad's work, the chicken plant," she said simply, dropping her eyes. She stared at the photo of the mangled body, praying she could see something to prove it wasn't her dad. The man didn't look African American, maybe more Mexican or Hispanic, but the photo was grainy, and she couldn't be sure.

She closed the file and pushed it away from her. "I can't look at this."

"Raelynn, I am not showing this to you to upset you. I want you to know what kind of people we are dealing with." Sharon's voice was firm, but Raelynn still felt the gentleness in it.

Her words drew Raelynn's eyes back to Sharon and she narrowed her eyes slightly. "What do you mean?"

Sharon took a deep breath and opened the folder again, pushing the photos to the back of the pile and turning them upside down. "About seventeen years ago, this group, a spinoff of some mafia-type gang, took over this particular plant. No one would stand up to them and a lot of people died trying to do the right thing and turn them in. The factory continued to run smoothly. They needed it to in order to keep their cover intact. If production waned, someone would take notice. The people who died weren't killed onsite, or it would have raised suspicions. You can only blame so much on 'work accidents.'" She gave a sad smile and made air quotes with her fingers.

"Officer Milton was a night guard at the time and would do some extra hours to help with security and make sure no one was doing anything they weren't supposed to. When he found out what was really going on, they threatened his family and then used it to keep him in line while the gang continued their operations."

Sharon took out the pages that Raelynn had pushed aside at first. She pointed to the names on the list and described each person's role in the operation. Most of it went over Raelynn's head as she tried to digest what she was being told. Did her dad get caught up in their operation or was he one who tried to turn them in? She couldn't believe that he was helping them to do anything illegal. But she also understood that people did desperate things when they were in a bad spot.

She suddenly thought about Creepy Guy and wondered if he was also working for them and was watching her. Maybe her dad was still being threatened and they were now trying to use her somehow. What about her mom and siblings, though? Are they also being used by this gang? Raelynn's thoughts raced around in her head from her life being in danger to her dad being held somewhere and tortured, while they showed him pictures of her and her family. She let out a shiver as she thought about her father being hurt.

Sharon's gentle voice pulled her from her spiraling thoughts, and she looked up to meet the older woman's eyes. "We didn't find your dad's body or any record of him being fired or quitting his job at the plant. One thing we do know about the Del Rios is that they are very loyal, and they could make someone disappear if they wanted to, much like the government's witness protection does for informants. One theory we have is that he was a participant in this gang. We aren't sure if he disappeared on his own or if they made it look like he did so he could continue to work for them."

Raelynn shook her head emphatically. "No. My dad didn't do this, Sharon. He was a good man; he wouldn't have helped them."

Sharon sighed. "I know it's hard to believe it's possible, but Rae—"

"No!" Raelynn stood, slamming her hands on the table. "My dad was not like this." She swung her hand over the file in front of her. "He cared about people. He would not have helped kill anyone. That's preposterous."

Beau reached out and took her hand and gently pulled her back to her chair. "Come on, Rae. Let's listen to what else Sharon has to say." He glanced at the older woman across from him and then back at Raelynn.

After a few minutes, Raelynn reluctantly sat back down. She stared at the table in front of her not sure what was coming next.

"Raelynn, I'm sorry. I didn't mean to assume he was a part of it, but he may have been coerced like Brad was. It is something we have to consider. But all I can tell you definitively is that he was not killed at the plant. The Del Rios keep pretty accurate records of their people and who had crossed them. I am working on getting those documents. But so far, we do not have anything saying your father died at their hands. I am working on some other leads to see where he went when he left for lunch that day and didn't return." Sharon said, closing the file folder.

At this, Raelynn looked up. "You know when he left work? When he failed to return?" When Sharon nodded, she added, "How?"

That information was more than what Raelynn had been able to find out in months of research. Sharon found out in less than twenty-four hours. Hope resurfaced in her heart as she watched Sharon's face soften.

"As you said, I know things. But mostly I know people." She gave Raelynn a smile and patted her hand. "I am going to go meet with a friend for brunch this morning. Why don't you go home and gather up all your *gifts* and notes from the past week and come back around eleven. Does that work for you?"

Raelynn nodded. "Yes, absolutely. Thank you, Sharon. You have no idea how helpful this is." They all stood, and Raelynn made her way around the table to give her a hug.

"Don't worry, Raelynn. We will figure this out. I promise," Sharon said sincerely, as they walked to the door.

Raelynn nodded again. "Wait," she said suddenly turning around as Sharon was about to close the door. "How do you know about the turtles?"

Sharon just smiled and then disappeared into her house again.

Beau chuckled next to her the bewilderment clear on her face. "She's something, isn't she?"

Raelynn grumbled about not getting an answer as they moved to her car and started out of the driveway. "Well, where to then?" she asked as they sat in the running vehicle.

"I don't know. Can your doggo stay with your brother longer?" he asked.

Not having to worry about Timmy might be helpful, she thought. "I'll check. My mom said she was only working a half day today, so maybe it will be ok. I don't know what Jericho has planned either."

As if somehow reading her mind, Raelynn's phone rang in her hand. She shot Beau a knowing look and answered it.

Bonded Blood

"Happy birthday, Rae!" rang out through her car speakers as her mom, sister, and brother all screamed into the phone.

Raelynn laughed. "Thanks guys. While I have you on the phone, can Timmy stay with you longer today? I have some stuff to take care of and it will be easier to not have to worry about him being left alone."

Jericho chimed in first. "I got this, sis! Consider it your birthday gift from your favorite brother."

Honesty laughed and then had to get back to work since they called her in on a conference call and Sahara was getting ready to go somewhere with Kiah.

"Well, that's taken care of," she said, turning to Beau. "Now what?"

"Now we go get your turtles and all the extras and head back. Maybe grab something to eat on the way?" Beau suggested.

They headed back to Raelynn's apartment and started to put all the statues in two of the bigger boxes. Raelynn grabbed all the notes and put them in an envelope. As she put everything together, she looked around.

"I think I have everything. Are you ready?" she asked Beau, who was doing the same thing.

"Yep. I was actually thinking, since we have a little bit until we need to be back at Sharon's, I'm going to run my car back to my place and grab a few things. If you're ok with following me."

Raelynn shrugged. "Are you sure you want to be without your car? I mean I don't mind driving you around, but I don't want you to feel stranded either."

Beau grinned at her. "Are you going to ditch me somewhere, Rae?"

Rolling her eyes, she groaned. "Maybe. But seriously you might get tired of hanging out with me and want to leave. Then what?" Her thoughts drifted to Serenity.

"Why would I get tired of hanging out with you? Heck we still haven't had our date. That was supposed to be yesterday too." He paused and tapped his lips and narrowed his eyes at her. "Are you trying to get rid me, Rae? Too afraid to be alone with me? Or maybe just don't want to be seen with me? That must be it. That's why we are always hiding out in your apartment, isn't it?" he teased, snapping his fingers.

"Pfft, whatever. I have been a little preoccupied lately. And who knows, maybe you have changed your mind," she said, as she glanced over at him. She was startled to see him staring at her.

Beau was quiet for a second and then shook his head. "Nope. I will wait for all this to be over, but we are going on that date, Rae. I wouldn't have asked if I didn't want to go. Nothing has changed in the last week for me to even think about changing my mind."

Raelynn didn't know what to say in response, so she just nodded. They made their way back outside to her car. She headed to the back of the car to put her stuff in the trunk.

"Hey, Beau, bring that back here, please," she called to him.

"Uh, Rae?" His voice came from the front of the car.

She closed her trunk and looked around to see what he needed. He was holding a small box in his hand and his face showed concern and maybe a little fear.

"What is that, Beau?" she asked, her voice shaky.

"I think it's another 'gift' Rae," he said.

They both looked around and didn't see anyone. They were only inside for a few minutes. How could someone have such perfect timing? Now that she had more information about this Del Rios gang, Raelynn couldn't help the lump in her throat or the sick feeling in her stomach. Were they watching her? For the first time in all these years, she was actually scared about finding her dad.

Chapter 21

Raelynn decided to wait to open the new package, dropping it on the backseat until she was with Sharon. She wasn't sure why, but she suddenly felt insecure about her safety and what these turtles could mean. Maybe it was what Sharon had revealed, but she just felt strange and even more like she was being watched. It didn't get past her that tomorrow was Halloween either. All kinds of weird stuff seemed to happen around that time of year and people thought it was funny to scare others. She secretly hoped that's all this was. Or maybe just her imagination going a little crazy.

Unfortunately, she also knew this was wishful thinking. Sharon was taking this seriously and she wouldn't be in on some sick joke, would she?

"Ugh," she groaned as she sat in her driver's seat outside Sharon's house, after dropping off Beau's car.

Beau turned to her. "What's wrong?" he asked. "I mean besides the obvious."

Raelynn chuckled darkly. "Yeah, the obvious. I'm just frustrated. It's like I've been spinning for so long and in just a week, I have all this stuff coming at me and I don't have any way to make sense of it." She turned to face him and tried to smile. "I'm glad you are with me though, Beau. Having a friend by my side is really helpful."

Raising his eyebrows, Beau leaned closer to her. "Is that all I am, Rae? Just a friend?"

Something in his voice made her catch her breath. She didn't know how to answer his question. Until she saw him and Serenity so close the day before, she had started to think about him as more than just a friend. But now, she didn't want to get in the way of her friend's happiness, especially after all Serenity had been through in regard to men.

When she didn't answer, Beau touched her hand lightly. "It's ok if you just want to be friends, Rae. I was just teasing you. I mean I would like to be more, but I can be ok with that if that's what you want."

Raelynn looked over at him and smiled, tapping his hand back. "It's not that. I just…well, last night…I don't know how to say this without sounding like a crazy person." She sighed and then looked down at their hands. "I kind of thought you were into Reni."

Beau pulled back and furrowed his brow. "What gave you that idea? Sorry, I mean, I am genuinely curious. Because I hope I didn't give her the wrong idea." He turned to look straight ahead, his face scrunched in concentration as he seemed to be replaying the previous night's events in his mind.

Not sure what to say right away, Raelynn looked out the front too. At that moment, Sharon came outside. Waving, she made her way to Raelynn's side of the car. She opened her car window and waved back.

"Hey, what are you two doing out here? Come on in!" she exclaimed and then moved toward the house again.

"Can we finish this later?" Raelynn asked Beau, who turned toward her again, an unreadable expression on his face.

"Yeah, sure. Let's go see what other bombs she has to share, shall we." Raelynn could tell he was trying to brush aside their conversation, but she didn't know what to say. The image of him and Serenity by the fire flashed through her mind again. How could she tell him what she was feeling without sounding like a jealous girlfriend?

"Hey, Rae?" Beau tipped her chin with his finger so she would look at him. "It's all going to be fine, ok? This thing between us we can talk about anytime."

Raelynn nodded and gave him a small smile.

They exited the car at the same time. Raelynn pushed her trunk release button while Beau reached into the trunk and grabbed the boxes and envelope they brought. Raelynn waited by the front of the vehicle and then they walked into the house side by side.

The house was quiet, and Raelynn peered around the corner just inside the door to see where Sharon had gone. She found her sitting in one of the chairs at the table with a couple more closed file folders in front of her. Raelynn glanced over at Beau with a questioning look, drawing a shrug out of him.

Raelynn motioned for him to set the boxes down on the table and then they sat next to each other, across from Sharon. She raised her eyebrows at the boxes before looking between them.

"Looks like we have a lot to talk about," she said with a smile. She then gave a nod at her folders as well. "Do you want anything to drink? I have more coffee and sweet tea."

Raelynn shook her head. "I'm good. I'm a little anxious to get going, if I'm honest."

Sharon nodded knowingly. "I understand. I think we have a lot to cover. What did you bring?" She motioned her head toward the boxes in front of Beau.

"I don't even know where to begin with all this," Raclynn said with a sigh glancing at the boxes. "I have been getting deliveries since last Saturday. But I think you already know some of that."

She opened the flaps of one box and then glanced at Sharon who was nodding. Raelynn narrowed her eyes. "I still don't know how you knew about these gifts as you called them."

Sharon chuckled. "I told you Raelynn. I know things. But I will never reveal my secrets or my sources." Her voice softened and she added, "But let me help you figure this out, ok?"

One by one, Raelynn and Beau removed the turtles from each box and set them in a row, facing Sharon. Thankfully, none of them had broken from the short trip, and they looked exactly as they had when she first received each one. Sharon looked at the group and then she hummed and nodded.

"Can I touch them?" she asked, eyeing each one, not looking up from her study.

"Sure," Raelynn said with a lift of her shoulder. She didn't think there was much that anyone could do to hurt them.

Sharon picked up each one and examined it closely. She turned it upside down and side to side. She studied the features and the materials as if she were appraising it for some potential fortune. Finally, she set the last one down and leaned back in her chair. For the first time in what felt like an hour, Sharon looked at Raelynn.

"So, tell me what you think these are, Raelynn," she said, looking between Raelynn and Beau.

Raelynn hesitated. She didn't want to be the first to speak about them. She wanted to hear what Sharon thought first. She had been spinning things in her own head for a week with no idea what they might mean. And she wasn't sure what to say anyway.

Seeing her hesitating, Beau spoke up first. "We really aren't sure what they mean actually. We have been tossing this between us for a few days." He motioned with his hand between the two of them.

Raelynn met his eyes and smiled, grateful for him stepping in like that. It gave her some time to come up with something to say.

She cleared her throat and looked back at Sharon. "I am suspicious about the turtles actually." She paused again and then looked at the turtles, adding, "My dad used to make these kinds of things with me before he went missing. We used to find random things and then he would help me glue stuff together and we made a turtle. I didn't bring any of the older ones, but these are similar, I guess. We would pick up shells on the beach with the intention of making a turtle when we got home."

"Do you think you could bring a couple of those to show me?" Sharon asked.

Raelynn looked up at her. "I mean, I can but why?" she asked. She didn't want to hope that Sharon might also believe these were from her father just yet. But that tiny flame flickered in her chest.

Bonded Blood

"I know this is hard, Raelynn, and I'm not saying it is him, but I would like to compare. I need you to stay safe though, because we don't know what your father's involvement is with the Del Rios yet. I need you to be very careful." Sharon's warning caught Raelynn off guard, but since Creepy Guy had obviously found out where she lived, she had to agree.

"Um, there's something else, Sharon," she said slowly. She looked to the side and slid the envelope with all the notes toward the center of the table.

Sharon raised her eyebrow and slid the package the rest of the way to her and opened it. Her eyes widened as she looked through the notes.

"Well, this is interesting. I would say someone is definitely trying to get your attention, dear. The question is *why*?" She studied the notes now all spread out in front of her tapping her lips in concentration. "We need to figure this riddle out as much as we need to figure out what the deal is with the turtles, Raelynn." She leaned back in her chair again and scanned the table.

Sharon focused her attention back on one turtle in particular. Raelynn followed her eyes as Sharon picked up the turtle with the tiny container as its shell. She shook it slightly, her brow furrowing. Carefully, she turned it over a few times, before seemingly satisfied and then set it back down with the rest. She wrote something down on a pad of paper Raelynn didn't notice she had before.

"Ok, I think I need to give Trish a call. Do you want to hang out here or take a break?" Sharon was pushing her chair back and watching Raelynn at the same time.

Raelynn felt like she was being dismissed and glanced at Beau. "I guess we could go check on Timmy for a little bit.

I need to call Serenity too," she said, glancing at the time on her phone. I can't believe its been two hours already.

"Ok, let's break for a bit and then we can see what Serenity found out too." Beau stood and Raelynn joined him.

They turned to Sharon who was standing now as well but was staring at the table in front of her. "This is quite the mystery. I have to admit I am excited to meet the mastermind." She laughed and then the trio moved to the doorway. "Come back in about an hour or two and we will continue, ok?"

Beau and Raelynn nodded. "Got it," she said as they moved outside.

Once seated in the car, Raelynn glanced at Beau, who looked lost in thought. "What are you thinking about?" she asked him.

"I'm not really sure actually. There seems to be so much more than what we thought before. Once you lay it all out and really look at it." He looked over at her and gave her a smile. "But I think we have the right person helping now."

Raelynn agreed. "I don't know Sharon all that well, but what I do know is she is very smart and sees things others don't. I just hope we can unravel this quickly." She sighed and started the engine.

They decided to stop in at her mom's house and see Timmy. Her mom was supposed to work a short day so she might be there as well. The ride was quiet, and Raelynn looked out the window now and then at the passing houses, once again in awe at the difference in size and style the further she got from Sharon's. She thought about having Beau drive, but he had gone straight to the passenger side, so she didn't bring it up.

When they pulled into her mom's driveway, Raelynn noticed her mom's car was there. They made their way out of her vehicle and went to the backyard to see if Timmy and Jericho were back there. She couldn't resist the smile when she saw her brother and pup laying in their favorite position on the lawn. Timmy was stretched out on the soft grass and Jericho looked like he was sleeping with his head on the dog's belly.

She decided not to disturb them and motioned for Beau to follow her to the front door. His grin told her he probably saw the same thing she did.

Honesty was sitting at the table in the kitchen when they walked in. She looked up from the papers in front of her when she saw them and smiled.

"Hey you two. What are you doing here?" She stood and moved around the table to give Raelynn a hug. "I thought you were busy all day." Honesty went back to her chair and motioned for them to join her.

When everyone was seated again, she raised her eyebrows as if asking her question again.

"We were meeting with Sharon, but took a break," Raelynn volunteered. She looked over at Beau and then added, "We are going back in a little bit. Just taking a breather, I guess."

Honesty nodded. "So does she have any information?"

Raelynn could tell her mom was as anxious as she was to get any information about her father. Unfortunately, they would both have wait longer. She wasn't ready to tell her mom about the gang that had taken over the factory where her dad had worked. She was questioning even more if he was still alive or if he was alive that maybe he wasn't the "good guy" she remembered. She also didn't want her mom to lose hope just yet.

"Not yet," she said, looking over at Beau. "She is going to call her friend over and we are going to go at it again in a little bit. We just thought we'd come over here while she waited for Trish." She tipped her head toward the window. "I see Timmy is being difficult for you."

Honesty laughed. "Yeah, such a high maintenance dog. He's good for Jericho, though. I worry about him being alone with only his friends around here. I liked having you girls here to keep him in line. Now he has the influence of all the social media and kids like Jamal to hang out with." She sighed and glanced toward the window. They couldn't see outside because of where they were sitting, but she still looked as if she could see through the wall of the house. A second sigh escaped her lips, and Raelynn knew what her mom was thinking.

If only her dad was here to give him some better guidance and offer Jericho two adults to look out for him and not one who always had to work just to make ends meet. Raelynn wished for the same thing if she was completely honest with herself. She wanted to be selfish and take her dad for just herself, but she knew he would embrace Jericho, even though he wasn't his blood. It wasn't any different than Honesty taking in Raelynn as her own. And her dad loved being a dad. *If only we could find him,* she thought glumly. She brushed aside the negative thoughts and tried to focus on the potential positives of finding him alive and well.

The group was quiet for a few minutes until Jericho came through the door. He looked around at the group and landed finally on Raelynn.

Bonded Blood

"Are you picking Timmy up, Rae?" he asked, looking a little disappointed.

Raelynn smiled and shook her head. "Nope, he's all yours still. We are talking to a few people today, so if you don't mind keeping him for me a little longer, I'd appreciate it."

Her brother made a fist bump in the air, grabbed something from the fridge, and nearly skipped back outside.

It was the tension break they needed as they all watched and chuckled at Jericho's exit.

"I guess we should get back," Beau said, somewhat reluctantly.

Raelynn nodded. "I'd like to grab some lunch or something on the way. I'm not sure when Trish was coming either. It feels like we just got here. I'm gonna go check on Timmy and then I can meet you out front." She stood and pushed away from the table as her mom and Beau did the same.

Throwing her keys to Beau, she turned and went through the door that her brother just used and made her way to her massive ball of fur.

"Timmy!" she called as she got close. Her dog lifted his head and gave her a yawn. "What a brat," she mumbled.

He stood and stretched, and then slowly ambled over to her. Once he reached her, he lifted his chin looking for head scratches. She chuckled to herself wondering what he thought of her. Was she his number one head scratcher or just the food lady? Deciding she didn't really care, she gave him lots of love and scratches.

"Has he been good, Jer?" she asked her brother.

Jericho shrugged. "He's a dog, Rae. What's he gonna do? He went potty like you said, and he ate his food. He also had a bunch of treats 'cuz he was doing a good job training before you got here," he shot the big dog a proud look which earned him a loud "woof" in response.

"Alright then I'm gonna go. Thanks, Jericho. You're doing me a huge favor," she said and ruffled his hair, earning her a glare.

She walked around the house and through the gate to meet Beau out front. He was in a quiet conversation with her mom on the porch when she came around. She stood at the car and waited for him to meet her.

"Everything ok with Timmy?" Beau asked as he jogged up to her.

Raelynn nodded and said, "Yup. I think I just found a new babysitter for the big lug." She looked around him and waved at her mom. "Everything ok with my mom?" she asked when she turned back to Beau.

He glanced behind her and nodded. "I think so, she's just worried about you. She thanked me for being here with you. I told her I wouldn't have it any other way."

Her eyes met his and she could see sincerity in them. "I'm glad you're here too, Beau. Thank you."

Beau nodded and then they moved to the car. He still had the keys and held them out to her. Raelynn shook her head. "No, can you drive? I'm so distracted," she raised her eyebrow in question.

"Are you sure? I don't mind but are you sure?" he asked seriously.

"Why are you worried?" she asked. "I just really don't want to drive."

He studied her face and finally nodded.

Once they were inside and buckled, Raelynn looked over at him. "Why are you so nervous to drive?"

"It's not that, I just don't like driving other people's vehicles." He put the key in the ignition and started it.

Raelynn watched as he made all the adjustments so he could see and then smiled. "I don't care who drives my car, as long as you are sober and have a license. If you aren't comfortable with it though, I will drive," she said, touching his arm softly.

Beau looked over. "As long as you are sure." Then he smirked and winked, saying, "I am sober, so there's that."

"And I know you have a license because you drove to my place multiple times this week," she pointed out.

Beau shrugged. "Maybe I just like to drive but never got my license," he suggested.

Raelynn laughed. "Right. I'm pretty sure your parents wouldn't allow that."

"Ah busted by my overprotective parents. Shall we? Where do you want to get lunch?" He shifted into reverse to back out of the driveway but stopped as he got to the end of it to look at Raelynn.

Biting her lip, she looked out her window. She honestly wasn't really hungry, but she didn't know how long this would go today.

"How about we go over to Food Lion, grab some ready-made sandwiches and some snacks in case it goes longer than just through lunch?" Raelynn suggested, turning back to Beau. "We can always have something delivered for dinner. I don't want Sharon to feel like she has to feed us, especially if Reni comes over too."

Beau thought for a minute. "That's actually a good idea."

Raelynn made a mental list in her head of what she might want to get as they drove the short distance to the store. Getting drinks would probably be a good idea, too. As they exited the vehicle, her phone alerted her to a text. Stopping to read it before they went inside, she froze. Beau looked over and read over her shoulder.

"Raelynn, I need you to hurry back. Trish has an idea, but we need you here." Sharon had sent it and Beau and Raelynn locked eyes.

"What could they have found so fast, Beau?" she asked.

He shrugged. "I don't know but we should hurry. It sounded kind of urgent."

Raelynn agreed. "I'll text her back and see if we have time to grab some things first."

After confirming with Sharon that it was ok, they rushed through the store grabbing what they needed, lunch completely forgotten as they checked out and hurried back to the car and headed to Sharon's.

Chapter 22

The group of four sat around Sharon's table with papers and statues spread out all over. Trish had her gray locks tied up in a bun on top of her head and the brown skin of her forehead was scrunched in concentration. Sharon was reading over the notes again, tossing each aside as she reread it. Raelynn and Beau were watching the two of them with confusion and interest at the same time, occasionally meeting each other's eyes.

Raelynn wasn't sure what to make of the scene in front of her. She remembered when Trish and Sharon helped with Beau's family in the summer, they worked so well together that they could just share a look and know what each other meant.

It was a moment like that that made her laugh out loud, drawing everyone's attention to Raelynn.

"Sorry," she said sheepishly. "You two just seem to communicate telepathically and I just thought it was funny." She moved her finger between the two women on the opposite side of the table.

Sharon looked at her surprised. "You mean, I didn't say that out loud?" she asked, looking over at Trish who was grinning at her and shaking her head.

"No Sharon. You do need to learn to use your words," she said with a smirk. "But I did understand what you were saying in my head. By the way, get out of my head. There are things in there you don't want to come across by accident." She wiggled her eyebrows at Raelynn, making the foursome laugh.

When Raelynn first met Trish, she was surprised to say the least. The older woman had a strange sense of humor and took a little getting used to. Ashley had told her the woman was a little freaky, not fully understanding what she meant. When Raelynn finally met her and set foot in her house for the first time, she understood immediately what her friend was talking about. Trish had a hardness about her, maybe more abrupt than most people, even for the east coast. But she had a heart of gold, and she hated "bad guys" deep in her soul. It didn't take long for Raelynn to understand that Trish had something tragic happen in her past, but she didn't talk about it.

Trish also had a strange appearance. Raelynn thought she looked a lot younger in her face than her graying hair suggested. It was almost like she made herself look older than she was. It was odd to Raelynn because most of the older women she knew wanted to look younger, not older. But then she never asked how old Trish was, so maybe it wasn't weird at all. She just maybe went gray early in her life or she had amazing face creams and products to keep her face looking younger. She also didn't need readers like Sharon did.

"I'm sorry," Sharon said, adjusting her glasses slightly. "I was looking at these notes and something is just odd about them." She pulled one out and pointed to the letters. "Do you see how some of the letters are bold or darker?" Sharon pointed to the "F" and "R" in the note that read "two for two."

Raelynn nodded. "I guess I did notice that, but it didn't really make sense. And I couldn't tell if it was on purpose or not. The notes are all kind of smudged and it was hard to tell for sure." She picked up another note and saw that it was the same way. If she looked closely, she could make out two letters in each one that looked darker than the rest. She picked up the first note and narrowed her eyes.

"Look," she said, pointing at the writing. "This one has four letters that look darker. Or maybe it's just me." She handed the letter to Trish who was right across from her.

Trish took it and smoothed it out on the table, studying the letters closely. Her brow furrowed as she squinted at the paper. Finally, she nodded and handed it to Sharon.

"Those are definitely part of whatever code this person is trying to send." She pulled out a notepad and a pen.

Nodding, Sharon made a pile of the notes and then handed the notes to Beau while Trish handed Raelynn the pad and pen.

"You guys write these letters down and see if you can make any sense of them," Sharon said.

Beau and Raelynn nodded and got to work on the notes while Sharon began studying the turtles one at a time. Trish and Sharon each took a turtle one by one, twisting and turning it in every possible direction. They were both concentrating hard, and Raelynn smiled as she watched them work. She was grateful to have these two helping her and silently wished she had thought of Sharon a week ago. Maybe even last summer.

"What do you think these are?" Trish asked, staring at the bottom of one turtle.

Raelynn guessed she was talking about the numbers scratched into each one. When Trish looked at her, Raelynn shrugged.

"I'm not sure. I was thinking, if it was my dad, the numbers would mean something to us. You know, like a birthday or an anniversary. But only one was a significant date, so I wrote that off. I honestly don't know what they are." Her frustration was evident, but she tried to hold it in as much as she could.

Trish and Sharon exchanged a look and then nodded.

Beau nudged her and grinned. "I see what you mean," he said, motioning between the two older women.

Raelynn snickered and nodded, drawing the attention to them.

"What?" Sharon asked.

But Trish just grinned back and nodded.

"Ok, let's see if we can unravel this stuff, shall we?" Trish said with a clap of her hands. "You two like puzzles?"

"I love puzzles," Raelynn said. "But this is more complicated than a puzzle, with all due respect Miss Trish."

Trish snorted and looked at Sharon, who let out a soft chuckle. "Yeah, it's just Trish, honey. Now this is what we call a big kid puzzle. You think you can handle that? No more little kiddie things here. This is real life puzzle work." She spread out the turtles in a row and tipped each one upside down.

"First, we have to figure out what these numbers mean, and there are a lot of them," Sharon confirmed.

Raelynn nodded. "I know and that's the hard part. None of them repeat and each turtle has two numbers. I already said none fit important dates either." She looked at the statues and then at the women across from her.

"I was thinking maybe they could be combinations to dates. For example, we are looking at a four and two being forty-two. But what if it is actually part of a four number combination? Like four then a two and then add another two numbers to complete a date. Three could be short for zero three, or two thousand three for example." Trish arranged two of the turtles to show what she meant.

Sharon picked up two other ones and put them together. "That could work. Maybe it is a string of dates with no real significance for us right now, but might later on, when we can figure out the rest of this."

"But like this one has a four and a four, and you can't put that with anything else because there aren't forty days in a month," Raelynn argued.

Sharon smiled. "Maybe, but if the four and four are April fourth and another is the year, it will work. Let's just see," she said as she started to look through the other numbers. "How about eighteen? Anyone born in two thousand eighteen that you know of? Or an anniversary?"

Raelynn thought for a second, but nothing popped into her mind as significant. Reluctantly she shook her head. "Maybe mom would know more dates that we could compare," she suggested.

"Hm, not a bad idea," Trish said. "Why don't you give her a call and ask her for all the important dates she can recall so we can start to compare them. That might give us a clue as to if this is your father or not." She gave a knowing look to Sharon who nodded her agreement.

Raelynn couldn't help but wonder what that silent communication was, but she just nodded and pulled out her phone to text her mom. "What does it mean if the numbers do mean things like dates that relate to my family?"

Sharon set down the statue she was looking at and let out a small sigh. "Well, it could confirm that it is your father sending these. But if the dates are common knowledge, or easily found, then there may be a more nefarious sender, trying to convince you they are safe."

The table fell silent as everyone processed the possibilities. The weight of decoding the numbers was stifling for Raelynn and she closed her eyes and took in some air. She was trying to stay positive, and she couldn't think about any other option yet.

"We also can't ignore the possibility that the dates are for more obscure things as well," Trish said, giving Sharon another knowing look. Sharon just nodded back.

"Maybe we should write down all the numbers too," Beau suggested. They had written all the letters down from the notes but hadn't done anything with the numbers yet.

The others agreed and each took a turn reading from the turtles while Beau wrote down the numbers on a clean sheet of paper. Once they were all written, he turned the list to the group.

"Does anything stand out to anyone?" he asked.

Everyone shook their heads, and a collective sigh sounded around the table.

"And then there is this," Trish said as she held up one of the cards. It was the one that Creepy Guy had dropped off one morning at Raelynn's work.

"Oh, yeah. That came from Creepy Guy," she said without thinking.

Sharon and Trish turned and looked at her sharply. "Who is this 'Creepy Guy'?" Sharon asked. She pushed back slightly from the table and leaned back in her chair, as if she were waiting for a good story.

Raelynn looked between them and then at Beau next to her. His face was filled with worry as he gave her an encouraging nod.

Taking a deep breath, she began to tell them about the strange encounters with the man. He only came into her workplace, until the day before when he met her outside her apartment. She looked over the turtles and picked up the one that was left outside her apartment's sliding door the same day with the note that came with it.

Sharon took the items from her and Trish leaned to look at them.

Trish spoke first. "Do you think he's the sender of these other things?"

"I don't have a clue," she said honestly. "But there's is something really familiar about him. I can't place it. His eyes aren't cold and malicious, if that's possible to see in just someone's eyes." She shrugged.

Trish and Sharon looked at each other again and this time Sharon spoke first.

"Do you think you could identify him again? Or if we could get some software in here, could you help us draw a picture?" Sharon asked, pulling a second pad of paper from a bag next to her.

"I'm not sure. I'm really bad at remembering details about people, when it comes to what they look like I mean.

I can tell you all about what he was wearing or how he smelled, which surprisingly wasn't gross like I expected." Raelynn tried to remember what color his eyes even were, but she couldn't be positive. "I would be a terrible crime witness," she said with a frustrated chuckle.

Trish patted her hand. "Sometimes those details are just as important as physical features. Things like which direction he came from or left can be very helpful in tracking people down."

Sharon snorted next to her and waved her hand at Trish. "This lady here is our right-hand hacker, Raelynn. If we have an idea of the direction this man went, she can track him pretty accurately. We have found many bad guys that way, haven't we old friend?"

"Who are you calling 'old'? Huh?" Trish asked defiantly. "I'm pretty sure you are older than me too." She crossed her arms over her chest and lifted her chin.

Raelynn wasn't sure if she was joking with her friend or not, so she just watched the two of them. Sharon swatted Trish's arm and laughed.

"Well now, how long have we been friends, Trish?" Sharon asked, crossing her own arms.

Trish raised her eyebrows at Sharon and then softened her eyes. "About three years after…" her voice trailed off and she abruptly sat up straighter and cleared her throat. "Ok, back to this."

Raelynn wanted to ask what happened to Trish that made her shift so quickly, but felt it was none of her business. It was clearly something that caused her a lot of pain though, as she watched Sharon put her arm around her friend's shoulder, giving it a quick squeeze, before letting go and focusing on the table.

Bonded Blood

"Ok, we need to get a timeline of when you saw this 'creepy guy' as you call him, at work," Sharon said, clapping her hands as if that cleared the air around them. "Have you seen him any other times, Raelynn?"

"Um…" she said, stalling. How should she answer this question? After making eye contact with Beau, she sighed. "Yes, I have." She cleared her throat nervously. "He, um, met me outside my apartment yesterday after work."

Neither older woman looked shocked or like they were about to chastise her. Trish just watched her while Sharon's face showed compassion and concern.

"Did he say anything?" Trish asked after a few minutes.

Raelynn shook her head and pointed to the last turtle. "He gave me the box with this one in it." She looked over the notes and pulled out the one that came with the last turtle. "And this card was with it."

She watched Sharon read the note and her eyebrow raised with concern. When her eyes met Raelynn's, she sighed. "This is a little more than just concerning, Raelynn. This one feels ominous, and I'm actually worried for your safety right now. Why would he personally deliver this one to you?"

"She could stay with me for a little bit while we figure this out," Trish suggested to Sharon.

"No, I'm not going anywhere. I have my dog, and Beau has offered to stay at my place with me. Creepy Guy hasn't threatened me at all, and maybe I am naïve, but he doesn't strike me as the kind of person out to kill someone." Raelynn didn't want to go into hiding or anything. She wanted to just solve this and move on. There had to be a reason this man was targeting her. And maybe it was nothing to even do with her or her dad. But if she could help someone else, she would at least try.

Trish sighed. "You're not being smart, child. This could all be a ruse of some sort, and this guy is just the messenger. The reason he's not threatening to you might be because he is just the delivery person for the real bad guy and maybe he feels bad about what might be planned for you."

Raelynn shuddered. She didn't even think of that possibility. She raised her eyes to meet Beau's, and it appeared he was thinking the same thing she was. She still didn't want to go into hiding. *Maybe just a few more days to see what happens*, she thought. Although she could ask Susiana to find someone to cover Sunday's shortened hours for her and she wouldn't have to be back at work until Tuesday. It would be a good time for a short-term disappearance.

"I don't know. I just don't want to go into hiding and then leave the target on my family's back," she tried to rationalize. "Jericho is too young to know what to do it if something happened and my mom's work schedule leaves him alone a lot." Raelynn bit the corner of her lip. She looked around the table and sighed. She honestly didn't know what to do.

Beau cleared his throat. "What if we set up some sort of security camera outside her apartment windows and doors?" he asked. "That package came to her sliding door. If the guy is staying outside and not getting into the building, the security must be pretty good. But the outside door, since Rae lives on the lower level, is the vulnerable point."

"That's right! I remember the security system you have set up at your place, Trish," Raelynn agreed. "Could we do something like that for now?" She tried to be hopeful as she silently wondered how much danger was lurking around her at the moment.

Sharon let out a loud sigh. "You know I strongly disagree with this plan." She looked at Trish who shrugged. "But ultimately, we can't force you to do anything. We can see what we can set up there. For now, will you just stay here until we get something figured out, Raelynn?"

Raelynn wanted to do a fist bump into the air much like her brother does when he gets his way. She hoped with these two on the case it wouldn't take long for them to figure it all out and it would be over soon. Until something happened, she would continue to hope and pray for a good outcome to everything. She had kept hope alive for nearly fifteen years, and she could do it for a little longer.

"I will be ok, Sharon. I appreciate the concern, though," Raelynn said softly, trying to reassure the older woman as much as herself. "If we can get something set up at my place and I have Beau with me, would rather stay there."

Sharon sighed and then nodded with obvious defeat.

Trish clapped her hands together. "Great, now that that part is settled, what are we doing about the rest of this?" She motioned over the table now spread with turtles and papers almost completely covering the whole surface.

Sharon picked up the one that Creepy Guy had hand delivered to Raelynn. She turned it every which way and then gave it a shake. Biting her cheek and wrinkling her forehead, she continued to flip it over. "Trish, this one has something in it, but I can't find an opening to get a look inside." She handed it to the other older woman.

Raelynn remembered she was studying it before as well. She furrowed her brows watching Sharon try to figure it out.

Trish took it and gave it a shake as well, furrowing her brow in the process. She continued to turn it over and sideways to examine it just as Sharon had.

"Hm. I mean you can see it's a container of some sort, but how do you open it?" She turned it upside down and grabbed a small flashlight from somewhere next to her and shined it on the underbelly of the turtle. "Yep, look at this."

Trish pointed to something, and Sharon leaned in close to see what it was. Raelynn couldn't see what they saw, but she watched them as Sharon took out a different tool, like a screwdriver of sorts, and in another thirty seconds, the bottom of the turtle opened up.

Both women wrinkled their noses and peered inside. "Huh, that's interesting," Sharon said, squinting at the small opening. "Grab me a—"

Trish handed her what looked like a tiny spoon before Sharon finished her sentence. Sharon looked up and smiled.

"That's definitely—" Trish started as Sharon nodded and finished the sentence with, "litter."

Raelynn just watched in awe of them. She had no clue what they discovered by just opening the small container, but they clearly discovered something meaningful. She also didn't know what cat litter had to do with anything. It looked like dirt to her. It seemed as if they knew what each other was thinking all the time. *I guess that's what makes them such a good team*, she thought.

She glanced over at Beau and noticed the same look on his face that she was sure mirrored her own. "Crazy, right?" she whispered, leaning over toward him.

Beau just nodded and smiled back.

The two woman across from them were extracting something that looked like dirt from inside the small container that made up the turtle's shell. Sharon put a tiny scoop of it on a white piece of paper and moved it around. Raelynn thought it just looked like black dirt from a garden. *How would that help anything*? She couldn't help wondering. Then she remembered her crime shows where they could trace a scoop of dirt to a certain area of the city and then find exactly who had been there and all that. But that was just TV, right?

Trish pushing away from the table snapped Raelynn out of her thoughts. She looked up as Trish was gathering some things and Sharon was dumping the small amount of dirt back inside the turtle. Confused, she watched as Trish took the turtle from Sharon.

"Ok, I'll be back in a couple hours or so," Trish said and then she disappeared out the door.

Raelynn looked at Sharon and asked, "Um, what did I miss?"

Sharon chuckled. "Trish has some equipment at her place that can analyze the substance and see what it is made of and where it came from. It shouldn't take her long, but I don't have that here." She turned her attention back to the table.

Raelynn looked over at Beau, who looked like he was enjoying whatever was going on. She wasn't sure if it was her not knowing what was happening or if it was these two women and their interactions making him smile.

Before she could think about it too long, her phone rang. Glancing at the caller ID, she quickly swiped to answer it.

"Hey Rae?" Serenity's hurried voice came over the line. "I found something at one of the galleries. I was going to go check it out after work. Should I meet you somewhere?"

"What did you find, Reni?" Raelynn asked. With what she was learning, she wasn't sure her friend should go alone. Maybe they could meet her there.

A slight pause met her question. Finally, Serenity said, "I think I know who the artist might be that was featured in that exhibit. But I want to make sure. It is kind of personal and I don't want to say anything unless I know. But I'll come over after I go there. Like four or four-thirty?"

Raelynn didn't know what her friend was hiding, but she wanted her friend to be safe. She looked at Sharon and hit the mute button on her phone. "Sharon, could my friend come here after work, like four thirty or so?"

After Sharon nodded, Raelynn turned the mute off again and gave Serenity the address for Sharon's house. They agreed to call if anything happened, and Raelynn told her friend to be careful and let her know if she needed anything. She didn't want to get into too much over the phone plus she knew her friend was still at work. She would have to sit and wait, hoping her friend was looking into something that wouldn't put her in danger.

She hung up the phone and sighed. When she looked up, Sharon was studying her closely making Raelynn feel somewhat self-conscious. Just as suddenly, Sharon looked away and cleared her throat. A text came through then too, drawing Raelynn's attention back to her phone. She read the message and then turned it to show Sharon.

"Oh, good. Your mom sent some dates we can start with," Sharon said. "Why don't you guys write those down and we will start to put numbers together to see what we can find."

Beau nodded and then looked over at Raelynn. "What about the letters?"

"I can see if I can find some words in them," Raelynn suggested. "I always liked those 'unscramble the letters' games as a kid. It might not be anything. But it's worth a shot, right?"

Sharon nodded. "Yes, it is. They are there for a reason. And if we compare them, it looks like the same person wrote them. The writing is similar enough that even without handwriting analysis I can see similarities in the strokes."

When Sharon mentioned the handwriting analysis, it reminded Raelynn about that letter from her dad to her mom so long ago. It didn't even occur to her to compare the writing to the notes. She was only focused on the outside of the box.

"Um, Sharon, there was one of the boxes, the one that showed up at my apartment. It was the only one that had my name handwritten instead of a printed label on it. My mom gave me a letter from my dad to her a long time ago to see if we could tell if the writing matched. I was wondering if you could compare the writing to see if they might be the same?"

After a few minutes, Sharon nodded. "We can sure try. It might match the letters too and then we will have a better idea if these are all connected to your dad or not. But I'd like to wait for Trish to come back first though, if that's ok. She has a better eye for that stuff than I do."

Raelynn nodded and then looked at the collection of letters in front of her. The group made no sense to her and as she looked, she wondered if there were even enough vowels to make words. She rewrote them in a vertical line, checking to make sure they got all the letters from the notes. She came across one that made her brow crease.

"Sharon?" she asked, not looking away from the note in her hand. "What do you think this means?" She pointed to the writing where there was a capital "D" in the middle of the word "hide". "None of the other letters are capitalized."

Raelynn handed the note to Sharon who looked it over a few times and then shrugged. "I guess we write it down like that for now. But let's put it somewhere else. Something is different about it. It's not bold and the other words with 'D's' aren't capital like this. It must mean something." She handed it back to Raelynn, who nodded and wrote the letter at the bottom of her page.

The only note she didn't know what to do with was the one Creepy Guy gave her that didn't have any words on it, just a drawing. She decided to set that aside for now and maybe it would make sense later.

The trio worked together in silence for almost three hours, when Trish came walking through the door again. Raelynn checked the time and noticed it was past two. Her stomach growled, letting her know she missed lunch after all the excitement when they first arrived.

"Maybe we should take a break so Trish and I can talk about what she found," Sharon suggested, likely hearing Raelynn's angry stomach.

Raelynn quickly agreed and Beau got up after her. They had put their bags from the grocery store on one of the islands in Sharon's kitchen when they came in, thankfully nothing needed to be refrigerated.

"What do you think?" Beau asked, as he leaned over the counter across from Raelynn.

She shrugged. "I don't really know. I mean, they are obviously really smart and know what they are doing. It's just weird. I can't explain it any other way. I am actually more curious about what Serenity is bringing."

Beau nodded. "I agree. I wonder who she thinks the artist is. The brochure she had said it was an anonymous person." He opened one of the bags of chips they had grabbed and took a few of the cans of soda out and put them in Sharon's fridge.

"Sharon?" Raelynn called. When she had the other woman's attention, she asked, "Could we borrow a couple of glasses and some ice?"

"Of course! Help yourselves," she said back and then was almost head-to-head with Trish.

Beau checked a couple of cabinets before finding the right one and filled each glass with some ice and then soda from the warm cans. Setting down one full glass in front of Raelynn, he looked over his shoulder at the two older women again.

"What do you think they are talking about, Rae?" he asked, as he started on the next glass.

Raelynn snorted. "I have no clue. These two are amazing and read each other's mind. It's crazy. I can't even attempt to guess."

"It's a little exciting though, isn't it? This stuff all means something to them, or at least they know what to do to find the answers," Beau said as he turned to watch them again.

Raelynn followed his gaze and nodded absently. "If it leads somewhere, then definitely."

"It will, Rae," Beau said softly, reaching out for her hand. "This is the best chance I think you've got to find out what the deal is with the statues, but also about your dad."

They watched for a minute and then Beau asked suddenly, "Hey, where is the package from earlier today?"

Raelynn focused back on him, confused for a second before realization dawned on her. "I completely forgot about it. Where is it?"

"I thought it was on the backseat, but why didn't we grab it when we got here? I don't remember seeing it," Beau said with a confused look.

Raelynn thought about it and nodded. "I know I put it on the backseat. I'll go look."

"Right behind you," Beau said, setting down his glass.

They let the other two know they were going outside, but neither acknowledged them. Beau tossed her the keys that he still had in his pocket, and she unlocked the door.

Nothing was on the back seat, which explains why they didn't think to bring it in earlier, but where had it gone then? Raelynn wondered.

Beau climbed into the backseat and looked under the seats, finding the small package tucked there.

"How did it get that far under the seat?" she asked surprised. They hadn't had any near collisions or anything, so how did it fly that far out of sight?

Beau shrugged. "It is pretty light, so maybe it just bounced around," he suggested.

Raelynn reached out for it and used her key to break open the tape. Once she had it opened, she looked inside.

Bonded Blood

Confusion clouded her features as she stared at the thing inside the box. "What the heck kind of sick joke is this?" she mumbled.

Chapter 23

Beau and Raelynn stared at the tiny wooden chicken carving now sitting in front of the row of turtles. Raelynn's chin was resting on her folded arms, staring at it like she was sure it would get up and attack her at any moment.

"I don't understand," she mumbled.

Beau lightly put his hand on her shoulder, drawing her eyes to his. "I don't get it either, Rae. I thought the thing with your dad was turtles. Why a chicken? Especially after all this?" He motioned to the collection in the middle of the table.

Sharon and Trish were lost in their own conversation away from the table. Raelynn wasn't sure what they were talking about, and she honestly didn't care. She just stared at the carving.

"I hate chickens," she groaned, sitting back in her chair, her eyes never leaving the small bird. "This is making me think it isn't my dad at all, and someone is messing with me. Like, badly messing with me."

"Raelynn, sweetheart, explain why you think that," Sharon suggested, moving back to the table where Beau and Raelynn were sitting. "What is it about chickens? Why do you think someone would send you this?"

Bonded Blood

Raelynn groaned again. "I don't know. I don't even remember why I hate them so much, but I hate the creatures. I love to eat them but avoid live ones whenever I can."

Trish sat down across from her again and gave her a questioning look. "Did something happen when you were younger?" she asked gently.

"I have no idea, I have just always hated them," Raelynn said with a shrug, still not looking away from the statue in front of her.

Sharon and Trish shared another look before Sharon asked, "Did anyone in your family own or run a farm when you were growing up, Raelynn?"

Raelynn shook her head. "No, actually I don't know anyone who had a farm growing up, I was a city kid, grew up in Salisbury and my parents and grandparents were the same." She thought for a moment and then added, "No one ever talked about being on a farm either."

An alert sounding on her phone finally brought Raelynn's attention away from the chicken. "Serenity is on her way, if it's still ok," she said, looking to Sharon for the confirmation.

Sharon nodded and then stood with Trish to continue talking in the kitchen. Raelynn sent a quick text back and gave her friend the address again.

"I need to focus on something else," Raelynn said abruptly. "Beau, will you put that thing back in the box and hide it somewhere?"

Letting out a soft chuckle, Beau did as she asked and put the box on the floor next to him.

"Actually, I'll take it," Trish called from the kitchen, moving quickly to take the small package. "I have about another hour before my analysis is ready at the house, so let me see what else we can get from this little monster." She took the box from Beau with a sly grin.

Raelynn turned to Beau. "Should we mess with these letters some more and see what we can find? I have only found a couple small words so far. But I am making a list. Maybe fresh eyes could help me out."

"I can try," he offered. "But spelling has never been my strong suit."

Raelynn smiled. "It's like 'Wheel of Fortune.' Just take a couple of letters and try to fill in others to make words."

She took out the notepad again and looked at the letters. She wrote down a "G" and then left some space and added an "N". She showed it to him to demonstrate her point. Then she wrote an "A" and "I" to make the word "GAIN".

"See?" she asked, holding it up to show him. "Easy."

Beau shrugged. "I'll give it a try."

They worked for what felt like just a few minutes before Sharon said Serenity had arrived. Raelynn got up to meet her friend so she wouldn't feel awkward knocking on a stranger's door. She got there right as Serenity got out of her car and started up the driveway, appearing as if she were trying to figure out which door to go to.

Raelynn noticed the relief on her friend's face when they made eye contact.

"I'm glad you are out here!" Serenity said with a smile that looked forced.

"Is everything ok, Reni?" Raelynn asked. Her friend looked a little spooked and it worried her considering everything else that was going on.

Bonded Blood

But Serenity waved her hand dismissively. "Yep, everything's fine. I think," she said, turning toward the house. "So, what are we doing here, Rae?"

Raelynn didn't miss the hesitation in her friend's voice but chose to ignore it for now. She knew her friend had some anxiety, especially meeting new people and going to new places. Raelynn knew Serenity would be safe here, so she put an arm around her friend's shoulder and guided her inside. She was looking forward to finding out if Serenity had gotten any information from the gallery.

They moved inside the house and Raelynn introduced her to Sharon and Trish. "They are helping me put the pieces together and hopefully figure out who is sending these things to me."

Serenity nodded and then gave Beau a small wave. He nodded in return and went back to his letter puzzles.

"Raelynn, dear, we are going to try to figure out what else these numbers could be trying to tell us. For that I need to go to my computer in the back. If you need anything, just give a shout, ok?" Sharon pointed to a hallway that must go back to her office, Raelynn thought.

"Ok," she responded. "Do you have the list of dates from my mom?"

Trish and Sharon exchanged a look and then Sharon nodded at Raelynn. *Ok, something is definitely going on that they aren't telling us*, she thought.

Serenity settled her things on the table across from Beau and leaned forward on her hands to see what he was working on. "What are you doing?" she asked finally.

Raelynn moved to stand next to her. "So, we figured out that each note has a couple of letters that were bolded.

So, we are trying to see if they make a word or words that will help us. We are just making a list of words that the letters make, like a massive word scramble, and then see if they mean anything."

"That actually sounds kind of fun. Can I help?" she asked, looking between Beau and Raelynn.

"I don't see why not. Maybe we will come up with different words and that will give us more to work with." Raelynn leaned over the table and grabbed her paper tablet and another pen from the center of the table. She handed them to Serenity and then moved back to her spot next to Beau.

They worked in silence for a while, and then Raelynn finally asked, "Reni, did you find out anything at the gallery?"

Serenity sighed. "The owner said that he couldn't reveal the artist because it was strictly an anonymous person who wanted to stay out of the spotlight. But he gave me more information on the style of art." She put her pen down and pulled out a stack of papers. She handed it to Raelynn and then picked up her pen again.

"Scavenger art?" Raelynn asked, looking up from the paper.

"Yeah. So, they call it different things, like scavenger, recycled, trash. They are all ways to describe the art I was asking about, he said. Artists use anything from literal trash they take out of the dump or trash cans to things they find anywhere. Like the beach, or an old shed, or an abandoned house. Stuff like that." She stopped and looked at Raelynn. "There are a lot of famous artists making this kind of art. There are also places to visit that are literal sculptures by these artists."

Serenity pulled another brochure out of her bag and handed it to her friend. "He said if I was interested, I should check out this place in Summerville, Georgia. The guy built a garden out of trash and old things. It's famous, I guess. He also used his art to design album covers for a few eighties' bands. Then he gave me a couple of famous names, but none of them are from around here that could help us."

Raelynn and Beau looked at the papers she had brought. "This is actually really interesting, though. Who would have thought this was a thing?" Beau commented, looking at the paper in Raelynn's hand.

Thinking, Raelynn said, "Did he know who a local artist doing this kind of art might be, someone who didn't want to stay anonymous?" She thought about her turtles, and they did look like they were made out of discarded things. She wasn't sure what they originally were or where they might have come from, but it could be a start.

"He did. None of them rang a bell for me…" Serenity hesitated and then sighed.

"Ren, what is it?" Raelynn asked quietly.

Serenity sighed again and looked at her friend's concerned eyes. "One of the names is someone I knew a long time ago, but he died when I was like ten."

"Who was he?" Beau asked, setting down his pen and giving Serenity his full attention.

Just then Sharon and Trish came out of the hall, talking animatedly.

"Trish is going to check on the sample back at her place. What have you kids found out so far?" Sharon asked as Trish gave a wave and left the house.

She didn't share what they were discussing, making Raelynn slightly nervous. She wanted to know what was going on. Raelynn got up and started to walk to the other side of the table.

"We were just talking about a gallery downtown and the kind of art these statues might be linked to," Beau said.

Sharon sat across from Serenity, taking Raelynn's chair, and raised her eyebrows. "Oh, and what did you find out, dear?" She folded her hands on the table and gave Serenity all her attention.

Raelynn could see her friend tense up, so she reached over and gave her hand a squeeze. "It's ok, Reni. Sharon is brilliant. She's just trying to help me figure this out."

Nodding, Serenity looked at their connected hands and took a deep breath. "Like I said, he gave me some names and one stuck out. He was an old friend of my dad's; they worked at the factory together." She looked up at Raelynn suddenly and added, "When our dads worked together, before…"

"You mean your dad also worked at the same plant Raelynn's dad did?" Sharon asked, surprised.

Serenity nodded and Raelynn looked at her shocked. "Our dads worked together? Why don't I remember that?" She pulled out the chair and settled next to her friend.

Serenity shrugged. "I don't know. Maybe it was too hard for you to remember everything from back then. It wasn't a long time that they worked together either. But I remember this guy went missing and then showed up dead by the river one night. They never found out who did it. I think it was a few years after your dad went missing. My dad didn't take it well and that's when he started drinking."

Bonded Blood

She shrugged again. "I guess he thought everyone around him was leaving somehow and he was losing his friends for no reason."

Sharon tapped her lips and stared out the glass doors behind Raelynn and Serenity. "I wonder…" her voice trailed off and then she suddenly stood and disappeared down the hallway.

The three watched her hurry away and then looked at each other confused. "Ok, that was weird, right?" Serenity asked.

Beau and Raelynn both nodded and then laughed.

Raelynn, turning serious again, said, "Honestly, Reni, I don't remember us being friends before like fourth grade. And that was after my dad was gone."

Serenity nodded. "We were in the same class since kindergarten but really didn't do much together before then."

"Serenity, dear, what is your father's name? And his friend, the artist?" Sharon called from down the hall.

Startled, Serenity answered her questions, giving the other two at the table a questioning look. They both just shrugged again, but smiled this time, knowing this wasn't the first time nor would it be the last.

"I know, it's weird, but trust the process," Beau said quietly.

"I don't have much choice, do I?" she asked with a nervous laugh.

They were quiet for a few minutes, each lost in their own thoughts. Raelynn was shocked to hear about the history she had with Serenity and her family that she had somehow forgotten. She wondered how many other things she had forgotten. She had been so focused back then that her brain must have compensated and blocked out unnecessary or traumatic things.

Raelynn jumped slightly when Beau touched her arm. He lifted his hands in the air and then smiled.

"What has you so on edge, Rae?" he asked.

She looked at him and shrugged. "I don't know. I guess I was thinking about all the things that I may have forgotten over the years." She motioned with her hand to Serenity. "I don't remember us being friends that long ago. I mean I remember things since my dad has gone missing, but nothing about what Ren has been talking about from before that."

Her voice sounded distant and detached as she tried to remember Serenity and her family before she turned eight. Was Serenity at her eighth birthday? It was the last birthday she celebrated before yesterday. She didn't remember anything except a lot of crying for her dad.

"Hey," Serenity's soft voice broke into her thoughts, "Rae, it's not a big deal. I mean there's a lot of my high school years I don't remember because of all that was going on. You shouldn't feel bad about not remembering something."

Raelynn looked up to find her friend still seated next to her. "I know, it's just that, I don't know, I just feel like there's so much more I am missing. Like, what else have I forgotten?"

Just then Sharon came flying back into the room. Raelynn watched her with wide eyes. There was no other way to describe what was happening. The older woman settled next to Beau at the table again.

"Ok, ok, listen up. I think we have found something. Well, I have anyway," Sharon said with a snort. When none of the others laughed, she waved them off. "Ok, well, Darius Brown, the man who was killed, he was a well-known artist around these parts for a few years. Everyone had high hopes for his future. I knew his mother, nicest woman you could ever meet. He was supposed to be the first of their family to go to college, art school at that. But then his dad was suddenly killed in an accident, and he had to quit school and go to work to help support his family." She paused and had a faraway look on her face.

Raelynn watched Sharon's face go from excited to melancholy as she thought of the misfortune of the family. She gently cleared her throat, and Sharon glanced over at her surprised, broken from her memories.

"Sorry," she said with a shake of her head. "His family was very active in our church, and we got to know them well. Gary and I used to meet with Darius' grandparents for breakfast now and then and convinced them to head up and organize one of the more vocal groups of black families addressing social justice around here."

She paused again and then cleared her own throat. "Anyway, a while after he had to go back to work, his mom had come to me and asked me to help him find a way back to his art, which meant he would have to also find a way out of his job. She knew there was something off about the plant, but no one knew then how bad it actually was." She let out a deep sigh and added, "He was killed just two weeks after that."

The four of them sat in silence, digesting her words.

"So where does that leave us, Sharon?" Raelynn hesitantly asked.

Sharon shook her head. "I'm actually not sure. But if Darius was the inspiration for your turtles, then maybe there *is* a connection to your father. Do you remember anyone your dad worked with, Raelynn?"

"No, I don't even remember Serenity's dad working with mine," she admitted grimly.

Sharon waved her hand dismissively. "It's ok. If there's a connection, I will find it."

"But how, Sharon?" Beau asked, looking between the three women at the table. "You said Darius died a long time ago. It's not like he came back from the dead to make these statues and send them to Rae."

Sharon chuckled. "No, I'm not suggesting that. I am just thinking about other possible connections. Maybe Lee, Raelynn's father, knew him and since Darius and Donte, Serenity's father, were friends, it is safe to assume that Lee also knew them." She stood and hurried back to the hallway and disappeared.

Serenity shook her head. "Ok, so she said some stuff, but none of it seemed any closer to anything. Did you guys get something that I missed?"

Raelynn and Beau both shook their head and sighed collectively.

"I guess we just keep working on this and wait," Beau said, tapping the pad of paper in front of him.

They had barely focused on the papers in front of each of them when Sharon appeared again, at the same time Trish burst through the back door. They met in the kitchen, almost as if they had been on the phone together or something because it was timed so perfectly. Both women were talking animatedly and fast, and only in half sentences.

Raelynn leaned forward and whispered, "Can anyone understand anything?" She looked between her friends and then the three turned to look at the older two in the kitchen not more than fifteen feet away.

It was crazy to watch as Sharon would say something, and Trish would nod, and then Trish would say something making Sharon nod.

"If I didn't know better, I would think they were a couple of teenage girls gossiping about the latest prom dresses," Beaus said with a laugh. "They just need to be holding hands and jumping up and down."

Raelynn and Serenity couldn't help but giggle themselves at the comparison, drawing Sharon and Trish's attention to them, earning the younger two a double glare.

"I will have you know this is very exciting stuff, youngins," Trish admonished them.

Sharon tapped her friend on the shoulder and tipped her head toward the hall. With a huff, Trish followed but not before putting her first two fingers to her eyes and then pointing them back at the younger folks at the table.

Raelynn let out a shiver. "She's kinda scary," she whispered, watching Trish follow Sharon.

"Ah, whatever," Beau said flippantly. "You have to admit it did look like two schoolgirls gossiping about whatever it was."

Serenity nodded. "I have to agree, Rae. It was funny to watch two old ladies acting like that."

Raelynn sighed. "Maybe, but that woman is not to be messed with. Bro, I have seen her house." She let out another shiver, making Beau laugh.

Giving them a questioning look, Serenity lifted her pad of paper in the air and suggested, "Let's see if we can make anything from our words."

Beau and Raelynn nodded and put their papers in front of them as well.

They compared lists and crossed out duplicate words, only one person keeping it on their list. They worked through all the words quickly and then decided to see if they could make any bigger words together. Most of the words they had so far were three, four, or five letter words. It was plausible to think the letters made one big word or maybe two smaller words. They had fifteen letters with five vowels. There had to be a few big words in there.

Serenity was the first to speak. "So, I found 'farm' before, but there are enough letters to make 'farming'. I wonder how many more we can do that with?"

"Interesting, I guess I didn't think of that. Maybe it is just adding to the words we have already," Raelynn agreed.

"I'm going to let you guys work that out," Beau said with a small smile. "How about I get us some pizza or something for dinner?" He pushed away from the table and stood beside Raelynn with a questioning look.

Raelynn looked over at Serenity. "I could eat. Reni, are you hungry?"

"I can always eat, Rae," she said with a laugh. "You know me."

The three of them decided on what to order and Beau stepped out to make the call.

"Do you think we should ask Sharon?" Serenity asked, looking toward the hallway. "It has been a little while since we have seen them." She bit her lip, looking back at her friend.

Raelynn wasn't sure if it was because she was nervous about the women coming back or that it might offend them if they didn't ask.

Bonded Blood

"I could ask I guess." She pushed away from the table and started to walk that way, just as the two older women stepped out of the hall, still talking animatedly. *They must have a soundproof room back there*, Raelynn thought, because they weren't quiet as they moved toward her.

"Trish and I are going to go check something out. Are you kids comfortable staying here for a bit alone?" Sharon asked.

Raelynn nodded. She hesitated, wanting to ask what they were checking out, but couldn't find the words.

Sharon patted her arm. "Don't worry dear," she said softly. "We will be back soon, and I will fill you in on everything. Did you want to order food or anything? Gary won't be around until late, so no need to worry about anyone showing up here."

Not knowing what to say, Raelynn just nodded again.

"Beau just went to order pizza," Serenity offered, when Raelynn remained quiet.

The older ladies just hummed and nodded, arguing their way out of the house about which one was going to drive. Trish complained about Sharon's car being too small. Raelynn knew she had a yellow Mini Cooper and Trish probably had good reason to complain. But Raelynn also knew she would likely lose the argument as well.

Beau walked back in and had a grin on his face. "That has to be the funniest thing I have seen in a while." He was pointing behind him with his thumb, probably talking about the older women getting into the tiny car.

Raelynn laughed in spite of herself. She had seen Sharon get out of the vehicle over the summer and had to admit she thought the same thing.

"OK, let's make some more words while we wait," she said with a clap of her hands. It had already been a long day, and she felt like they weren't any further along than when they started.

Chapter 24

Raelynn had completely forgotten it was her birthday until Beau pulled out a dessert pizza from the restaurant and insisted that he and Serenity sing happy birthday to her.

"Seriously, you're being weird," she said, laughing at their terrible singing. "We had a party last night. I don't need all this too."

Beau shrugged. "It doesn't matter. Today is the day and that is important." He took both of her hands in his and squeezed. "I'm glad I am here with you today, Rae." The sincerity in his words almost made her blush. Almost.

A sudden ringing on her phone brought Raelynn's attention away from her friends. She was surprised to see it was her boss.

"Hey Susiana! Is everything ok?" she asked anxiously. Susiana rarely called so Raelynn was on high alert hoping something terrible didn't happen.

"Oh, hi, Raelynn," her boss said with a chipper voice. Letting Raelynn relax slightly. She wouldn't sound happy if the café burned down or something, she thought. "Listen, I just decided to close up tomorrow so you don't need to come in. I am setting up pickup or deliveries with everyone who placed cookie orders. Have a happy Halloween!"

To say she was surprised was an understatement. Susiana never closed up, and she couldn't help but wonder why she was tomorrow. The line clicked and she pulled the phone from her ear and stared at it.

"Is everything ok?" Serenity asked.

Raelynn just nodded. "Susiana closed the café tomorrow. So, I don't have to work. She never does that!"

"I'm sure it's because of Halloween," Beau said. "She has a young son, right? No one likes to go out past dark anymore. I'm sure that's why." He sat next to her at the table and waited for her to reply.

"I guess. It's just odd," she confirmed. "I guess I should enjoy the extra day off and not ask questions." She finally gave a shrug and looked at the papers in front of her. "Although a break from this would be nice," she grumbled.

"Maybe we should take a break and get out of here for a while?" Beau suggested. It was around five thirty and Sharon and Trish had not returned. "Maybe just go to the park and walk for a little bit. I could use some fresh air."

Serenity nodded. "Me too. C'mon, Rae." She pulled Raelynn's arm until she got up from the chair.

"Ok, Ok," Raelynn said with a laugh. "I'll just leave them a note in case they get back before us."

She quickly scribbled a note to Sharon, and then Beau and Raelynn got into Raelynn's car. Serenity decided to drive herself because she wasn't sure how long she would be able to stay. They headed out in the direction of the city park that sat alongside the Wicomico River. At this spot, the river was pretty narrow and there were a few cute bridges that crossed the river around the park. The walking path felt like it was deep in the woods because it sat below the level of the street with a lot of tree coverage.

They walked in silence for a while, the path a rough one. It wasn't paved and widened and narrowed as the trees did the same. It was still wide enough for a few bikers as well as walkers.

Raelynn pulled her jacket a little closer to herself as she felt a chill from the breeze. *It's definitely fall on the Shore*, she thought. She noticed the number of people around was smaller than normally would be on a summer evening.

Out of nowhere a small blur came running toward them. Raelynn was lost in her thoughts, and the sudden movement startled her. The animal couldn't have been more than two feet tall and just as long. But she saw it out of the corner of her eye, and she didn't recognize it as a dog at first.

She jumped and let out a little screech as it came barreling toward them. She didn't miss the look of surprise on Beau's face as she hid behind him.

"Rae?" he asked confused. "It's a dog. Yours is like ten times this size!" But he still reached back to hold her there protectively.

The tiny dog came up to them and sniffed their feet. Raelynn snorted at her ridiculousness and reached down to pet the small pup. Soon a young boy came running, calling out to it. Raelynn figured it was the dog's name. She waved him over and with relief, he clipped a leash on the reluctant pup and thanked them, racing away again.

Once they were out of sight, Beau turned and looked at Raelynn. "Are you ok? I didn't think you were afraid of dogs, unless you consider yours a small horse, then I guess I get it."

Serenity suddenly let out a giggle, which led to a fit of giggles, leaving Beau and Raelynn staring at her.

She waved her hand, trying to catch her breath. "Sorry," she said, in between giggles. "It's just…like…when…we…" Serenity hunched over, putting her hands on her knees trying to calm herself.

"Reni, you are making no sense. What is so funny?" Raelynn asked, now standing with her arms crossed over her chest, somewhat defensive at being laughed at.

Taking a deep breath, Serenity stood up and looked at Raelynn. "Oh my god, that was funny."

"No, it wasn't!" Raelynn insisted. "And it just startled me, that's all."

Serenity waved her hand again. "No no, not that. Don't you remember when we went to visit my poppop's farm and the chickens chased you all over the yard?"

"What are you talking about?" Raelynn asked, confused. She didn't remember anything about going to a farm when she was little and definitely not being chased by crazy chickens.

"Oh, ok." Serenity looked a bit confused, and something crossed her face. Raelynn thought it might be sadness, maybe because she didn't remember.

She reached out to take her friend's hand. "I'm sorry Reni. I just don't remember." She thought for a minute and then gave her a sheepish look, adding, "Maybe that's why I hate chickens so much."

Serenity let out another laugh as Raelynn pulled her into a hug. "Rae, I think I have some pictures actually," she said, pulling away and smiling.

"I would love to see them," Raelynn said sincerely.

"How about I go get them from my place and meet you back at Sharon's?" Serenity suggested as she rocked on her feet like a child waiting for permission to get candy.

Raelynn chuckled at her friend. "I would love that actually."

Serenity nodded and hurried off. Raelynn and Beau watched her go with humor and then turned back to walking.

"Where are we walking to?" she asked.

Beau shrugged. "No idea, just walking. We could go to the zoo," he suggested.

Raelynn walked to one of the any picnic tables set around the park. Sitting down, she said, "How about we just sit for a little bit? I just want to be outside."

"Ok," he said and settled next to her.

They sat in silence for a long time, listening to the birds and wind blow through the trees. A curious squirrel ran by at one point, making Raelynn notice that the skies were darkening.

"Maybe we should get going," she said more like a question than a statement.

Beau simply nodded and grabbed her hand as they stood and made their way toward the car. Raelynn was lost in her thoughts, pondering the revelation Serenity made that they had gone to her family's farm when they were young. So many things were coming to light that was making Raelynn concerned about her mind and memory.

As soon as she was buckled in her seatbelt, Raelynn's phone beeped with a text alert. She pulled her phone from her pocket before she started her vehicle to see a note from Sharon.

"Apparently Sharon and Trish have found something new," she told Beau. Turning toward him, she added, "They want to know when we will be back."

"Good thing we are already on our way, huh?" Beau said with a smile.

* * * * *

The group sat around the table again, Raelynn looking expectantly between Trish and Sharon. The two women had their heads together across from her and Beau, as if the younger two weren't even there.

She sat back and huffed out in frustration. Sharon glanced up and Trish gave her a scowl.

"Be patient child," Trish said.

Sharon touched her friend's arm and raised her brow as a hidden reprimand. She then turned to Raelynn and gave her a soft smile. "Just give us a couple of minutes, honey," She nodded and then went right back to locking her head with Trish's.

Beau reached over and put his arm around Raelynn's shoulder and pulled her toward him. She was so tired, she just let him and leaned into his embrace. Raelynn closed her eyes and tried to let herself relax as much as she could. She couldn't do anything at the moment, and she just wanted it all to end.

A loud clap of hands startled Raelynn and she opened her eyes, staring at Trish who now had a wry glint in her eyes while Sharon was just shaking her head. Raelynn sat up straight and looked at the other two women.

"Ok, so we are operating off of a couple hypotheses," Sharon began, after giving her friend another look. "We are still trying to figure out the letters and what they mean. But I think we have a lead on the numbers."

Sharon paused and pulled out a sheet of paper with a bunch of numbers listed. It looked like they had put them into some computer program and then printed them out a million times. Raelynn couldn't make any sense of what they seemed to be seeing in the unending list, but she would trust them and hoped they explained it.

Raelynn glanced over at Beau who had the same look on his face. He met her gaze and gave her a small shrug with his shoulder and smiled.

Trish stood and disappeared into the back hall and returned with the box of turtles. She set the box on the table and then proceeded to set them up in a row, one by one. She finally set the small hand carved chicken at the end of the row, making Raelynn shudder slightly.

Her eyes met Beau as realization sunk in. "I hate chickens, and now I think know why. But who would send this to me knowing that they scare the daylights out of me?" Her voice was barely above a whisper as she stared at the wretched creature.

Sharon picked up the chicken and turned it around and upside down. "So, this one is puzzling. Not only is it a completely different animal, but it doesn't seem to have the numbers like the others do."

"Can I see it?" Beau asked, reaching out for it.

Nodding, Sharon set it on his hand and looked over at Raelynn. She wasn't sure if it was sympathy or something else, but Raelynn dropped her eyes to her own hands on the table.

"You didn't find any numbers on this one, Sharon?" Beau asked.

"Nope, but there are three little notches on the side, almost like it makes a wing. But the other side doesn't have it, so it could be something." Sharon watched Beau turn it over and around in his hands.

Raelynn looked over at the wooden piece and sighed. She remembered the one that had the scratches above the eyes, making it look like an eyebrow instead of a number. She reached over and took the chicken from Beau. She looked closer at the wing that Sharon mentioned. She could see what Sharon was talking about because she couldn't make out anything but three short lines as well. She turned it upside down and squinted at it.

"It could be a seven and a one," she suggested.

"Show me," Sharon said, reaching across the table.

Raelynn pointed to the tiny line that came out above one of the other ones. It was a little cock-eyed, but she could make a case for it looking like a seven.

Sharon put her glasses on and squinted at the spot Raelynn pointed to. She took it from her hand and leaned over to show Trish. They whispered something and then they both nodded. Sharon looked up and smiled.

"I think you are right, Raelynn," Sharon said. "We just need to add those numbers to our list then and rerun the numbers.

Raelynn's forehead creased and looked at Sharon curiously. "What are you running numbers for, Sharon?"

"Oh, I should explain. So, we are looking for anything that would make these numbers together mean something," she said. Pulling the sheet out again, she pointed at the first ones. "The numbers could be anything. We are trying to figure out if small groups of them could be something instead of or maybe as well as dates. These four together make up your sister's birthday, but none of the other combinations seem to mean anything significant, at least with the dates your mom gave us."

Trish cleared her throat. "So, we are also looking at other dates, maybe dates in history, that might mean something or have significance. And addresses that could have meaning."

The group was silent around the table. "What if they are just one big number?" Beau asked slowly. "Or two maybe?"

Sharon looked at Beau and then at Trish. She let out a small chuckle and looked back at Beau. "Well, we kind of didn't even consider that. That's actually a huge oversight on our part."

"In all fairness, we didn't have enough numbers to make it mean anything," Trish said, justifying the miss.

She pulled the sheet out again and pointed to one list. "With this many numbers, we could be looking at a location, Sharon." She raised her eyes to meet Sharon's.

Raelynn watched the two of them, her excitement and worry building simultaneously. If the numbers pointed to a location, could it be where her dad is? Or could it be a trap for her for some weird reason? She swallowed hard and looked over at Beau.

"Well, I guess we will have to look at this again," Sharon said, scratching her chin.

Trish thought for a moment and then said, "Maybe not." Her eyes traveled to Raelynn and then down to the statues in the middle of the table.

All eyes turned to look at Trish expectantly. She looked up and gave the group a sly grin. "What if the order of the deliveries is the order of the numbers?" she asked slowly.

Recognition crossed Sharon's face, and her mouth widened in a grin. "Ok, that could be a good start." She turned her attention to Raelynn. "Do you remember what order they came in, Raelynn?"

Raelynn bit her lip. "I think I can figure it out," she said staring at the figures in front of her.

She pulled all of them toward her and subconsciously left the chicken alone, not really wanting to touch it. Taking a deep breath, Raelynn looked at each turtle and tried to piece together when she received each one. She knew the first one she got last Saturday because it was such a surprise. Raelynn set that one at the center of the table.

She looked at remaining six turtles. She remembered the two that came together, which meant those were next because Raelynn knew there were no deliveries on Sunday. Now the four that were left she had to think about.

Raelynn stared at each one carefully, setting her chin on her folded arms. Then she remembered the one with the container as the shell came the day before and the heavier one, made of the thicker metal was right before that on Thursday. She put them in the right place and stared at the last two. She did remember that the two metal ones didn't come right after each other, so that made it easier to put them in order.

Satisfied, she sat back in her chair. "I think this is it," she said, looking up at Trish and Sharon.

Sharon gave her a smile and stood with Trish to start putting the numbers from each statue in order on their paper. Once they had them all written, Trish dashed to the back room.

Raelynn suddenly wondered where Serenity was. It had been a long time, and the sun had almost completely disappeared from the sky. Sharon had turned the lights on, and the entire space lit up as if it were daytime.

"I wonder where Reni is," Raelynn asked Beau, who just gave her a shrug in return.

Trish reemerged from the hall and had a new sheet of paper in her hand. "Sharon, I'm not sure if this is correct, but it is worth checking out. The location isn't absolute, because we don't know which direction we are looking at yet, but I have run all possibilities with these combinations. We just need to somehow narrow down if we are looking at north or south and then east or west."

Sharon nodded in agreement.

"How are we going to figure that out?" Beau asked.

Both older women looked at him and smiled. "First, I need to run back to my place and get my results from the litter sample and then I ran a set of fingerprints from a piece of tape from the box that was smudged. I was able to get a good print that we are hoping to get a hit on."

Trish turned to Sharon then and added, "I'll be right back."

As soon as Trish disappeared, Sharon's phone buzzed with some sort of alert. She looked up after glancing at her phone and nodded to Raelynn with a smile. "I think your friend is here."

Raelynn stood to meet Serenity and Sharon headed back to the hallway again. Serenity looked flushed when Raelynn met her at her car.

"Is everything ok?" she asked her friend.

Serenity nodded but shifted her eyes around. Raelynn wrapped her arm around her friend's shoulder and guided her into the house. Neither spoke as they entered the brightly lit kitchen. Beau looked up and gave both girls a smile and a nod and then went back to what he was studying. Sharon was still missing, but as if she sensed someone, she appeared as soon as Raelynn and Serenity sat down.

"Hello, dear," she greeted Serenity.

Raelynn noticed her friend's eyes were still wide like something had spooked her. She put her hand on top of Serenity's, drawing the other's eyes to meet hers.

"Reni, what happened? You look like you've seen a ghost or something," Raelynn asked her gently.

That seemed to grab Sharon's attention. She moved to the table and stood at the edge. "Serenity, honey, what's going on?"

Serenity looked from her friend to the older woman and back to Raelynn again. "I…I'm not s-sure," she stumbled. Closing her eyes, she took in a breath of air and then opened them again, looking at Sharon. "My mom called on my way over here. My dad is missing. He's been gone for almost three weeks, and she didn't tell me."

"What do you mean, Ren? When did you talk to him last?" Raelynn asked, turning to Sharon with pleading eyes.

Serenity looked down at her folded hands. "I don't even know. We got into a fight about three weeks ago and I haven't talked to him since. He started acting really weird and I knew I was moving out soon. I told him he needed to grow up and start providing for mom 'cuz I wasn't going

Bonded Blood

to be able to help out with my own place and his." She sniffled and shook her head.

When she spoke again, it was barely audible as she said, "I think he got back into his gambling and drinking because he just kept going on about some big score, and it was close, blah, blah, blah." She waved her hand around and laughed bitterly. "Same old story he always used to say before. And then he would come crawling back to my mom and beg her forgiveness. Only I told him—"

Raelynn put her hand on Serenity's back and rubbed gentle circles. "It's ok, Reni. We all say things we don't mean when we're upset. I'm sure he understands."

Her friend turned a sharp gaze at her. "No, I meant it, Rae. I told him he was nothing to me if he did this to mom again."

"I'm so sorry, Reni," Raelynn said, pulling her friend close in a tight side hug.

Serenity tried to shrug, but there wasn't much strength behind it. "I just hurt for my mom. I'm going to have to figure out how to support her again." She let out a frustrated and pained sigh.

The group was silent for a few minutes and then Sharon straightened. "Serenity, dear. Do you know what your father was talking about?"

Serenity looked up at her and shook her head. "No, but he always had some get-rich scheme in his head. I'm sure it wasn't anything serious."

Sharon's phone rang at that moment, and she answered it as she walked back down the hall. All Raelynn heard was "I was just thinking that. Come back here as soon as you can, Trish. We have a new issue." Raelynn met Sharon's eyes as she turned around right before disappearing into the darkened hallway.

"They have this weird secret code I really wish they would share with us," Beau grumbled from across the table.

Both girls laughed and agreed whole-heartedly. Raelynn wondered what Sharon and Trish's sudden epiphany was about but knew it didn't do much good for her to ask. Sharon would tell them when she was ready. Instead of dwelling on it, she tugged on her friend's sleeve.

"Did you bring the pictures?" she asked, nodding toward the bag Serenity had in her lap. Maybe a good laugh would be a decent distraction from whatever was going on down the hall.

Serenity laughed and nodded. She reached into her bag and pulled out a small photo album. She set it on the table, putting the now empty bag on the floor. Turning back to the book, she gave her friend a sly grin. "Ready?" she asked.

Raelynn nodded with her own grin. She watched Serenity open the cover and immediately she was met with a photo of herself at around seven years old. She had a smile so full of joy on her face that Raelynn herself didn't remember feeling in a very long time. She realized something as she stared at the photo of the two of them.

"Reni, this was before my dad disappeared. Look, he's right there in the background," she said, her voice laced with shock and confusion. "We were friends before."

Serenity nodded slightly but gave her friend a sympathetic look. "I think our dads were friends actually. This is the first time I remember really hanging out with you. My dad invited you guys to his parents' farm with us. I think that's why the book starts with this picture, if I'm completely honest," Serenity admitted.

"And these chickens in the background are the wretched creatures that have given me the fear of chickens, huh?" Raelynn stifled a chuckle as she pointed to the group of animals in the background near where her dad and someone who had their back to the camera stood. She thought it was likely her friend's dad.

Serenity laughed. "I guess so. Wait there's a better picture," she said and flipped the pages past some group pictures of Raelynn and Serenity with Serenity's older brothers and Sahara.

"Here!" Serenity said with glee, pointing to a photo.

Raelynn looked at the photo of her younger self being chased by a chicken across the yard. "Yep, I look terrified. Who thought it would be funny to record this terrible event in history?" she asked playfully, holding in her shudder. The memory along with the trigger of the picture reminded her brain that this did in fact happen and she could feel her fear in the photo.

"Let me see that," Beau said, reaching across the table to take the album. As he did, Raelynn glanced at the opposite page and gasped.

"Wait, who is that?" she asked as she stared at the deep eyes that she had seen more over the last few days than she cared to admit.

At that moment, Trish came flying through the door and grabbed the photo album and continued into the hall to meet with Sharon. "Hold that thought!" she said over her shoulder. Her movements were so fluid, the other three were stunned into silence and just watched her go by.

Chapter 25

"Ok, I think we are on to something here," Sharon said clapping her hands together. "We just need to figure out the letters. Have you kids made any progress with that?"

Raelynn looked between her friends and shrugged. "Well, we have a list of words, but nothing that is earth-shattering." She pulled out the sheet of paper they had compiled a while ago. Heck, it seemed like days ago.

"I am still trying to figure out if there is anything special about the litter, but let's focus on the letters and these notes. The last one being the most ominous if you ask me," Trish said, pulling out the note that read "Out of time." She stared at it and sighed. "You are still here, Raelynn, so it might not have anything to do with you directly."

Sharon nodded. "I haven't noticed anyone hanging around here that shouldn't be. Have you gotten any phone calls or notice anyone hanging around you guys at all?"

Raelynn shook her head. "Nothing really." Then she widened her eyes as she realized something. "But I haven't heard from my mom or brother in a while. Is it possible they are the ones in danger and not me?" She picked up her phone and debated if she should call, and then what would she even say. If her family was safe, she didn't want to scare them unnecessarily either.

"They do still have Timmy, right, Rae?" Beau asked, as if he was reading her mind. "Just make sure he's doing ok and see if he can stay a while longer. Maybe even overnight again."

Raelynn nodded and tried to give him a smile. It likely came out as a grimace though as she was now worried about their safety.

Sharon sighed and looked at Trish. "Raelynn, I, well, *we*, think this is not about you or your family."

"What do you mean?" she asked, not really understanding what Sharon was trying to say. Of course it had to do with her. The deliveries were made directly to her, the notes were handed to her personally.

"Let's start with something easy." Sharon pulled out the letter from Raelynn's mom and a photo of the writing on one of the boxes. "As far as we can tell, the writing doesn't seem to match your dad's. At least not on this package. But on this first note you received the writing looks similar enough that we could say with a certain amount of confidence that your dad could have written this note."

Raelynn sucked in her breath. *That means my dad is alive*, she thought, unsure of what else was coming. They were words she had been hoping to hear for so many years. A throat clearing brought her attention back to the table.

Sharon tapped the note to show Raelynn which one she was referencing. "The rest of the packages, aside from this one, you mentioned were on printed labels, so no other writing samples could be used. But the notes all appear to be hand-written. We aren't sure how they were able to get printed labels, but it is pretty clear there may not have been access to computers or printers to type out the notes."

Trish pulled out her own notes and pointed to the list of numbers they had printed out. "The other issue we have is where these locations are. I needed to finalize the analysis of the sample we got from the small container to see if we can narrow down the area we are looking. I had to add a couple more tests to see if there was anything unique in this sample that would distinguish it somehow."

Raelynn looked up with a question in her eyes. "What are you looking for?" she asked, her eyes dancing between the two older women.

Trish and Sharon shared a look and Sharon finally spoke. "We think your dad might be alive. But we don't know where or how. There is no trace of him anywhere. We have not been able to find him on any cameras around like traffic cams or doorbells. So, we suspect he might be getting help or at least has somehow gotten access to money in order to survive off the grid for so long. It may be money through the Rios as one of their guys, or it could be the opposite. But until we can figure out some of these things, we are operating as if he is an accomplice and is dangerous."

Sharon's words were like a knife cutting through Raelynn. She felt her breath stall and suddenly felt ill. Could she believe her dad was a bad guy? That he was capable of killing people? She shook her head hard, making her dizziness worse. She was just told he was alive, but they are tarnishing his image calling him evil and capable of the brutality in the photos she saw. But Sharon did say before that the Del Rios could help someone disappear if they wanted to. Is that what her dad really wanted?

Beau, now sitting beside her, pulled her into his side and rubbed her arm soothingly.

"Rae, it's a precaution more than anything right now," Sharon said quietly. "We have to be very careful."

Raelynn just closed her eyes and tried to relax into Beau's shoulder and calm her racing mind. She needed to focus. The important thing she needed to take away is that he is alive. Now she had to help find him and hopefully find out the truth about everything.

With renewed determination, she opened her eyes and straightened in her chair. "Ok, what do we need to do?" she asked, folding her hands in front of her.

"Well," Trish cleared her throat, "The first thing we need to do it figure out where this litter came from." She held up the small turtle that had the container of dirt in it. "I have an analysis of what it contained, and there is something unique in it, but I haven't quite figured out what it is or how we go about finding out more. But we are working on that."

Sharon picked up another photo and held it up. "One of the boxes had smudges on the tape and we were able to get a decent print that I am currently running to see if it's anyone in the system that could help us out."

Raelynn smiled to herself. She had thought that it might help and was pleased with her thought that it could be used. She had forgotten about it but when she brought all the statues, she had inadvertently brought that particular box. *So, we got a stroke of luck*, she thought.

"Raelynn, you might want to see about your dog. We can either keep going on this tonight or we can get some sleep and come back in the morning." Sharon looked at Raelynn, who then looked over at Beau.

Beau shrugged. "I don't have to work tomorrow, and your boss gave you the day off. I'm good with whatever you want to do," he said with a grin.

Serenity smiled as well. "I know no one asked, but I am available too."

"Oh, Reni, of course we want you here!" Raelynn laughed and squeezed her hand. "I can use all the support I can get right now. But if you need to be with your mom, I do understand."

Sharon cleared her throat loudly. "I actually think you should stay here too Serenity, dear." She glanced over at Trish and Raelynn noticed an almost imperceptible shake of her head, making her lift her brow.

Serenity shrugged. "I'm ok with staying. I don't know what I can do at home anyway."

Raelynn didn't look at her friend, but was watching Sharon and Trish have their silent conversation, curious about what they weren't saying. She assumed it had something to do with her friend, but she was hesitant to ask. She looked over at Beau who was watching her with the same curiosity she knew she was watching the older women. She raised her eyebrow at him, and he gave her a grin and a lift of his shoulder.

Shaking her head, she looked away, not able to hide the grin on her own face.

"Ok, so while we wait for the fingerprints to come back, let's look at these words." Sharon clapped her hands together and looked at their list.

Trish settled into a chair at the head of the table and pinched her chin with her finger and thumb. "I think we need to look at anything connected to chickens or farms or something."

Raelynn looked over at her and squinted. "Why chickens and farms? I am still traumatized by the chicken carving and some person's weird taunting." She let out a shiver and both older women looked over at her.

"That's it!" Trish said, slapping the table. "The chicken is the last clue." She glanced over at Sharon, who nodded and smiled.

Raelynn again looked between them and let out a frustrated breath. "You two have that weird silent telepathy going on again and it is seriously annoying. What does the dang chicken have to do with anything?" She sat back in her chair and dropped her head back to stare at the ceiling.

"Well, we think the chicken is the clue that will tie everything together." Sharon started to explain after she let out a chuckle.

Trish picked up after Sharon and added, "The chicken carving seems to confirm that we are looking for a chicken farm. We know the litter from the container came from a chicken farm. But there is something in it that we couldn't place. We are hoping it will give us a clue as to where the litter came from, so we have a starting place to search."

"What do you mean 'search'?" Raelynn asked quietly, fearing the worst.

"We need a place to start. We are hoping these letters and numbers will lead us somewhere. But we aren't sure yet what we are searching for. It could be your father, or it could be a trap. We just don't know," Sharon explained.

Raelynn looked up at her and resisted a shudder. "But you think my father is alive? I will be able to finally see him and hug him?" For so long she had been hoping for someone to believe her, believe her father was still alive, but no one had given her this much hope before, let alone said it out loud. She felt like her lungs were closing in on her and she couldn't breathe.

Beau put his arm around her shoulder and leaned into her. "Breathe, Rae. It's going to be ok," he said softly, calmly holding her close.

"I am optimistic, Raelynn. That is the best I can say right now. I am not positive it isn't a trap either though, so we have to be very careful with our information." Sharon leaned across the table to pat her hand as well. "And we have to be careful who we trust." She glanced at Serenity and added, "I am not positive your father is not also involved, so I would like you to stay here and be safe, if you are ok with that."

Serenity's face clouded over, and she scowled at Sharon. "How can you think my dad could do something to put my friend, *his* friend in danger or worse, or be the cause of her dad going missing! You don't even know him and you are making a judgement based on what exactly?" She stood and crossed her arms over her chest.

Raelynn had never seen her friend so angry before. It caught her completely off guard. She stared at Serenity and wondered what had suddenly happened. She thought Sharon just wanted her to be safe, but maybe she had misunderstood.

"Dear, don't be angry. There are things going on that we don't fully know yet. I need you to stay calm and help us figure it out. We don't know anything for sure yet," Sharon stood and tried to calm Serenity, who just pushed her away.

Serenity shook her head. "You have nothing to tie my dad to this." She swung her hand over the table with everything covering it.

"We have his fingerprints," Trish blurted out, crossing her arms across her own chest as if challenging the younger woman.

Serenity stared at her. "What?"

Sharon sighed and moved to Serenity's side. She shot a glare at Trish over her shoulder. "We don't know for sure yet, but we have some other things that tie him to the death of his friend. Please let's sit down and talk about this, ok?"

"You're lying," she said defiantly. "My dad would not do anything like this. He was friends with Rae's dad."

Sharon sighed and shook her head. "Look, I know we are just starting to figure this all out, but there is a connection to the three men and the Rios. I am not pointing fingers yet because I know we don't know everything. But I am hoping if we can find where this all leads, we will get all the answers."

"Fine," Serenity gave in and dropped herself back in her chair. She was clearly frustrated, but she seemed to also understand there was a lot more at play in the situation.

Raelynn watched her friend and wasn't sure how to feel herself. She was scared for the first time that she was going to find out that her father was actually one of the bad guys and not the perfect dad she remembered. What would she do then?

Sensing her sudden shift in mood, Beau pulled her close again. "Rae, it's going to be ok. No matter what happens, you will get through this. And I'll be right here by your side."

She grabbed a hold of his hand on her shoulder and squeezed it. "Thank you, Beau." She gave him a weak smile and a nod.

"So, what do we need to do now?" Beau asked the group.

"Well, we need to wait for the analysis and confirmation on the prints. Until then we need to see what else we can get from this." Trish looked back at the piles on the table.

Serenity let out a huff and leaned forward. She shuffled through the papers and notes, laying them out. She had them in a line and then she froze. Raelynn followed her gaze and landed on the hand drawn picture she had gotten from Creepy Guy. It was the only note that didn't have words on it.

"Reni, where are the photos from the farm?" she asked with a shaky voice.

Serenity seemed to sense the same thing and flipped through the book to find the photo she knew her friend was looking for. She took the photo out of the sleeve and handed it to Raelynn with a grim expression.

Raelynn picked up the hand drawn note and set it next to the photo. It was a match.

Sharon gasped. "Where is this, Serenity?" She picked up the photo and the drawing comparing them.

"It's my grandparents' farm. Rae and I went there when we were young." Her voice was soft and dejected as she realized her dad had to be involved somehow if this was part of everything.

Trish took the papers from Sharon and studied them. "Where is this?" she asked, without moving her eyes from them.

Bonded Blood

"I don't know. My grandparents died in a fire on the property a long time ago. I don't think I have been there since I was eight or nine. My dad never wanted to go back, and my uncle moved across the bridge after. That's like thirteen or fourteen years ago I guess. Maybe longer." Serenity's eyes never left the table in front of her as she spoke.

Sharon and Trish once again locked eyes and Trish spoke first. "We need to find this place as quickly as possible."

Sharon nodded. "You don't know where it is though, Serenity? Was it a long drive to get there?" She started to ruffle through the papers and finally found what she was looking for. She stared at the list of numbers again.

Serenity shook her head. "I'm sorry. I was little. I just remember getting in the car and riding. We played 'I Spy' games, and I always looked for this one farm that had horses. I always loved horses growing up. I know it didn't take us all day to get there, now that I think about it. We usually left in the morning after breakfast and then we ate lunch with Poppop and Granny on the back porch." She paused for a second and then added, "But I always got to feed the horses before that. So, it couldn't be too far away, right?"

"Did you live near Raelynn at the time?" Trish asked.

Serenity was quiet for a minute and then looked at Raelynn. "Actually, we moved by Rae right before we visited the farm. We used to live down by Pocomoke before that."

Trish and Sharon put their heads together and were mumbling quietly, pointing at the sheet.

"Can you *please* share what you are talking about?" Raelynn asked. She was getting increasingly frustrated with the older women and was struggling to be polite about it. There was more that they weren't telling them, and it bothered her a lot.

Sharon let out a soft sigh. "Ok. I will try to explain it. We have quite a few different options for these numbers, if we assume they are coordinates to a location. We have to first figure out the order, which group comes first and then if it is north or south, and east or west." She pointed at the photo from the farm and added, "and we have to see if we can figure out where this is and if it is listed on a registry or anything."

"Without the name, it is going to be difficult to find this farm though." Trish raised her brow at her friend, who nodded in return.

"Maybe that's what the letters are," Raelynn said suddenly. "Maybe they are jumbled up and if we unscramble them, they spell the name of the farm." She was finally starting to see something come together. It didn't seem like such a long shot any more.

Serenity nodded and then moved to the same side of the table as Raelynn and Beau. The three put their heads together to go over their list of words. Trish and Sharon did the same with the numbers, trying to figure out what the options were for a location not far away, but not too close either.

They all worked in silence for about fifteen minutes when Raelynn sat back in her seat, Serenity on one side of her and Beau on the other.

"Well, we have some options, I guess," she said, stretching her arms above her head. "Most of the farms out here seem to have the word 'farm' or 'farming' in their name. So, we can take 'farming' as one of our words."

Bonded Blood

She started a new sheet of paper to help them organize their words into potential farm names.

Serenity bit her lip and then said, "I see 'four'. My dad had one brother who worked on the farm and then with him and his parents that could be part of it, right? But 'four farming' doesn't make sense."

"It's a start though," Beau said, encouraging her to keep going. He studied the words and suddenly asked Serenity, "Did all of their names start with the same letter? Or a family last name or something?"

She thought for a second. And then smiled. "Yep! They all start with the letter 'D' actually. Donte, Darryl, DeShaun, and Dede. Their last name is the same as mine."

"OK, so let's pull out the letters we know for 'farming' and 'four' and let's just take the letter 'd' for now. What do we have left?" Raelynn asked. "Wait. Remember the one capitalized letter? Here! 'D'. This has to be it." She rewrote the capitalized letter by the words "four" and "farming".

Beau looked at the papers and watched as Raelynn wrote the words out. "If we go with 'Four D Farming' we still have letters left though."

"It looks like we have 'big' left," Raelynn said with a sigh. "'Big Four D Farming'?" she asked as she looked around the table. "Or 'Four Big D Farming'?"

Serenity smiled and shrugged. "It could be either and it would still make sense. They were a really close family. I know my dad always talked about how much that farm meant to his dad and family was the most important thing."

Trish tapped her chin. "That makes sense then, with the four hands on the design." She nodded and turned to

Sharon who at some point had disappeared and reappeared with a laptop. "Try both and see what we get."

Sharon got to work typing on her keyboard. She let out a frustrated huff after a few minutes.

"I don't see either name anywhere," Sharon said as she typed. "But that doesn't necessarily mean anything. If it's not an active farm, it may not show up. So, let's work on the numbers." She turned back to Serenity.

"How many games did you play, or songs did you sing, Serenity?" Trish asked. "It might not seem like it means anything, but we are looking anywhere from Philly and New York to right here in Wicomico County."

Sharon nodded. "Do you remember if you had to stop for anything along the way?"

"I don't think so, but I honestly don't remember. I'm sorry." Serenity dropped her head in frustration.

Raelynn put her arm around her friend. "Hey, it's ok. We were little. Heck, I don't even remember going, so at least you remember that much more than me," she said with a sad chuckle.

Trish sighed. "If we can figure out what this extra substance is in the litter, we will be closer. We will have to work on that."

"What about the fingerprints?" Raelynn asked. "Will that tell us anything?"

"We are working on confirmation," Sharon said with a frustrated sigh. "But there is still another way." She had a glint in her eye that Raelynn couldn't quite decipher.

Raelynn's phone suddenly rang, and she looked at the caller ID and saw it was her mom calling. She realized she had forgotten to call and check on Timmy. Feeling

Bonded Blood

guilty, she answered it as she got up and moved away from the table.

"Hey, mom," she answered.

A snicker on the other end made her stop walking. "Not mom," her brother said, laughing.

She resisted an eye roll as she groaned. "What's up Jericho?"

"Mom told me to call and see what the plan was with Timmy. I want to keep him tonight again, but mom said I have to ask you because it's your dog, blah blah." His sarcastic preteen voice made Raelynn smile. She was glad they were ok, and it seemed as if everything was fine there.

"If mom said it's ok, then he can stay tonight. I am still working on this thing with Beau anyway. Can I talk to mom?" She bit her cheek as she listened to her brother give a shout of excitement and then waited for her mom to answer.

"Is everything ok, Rae? You have been at it all day," Honesty's concerned voice came over the line a few seconds later.

Raelynn sighed. "I know. It's been a long day. But I think we are making progress. Um, mom, is everything ok there?"

"Yes. Your brother thinks Timmy is his dog now, and you might have a hard time getting him back," she said with laughter in her voice.

Raelynn smiled, but she knew it was forced. She was worried but didn't want her mom to worry too, especially if it wasn't anything. She wanted more information before she divulged too much. "And nothing else has come to the house, right?"

The other end of the line was silent for a few moments before her mom's voice came through again. "Rae, are you sure everything is ok? Nothing has come at all. But you sound worried."

"No, it's ok. I just didn't want to miss anything just in case." She forced herself to be positive as she waited for her mom to call her bluff.

Instead, Honesty sighed. "Ok, sweetheart. Please be careful."

"I will. Love you mom. Take care of *my* pup for me," she said stressing the possessive, making her mom chuckle.

She hung up and turned to the table again. Sharon was staring at her computer screen and the other three were staring at Sharon.

"What happened?" Raelynn asked, moving closer to the group.

"Well, we have a problem, and I think I know why the last note says 'out of time.'" Sharon said, turning her screen to show Raelynn. "There's a major court case coming up on Monday regarding the Del Rios, right here in Salisbury at the courthouse. We may actually be out of time, Raelynn."

Chapter 26

"I am confused. What does a major case with the Del Rios have to do with my father?" Raelynn asked.

Sharon looked at Trish and then at Raelynn. "I am going to guess that the case they have been trying to delay for years is finally going to be tried. I am going to look into it more and I have a couple of contacts I can call. But if I were to guess, I would say whoever has been reaching out to you is hoping to use you somehow in the trial."

Raelynn scowled. "There is nothing I am good for. I don't know anything, and this is the first time I have ever heard of them." She shook her head and slouched in her chair. Just when she thought they were getting somewhere something new came up.

Trish was busy tapping away at the keyboard of the laptop. She huffed out a few curse words here and there and then tapped away some more. If she weren't so stressed about everything, Raelynn would have laughed at her.

Sharon leaned over as Trish pointed at something on the screen. Both women then looked at Raelynn.

"What?" she asked. "Why are you looking at me like that?"

"I'm afraid what Trish has found doesn't look good for you, or your dad," Sharon said quietly.

"What do you mean?" Beau asked for Raelynn. Grateful for not having to ask again what was going on, Raelynn shot him a small smile.

Trish let out a puff of air and pushed the screen toward the center of the table. "So, I was able to hack into the court system to get more information." She paused to give Sharon a glare when the other woman cleared her throat loudly. "Anyway, the prosecutor is charging your dad with murder and corruption and a bunch of other things that we know the Del Rios are guilty of. But this names him specifically in the death of Darius Brown and Jervante Davis."

"This isn't happening," Raelynn groaned. "So even if he's still alive, which it sounds like he is, he won't be coming home anytime soon."

Sharon stood and moved to stand behind Raelynn. "Dear, I think this may be a trap. I'm not sure why they want your dad, but if we can somehow prove he is innocent, and we can find him before Monday, we might be able to save him. But we are going to have to be careful."

"Oh, this is not good," Trish groaned as she continued to tap the keys. "It looks like the county attorney has the list of witnesses and one of them is Officer Milton."

Raelynn felt her blood run cold. "What? He's helping them convict my dad? Why?" She couldn't believe that he would turn on her like that, but it made sense now why he sent her to Sharon instead of helping her. He was in on it. Maybe he was actually leading her on and wanted to lead her to her dad and catch him or kill him for what he has supposedly done.

"It looks like there are plenty of other charges they are trying to convict him of as well." Trish looked up at Sharon.

Bonded Blood

"This stinks like something out of the you-know-where. There has to be something we are missing." She continued to angerly type away at the keyboard.

After a few more minutes of no sound except the keys being aggressively pounded on, Trish groaned. She looked at Sharon and spun the screen to face her.

"Apparently there was a large sum of money that went missing quite a few years ago and the Rios are looking for it. They may be trying to find it and believe your dad took it before he disappeared." Trish said quietly.

Sharon stared at the screen and then looked at Trish. "It could be what he has been living off of for so long."

"It could also be hidden somewhere, and no one knows where." Trish reasoned. Then she glanced at Serenity. "You said your dad kept saying there was a big score or something, right?"

Serenity just nodded, a look of horror taking over her soft features as she realized her father was possibly involved in trying to find the money and then take out Raelynn's father at the same time.

Sharon was quiet for a moment. "I think we need to figure out the location of these numbers. Maybe there is something there, a clue or some evidence to prove your dad's innocence or implicate someone else."

"Maybe," Trish said slowly. "Or it could be a trap to catch someone else to then lure out Lee." She raised her eyebrows with slight nod toward Serenity, who dropped her head.

"But how can we find out where the farm used to be if it's not listed anywhere?" Raelynn asked, turning the conversation in a different direction. She reached over and grasped her friend's hand, not wanting her to go down that path just yet.

Trish shrugged. "The analysis shows it was definitely chicken litter in the container. It is likely from a farm that hasn't been active in a while as the numbers weren't consistent with what a fresh flock would have dropped."

She pulled out a form with numbers and charts. "There are no traces of salmonella, which suggests the litter is older, but also protected from the elements. I know from some research I have recently done for another reason that we have between 1500 and 2400 abandoned chicken houses on just the Eastern Shore. So even if we limited our search to old, abandoned farms, we are still looking at a monumental task. We need to narrow down our search to a smaller geographical area."

"If we can identify something that is specific to a certain company or location, we would limit our search to a group rather than every house on the shore," Sharon added. "Trish was there anything in the sample that would suggest if we should be looking in Maryland versus Delaware or Virginia?"

Beau jumped in before Trish could respond. He had a thoughtful look on his face as he listened to the older women talk. "I might be able to help," he said slowly, still thinking. "I have a degree in animal science from UMES. Maybe I could do some digging on some of the other companies on the shore who run chicken houses, and we can figure out which ones use which feed, et cetera, to narrow our search."

Trish snapped her fingers and Raelynn looked between them in complete confusion. "I am so confused right now," she mumbled.

Bonded Blood

"I know, this is a lot," Sharon said, "but Beau is right. For example, if we can narrow down which companies use vegetarian diets for their flocks, we could easily eliminate some farms." She lifted her paper and squinted at the words.

Trish picked up where Sharon left off. "There are large amounts of potassium, nitrogen, and phosphorus, along with traces of feathers and dander, which confirms it came from a chicken house."

She looked over and gave Sharon a nod before continuing. "There is some evidence of certain proteins, which suggest that the company did not use a vegetarian feed, which you already mentioned. I know at least one local company that only uses vegetarian feed, so we can rule them out right away. But the biggest question is this 'Azomite.' I don't know anything about it, but it is present in the litter so it must mean something." Trish stared at the paper, as if she were making sure she was reading it correctly.

The group was quiet and then Beau slapped the table. "Wait. I did my research paper on chicken gut health and unique minerals to help improve it."

Raelynn groaned and wrinkled her nose, making him laugh. "Ok, I know, weird, but it might be helpful now." He turned to Trish. "There's a substance called azomite that is actually a group of minerals and traces of other elements. It is difficult to come by since it is only mined and produced in Utah. The company that developed it put it on the market and then sold their patent and all their stock to one chicken company. That company now only produces it for this one chicken company and no one else can get their hands on it."

Sharon and Trish nodded along with his explanation as Trish started to tap away at the keyboard again. "I remember reading about this a long time ago. I think there was some sort of lawsuit the other companies tried to bring forward as a non-monopoly type thing to be able to get their hands on it, but they lost. Beau, do you remember which company bought it? I bet they still use it today, or at least did when this farm was still active. If we can get into their system, we might be able to identify their chicken houses and possibly find where this sample came from." Sharon held up the small turtle with the now empty container.

"I don't but I have everything on my drive. I might even have it on my phone. Just give me a second and I'll try to find it." He pulled out his phone and started searching.

While everyone was searching for something, Raelynn glanced over at Serenity. "Are you ok, Reni?" she asked quietly.

Her friend just shrugged. "I don't know how to feel actually," she admitted. "I was angry at my dad and then worried and now I'm angry again. I'm so sorry, Rae. What if he is the one after your dad and ends up doing something terrible? I couldn't survive knowing my family caused you that kind of pain."

"It's not your fault, Reni," Raelynn said trying to comfort her friend. "We will get through this, whatever this is, together ok?" She gave her a side hug as Serenity nodded.

"Got it!" Beau said suddenly. "It was Amery Farms. They have hundreds of farms on just the shore though."

Trish started to excitedly tap on the keyboard. "Ok, we have narrowed it down a little bit. How about are there any in Pennsylvania?" She didn't even look up from her screen as she shot out questions.

Bonded Blood

Beau and Sharon were both on their phones. Raelynn glanced at Serenity and nearly laughed. She had the same lost look Raelynn was positive was on her own face as she watched the trio do their research. Serenity made eye contact with Raelynn and they both laughed, bringing the attention back to the younger two.

"What's funny?" Trish demanded, finally looking away from her screen.

Raelynn waved her hand at the three of them and shrugged. "I feel kind of useless right now and you three seem to know what you are doing, so I just thought it was funny. Me and Reni are just lost and watching."

"I didn't mean to be disrespectful or anything, we just thought it was funny that we seem to be just sitting and watching you all work," Serenity added with a wave of her hand between herself and her friend.

Trish snorted and went back to her laptop and Beau bumped shoulders with Raelynn and grinned. "Hey, I finally feel like I can help. Who knew such a weird major would come back to potentially help out in a big trial?"

"Nothing in PA," Sharon announced. "That leaves us with the Delmarva Peninsula. Unfortunately, it still leaves us with a lot of farms to check out. There isn't much around here that is more than a couple of hours from Salisbury."

Trish tapped her lips with her fingernail. "Maybe I can get into their old files and see what farms are no longer active," she suggested, and then started typing again.

"What about the news?" Raelynn suggested. All eyes turned to her, and she shrugged and looked over at Serenity.

"You said your grandparents died in a fire on the property, right? Well, if there was a fire that took lives, it may have been on the news." She looked between the others at the table.

Sharon nodded. "Good idea, Raelynn." Then she started to tap away at her phone again.

Not even five minutes later, Trish clapped her hands together. "Got it. Amery only has about 20 non-active farms. If I can go backwards to see what they have now and what they had say fifteen years ago, maybe that will help us narrow it down. If I can go back further, we might be able to get the location of the farm since we now know the name. This list doesn't give me the names of the inactives, just the locations—which is odd actually."

She continued doing whatever it was she was doing without looking up and then finally said, "Sharon, I printed off a few lists. Can you go grab them? If I had my setup, we could compare them over the different screens. Paper will have to do for now." She let out a long and dramatic sigh, giving Sharon an exasperated look.

Raelynn couldn't tell if she was complaining or just grumbling to herself.

Sharon came back and gave the papers to Trish then sat back in her chair. "I have figured out the configurations for the numbers. If we just assume they are coordinates, I have ruled out most of the combinations. I have narrowed it down to most likely this location in Snow Hill." She turned the paper to show Trish.

"Ok, let's see what Google Earth says is there," Trish said with a grin. She typed in the numbers and then hummed to herself. "There's nothing there. Definitely not a chicken farm or even a chicken house."

Raelynn looked at the numbers and then looked at them again. Serenity looked over as well.

"I don't think that's right though. I know when we went to Snow Hill it was always a busy road, like going down 50 or 13. When we went to the farm, it was like driving on the old country roads," Serenity offered. "And it would have been closer to our house back then, since we weren't in Salisbury yet."

Raelynn studied the numbers and then the statues. "What if we mixed up the order of the numbers?" she asked.

"What do you mean?" Sharon asked. "I thought we put them in order."

Everyone turned their attention to the turtles in the middle of the table.

"Yeah, we did. But I got two of them the same day. What if we mixed up the order of those two? Would it make that much of a difference?" she asked, staring at the second and third ones she received almost a week ago.

Trish shrugged. "It would make the location close but definitely different. Sharon, give me the numbers with those two switched and let's see where we end up."

Sharon picked up the two and switched their places and then read those numbers to Trish who typed them in.

"We can compare that to any news articles and see if the locations match up. Serenity, do you remember about how long ago the fire was again?" Sharon asked.

Serenity shook her head. "I can't be sure. I think I was in third or fourth grade. And it was spring if I remember right. Sorry, I am bad at remembering stuff like this."

"It's ok. Every bit of information helps narrow things down, dear," Sharon replied, comfortingly. "I'll do a quick search on farm accidents." She started to do a search on her phone.

Beau spoke up first. "I did, there's were two farm related fires in the spring of 2012. Only one had any fatalities though." He turned the screen to show Sharon and Trish. They both nodded and smiled.

Sharon pointed to a number and Trish nodded, turning back to her keyboard.

"Huh," Trish said. "This might just be it."

She turned the computer toward the group. "This is in Wicomico County, not Somerset, which is closer and definitely off the beaten path. I will get the address, and we can go for a drive." She grinned at Sharon, who nodded her approval.

"We just have to be careful," Sharon warned. "We don't know yet what we are walking into."

The two older women stood and stretched, while the younger three looked on, not sure what to do.

Finally, Raelynn spoke. "Can we come along?"

"Of course, but stay close and don't get out of the car unless we say it's ok, got it?" Sharon warned.

"I should get some equipment from my place on the way," Trish said quietly, only really wanting Sharon to hear her it seemed.

Sharon nodded and then they gathered the laptop and a few papers, and the group headed out.

Raelynn felt a mixture of fear and excitement. She wasn't sure what they would find but hoped it would finally lead her to her dad. She folded and unfolded her hands so many times, she was afraid she would wear the skin away.

Beau took hold of one of her hands and squeezed. "Relax, Rae. We are getting closer to finding your answers." He rubbed gentle circles on her hand, and she just nodded.

She knew everything they were walking into may not be what she wanted, but she would give just about anything to see her dad again. She didn't believe he was capable of hurting anyone, but he had been gone for so long, and who knows what desperation can do to someone especially if their loved ones were being threatened.

Raelynn couldn't help but fantasize about how he got caught up in some sort of gang crossfire and tried to turn them in or something and instead they ended up framing him for their sins and expected him to take the fall.

She felt a shudder inside as she thought about the possibility of not finding evidence to clear him. What if they found evidence to implicate him further of all the terrible things they were accusing him of? She had been painting him as saint in her mind for so long and hoping for a good solid male role model for her little brother but what if her dad turned out to be just as bad as his biological father.

She didn't want to think about the possibility of him being a dangerous criminal. She couldn't believe it even if the evidence did in fact point to him. Raelynn refused to think about it anymore. She shook her head hard and closed her eyes, trying to even out her breathing.

"Are you ok, Rae?" Beau asked quietly. She was sitting between him and Serenity in the back of Trish's small SUV.

Raelynn just nodded, not fully trusting her voice. Her mind was reeling with all the possibilities, and she wasn't going to entertain the bad, she decided. She'd stand firm in support of him until someone proved her otherwise. She didn't have any other choice at this point. She had waited too long to see him, hug him, tell him she loved him to let someone else tell her he was actually an evil man.

The vehicle slowed as they turned on a narrow and dark street. There weren't any streetlights, and Raelynn noticed the sign as the headlights hit it. She gave a slight shudder, even though she had been here before. The ominous sign that read, "Prepare to meet thy god" always gave her shivers. The darkness around her didn't help with the feeling of dread in her chest.

Trish was driving since she had a bigger vehicle, and she chuckled quietly. Raelynn assumed Serenity must have also read the sign because she let out a gasp.

A "tsk tsk" came from the passenger seat and Sharon looked over at Trish. "I think you leave that darn sign up for effect, Trish," she said with humor in her voice.

"Damn straight I do," Trish said emphatically. "Keeps the crazy out."

Raelynn saw her shrug in the darkness, and she just shook her head. Trish was a very mysterious woman, but Raelynn knew better than to ask questions. She also knew Trish was deadly as sin with a gun, so she just sat back and looked into the darkness outside the car.

Eventually they stopped outside of a small house, much like her mom's. But Trish's house was nothing like anything she had ever seen before. She hadn't been here in a few months and then only once.

"You kids stay here. I will be right back," Trish said as she looked at Raelynn in the rearview mirror.

Sharon got out of the car as well and the two women disappeared into the house. Raelynn let out a breath as she looked around. It was dark out and there wasn't much light from anywhere. Even the clouds above covered any light the moon might have given them.

Bonded Blood

She suddenly felt like they shouldn't be going anywhere. Maybe it was the darkness or the fear of what they would find at the old, abandoned farm, but she had a sudden desire to go home. It would probably look a lot like this place, with little to no light. Maybe they should be coming back in the daytime, she suddenly thought.

The property they were on had corn fields surrounding it. There was an old garage at the back, barely visible behind the house. Raelynn knew there was an abandoned chicken house somewhere on the property, but it was invisible now with the darkness. She looked over at the house. There was a large porch across the front of the house that blocked the view to the front door.

She glanced at Serenity, wondering what her friend's reaction would be if she could see the millions of eyes staring at her as she walked onto the porch. The odd collection of dolls was the creepiest thing Raelynn had ever seen, and she was glad to sit and wait in the car rather than walk through that again, even though it was dark outside.

There was a single and faint light on in the house, making it difficult to see into the house or porch at all. She couldn't even see shadows as she studied the house.

"This place is kind of creepy," Serenity whispered. "I feel like we are in a horror movie and the bad guy is going to jump out any second and attack. We're doomed, stuck in this car too." She let out a small shudder.

Beau chuckled. "Oh, you have no idea. The outside is mild compared to the inside."

"Oh my god, I was just thinking about the dang porch," Raelynn said quietly with a soft chuckle. "It is like nothing you have ever seen before, Reni. Like haunt your dreams, type of creepy." She gave a soft shudder for emphasis.

Serenity looked between Raelynn and the house. "Well, now you have just made me more curious. You know how I like a good horror movie." Her grin in the darkness was unmistakable.

"Yeah, I remember. One of the few things we could not agree on growing up!" Raelynn agreed. She rarely watched movies with Serenity because she loved the genre and Raelynn hated it. Raelynn thought it might be a coping mechanism from all of her own trauma. Someone had it worse than she did, she used to say, even if it was a movie and all fake.

Trish and Sharon finally came out of the house carrying a couple of boxes. Trish opened the trunk, and they emptied their hands before she closed it tight, and moved back to their seats inside the car. Raelynn couldn't help wondering what they had brought.

Sharon turned after buckling her seatbelt and smiled. "Are you all ready?"

Chapter 27

The vehicle was silent as they drove through the dark roads. They stayed primarily on the backroads and the darkness was thick with nothing visible aside from the limited illumination of the headlights. Raelynn sat in the middle seat between Beau and Serenity. Beau had a tight hold of her hand the entire car ride, making her feel safe and calm.

Eventually, Trish slowed down and pulled off the road. Raelynn looked around and couldn't see anything aside from trees and overgrown fields with what likely used to be corn. There wasn't a shoulder on the side, which was pretty common on these back roads. It was barely wide enough for two cars to pass each other.

Where Trish had pulled aside, there was a very small, barely visible opening in the field. It looked like a common place for people to turn around or pull over for an emergency. Raelynn didn't see it until they stopped, but Trish must have known it was here.

"Why are we stopped?" she asked the two women in the front.

Sharon sighed. "I was hoping there would be a driveway visible or something. I don't think we should venture out into the unknown in the dark."

Trish nodded. "I agree. Let's get some sleep and meet as soon as the sun rises tomorrow. That will give us a head start on anything we might find and if anyone is watching your schedule, they won't know that you don't work tomorrow until you don't show up." She glanced back at Raelynn, who just nodded.

"Ok, I don't know what we are even looking for, but it makes sense to do it in the light." She looked at Beau and then Serenity. "We can all crash at my place tonight if you want," she suggested.

Beau smiled. "You already know I'm not going anywhere." He gave her hand a squeeze and she just nodded and grinned back.

"I think I will head to my place. We aren't far away from each other, so if anything happens I'm close." Her gaze was focused on the window and her voice was barely audible.

"Reni, are you ok?" Raelynn asked. "I am worried about you."

Serenity turned to face her friend. "I'm ok, I think anyway," she admitted quietly.

"None of this is your fault, so don't feel guilty or bad about any of it," Raelynn reassured her. "If anything, you have saved us a lot of time trying to find the farm."

Serenity sighed. "I guess, but what if my dad is up to something?"

"Try to stop worrying about that. You are one of my best friends, Ren. I don't care what your dad does. It's not you." Raelynn put her arm around Serenity's shoulders and pulled her into a tight hug. "Friends forever, remember?"

Snorting, Serenity agreed. "Forever. But I'm still going to go home tonight."

The car pulled onto the road again and they headed back to Sharon's house, Raelynn guessed. She didn't plan to bring anything home with her to avoid anything getting broken. They might need the statues or notes still. She knew this was far from over.

It seemed like only a few minutes before they were pulling into Sharon's driveway. They piled out as soon as Trish turned the ignition off, and Serenity was quick to wave and head home.

Raelynn sighed. "I'm worried about her," she admitted quietly to Beau.

He nodded and watched the last of her taillights disappear down the road. "I know. But we don't know everything yet. So, we just have to stick together until we have the answers."

"Yeah," she said simply.

"OK, let's meet back here around seven. Is that too early?" Sharon asked the remaining group.

Raelynn shook her head. "Works for me. I will text Serenity and let her know."

Sharon watched her carefully and then just sighed. Raelynn wasn't sure what that was about, but Sharon didn't tell her *not* to tell her friend, so she would keep her in the loop. Raelynn couldn't help but wonder if Sharon was worried about her friend's dad being another "bad guy" in this whole thing. But Serenity had as many questions as Raelynn did and deserved to have them answered as well.

Raelynn and Beau drove back to her apartment in silence. She didn't know what to say or what to think as she stared out the window. Thankfully Beau had asked if she wanted him to drive. She leaned her head against the cool glass and stared at the passing houses and occasional streetlight.

Her thoughts were a jumbled mess as she tried to make sense of everything she had learned throughout the day. It had flown by, and she couldn't believe the amount of information Sharon had found in less than twenty-four hours. She had been struggling with the deliveries and notes for a week and in just a few hours they had figured out the significance of the numbers and letters.

She wondered what had happened to her father all these years and what he was really like now. Did he have the same gentle smile and brown eyes full of life or had his experiences dulled them? She couldn't block out the dark thoughts and possibilities that he was a dangerous man now who was capable of brutal things. She closed her eyes tightly and tried to take deep breaths. She didn't want to think about the possibility that he wasn't the father and man she remembered.

"Rae?" Beau's soft voice broke into her thoughts, and she opened her eyes with a start. "We're here."

Raelynn looked around and saw that they were already parked in her apartment's lot. The darkness felt stifling, and she sat up straight in her seat, but didn't move to exit the vehicle. The lone streetlight in the lot was flickering in the distance giving the darkness an even more eerie feeling. She wanted desperately to get inside her place but felt frozen, not wanting to move out into the dark night. Sitting next to Beau, she felt safe.

He seemed to understand because he hadn't shut off the engine yet. She felt his eyes on her, but she just stared straight ahead, wondering why she felt so stuck.

She felt his hand touch hers and she looked over.

"Let's get inside, Rae," he said quietly. "Maybe a hot shower and sleep with help."

Raelynn nodded and reluctantly got out of the car. She couldn't help but look around, even though there was nothing but darkness surrounding her. She heard Beau lock her car and then hurry around to stand next to her. He took her hand and gently led her to the door.

She felt like she was in a trance of some sort. She didn't feel the chill of the evening or the pavement under her shoes. All she felt was the warmth of Beau's hand holding hers tightly, but still gentle. She glanced up and was startled to see he was watching her.

"I'm right here, Rae, and I am not going anywhere," he said, staring at her. "And if you want to go get your dog, we can do that too, if it will help you feel better."

Raelynn forgot about Timmy not being home and she wondered if it would make her feel better. But then again the big lug was so lazy it probably wouldn't matter, and her brother would be so disappointed.

"No, it's ok. I'll be fine," she replied, looking back toward the big glass doors. "Let's get inside."

They walked to the door and Beau handed her the keys. Opening the door, she stopped suddenly.

"You need your stuff from my car," she said.

Beau grinned and lifted his shoulder that had the strap from his duffle bag over it. "Already ahead of you."

She smiled back and nodded. They made their way into the building, and she quickly walked to her apartment. Multiple scenarios ran through her head as she neared her door. Was it safe to go inside? she wondered. What if someone was waiting inside to grab her and drag her off somewhere. Would they torture her like the people in the photos?

Raelynn shivered and Beau instinctively wrapped his arm around her. "Hey, are you ok?" His voice held so much worry that she just nodded and put her key in the lock.

She hesitated before she opened the door, and she cringed when she realized Beau saw it.

He put his hand on her shoulder. "Rae, it's ok. I'm right here. No judgement."

Raelynn nodded and took a deep breath, closing her eyes for split second. She pushed the door open all the way and they moved inside. Beau quickly closed and locked it behind them. Raelynn stood frozen to her spot, not sure where to look first to make sure they were alone. Beau moved around her and put something in her fridge and then disappeared into the hallway.

She glanced around the living room, and it all looked exactly as she had left it. She took a deep breath in again and then moved to check the sliding door to make sure it was still locked and secure. Finding it was, she let out a sigh of relief and shortly after Beau reappeared.

"Everything looks ok," he said, his hands resting on his hips. "I could use something to eat. Want some popcorn and maybe watch a movie for a little while? I'm thinking a distraction before we try to sleep would be good." His eyes held the question, and he waited for her to answer.

Raelynn knew he was doing his best to distract her, and he could probably tell she was on edge. She just gave him a nod and he disappeared again into the kitchen this time.

Bonded Blood

She moved to sit on her couch and grabbed one of the blankets she kept there. She spread it across her legs and then pulled them up and under herself. She stared at the blank TV, but didn't move to turn it on. She just waited and listened to the popping of the kernels in the microwave. It didn't take long, and Beau was making his way back into her living room with a bowl overflowing with popcorn and balancing two cans of soda in his hands.

Raelynn laughed and moved to help him. She finally felt a little bit of tension release from her body as she settled back on the couch with the drinks on her coffee table in front of them.

"It is good to hear you laugh, Rae," Beau said as he sat down next to her. "This has got to be a lot."

She resisted an eye roll, considering what he went through last summer. A chuckle escaped her lips drawing his attention back to her.

"What's funny?" he asked, grabbing a handful of popcorn.

Raelynn shook her head. "Just thinking about what you said. This *is* a lot, but not any worse than what you went through last summer."

Beau nodded. "Oh yeah that was something. Talk about emotional rollercoaster in a matter of hours." He stopped for a second and then grinned. "Looks like we have something to bond over that most people would never understand, huh?"

Raelynn laughed again. "Sad but true," she said with a lift of her eyebrow.

They settled on an old Eddie Murphy comedy to try to relieve some more of the stress. Raelynn settled next to Beau on the couch and moved her blanket to cover both of them. They shared the popcorn until the bowl was empty and she was reminded of the old "Lady and the Tramp" Disney movie from when she was little. Their hands touched and she looked up and smiled.

By the time the movie ended, she felt much more relaxed and thought she might even be able to sleep. She yawned and stretched her arms high above her head and then leaned back against the couch.

"Tired?" Beau asked, with a smile on his face.

Raelynn nodded. "I guess so. Thanks for staying. I know if I was here alone I would have gotten stuck in my head."

She was surprised to see it was after eleven when she looked at her phone. "Six is going to come early tomorrow," she mused, more to herself than to Beau.

"Eh, it'll be an adrenaline filled day. I think we will be ok," he said with his own stretch. "I'll crash here again and then you can have your bed. Maybe you will sleep better there anyway."

Raelynn just nodded. "I'm not sure if I'll sleep without my big ball of fluff taking up most of the bed, though," she said with a smile.

Beau laughed and started to clean things up from the living room and place them in the kitchen sink. When he turned, he was surprised to see Raelynn right behind him. "Everything ok?"

"Yep, just wanted to thank you again," she said softly, feeling vulnerable--and uncomfortable knowing it.

Beau nodded and reached out to give her a hug. "It's fine. I would rather be here than somewhere else worrying about you. Go use the bathroom first and get to bed." He released her and she turned to head to her room.

"I'll have my alarm set for six. What time do you need to be up?" she asked over her shoulder.

"I'll set mine for six too. Then we can eat something before we go since I have no idea what those two women have planned." He gave her a wide smile, and she knew exactly what he meant. If they had a plan it was kept between the two of them and not shared with the "youngins."

Raelynn smiled back with a nod and disappeared into the bathroom. She stared at her reflection in the mirror and wondered what would happen once this thing was over with Sharon and Trish. Would she want to start something more with Beau? She still needed to clarify what Serenity and Beau felt about each other. She wouldn't stand in her friend's way for anything.

Shaking her head, she focused on the task at hand. She quickly got herself ready for bed and exited the bathroom, letting Beau know she was finished, and the bathroom was his. She closed her door before he made it to the bathroom and climbed into bed. She stared at the ceiling for what felt like hours before she finally fell asleep.

* * * * *

The annoying beeping of her alarm woke her after what seemed like mere minutes. She reached over to turn it off and sighed, her eyes still closed.

The smell of bacon wafted into her room, and she took a deep breath in through her nose. Her eyes suddenly widened as she remembered Beau was here. Raelynn picked up her phone and saw that it was only six. *What time did he get up?* she wondered. She threw the covers off her body and stretched. The room was still dark, and she thought about sleeping for a few more minutes.

But then she remembered what they were doing today. She might see her father for the first time in forever today. She sprung from the bed and ran to the bathroom. Raelynn didn't need more than twenty minutes to get ready. She would be braiding her hair to make sure it stayed out of her face for the unknown events to come.

A surge of excitement and nervousness flowed through her blood. Her thoughts were all mixed up and she couldn't think clearly about what might happen later. But she shook her head and washed her face with cold water to shake off her sleep and focus. Raelynn braided her hair tightly down her head and tied it with a hair tie. A few loose ends dropped from their places, but she just shook her head lightly to loosen any others. The strands framed her face subtly and she smiled at her simple reflection. Then she quickly got dressed and headed to the kitchen.

Beau looked over at her when she came into the space and smiled. He handed her a slice of the cooked meat with the tongs. She took it with a smile and moved around him to start the eggs like they did the day before. Raelynn was surprised with how comfortable she was having him there and making breakfast together. It just felt right, and the thought shocked her since they barely knew each other. She wasn't one of those hopeless romantics who believed in love at first sight, so her comfort was a little unsettling.

"What are you making, Rae?" Beau asked, startling her.

She nearly dropped the pan she was holding. "I thought I'd make scrambled eggs like yesterday." She shrugged and turned to grab the eggs from the fridge.

Raelynn set the pan on the stovetop and turned to see Beau leaning against the doorframe watching her. She gave him a small smile and then reached above the microwave for a bowl to mix the eggs.

"Do you want eggs or French toast? It doesn't take any longer to make," she asked as she looked around for her bread.

Beau shrugged. "Doesn't matter to me. Surprise me."

"Ugh," she complained. "Fine. I'll just make what I want." She shot him a playful glare and pulled out her bread and cinnamon.

While she got busy making the French toast, she noticed Beau disappeared. She assumed he was going to get himself ready while the rest of the breakfast finished cooking. A quick glance at the time showed they only had about twenty more minutes to eat and leave if they were going to be on time to meet Sharon.

She flipped the bread one more time after adding a generous amount of cinnamon. Beau reappeared and smiled, moving around her to grab plates. He held one for her to put two slices on and then gave her the other one. He then moved to put bacon on each and carried them into the living room. Raelynn filled two glasses of juice and followed him.

As she set them down, her phone beeped with an alert. Raelynn went back into the kitchen to get her phone and on her way back opened her texting app.

After she read the text, she looked up at Beau. "Serenity isn't going to make it this morning. She said she would connect later on today and meet us wherever we are."

"Is everything ok?" he asked as he put a huge piece of French toast into his mouth. "Wow this is really good, Rae. I've never put cinnamon on it while it was cooking before."

She smiled and gave him a nod. "Oh, I forgot the brown sugar." She got up and went to grab the small container. Before she reappeared, she stuck her head out and asked if he wanted anything else.

Beau shook his head and gave her a weird look. "I am actually more curious about what you are going to do with brown sugar on French toast." He put another piece in his mouth and then leaned back against the cushions.

Raelynn just shook her head at him and moved back to sit next to him. "It's actually better when they are warm, but the sugar melts into the toast. It's so good. Better than syrup any day."

She scooped up a spoonful and sprinkled it on her toast and then handed the container to him. "Just put it on a small piece and see if you like it."

"Ok, let's see about this," he said skeptically. He put a small amount of brown sugar on a corner and then cut it with his fork. He gingerly brought it to his mouth, giving her a strange look. He put it in and slowly chewed.

Raelynn grinned at him when she saw the realization on his face. "Good, right?" She cut into her own and started to eat as well.

Nodding, Beau spread more of the sweet stuff on his remaining pieces. "So, what's up with Serenity? Is everything ok?"

"I don't know, she just said she will try to meet us later. She didn't gave me any details. I hope it isn't something with her dad," she said quietly. Her thoughts and emotions were so conflicted with everything that they had found out the day before. And now she worried about her friend's dad and what he was up to. "I'm trying to wrap my head around all the possibilities from my dad being framed to him being a bad guy, and now with Reni's dad disappearing there's just so much. I hope he's not up to something dangerous though."

Beau nodded his agreement, and they finished eating in silence. As soon as she finished, Raelynn gathered the dishes and headed to the kitchen to rinse them and then load the dishwasher. Beau was folding the blankets he used from the couch. They met near the door with a smile and a nod and then headed out without a word being spoken between them.

Raelynn knew it was going to be another rollercoaster of a day. She took a deep breath and, not even realizing it, looked around to make sure they weren't surprised by anyone. She could feel her anxiety rise as she watched for Creepy Guy to pop out from somewhere like before.

The sun was just starting to rise and the orange and red glow from the start of the sunrise caught her breath. She was again reminded of her favorite time of the day. Pulling her hoodie up over her head, she rubbed her arms. It was a chilly morning, but she wasn't sure if it was the air or the sudden feeling of being watched again.

Raelynn hurried to the car and unlocked it, sliding inside quickly. She turned on the engine and cranked up the heat. Her eyes scanned the parking lot, but she didn't see anyone. Beau had buckled his seatbelt and put his hand on hers tightly gripping the steering wheel.

"Are you ok, Rae?" he asked.

She nodded but continued to scan for any sign of anyone.

Raelynn glanced in her rearview mirror to make sure there wasn't anything sitting on the back of her car. She had already checked the front and didn't see anything. She put the shifter in reverse and pulled out of her parking spot and headed for the driveway exit.

Beau was quiet next to her, but she could feel his eyes watching her. She couldn't put into words what she was feeling anyway, so she appreciated his silence. She tried not to look at him while she drove, so she didn't have to answer any of his silent questions.

Once they were out of her apartment lot and on to the main street, Raelynn breathed in deeply and settled back in her seat.

"Still a little freaked out about that guy, Rae?" Beau asked quietly.

Surprised he understood that already, she looked over and gave him a small nod.

"Did you see anyone?" His face didn't turn away from hers as he watched her.

Raelynn looked over again and shook her head. "No, but I felt like someone was watching me. It might just be in my head though. I didn't see anyone or anything weird." She shivered and turned the heat to a warmer setting.

Beau looked out the window and then back to face her. "Rae, I hope we get things answered for you today. I know when Ki and I were doing our search, it was torture waiting and wondering what was going to be thrown at you next." He smiled and squeezed her arm. "But it worked out perfect in the end. I know it will all be the way it is supposed to be for you too."

"I know," she said quietly. "I just worry that all my idealistic views are going to be burned to ash when we finally get the answers to everything."

"Well, I'll be right beside you through it all, ok?" Beau said. "But I trust Sharon and Trish after last summer, and they will get it all right. I am sure everything will be ok."

His confidence made Raelynn smile. "I hope you're right, Beau. I hope you're right."

Chapter 28

The drive back to the old, abandoned farm felt different in the light of the rising sun. The roads weren't nearly as creepy as the night before and the canopy of trees gave it a homey feel rather than an ominous one. Raelynn hadn't realized they were basically driving through a tunnel of trees high above them the night before. The overgrown fields looked neglected, but not like they were hiding anything and everything from view as the car drove by.

Sharon had explained that she felt there may be others trying to get the information they had discovered, which was why she was worried about Raelynn's safety. She wanted to get going early so that hopefully no one would be following them at this time of day and there would be limited danger, but also adequate light to ensure safety. She didn't explain any further about her concerns and Raelynn and Beau didn't ask.

Trish slowed as she came to what Raelynn assumed was the same small space in the fields that allowed for a convenient turnaround spot or an emergency stop. This time though, she didn't stop but turned as if she were driving right into the field. Raelynn gasped as she waited for the long, dead foliage to scratch along the car. But it quickly gave way to a small clearing.

Bonded Blood

Looking around, Raelynn saw quite a few buildings, all in disrepair. There was a house, but it looked like the upper levels had been demolished and only the main floor still stood. She remembered Serenity saying there was a fire, and it looked like the house had remained untouched all these years. She also noticed a tree had begun growing right through the center of the house, reaching out through the front door.

Trish drove up to the dilapidated building slowly and eventually stopped the car. Raelynn noticed that she didn't turn off the engine though. She glanced over at Beau who looked back and shrugged. Sharon turned to look at Trish and they shared their silent language about something. Trish huffed a little and then started to move the car again.

Raelynn noticed she turned it around and was now facing the way they came in and then she pulled it almost into the field, keeping it hidden from the road. She turned it off and then pocketed her key.

"I want you two to stay close," Sharon began. "We are not sure what we are walking into here. I honestly don't want to find out something or someone is waiting for us, and we happen to be separated." She lifted her brow at both of the backseat passengers and once she had a nod of agreement, the foursome exited the vehicle.

Beau let out a chuckle and when the others looked at him, he just shrugged. "You know, never separate. Like the horror movies teach us."

Trish snickered and Sharon just shook her head. Raelynn gave him a wide smile, grateful for the comedic relief.

"And if I *did* watch horror movies, there's no way I would be anywhere near this place right now," Beau whispered in her ear as she slid over to his side to get out.

Raelynn laughed and nodded her agreement. She took his outstretched hand to help her out.

Sharon and Trish had already moved away from the car by the time Raelynn and Beau had gotten out. Beau leaned over and whispered, "So much for staying together."

Raelynn laughed and they quickly caught up to the other two. Sharon was studying the outside of the charred house. Now that they were close, Raelynn could see where it had been burned.

"Probably a kitchen fire they just couldn't get a handle on in time," Sharon mused to herself.

Trish nodded. "This whole side is gone. It probably went right up this side of the house and then it just collapsed inward. So sad," Trish added.

Raelynn looked where the older women pointed and wondered how they could tell. To her the entire building was a mess with a massive tree growing through the floor and out the door with a multitude of branches expanding everywhere. Raelynn found herself wondering what it must have been like when the fire broke out. She imagined they would have been trying to put the fire out frantically before it just consumed them. She stared at the structure and could imagine the fear and pain of the family and the older couple who perished in it.

Shaking her head, she followed Trish and Sharon who had moved to the back side of the family home. There were three or four chicken houses in varying stages of disrepair she saw as they moved past the house. She could only see two, but a third peeked out behind one of the front buildings and she guessed there was probably a fourth behind the other.

Bonded Blood

The buildings in front of her were barely standing. Raelynn could only see the front two houses, but the roof on one looked like a tornado had taken it off. There were pieces of the sheet metal roof that had been taken off in some places but not others. The sides had some fabric blowing in the breeze, almost like windows that were covered at one point with curtains, but the glass had been blown out and the fabric just blew in and out of the open space.

The sides looked like there was a long line of shrubbery that was intended to be decorative at one time, but now it was just overgrown and unruly. The bottom of the chicken house, below the windows, was completely covered by shrubs and weeds. There was a bright yellow sign staked into the ground that warned of trespassing. As she looked around the property, she noticed many more of those signs scattered about.

At the end of the chicken house, the part that faced the group, there had been a large door at one point. Now though it was completely bare and open, as if the door had been either removed or just fell off the hinges, tired of hanging on for no reason. The space where they were standing was open aside from the overgrown grass and weeds. Raelynn could recognize this as the place in the photos that Serenity brought. This was where they had run and played, and where the wretched animals chased her relentlessly.

The memory gave her a chill as she thought about the terror on her little girl face in the photo. Standing in the yard, she could feel the familiarity. She still couldn't remember the details, but the photos helped. She turned around in a spinning motion, and looked at the property as much as she could see with the overgrowth.

Beau came up next to her, staring straight ahead at Trish and Sharon. The older women were walking toward one of the chicken houses, seemingly laser focused on something.

"Should we follow them?" she asked him, reminded again that it was Halloween and of the horror movie mantra. There might be some crazy killer in there hiding behind something ready to chop them up in a million pieces with a chainsaw or something. She shivered as she thought about it.

Beau met her gaze and smiled. "It might be Halloween, but these two aren't stupid. They know something." He glanced back in their direction and tipped his head. "C'mon, let's go see if they'll tell us anything."

Raelynn just nodded and bit her cheek. "I swear if you are leading me to my death I will haunt you forever." She poked her finger into his chest.

He laughed and grabbed her finger. "I look forward to it," he whispered with a glint in his eye.

Rolling her eyes, she pulled her finger from his and grabbed his hand. They reached the other two just as they were about to disappear into the semi darkness of the abandoned building. As she entered, Raelynn noticed the pieces of what looked like a blue tarp at one point flapping in the breeze. It had been ripped apart over the years. She wondered why it was there to begin with. Why was someone trying to salvage it but then just give up.

There were multiple openings in the ceiling showing the sun shining through a few clouds. Aside from the pieces of blue plastic swaying in the breeze, the shreds of fabric waving on the windows drew her attention. She wasn't sure what it looked like before, when it was a thriving farm, but something told her this wasn't supposed to be like this. She wandered toward it and touched a piece.

"This is one of the things on the turtle I got," she said suddenly, turning to Beau.

He walked over and looked at it. He nodded. "It sure looks like it. I wonder what else is here." Beau looked around thoughtfully and turned back to Raelynn.

She was looking up and noticed something else. "Look at those," she said, pointing right above her. "That bowl like thing."

Beau came over to stand next to her. "Those are the feeding bowls for the chickens. They can be raised and lowered based on when the chickens are supposed to be fed. Next to it, those tiny metal tubes, that's the water line." He looked toward the end of the building, as if he was looking for something.

She followed his eyes but had no idea what he was looking for. He moved suddenly and walked to the end of the building. She looked down at the dirt they were walking through, wondering if this was what Sharon and Trish were talking about, the stuff in the tiny container.

Raelynn glanced around to see where the older two had gone. They were still in the building, and she noticed that Beau had walked to them and the three of them were having an animated conversation. She glanced around and then made her way to them as well.

"There should be a manual way to bring these down," Beau was saying.

Trish nodded. "There is, but I don't think that is our main concern right now."

"Trish is right," Sharon said. "I agree this is exactly what we are looking for. It appears all of the materials from the statues Raelynn was gifted are from here. Or at least from a chicken house somewhere."

"But if the azomite can be traced to this farm, that would make sense, wouldn't it?" Beau asked. "We could see if the materials from the turtles are missing from here and that would also help our case right?"

Trish slowly nodded. "Yes, but we have to go through all four houses." She said as she looked around. "This one is pretty open to the elements. The sample I tested was purer, meaning there was more protection for that litter."

Sharon was thoughtful for a while and then turned to Raelynn. "Do you remember what materials the other turtles were made out of, Raelynn?"

"Then we can look for those specific things," Trish agreed.

Raelynn looked over at the trio and shrugged. "I don't know. I guess one had a thick metal shell, another was a thinner metal. The one with the tiny container, I guess I would assume this dirt is what you found inside." She kicked at the ground loosening up the stuff under her foot.

"Yes, this is the litter that lines the entire house floor. The farmers typically will turn it over after every flock, but they don't replaced it. That's why we can see what kind of feed and all that is used over the years." Trish explained as she looked at the ground as well.

"So, it's called litter but it's actually dirt?" Raelynn asked. "I guess I figured litter would be what you put in a litter box for a cat or the shavings you use for guinea pigs or something. It's kind of gross that they don't change it or replace it, isn't it? So, we are literally walking in chicken poop and pee." She made a face thinking about how gross it was that her shoes were now covered in chicken feces.

Sharon chuckled. "It is. But chickens don't urinate, so it is just their poop. And it is actually healthier for the flock if the litter isn't fresh. Anyway, something for another day," she said and turned to look at Trish. "How do we get started?"

Beau looked up again. "I think we can just walk the perimeter and see if any of the bowls are missing from here." He moved to walk a line looking straight above him at the bowl things Raelynn had noticed were placed every few feet apart.

"Ok, you two go do that. I'm going to check the fans and see if there are any tools around. This one looks like it was emptied out and then just never got another flock, like when the fire broke out they were between flocks. If it wasn't used as a chicken house before the fire, this would likely be more of a storage shed," Trish mused to herself still looking around.

Sharon nodded. "I agree. But we do have three more houses and one of those could be the storage."

Beau took a hold of Raelynn's hand and pulled her along with him, breaking her off from the conversation between Trish and Sharon.

He pointed above their heads. "We are looking for any of these bowls that might be missing, Rae," he explained. "They should be evenly spaced out. If there's a spot that's missing one, we can assume that it is the one used for your turtle."

Raelynn nodded and followed along beside Beau. They made their way along one side and then the other, not finding any of the feeding bowls missing. Raelynn looked around and found Trish and Sharon had disappeared. She felt that all too familiar chill run through her. Instinctively she reached out and grabbed a hold of Beau's sleeve.

"What's wrong?" he asked, looking down at her.

He was only a few inches taller than she was but right then she felt like she was a foot and half shorter. She felt like a scared little kid.

"We are alone, Beau," she whispered, looking around frantically.

Beau patted her hand gently and smiled. "They told us they were moving to the house next door just a few minutes ago. It's ok, Rae," he said. He removed her fist from his sleeve and weaved his fingers in between hers. "Come on, let's go meet up with them."

He led her to the house behind the first one. There was a door on the side of the building leading out that was missing. Beau held her hand the entire time they walked from one house to another. This house looked similar but the doors and roof were still intact. The growth of weeds and small trees spread around all of the buildings, but this one seemed a little less encompassing. She could see the metal of the siding and the openings she thought were windows were covered, where the other house didn't have much of that left.

They entered this house through the side door and Raelynn was struck by how quiet it was. Looking around she saw that this one was darker than the other. There were even a few lights on, which surprised her.

Raising her eyebrow at Beau, she asked, "How is there electricity?"

Bonded Blood

"A wonderful question, Raelynn," Sharon called from the opposite end of the building.

Raelynn looked down at Sharon, who was standing next to a door. Confused, she looked up at Beau, who started to move toward the other two. She didn't let go of his hand and followed slightly behind him.

Trish had a grin on her face that made Raelynn shiver. "This is the most interesting thing I have seen in a long time," she said. "Someone has been living here." She made the statement and then turned around to face a door.

Raelynn suddenly realized that this building was slightly shorter in length than the other one. She hadn't noticed and wouldn't have if it wasn't pointed out to her.

The door looked like a regular storm door that would be on a garage or house. She was curious about it but also a little anxious about what they would find behind it. The photos Sharon had shown her yesterday came flooding back. What if this was a torture chamber for the Del Rios? The thought made her shrink back a little and look for a way out.

Trish had a tool of some sort and looked like she was breaking in. Raelynn unconsciously let out a small gasp and Beau looked down at her.

"Hey, you ok?"

Raelynn nodded. "I'm a little scared, if I'm honest," she admitted.

Beau just nodded and pulled her next to him. "I have to believe they wouldn't do this unless they were sure it was ok."

Not really knowing what to say, Raelynn focused on Trish and her breaking and entering tools. The inside of the building was almost silent, even the noises of nature were blocked out. The small click of the lock giving way made Trish turn around and grin. She waved her hand to Sharon, as if to give her the privilege of entering first.

Sharon chuckled at her and pushed open the door. Raelynn was shocked at their relaxed dispositions and glanced around. The older two moved into the space and Raelynn heard Trish gasp. She moved into the small room quickly, dragging Beau with her. She had to know what they found even if she was terrified at the same time.

"Fascinating," Trish mumbled as she looked at the walls and appliances. "There is actual electricity running through here. How is that possible, and only contained in this small space?"

Sharon smiled and pointed to a window. "Someone is a genius, Trish." They walked to the window and Raelynn watched them. "See that windmill? Someone has hooked it up to an old car engine, likely the alternator, and created a small generator that will likely produce just enough power to run everything in here—and no one would ever figure it out." She gave her head a slight shake and quietly added, "It is completely silent, powered only by the wind."

Trish chuckled. "Brilliant. That's how they have stayed off grid for so long."

Raelynn watched them, not really understanding what they were talking about, and then turned back to the room. It looked like a fully functioning apartment and actually reminded Raelynn of the apartment at Sharon's house. There was a small kitchen with a small fridge, stovetop on the counter, and a few other small appliances. The countertop was small but had a small extra lip where a single stool was set up for eating. There was a couch and a bed with a small TV along the opposite wall.

What caught her attention was also what Sharon and Trish were staring at now that they moved away from the window. The far wall, end to end, was plastered with photos. Pictures mostly of Raelynn in different places and at different ages, she noticed as she slowly walked closer and really looked at the wall. She saw her high school graduation picture with her mom by her side. Her hand started to shake as she looked at each photo. There was another one outside her apartment on the day she moved in. Her mom had wanted a picture of them all.

Raelynn looked around and couldn't make sense of her emotions. A sudden fear took over as she turned in a circle in the room. Who was watching her and for how long? And where were they now? She suddenly felt like something was off and that all too familiar shiver covered her skin. A movement caught her attention at the door and her eyes suddenly met Creepy Guy's, who was staring at her.

Raelynn's gasp brought everyone's attention to her and then the man standing behind them at the door.

"What do you think you are doing?" he demanded, stalking toward the group dangerously. His voice was deep and rough, like he hadn't talked in ages. His eyes moved between the group but came back and landed on Raelynn. His face was scrunched in a scowl.

Raelynn shrunk further into Beau's side, and he gently moved her closer to Sharon and Trish. Sharon let out a dark chuckle as she made eye contact with the newcomer.

"Well, you led us here, so why are you surprised?" she asked, folding her arms across her chest.

Trish took a similar stance, but her smile looked even scarier than Creepy Guy's. Raelynn was reminded of the first time she had met Trish and the natural danger the woman gave off until she knew you were trustworthy.

Raelynn watched with fear, but also interest. She wondered how they knew Creepy Guy was behind this and then the thought about her father not even being involved made her catch her breath. Was he really gone? She suddenly felt dizzy.

Beau reached over and lifted her chin for her to look at him. "Rae, are you ok?"

Creepy Guy snorted, drawing their attention to him again. "Oh, baby girl, you have a lot to learn. But right now, I need you all to leave. Or I will not be responsible for what happens next." He made another move toward them.

Trish scoffed. "Yeah, right. Listen here boy, we are not leaving until we get what we came for." She took a couple steps toward him, making him stop and stare at her.

"What are you looking for?" he asked her, his eyes narrowed.

"Whatever it is that you wanted us to find. Give us that and we will go," Sharon said defiantly, lifting her chin in his direction.

Creepy Guy took off his dirty hat and scratched his head. He looked behind him and then suddenly disappeared through the door.

Raelynn breathed a small sigh of relief, but it was short lived.

He showed up less than a minute later with a gun in his hand and dropped a piece of paper. "Leave. Now. I won't be responsible for what happens if they find you here."

He motioned with his gun for them to exit the door, but his eyes locked on Raelynn's.

As they walked by, he gave her a look that she almost thought was sympathetic, the same look he had given her before. She shook it off and hurried through the door. This time she was dragging Beau behind her.

Trish and Sharon came through the door with huge grins on their faces. Raelynn was confused and just stared at them.

"How can you be smiling?" she asked them, almost angry about their obvious giddiness.

Sharon waved her off. "It's ok. It's just fun to show these men who think they are superior to us women that we are not to be messed with."

Trish was studying something in her hand and showed it to Sharon. They made eye contact and then nodded toward the house. Or maybe it was the street. She wasn't sure. She just followed them, looking behind her constantly.

Creepy Guy didn't follow them, which she was thankful for, but she wasn't letting her guard down.

Trish and Sharon detoured and started walking through the thick overgrowth. Raelynn stopped at the edge and then looked at Beau. "Are we supposed to follow them?"

Beau just shrugged but didn't move to follow either. He leaned down and whispered, "Do you know it only takes going in like five rows of corn before you get disoriented and easily lost?"

"Seriously?" Raelynn asked, as she noticed that the older women were no longer visible. "I'm definitely staying out here. Plus, ticks," she added, with a shrug of her own.

They stood in silence, glancing around now and then, for a few more minutes before both women emerged from the foliage looking proud. Trish was holding something in her hand, while Sharon had a piece of what looked like a sign. They were both smiling.

"Alrighty, let's get out of here," Sharon said and then waved for them to follow her to the car. Neither of them seemed worried about Creepy Guy or anyone else for that matter. They were acting like nothing out of the ordinary just happened.

Raelynn just shook her head. She wished she could have that kind of calm, and she also wished it wasn't Halloween.

Sharon threw something in the trunk and then slid into the front passenger seat. Trish was already in the driver's seat, and they shared a satisfied grin. Trish started the engine, and then started moving down the driveway, or what used to be, Raelynn thought.

Suddenly remembering Serenity, she leaned forward. "What if Serenity goes there looking for us and Creepy Guy is still there?"

Sharon looked at Trish and then at Raelynn. "*That* was your 'Creepy Guy'?" she asked, seemingly surprised by the information.

Raelynn looked between them and just nodded.

"OK, then," Trish said with amusement and then the front seat was quiet. "I think it will be ok, but text her and tell her to meet us at Sharon's house."

Raelynn looked at Beau and let out a frustrated breath. She sent a text to her friend and then looked out her window as the car started to move on to the road. As they turned, she caught sight of something in the long weeds.

"Wait!" she shouted causing Trish to slam on the brakes and glare at her through the mirror. "Sorry, I didn't mean to yell. But what is that?" she asked and pointed to what she saw.

Sharon looked out her window and agreed. "Let me get out and take a look," she said to Trish.

Trish backed up and parked with her window nearly buried in the weeds. Sharon jumped out and jogged across the street. The farm property was now on her side and Raelynn watched anxiously as Sharon waded through the greenery to pluck out what looked like a sign, after she had cleared the area.

She easily pulled it out of the ground since it looked like it was on just a couple of metal spikes. It was faded, but Raelynn could see a familiar image on it. Sharon shared a grin with Trish as she held it up and then ran back across the road. She tapped on the trunk and Trish pressed a button opening it up for her.

When Sharon slid back into her seat she gave Trish a nod. "I think we have everything now. Let's go back and see if we missed anything."

Trish nodded and then pulled back out onto the road. The car was silent the entire ride to Sharon's. Raelynn was almost afraid to ask any questions, even though there were a million swirling in her brain. She felt Beau next to her and realized just having him around made her calmer. She resisted leaning into him and stayed in her seat, but glancing over, she noticed he was also lost in his own thoughts, staring out the window.

They were finally parking in her driveway and Sharon turned to look at her. She gave her a smile. "Are you ready to figure out this whole puzzle, Rae?"

"You have no idea," she said with a small smile of her own. "I have so many questions and don't even know where to start."

Trish snorted. "Well, let the games begin. Hold on to your hats! This is gonna be a ride!"

Chapter 29

Trish dropped a bag full of equipment onto the table and Sharon rushed back to her office to grab her laptop. Gary was in a chair in the sitting area of the large open space and just watched with his face full of humor.

"Well, I guess I will go find a good book to read or something," Gary said with a grin. He gave Sharon a quick peck on her cheek as she rounded the corner from the hallway.

"Probably a good idea. You will be bored," she said with a smile. She gave him a quick hug and then he disappeared into a different part of the house.

Raelynn and Beau sat down at the table and waited for the other two to join them. It was like the women were preparing for some secret mission the way they moved around so quickly. They never met in their preparations, just move fluidly around each other.

Finally, they settled in front of the younger two and smiled.

"We have a lot to discuss," Sharon said and turned on her laptop and typed a few things on her keyboard and then waited.

Trish leaned over and looked at the screen and nodded. They sat like that for a few more minutes and then Trish turned to her bag of things and pulled out something handing it to Sharon.

"Hopefully this is what we are looking for and it's not some distraction or trick," Trish mumbled as she watched Sharon plug something into the side of the computer.

Sharon handed it over to Trish then. "This is encrypted. You're turn." She grinned and pushed back from the table as Trish pushed up her sleeves and wiggled her fingers. "You kids want anything to eat or drink?"

Raelynn stood with her and moved to the fridge. "Can you tell me what you are looking for? Or why you were so ok with what happened at the farm? I'm so confused right now," she said quietly, leaning back against the counter between them.

Sharon sighed and reached out to pat her arm. "I know this is a lot. I just want to make sure we have everything in order before we say too much. It may be hard for you to hear, and I want to make sure we are one hundred percent correct before we give you any kind of hope. Trust me, we are doing this as fast as we can."

"I am trying, and I do trust you," Raelynn replied. "But that man has been freaking me for a week now and you guys just basically laughed at him."

"Oh, yes. He's something," Sharon said with a smile. "But no worries. He knows who we are, and nothing will happen. He knows now that you are with us, and we will protect you. Stay patient, dear. All will be revealed soon." She reached into the fridge and grabbed a large pitcher of tea and two glasses. "Help yourself to whatever you like. I think you left some of your drinks here last night too."

Bonded Blood

Sharon poured the glasses full and then returned the pitcher to the counter and carried the glasses to the table for her and her friend.

With a sigh, frustrated she wasn't getting more out of Sharon, Raelynn pulled on the fridge handle since they had left some cans in there, she grabbed two and then headed back to the table as well.

Beau gave her a silent thank you and then turned back to watch Trish tap away at the keyboard. Raelynn had to admit it was somewhat cathartic listening to her tapping. She sighed and opened her can and took a long drink from it. The sweetness of the soda gave her a little boost. She glanced over and saw Beau do the same.

"Maybe we should get some food too," he suggested.

"Hold that thought," Trish said and then motioned for Sharon to join her. "There is a lot here. Might take a minute to go through it. But it is all here." She leaned back and gave herself a heartly pat on the back, making Sharon laugh and give her a friendly push on the shoulder.

"We aren't done yet, Trish," she scolded. "We still have to link this all to Lee and Donte." Sharon's eyes glanced up at Raelynn and then she looked back at the screen.

Trish tapped her lips with her fingernail. "Ok, where do we start?"

Sharon pulled out a folder from the bag Trish had carried in. "We start with the charges." She opened it and started to run through dates and charges.

Raelynn froze. Were they trying to convict her dad? They had been helping her but it seemed only to find the information and send him to jail forever. The realization struck her right in the chest, and she suddenly felt like she couldn't breathe. She trusted them and thought they believed her. She thought they even agreed that her dad was being framed.

She laid her head on the cool table and tried to even her breathing. She needed to leave, but where would she go. Was Beau part of this? What about Serenity? Raelynn knew she was being a little crazy, but she couldn't help her thoughts racing around.

Finally feeling like she was able to stand, Raelynn pushed away from the table and moved toward the door. Beau was quickly by her side.

"Where are you going, Rae?" he asked, his voice sounded worried, but she didn't know what to think at the moment.

She looked up at him and then at the two women who were buried in the computer and files.

"I need to go. This was all a setup," she said quietly, trying to contain her tears.

Beau grabbed both of her arms and shook his head. "No Rae. You are misunderstanding. They are trying to prove your dad is innocent. Didn't you hear them?"

Raelynn looked up into his eyes looking for any kind of deception. But she didn't see any. "What?" she stammered, looking between the two at the table and Beau.

He nodded and smiled. "They have to compare everything to make sure it doesn't match what the accusations are. If he goes to trial tomorrow, they need to be able to prove he didn't do these things."

"But how?" she asked. "He's nowhere to be found. Even if they clear him, we still don't know where he is." She felt the despair and disappointment surrounding her and she felt like she was going to pass out from the stress.

Sharon suddenly spoke up from the table, checking something on her watch. "Rae, I think your friend is here." She then went right back to her conversation.

Shaking her head, Raelynn moved to the door. She greeted Serenity just outside and gave her a hug.

"I have no idea what is happening in there, but I am glad you are here," she told her friend.

Serenity was a little stiff as she hugged her friend back.

Raelynn pulled away and creased her brow. "Reni, are you ok?"

"Not really," she said with a shake of her head. "Something is wrong, and my mom isn't telling me. She was meeting with a lawyer this morning and basically sent me out the door not long after I got there."

They stayed outside for a few minutes before Beau came out to get them.

"Uh, you guys are gonna want to come in for this," he simply stated and then turned back to the house and disappeared.

Serenity and Raelynn locked eyes and simultaneously took deep breaths.

"I don't know what is going on either, but it seems they are trying to clear my dad's name in this trial. But they aren't sharing much more." Raelynn was beyond frustrated. She knew it was showing but she also didn't care. Serenity was her friend and would understand.

Serenity just nodded. "Should we go inside?"

"I guess so," Raelynn grumbled.

They headed into the house. Raelynn wasn't sure what would be greeting her. She felt like she had already had one round on the rollercoaster and wasn't really interested in a second. She went right to the fridge to grab Serenity a drink and then the duo headed to the table. Beau looked up and moved so Raelynn could sit next to him and Serenity took the chair Sharon had added to the end of the table.

Trish looked up from her screen and gave the group a grin. "Looks like we have everything." She looked around and turned the computer. "We have everything we need to take the Del Rios down."

Raelynn thought for a moment and then asked, "Who has been sending me the statues? Creepy Guy called me 'baby girl' just like my dad used to. So, I guess it is plausible that he is behind all of this. But he clearly didn't want us there. So, if he is behind it all, why would he lead us there only to kick us out again?"

Sharon gave her a soft smile. "Well, your mystery man isn't such a mystery, Raelynn."

Raelynn gave her a puzzled look. "Do I know him?" She felt her nerves on edge and really wasn't in the mood for games.

"Maybe, but let's take a look at this first," Trish said, turning to Serenity. She handed her a folder and turned her screen to face them. "Recognize him?"

Serenity gasped and covered her mouth. "Wh-why do you have a file on my dad?"

"Oh, that's not even the surprising part," Trish said with a grin, pointing at the screen where a picture of Creepy Guy filled it.

Raelynn looked from Serenity to Trish, reaching for the folder. Was Creepy Guy really Serenity's dad? The man who has been stalking her and giving her creepy messages?

Bonded Blood

She couldn't believe it was the same person. She stared at the photo in front of her. The green eyes were definitely the same. She dropped the file on the table.

"I don't understand," Serenity whispered.

Sharon came over and patted her shoulder sympathetically. "I know, dear. We have found out a lot of information and wanted to be sure before we shared it with all of you." She gave Serenity's shoulder a squeeze and then moved back to her seat.

Raelynn met Serenity's eyes and gave her a small nod. She needed her friend to know that she meant what she had said the night before. Serenity was not her father, and she would just have to keep reminding her of that.

"Please, explain what all this means," Raelynn pleaded with the older women, who seemed to enjoy keeping the suspense going.

Sharon pulled out another folder that had what looked like more photos and Raelynn felt her stomach drop, worried about the last time she was shown photos. She felt sick as she wondered if these were pictures of her dad now. She didn't think she would be able to look at them. Closing her eyes, she tried to calm her racing heart and breathe.

"These were pulled from surveillance cameras in the area last week, and as recent as yesterday," Sharon said, laying the photos out on the table.

When Raelynn didn't open her eyes, terrified of what she was going to see, she heard Sharon speak to her. "Raelynn dear. You are going to want to look at this," she said gently.

Reluctantly, she opened her eyes and focused on one photo immediately. It was a picture of two men. They had their hands tightly clasped together and one was holding one of her turtles. She could clearly see Serenity's father, but the other one was slightly blurred, as if they were turning away quickly.

She looked up questioningly. "Who is this?" Raelynn could feel her voice trembling, not sure what to think at the moment.

"We believe that is Cornelius Jacobs, the third. Also known as Lee," Trish said with a satisfied smile.

Raelynn was speechless. So, her dad and Serenity's dad were actually working together. She leaned back in her chair. "The bad guys," she breathed out.

Trish chuckled in her seat, drawing Raelynn's glare her way. "I don't think it's funny, Trish. I just found out my dad is actually alive and is one of the bad guys and you laugh." She scowled and gripped Serenity's hand tightly. They would get through this together. She glanced over at Beau and was shocked to see humor on his face as well.

"What is going on?" she demanded, looking around the table.

Sharon cleared her throat. "Ok, I'll help you sort this out. While we were at the farm, Donte gave me a slip of paper telling me where to 'find' a drive that contained information to not only clear your father but implicate the entire Del Rios organization in so many crimes that they should all be put away for a long time.

"You father has been in hiding since they accused him fifteen years ago. He couldn't come out of hiding or they would have killed him. He knew what they were up to and when he got to work that day so many years ago, he found out they had plans to accuse him of stealing money and then stage a killing. He left for his lunch break and never came back."

"But I thought he was working with them?" Raelynn asked quietly, trying to absorb all the information.

Trish jumped in. "He led them to believe he was on their side so he could get more information. He never participated in any killings or other harm to people. They had threatened if he ever turned on them they would come after his family. According to Donte, who had just recently found out where Lee was hiding, he never did any of what they accused him of. This was just their way of getting ahold of him, drawing him out. He disappeared on them as well and they were worried. So, Donte and Lee have been in hiding for a few weeks now together. Lee believed Rae would find the right people to help her figure this puzzle out and knew of our interactions over the summer. Donte is the one who told Brad to lead you to Sharon, Rae."

Raelynn took a deep breath of air in and held it for a moment before asking the next question on her mind. "So, we have been in danger for years and didn't know it?"

"No, because your dad never turned over any evidence. But they have been watching carefully to make sure there was no contact between your family and him. That's why Donte wanted us to leave today, so no one would possibly see you with your dad." Sharon dropped her eyes and added, "We also found out who your brother's father is. He actually died of mysterious causes about seven years ago."

Raelynn met her eyes and noticed a trace of mirth there. She didn't care how the man died, it felt good to know he was no longer around. She hoped it would help her mom heal as well. She gave Sharon a nod, even if she wasn't responsible.

She was slowly starting to understand. The photos weren't actually stalking photos, they were the only way he could watch her grow up.

"So, my dad isn't working with the gang?" Serenity asked quietly.

Trish shook her head. "Nope. But he is going after a big payout, just like he said."

Just as Serenity dropped her head, Sharon added, "There is a significant reward for the information your fathers have been collecting. The state, feds, and company they have been operating out of are anxiously awaiting information that we now have. And they are paying heftily for it." She held up the USB drive with a smile.

Raelynn looked around the table. She wasn't sure what to think. Everything was coming at her in waves and the emotions were no exception.

"So, what do we do now? Are the Del Rios going to come after us?" Serenity asked, her voice slightly shaky.

She gripped Raelynn's hand tightly and they looked at Sharon and Trish.

Trish sighed. "Well, we aren't sure yet. We are going to make multiple copies of this, actually that's already started, and then we are going to go to the trial tomorrow. The Del Rios are hoping the charges draw you, your family, or even your dad out. We won't let that happen. As far as you know, nothing is happening tomorrow. Do you understand?" Trish asked, her voice dangerously stern.

Raelynn nodded. As much as she wanted to see her dad, she knew she couldn't jeopardize anything.

Bonded Blood

"If they see your dad show up, they will most likely kill him on sight, probably will have multiple snipers set up all over downtown. So, through Donte, we will be presenting the evidence against the Del Rios and then exonerating your dad at the same time." Sharon said with an eyebrow lifted.

"Lee will stay in hiding for a few more days to make sure all the suspects are rounded up and then he should be clear to return home," Trish added, waving her hand as if this was no big deal.

Serenity looked at Raelynn and Raelynn squeezed her hand. "What about my dad? Will he be ok?"

"He will stay with Lee until this is all taken care of. The police and feds are covering all over downtown to hopefully grab as many as they can before the trial even starts. I have contact information for both, but I will not share it until they are in the clear. I don't want someone to get tipped off before they are safe." Sharon's serious face and raised brow told them all they needed to know.

Eventually her face softened, and Raelynn saw her come out of agent mode and be the sweet grandmotherly woman again. She reached out across the table and held both girls' hands. "This is almost over. And when the reward comes out, I think you will both be very well taken care of, as well as your families."

Raelynn sat back and looked over at Serenity. Her friend had a mix of emotions on her face, and she suspected one was regret. Raelynn remembered the last fight she'd told them about with her dad and her heart was hurting for Serenity. At least she would be able to repair it.

"Hey, it's gonna be ok, Reni. Your dad was doing a good thing this time," she gave her a weak smile.

Serenity let out a dark laugh. "Yeah. But can he stay on the good side?"

"I think he has finally found the friend he thought he lost so long ago," Sharon chimed in. "He was lost and now that they are together and going to be alright, he is much better, Serenity dear. I think you and your family will be ok."

"But my mom was talking to a lawyer today. What if she's going to divorce him?" She slumped in her chair. "Because of me and my big mouth," she muttered to herself.

Trish cleared her throat. "I don't think that's the kind of lawyer she was talking to. Don't worry, child. Have faith."

Serenity just nodded and shared a look with Raelynn.

"I'm starving. Let's break for a few hours and remember, don't say anything to anyone outside of this room," Sharon warned. "We are so close. I don't want anything to prevent this from ending tomorrow."

* * * * *

Raelynn, Beau, and Serenity sat around the unlit fire pit in Raelynn's mom's back yard. They were lost in their own thoughts after what Sharon and Trish had shared. Honesty had to work part of the day, reminding Raelynn that maybe soon she wouldn't have to work so much. What would it be like to have her dad home again? Should she move back home?

Her mind was swirling with questions. After a while, they started to turn darker. What if the police didn't get to the gang members in time. What if they found out where her dad was hiding? What if she had to mourn her dad a second time?

She finally just shook her head hard and got up. "I'm going to get some drinks. When is the pizza going to be here, Beau?"

He glanced at his phone in his hand and said, "About ten minutes."

Serenity stood as well and moved with Raelynn into the house. Jericho was still upstairs when they got there, and she assumed Timmy was too. It wasn't much past ten and she knew he would be up soon. They were surprised to find a pizza place open this early, but it felt like she had been up for three days straight.

As if on cue, Jericho's door opened and a combination of his and Timmy's footsteps were heard on the stairs. The big ball of fluff came right to Raelynn and sat in front of her, lifting his head for scratches. She chuckled as she gave him what he wanted. *At least he hadn't forgotten about me*, she thought.

When he got his fill from Raelynn, he turned to Serenity, who put her hands in the air, trying to discourage him from coming to her.

Raelynn grabbed a hold of his collar and gave Serenity a nod. "He's pretty gentle, but he is big and not for everyone."

"I'm not afraid of dogs, but ones that outweigh me make me nervous," she said with an anxious giggle.

"I'll hold him if you want to pet him. He just wants love," Raelynn said with a laugh.

Gingerly, Serenity reached over and gave Timmy a small scratch on his head. He leaned into her a little further and nearly knocked Raelynn over trying to hold him. "He's got this big dog lean thing, where he tries to get as close as he can, and usually I end up sitting somewhere involuntarily." She laughed as she struggled to hang on without toppling over.

Jericho came over with his food and water. "Come on, boy," he called, and Timmy dutifully followed.

The girls watched the big beast gulp down his food and water and then Jericho took him outside to do his business.

After a few minutes of silence, Serenity quietly cleared her throat. "Hey, Rae? Do you think everything is going to be ok?"

Raelynn turned to her friend and nodded. "I think so. I have to believe it will anyway. It has been so long though. I feel like I don't want to get my hopes up. You know?"

Serenity nodded and they were quiet again. A yelp from outside drew there attention to the window and Raelynn laughed when she saw Beau and Jericho trying to wrestle a ball from Timmy.

"So, what's the story with you and Beau?" Serenity asked, still focused on the window.

Raelynn sucked in a bit of air and closed her eyes. Keeping them closed, she asked, "What do you mean?"

Serenity laughed. "Come on. I know you probably better than anyone. You can tell me, Rae. But I think I already know."

Raelynn opened her eyes and looked at her friend. Serenity's face was full of humor. Raelynn narrowed her eyes. "What do you know?" she asked slowly.

Letting out a series of giggles, perfect for a high school cheerleader gossiping about her crush, Serenity bumped her shoulder. "You like him don't you?"

Raelynn swallowed hard. She wasn't sure how to answer, especially if Serenity was interested in him. Finally sighing, she asked, "I am not going to get in your way if you are interested in him, Reni."

She turned back toward the window and waited for her friend to confirm her suspicions. She didn't expect Serenity to start laughing uncontrollably.

Turning to face her, she leaned her hip against the counter and crossed her arms over her chest.

Serenity continued her fit and waved her hand around. Finally, she shook her head and gasped for air, irritating Raelynn.

"S-sorry, Rae," she said, still trying to get her giggling under control. "I guess we haven't talked for longer than I thought."

Raelynn furrowed her brow. "What are you talking about? Did I misread something?"

"Griff is moving back, Rae. We have been talking again, and he's planning on staying. Now that we are adults, we can do what we want. He's always been the only one for me. I guess I thought you knew. So, no, I'm not interested in Beau." She smiled and gave Raelynn a hug. "He's all yours," she whispered in her friend's ear.

Loud barking drew their attention out the window again. Timmy was barking like a crazy dog, and Raelynn went on high alert. Timmy had never barked like that before. She ran outside, with Serenity close on her heels.

Beau and Jericho were staring at one of the neighbor's yards and Timmy was still barking at something in the same direction.

"What happened?" she asked Beau.

He turned and shrugged. "I'm not sure. Timmy just started going berserk."

"Let's go inside," Raelynn suggested, pulling on Timmy's collar. The big dog refused to budge and for the first time, she wished she had a small dog to lift and carry away.

She was about to call Sharon when Timmy suddenly lay down on the grass and huffed. He was still laser focused on something in the distance. After a few more minutes, he finally got up and the group went into the house.

They had barely made it inside when her phone rang.

"Hi Sharon," she answered.

"Raelynn, are you ok? I just got a report of someone trying to get to your mom's house." Her voice was worried but still calm somehow.

Raelynn looked at the group gathered. "We are ok. I think my dog scared whoever it was away."

Sharon chuckled. "Good boy. You should come back here for a while so we can make sure you are safe."

"I don't think they are coming back. But I will leave my dog here until we get through this," Raelynn said definitively.

After she hung up, Beau laughed. "I guess we figured out when he barks. He must know when someone is up to no good or is a danger."

Raelynn looked at her pup, now sprawled out on the floor ready to nap. "I guess so. And now he needs a nap."

They laughed as they watched him start to snore.

Chapter 30

Sitting around the all too familiar table again, Raelynn looked around at everyone. Trish and Sharon were trying to explain everything that they had discovered, and she was having difficulty focusing on it all. She noticed Beau seemed to understand and Serenity had decided to go home and see what her mom had been up to earlier that morning.

"So tomorrow morning, I will need you to stay out of sight. Go about your normal routine as if nothing is different," Sharon was saying.

Raelynn looked over at her with a confused look on her face. "What do you mean? We can't go to the courthouse? I mean it is my dad on trial right?"

Trish snorted. "Girl you need to pay attention. We talked about this earlier."

Raelynn couldn't help the scowl that must have crossed her face.

"No, I don't want you anywhere near downtown, Rae," Sharon said sternly, but more patient than her friend was. "I don't want there to be any reason for the Rios to come after you. If they suspect anything, I don't think they will hesitate to act impulsively. They are dangerous without a threat, but I don't want to find out what they will do if they think we are on to them."

Beau took her hand in his and nodded to Sharon. "We act like we don't know anything about any of this, including the charges being brought against Rae's dad so they aren't tipped off." He turned to meet Raelynn's eyes. "We didn't know about this until Saturday, Rae. If Sharon and Trish hadn't found it, we still wouldn't know. We have to act the same."

Trish turned to look at Raelynn, a thoughtful look on her face. "Raelynn, did your mom ever say anything about the trial or court or anything related to your dad over the last few days or weeks?"

Raelynn thought for a second and then shook her head. "No, not that I remember. Why?"

"I was just wondering if the court sent anything to her house and she just disregarded it since he hasn't been there in so long." Trish looked over at Sharon, who suddenly nodded and hurried to the back hall.

Sighing deeply, Raelynn leaned back in her chair. She put her hand on her forehead, fighting a headache. "What am I missing now?" she mumbled, making Trish chuckle at her.

"It is odd that no summons went out to him, even if he hasn't lived there in years. It is his last known address," Trish briefly explained.

Sharon reappeared with a frown. "We may have a problem. Trish, I need you to stay here. Raelynn, we need to go talk to your mom." She quickly disappeared again and reappeared with such grace Raelynn thought she could pass for a witch teleporting between the rooms.

It was Halloween after all, she thought with a smile.

Sharon waved for her to follow and then she disappeared out the back door. This time, Raelynn didn't hide the chuckle that came out of her mouth, drawing Beau's attention to her.

She shrugged. "I was just thinking about how she kind of jumps from here to there. You know like a teleporting witch, on this fine Halloween day," she said with a laugh. She wasn't sure why she wasn't freaking out at the moment with so much going on, but she figured it was just so much that she was overwhelmed, and part of her cognition was just shutting down. Self-protection maybe, she guessed.

Beau climbed in the back seat and Raelynn slid in next to Sharon. She had to laugh at Beau's large frame in the back of Sharon's mini cooper, but he had insisted she ride up front. She glanced back at him and gave him a teasing smile.

"Need more room, Beau? I can move my seat up—a tiny bit," she said as she realized there really wasn't a lot of extra room anywhere.

Laughing from the back, Beau said, "Yeah, sure. How about getting me about six or seven more inches, Rae?"

"Ha ha," she shot back. "I told you I would sit back there."

"It's fine. We aren't going far anyway," he said, looking out the window. He had situated himself sideways on the seat, still not gaining enough space for him, but it looked a bit better than when he was essentially kneeing himself in the chin.

Sharon just chuckled to herself at the two of them, drawing Raelynn's attention back to her. She prepared to give Sharon directions, but she noticed the older woman didn't even ask.

Turning a skeptical eye to the driver, Raelynn asked, "Do I even want to know how you know where my mom lives, Sharon?"

"I know things, Raelynn," she said simply, and continued her focus on the road.

Raelynn just shook her head and leaned back in her seat. She wondered what was so important that they had to go visit her mom right then, but she decided not to ask questions. If she had learned anything the last couple of days, it was to not ask too much. Sharon had a purpose for everything she did, and she would let Raelynn in when it was necessary. It didn't change the fact that it annoyed her, she just knew there was nothing she could do about it.

It didn't take long for them to park on the street alongside Honesty's home. It was after twelve and Raelynn hoped her mom would be home from work. She suddenly felt like a neglectful dog mom as she thought about how long her pup had been at her mom's. It had only been two nights, but it felt like it had been so much longer.

She noticed her mom's car in the worn driveway. The old car was still running after so many years, but Raelynn knew her mom took extra care with it and had a friend who was a mechanic. She couldn't afford for it to break down. She wondered if her mom would be able to get a new car after this was all over.

Sharon parked along the street and Raelynn hopped out of the car as soon as she turned off the engine. She didn't want her mom to be startled by the newcomer. Her mom appeared at the door as she approached and opened it for Raelynn and the other two as Raelynn took the first step.

"Rae, what's going on?" Honesty asked, looking at Sharon.

Raelynn motioned inside. "Can we come in for a few minutes? I'll explain everything. Well, actually Sharon will," she said motioning to the older woman standing behind Beau.

They moved into the kitchen and settled around the table. Honesty took a pot of coffee from the maker and grabbed four coffee mugs by the handles. She set everything in the center of the table and then sat down next to Raelynn. Honesty folded her hands on the table and stared at them.

The four of them were quiet and suddenly Raelynn wondered where Timmy was.

"Mom, where is Timmy?" she asked, looking around.

Honesty looked up and then smiled lightly. "I think Jericho took him upstairs. He loves that animal so much. It's so cute to see. He treats him like a little brother." She chuckled and then glanced at Sharon. "What is going on, Miss Sharon," she asked.

Sharon smiled. "I think you might already know why we are here, Miss Honesty, dear," she said simply.

Honesty's face showed confusion and then she sat up straight and looked to her side where she had a calendar hanging from the wall. Realization seemed to sink in, and she nervously glanced at Raelynn.

"Oh, I guess I am not positive," she said nervously.

Raelynn noticed her eyes shifting from Sharon to hers. Raelynn looked at Sharon who just nodded slowly.

"It's ok, Honesty," Sharon said softly. "Raelynn knows."

Honesty's eyes shot up and met Raelynn's equally surprised ones. Her mom knew about all this? Did she know the whole time Raelynn was trying to figure out the turtle mysteries?

Honesty shook her head. "I didn't know about this, Rae," she said softly, as if she were reading Raelynn's mind. "I had called Sharon when you said she was helping you. I'm sorry I didn't tell you. I didn't want you caught up in anything else."

"I don't understand," Raelynn mumbled.

Sharon sighed and then began to explain. "Your mom received a letter of summons a few weeks ago. She hadn't done anything with it because she didn't know what it was about. When you and I first talked, I asked Brad about anything more we should know. He told me about the gang, but nothing more. He had to keep his hands clean for plausible deniability and the safety of his family. When Honesty called me, she explained the letter she received and was worried about possibly being in danger.

"I assured her I would look into everything and that's when I found out the specifics we were discussing earlier. Honesty, I need you to act as if you know nothing about the hearing tomorrow," Sharon said, just as she had told Beau and Raelynn earlier. "We don't know what all is known at this point and since you haven't heard from Lee or seen him in years, if you don't show up, no one will suspect anything different."

Raelynn watched between the two women and then glanced at Beau. He was looking at her with concern. She turned to Sharon and asked, "Does mom know the plan?"

"She will as soon as we tell her," Sharon said with a smile. She then turned to Honesty and placed her hands over Honesty's. "We have a plan to bring Lee home to you, Honesty."

Bonded Blood

Honesty let out a small gasp as she locked eyes with Sharon. "What?" Her voice was barely a whisper.

Sharon nodded. "We have a plan. But we need you to act like everything is normal and let us take care of everything. I will let Raelynn know when everything is safe again and we will bring him to you, free and clear with nothing hanging over his head."

Honesty nodded, tears filling her eyes. She looked back down at their still connected hands. "I am worried about my family's safety if this goes bad," she admitted quietly.

Raelynn noticed her mom was now holding onto Sharon's hands tightly. She felt tears threatening to spill from her own eyes as she watched her mom's face. This was what they had been dreaming about for so long. She could hardly believe it was actually going to happen.

"I promise to do everything I can to ensure their safety. Tomorrow and the days after will be difficult as we wait to clear everyone we can legally take care of. But I need you to be patient and give us the time to do it right. We *need* to do this right, for everyone involved and especially Lee and your family." Sharon leaned forward and squeezed Honesty's hands. "We are so close, Honesty. So close."

Raelynn continued to watch as her mom's tears spilled over and splashed on the table and the connected hands. Beau put his arm around her shoulders, and she leaned into him. She was grateful for the support and knew he would be there for her through this. And then she would be there for her mom. And she would be there for her dad when he finally came home.

These next few days were going to be as difficult as the first days after he disappeared. But this time it would be worth it.

* * * * *

Raelynn was torn about having Timmy stay again at her mom's, since he'd shown that he would protect if he felt a threat—making her feel relieved—but her mom insisted that he go home and be as normal as possible. She was nervous though leaving her mom without any kind of protection.

Trish came through however and offered about three of her surveillance cameras to put around the property. Since it was Halloween, they worked perfect with the décor—creepy dolls and clowns were great for the festive holiday. It also wouldn't raise suspicions if anyone was watching the house for signs of anything out of the ordinary. Trish said she would keep tabs on the cameras and would notify authorities immediately if there was a threat.

Beau stayed with Raelynn again, after giving his parents a brief synopsis of what was going on. Knowing that his uncle and dad were previous coworkers at the FBI, he knew they would use discretion where needed. His parents also offered support to Sharon and Trish if needed. They had offered for Raelynn to stay there, but she refused saying that might raise suspicions if she isn't at home like normal.

By the time dinner had rolled around, Beau and Raelynn were settling in at her apartment. Timmy was spread out on the floor in the living room, obviously missing his home. His snores were loud and made Raelynn smile, glad her pup was home with her.

They had all agreed not to share what they knew with Sahara or Jericho. It was too risky, especially knowing her brother, he would try to do something or look for the people watching them. He was known for his big mouth and that could blow the whole thing up.

Raelynn had settled for picking up takeout from a local diner. It was easier than trying to cook something. And she really just wanted to get back to her place before it got too dark. She was trying not to get spooked about everything, but she didn't like the feeling of being watched and felt even more like she was every minute that ticked by.

A knock at the door made her jump. Beau chuckled.

"It's probably trick or treaters, Rae," he explained.

Raelynn laughed nervously. "Oh yeah I forgot. I got candy like three weeks ago. With everything going on, I kind of forgot." She went into her room to take the bags out. She was actually surprised she had kept it for this long without sneaking any.

She had been told by a few tenants when she moved in that they had a lot of kids come. It was all inside, which helped, and they could hit a bunch of people in a short amount of time. She ran back out to find Beau entertaining a group of three little kids, all dressed as superheroes. He was "testing" their superpowers as he waited for her to get back.

"Ok, ok, I made it! Here you go," she said as she dropped a few pieces in each child's bag.

They waved and said thank you as she closed the door.

"This could be a long night," he said as she moved back to her kitchen. She emptied the bags into a big bowl and mixed them up.

She set the bowl on the small table where she tossed her keys and nodded. "I guess so. We should eat fast before the next group comes."

Just as she was about to move back to her couch, a knock sounded again. She caught herself from the fear that seemed to just be lying under the surface and reminded herself it was going to happen all night.

Raelynn picked up the bowl and lifted it in his direction with a smile. "We might need to take shifts."

Beau nodded his agreement and dug into his food as she turned to open the door for the next group.

After about an hour, with them taking turns so they could both eat, it finally settled down and there was a lot more time in between knocks. They had just turned on a movie when there was a knock. Raelynn rolled her eyes.

"Ok, I get this is fun and everything, but I'm tired and want to just go to bed, you know?" she complained.

Beau laughed and gave her a light push off the couch. She turned and stuck her tongue out at him in return, making him laugh harder.

A second knock came and for some reason, Timmy stood up immediately and almost knocked Raelynn over when he ran to the door. Confused, she looked over at Beau. She looked back at Timmy who was now sitting in front of the door staring at it. At the same time, her phone rang and startled Raelynn.

"What the heck is going on?" she muttered, moving to pick up her bowl.

Beau grabbed her phone from the coffee table and showed her the screen. "Rae, hold on," he said quietly.

Raelynn stopped and looked to see it was Trish calling. The knock at the door was more forceful the third time. She looked at Beau with panic in her eyes. Timmy was silent but was still frozen at the door.

She moved and answered the phone. "Hello?' she said quietly.

"Raelynn do not open the door. The police are on the way, should be there in less than a minute. Do you hear me?" Trish's voice was very short and serious.

Nodding, she said, "Yes, I hear you. I understand."

Beau raised his eyebrows at her. She turned her speaker on, lowering the volume so he could hear too.

"How did you know, Trish?" Raelynn asked quietly.

The older woman chuckled. "Silly girl. Did you think we would leave you unprotected? Although that doggo of yours is pretty scary. Is he staring at the door like the good dog he is?"

Raelynn and Beau locked eyes in shock. "How…?"

"That's what he is supposed to do, Raelynn. His breed are natural protectors. He knows what to do on instinct when he senses a threat," Trish explained.

They heard what sounded like a scuffle outside her door, and she resisted the urge to look out the peephole to see what was happening, but once again her love of crime shows made her think twice. Because what if he had a gun and shot through the door and she was standing there?

"Ok, you should be good now. I told the officers to take care of things carefully and quietly to not raise any suspicions. I have my favorite Bessi standing guard for you, Raelynn. Be nice to her. I will pick her up in a few days." The line then went dead, and Raelynn stared at the phone.

She looked up at Beau and when they locked eyes, they both started to laugh. She wasn't sure if it was from nerves or just everything, but they couldn't seem to stop.

Chapter 31

Monday came and went without any word from anyone. Beau had to go to work and Raelynn stayed home with Timmy all day. She didn't want to go anywhere and after the night before, she didn't want to be left vulnerable and alone. The comfort of her big lug of a dog cuddled up next to her all night helped her sleep. She had set up an air mattress on her floor because she didn't want Beau to sleep alone in case someone came through the glass doors, at least that's what she told him.

By Tuesday, she was on edge. She had to work and needed to act as normally as possible. But she wasn't feeling normal. She got up and went through her morning routine as if on autopilot. Timmy was acting like his usual lazy self, and he hadn't had any more behavior like Sunday night. She wasn't sure if it was a fluke or if what Trish had said was true. But she did observe him twice acting very protectively.

As she left her apartment for work, Raelynn couldn't help but look in all directions. She almost wanted to bring Timmy to work with her but knew that wouldn't fly. She hadn't left except to let Timmy out and she nearly screamed when she saw a doll with bright red eyes staring at her when she turned to lock her door.

Bonded Blood

She laughed when she remembered Trish's words about Bessi. No wonder Trish knew everything that was happening. She wondered if the older woman had left anything outside her sliding door as well.

She quickly walked to her car and unlocked it before she reached it and slid into the seat, locking the doors immediately after. She was annoyed with herself. She wasn't a paranoid person, but then the photos Sharon had shown her came back and she decided this wasn't paranoia but natural protection for her safety.

Satisfied, she started her engine and looked around the dark parking lot. It was a lot darker now with daylight savings kicking in the day before. The lone streetlight in the parking lot still flickered ominously. Raelynn put her car in reverse and moved quickly out of the parking lot and onto the main street. She would feel better once she got to work and was around her people again.

The drive went by quickly, which she appreciated. She knew her boss would have plenty of extra goodies considering the shorter day Monday and the shop being closed on Sunday. Susiana would feel like she has to make it up to her customers.

Just as she predicted, when she pulled into the lot at the café, her boss was already there struggling with multiple bakery bags of goodies. Raelynn hurriedly parked and jumped out to help.

They struggled to get all six bags into the café and Susiana let out a laugh as they made it inside without dropping anything.

"It's been a while since I have made so much," she said looking around. She had her hands on her hips surveying their haul.

Raelynn laughed with her. "Why so much, Susiana? It seems like way more than we usually sell."

Her boss shrugged. "I just have a feeling about today. And I felt inspired by the day off." She then moved to start packing things away.

Raelynn moved to behind the counter to see what she needed to refill and get ready for the day. For a few minutes she forgot about the cloud hanging over her head. She focused on work and by the time the first customer came in she was in work mode.

Mister Adler was the first one in the door and he stepped into the café with a smug look on his face, seeing that it was completely empty.

"Ah, feels good to be number one, eh sweetheart?" he said with a broad smile.

Raelynn returned his grin and nodded. "Your usual, Mister Adler?"

"Of course!" he exclaimed. Just as he turned to go to his favorite seat, the bell above the door jingled.

A second older gentleman walked in and gave the first a glare. "Gerald! You are a thorn in my side!" he shouted as Mister Adler hurried to his seat.

Raelynn chuckled at the two of them and gave the second man a nod. She quickly made their drinks and then dropped a pot of black coffee on their table.

The steady stream of customers kept her attention for most of the morning and when Chrissy came in, she was surprised to see the time.

"Hey Chrissy. How was your weekend?" she asked, as she handed a customer her drink. She wiped up the small spill and turned to her newly arrived colleague.

Bonded Blood

Chrissy shrugged. "It was ok. Not much happening in my world actually. How about you? Oh, happy birthday, by the way!" She came over and gave Raelynn a tight hug.

Raelynn hugged her back and thanked her, just as another customer walked in. She rolled her eyes at Chrissy and turned back to the door as her coworker hurried off to get ready for her shift.

"Can I help you?" Raelynn asked, not looking up yet as she fumbled with the rag in her hand still. Tossing it behind her, she finally made eye contact with her new customer.

But as soon as she did, her breath caught in her throat, and she froze. *It can't be possible, can it?* she thought.

The man before her smiled, and she just stared. "Hey baby girl," he whispered, his eyes filled with tears as he watched her realize who he was.

"Dad?" Raelynn whispered, as a steady stream of tears ran down her cheeks.

Other works by this author

Bellbrook Springs Series
A Journey of the Heart
A Journey of the Mind
A Journey of the Soul
A Journey for Justice—in the works
A Journey for Peace—in the works

The Sense of Belonging Series
Shared Blood, Book 1
Bonded Blood, Book 2

Coming Next
Mixed Blood, The Sense of Belonging, book 3

Following me on
Instagram at brendabenningauthor
TikTok @brendabenningauthor
Website: brendabenningauthor.org

www.ingramcontent.com/pod-product-compliance
Lightning Source LLC
Chambersburg PA
CBHW030555110725
29382CB00001B/3